HEART
QUEST®

WHAT READERS ARE SAYING ABOUT PREVIOUS BOOKS BY PEGGY STOKS:

"Heart-wrenching, heartwarming, honest and pure."
▪ Johanna Asmi ▪
Washington

"Ministered much to my soul. So encouraging, so real."
▪ Twila Simonson ▪
Minnesota

"Oh, how I wished it had been longer! I don't ever recall reading another book that has held my attention like this one."
▪ Edna Bell Winland ▪
Ohio

"Written from the heart, written beautifully. Captivating and real, and I believed every moment."
▪ Terri Gross ▪
Minnesota

"I'm keeping this book to read again and again. Thank you."
▪ Rachel Donahue ▪
Oregon

"I laughed, I cried, I rejoiced. It was wonderful."
▪ Sattie JoAnn Trusiak ▪
Pennsylvania

"Couldn't wait to get to the end—then I was disappointed it was over."
▪ Ruth Bennett ▪
Minnesota

"You can't stop now—you must write another book!"
▪ Pat Doocy ▪
Minnesota

"Thank you so much for the great entertainment you have given me this week!"
▪ Lee Ann Cline ▪
Missouri

HEART
QUEST®

romance the way it's meant to be

HeartQuest brings you romantic fiction
with a foundation of biblical truth.
Adventure, mystery, intrigue, and suspense
mingle in these heartwarming stories of
men and women of faith striving to build
a love that will last a lifetime.

May HeartQuest books sweep you
into the arms of God, who longs for you
and pursues you always.

A VICTORIAN *Christmas* COLLECTION

PEGGY STOKS

Romance fiction from
Tyndale House Publishers, Inc., Wheaton, Illinois
www.heartquest.com

Visit Tyndale's exciting Web site at www.tyndale.com

Check out the latest about HeartQuest Books at www.heartquest.com

A Victorian Christmas Collection published 2002.

Library of Congress Cataloging-in-Publication Data

Stoks, Peggy.
  A Victorian Christmas collection / Peggy Stoks.
    p. cm. — (Victorian Christmas anthologies)
    ISBN 0-8423-6013-1 (sc)
    1. Historical fiction, American. 2. Christmas stories, American.
  3. Christian fiction, American. 4. Love stories, American. I. Title.
  II. Series.
    PS3569.T62237 V43 2002
    813'.54—dc21   2002005255

Printed in the United States of America

08 07 06 05 04 03 02
9   8   7   6   5   4   3   2   1

Contents

Tea for Marie

For Mary Strand—
I didn't forget.

ONE

Grandma Biggs sniffed with disdain, stretched herself to her full four feet, ten inches, and thumped the wide oak planks of the porch with her cane. "Marie Katherine Biggs! Were you out driving with that Farrell boy?"

"Goodness, Grandma," Marie replied. She watched the stylish black carriage retreat down the country lane, drawn by a perfectly matched set of bays. A cloud of dust rose in its wake in the golden October sunshine. Still tingling with excitement, the nineteen-year-old danced up the three steps to the porch and removed her bonnet. "A person would think you didn't care for Chadwick Farrell."

"I don't. The boy galls me." Grandma's snapping brown stare met her own as the cane struck the porch again for good measure. "He's good-lookin', I'll grant you, but he's got nothin' more inside him than hot air and horsefeathers."

"He's got so many wonderful ideas, Grandma."

"Oh, I imagine the boy can talk pretty enough. He always did. I'm also certain his term at the university only made that worse. I'm just wondering what he's all about. All these years, he comes, he goes. We see him, we don't. It's no proper courtship, Marie." She lifted slender, snow-white brows. "I'm wonder-

ing, too, what he tells you about his family—and why you're
never invited over there."

Marie sighed and set her hand on her grandmother's shoulder, her pleasure at the afternoon drive through the countryside
beginning to fade. "I think the least I can do is give him a
chance. He's very nice."

A wrinkled yet still strong hand came up to cover her own.
"He comes from money, Marie; don't let that be goin' to your
head. 'Tain't no secret his mama threatened to jump right into
the Minnesota River when she found out her boy had taken a
fancy to you. 'Imagine,'" she said in a high tone dripping with
mock disdain, her pinched expression mimicking the one
Imogene Farrell wore as a matter of fact, "'my son taking an
interest in a farmer's daughter. It is simply not acceptable.'"

"I'd best help Mother with supper," Marie said. The remainder
of her enjoyment of the afternoon's outing had dissipated. Several
uncomfortable questions about Chadwick Farrell once again arose
in her mind, questions she'd worked so hard at putting aside
during the drive.

"Now take Harald Hamsun there, across the way," Grandma
continued, hooking her cane over her wrist and tugging Marie's
arm until she was forced to turn around. The fair Norwegian
farmer was barely visible, leading a team of oxen and a heavily
loaded wagon from his fields. "A nice, honest man, he is. Hardworking. Just like his uncle Einar, afore he took sick." She nodded
with approval, a mischievous twinkle appearing in her eyes for
just a moment. "A set of fine, broad shoulders the young man
has, too."

"Yes, ma'am," Marie agreed, hoping her grandmother had
finally finished rendering her opinions. "I'd best go help Mother
now," she offered once again, wanting nothing more at that
moment than to occupy herself with some task and quell the
busy debate her reason was waging regarding Chadwick Farrell.

"Go on and help your mama, then." Grandma's voice softened, and she gave Marie's arm a gentle squeeze before shifting her cane back into her hand. "I think I'll just enjoy a little of this weather before it turns nasty for good. Prob'ly only a handful of decent days left." With that, the elder Mrs. Biggs adjusted her shawl and made her way down the porch steps. Somewhat relieved, Marie stepped into the kitchen, not entirely trusting she'd heard the last of her grandmother's opinions concerning her choice of suitors.

✳ ✳ ✳

By the time the Biggs family sat down for supper, much of Marie's pensiveness had yielded to her normally optimistic disposition. The good-natured banter of her younger brothers and sisters, combined with the delicious aromas wafting from the kitchen, did much to settle her disordered thoughts. The issue of Chadwick Farrell seemed much further away, and a feeling of peace stole over her while Father asked the blessing.

"How was your ride with young Mr. Farrell today, Marie?" Father inquired in a genial tone, as he sliced the roast pork and passed the platter. Strands of gray battled evenly with the rich chestnut color of his hair and beard. His deep brown gaze sought hers. "He seemed to leave in a hurry."

"He always leaves in a hurry," twelve-year-old Hugh commented, bumping Marie's elbow to indicate that she should take the bowl of mashed potatoes.

"The way he flies out of here." Anthony, two years older than Hugh, spoke in a voice already much lower in timbre than it had been a year ago. "I think maybe he doesn't like us."

"Well, he likes Marie," Sarah, nine, chimed in. "And he sure has a fancy carriage. If you marry him, Marie, will you have fancy things, too?"

"Hush, Sarah," Mother admonished gently. "No one said

anything about Marie marrying Mr. Farrell. Now take some corn and pass it on." She glanced around the table at her brood, giving them a wordless warning not to tease their oldest sister. "How was your ride, dear?" she asked. "We didn't get much of a chance to talk when you came in."

"Oh, it was . . . fine," Marie replied, scooping a small spoonful of potatoes onto her plate. She felt the eyes of all upon her. "The sun was actually very warm."

"Maybe that's why she suddenly got a sunburn on her cheeks." The musical voice of Rosemary, nearly seventeen years old, was laden with laughter.

Good-natured giggles, chuckles, and chortles broke out around the table. Seated between Hugh and Rosemary's twin, Raymond, Grandma Biggs loudly cleared her throat. "Well, you people can hee-haw all you like." She glared at her son. "I do not understand, William, why you let Marie say no when Mr. Hamsun called, askin' to court her. I'm tellin' you, that Farrell boy is nothin' but a skunk."

"Does he stink, Gramma?" Three-year-old Julia's innocent question produced another round of laughter from everyone but Marie.

"To high heaven, child," Ruth Biggs replied, nodding approvingly while Hugh pinched his nostrils and pulled a face.

"That will be enough," Father said. His voice was stern enough, though a trace of a smile lingered at his lips.

"I think we should change the talk from skunks to squirrels," Mother offered diplomatically, with a slight nod toward her mother-in-law before turning to her husband. "I'm quite certain I've been hearing more activity on our roof than I ought to, William. I'd like you to go up there and take a look. . . ."

"May I please be excused, Mother?" The peace that had settled over Marie during Father's prayer had long since fled. A lump had lodged itself in her throat, and unshed tears burned in her eyes.

"Yes, you may," her mother answered. "Would you go out and put the hens in for me? I'll keep a plate for you, dear."

There was a hush at the table as Marie pushed back her chair and rose. When she reached the back door, she heard a sudden buzz of conversation start up at the table. Julia's piping voice asked, "Is Marie going to cry?"

No, she wasn't going to cry, she vowed, closing the door quietly and stepping out into the evening. The temperature had cooled dramatically in the past few hours, making her regret she hadn't taken a wrap. Walking toward the hen yard, she wished her family would be more receptive toward Chadwick. Mother and Father had allowed him to pay call again since he'd returned from the university, but she could sense their reservation, no doubt having to do with the on-again, off-again manner in which he'd called upon her over the past several years.

They were from two different worlds, she and Chadwick, but if only her family could know the Chadwick she knew. A restless but bright-minded thinker, he flew through his high school courses and embarked upon his higher education with relish. He was an exciting person to be around, bold and so certain of himself.

The Chadwick her family didn't know worked hard at his father's bank and spoke eloquently about all the plans he had for social improvement and reform. He wanted to improve the Mankato area in south-central Minnesota and progress some-day throughout the state and country. Even in high school he had talked of such things, but since he had returned from the university, he seemed so much more determined to carry out his altruistic ideals.

With twilight approaching, the hens were only too happy to run into their coop and roost. As Marie closed the door and latched it, her mind's eye recalled the afternoon's events. Her heart did a little flip-flop as she remembered the way Chadwick's lean, neatly manicured fingers had lingered over her hands when he'd passed the reins to her. Briefly, she allowed herself to wonder if he was ever going to kiss her. He'd exhibited nothing but gentlemanly behavior toward her, but she sensed his interest. He liked her first of all, he'd told her many times, because she had such a pretty smile, but he liked her most of all because she was a good listener and asked intelligent questions.

Shivering, she crossed her arms and rubbed her palms over her upper arms as the chilly breeze intensified into a gust. Glancing up at the sky, she was surprised to see the setting sun almost entirely obscured by a layer of gray clouds. Rain tonight, maybe snow if the mercury dipped below freezing. The month had already been visited by one good frost, which had nipped many tender vines.

The glow of yellow light was visible from the Hamsun farmhouse, warm and beckoning against the deepening shadows. Einar Hamsun had built his sturdy home many years before on an L-shaped plot of two hundred acres in the heart of Blue Earth County. Graced by a mix of woods and fields, the land lay just south of the twisting Le Sueur River.

Long-ago widowed with no surviving children, the elder Mr. Hamsun had suffered a severe stroke just two years before, succumbing to death a short time later. Within a few weeks his nephew Harald had come from Illinois to take over the farm. As Marie understood things, he had bought out all interests from Einar's two surviving brothers.

Harald Hamsun was a nice enough man, she supposed, though she really didn't know him very well. He was typically Scandinavian in appearance with blond hair and blue eyes, and she guessed him to be somewhere in his mid-twenties. He wasn't as tall as Chadwick, and whereas the younger man's lines were long and lean, everything about Harald seemed broad—his face, his shoulders, his hands. He was a quiet man, unassuming, yet Father held a great opinion of him.

The only places she saw him were about his farm, in church, and occasionally at the table when Mother invited him for Sunday dinner. How he could make up his mind that he wished to court Marie based on the small amount of interaction they'd had made no sense to her at all. He was just lonely, she decided, living over there all by himself.

"Ooh, it's gotten cold! Looks like it might rain, too." Lost in thought, Marie hadn't heard Rosemary's approach. "I'm awfully sorry for teasing you, Marie," Rosemary continued, linking her arm through Marie's. "We were only having fun, but things just seemed to go too far at your expense. Everyone's sorry . . . well, except for Grandma. Mama's still talking on about squirrels, but now Grandma's decided Mr. Farrell is closer to a ferret than a skunk."

"It's all right," Marie said, feeling a crooked smile steal across her lips. Exasperating as her family was, she loved them dearly.

"Are you in love with Chadwick?"

"I'm not sure," Marie answered slowly. "I know I feel excitement when I'm with him, but it doesn't feel like the kind of love I have for you or Mother or Father."

"It's not supposed to, silly." Laughter bubbled up from deep inside the slender, dark-eyed young woman, and she gave Marie a playful shove, knocking her off balance.

"And just what do you know about that?" Straightening, Marie planted her hands on her hips and gave Rosemary a searching look.

"Maybe more than you do," Rosemary answered coyly, tossing her dark braids. "Race you to the house." With that, she was off.

Shaking her head yet unable to resist the challenge, Marie picked up her skirt and outraced her younger sister by three whole steps.

❄ ❄ ❄

Lying in bed listening to Rosemary's deep, even breathing beside her, Marie sighed and turned from her side to her back. She'd said her prayers and asked the Lord for his peace, but her mind simply wouldn't rest. The unpleasant questions about Chadwick had come back, as they always did.

What *were* her feelings for Chadwick? And if he liked her so much, then why didn't he invite her to spend time with his family? Mama was always inviting him to stay for a meal, though he scarcely did. Was it really true that Imogene Farrell disdained her as much as Grandma said?

Eventually, fatigue overtook her, and she dozed.

Coughing and choking, Marie awakened, disoriented. Beside her, Rosemary was coughing too. Someone was shouting frantically, a surreal, bizarre sound, accompanied by muffled crackling noises. Shrieks of terror came from elsewhere in the house as her lungs struggled for pure, clean air.

"Everybody out! The house is on fire!" Father burst through the door, a lamp in one hand. Thick black smoke whirled about his hurried movements like a horde of writhing demons. "Get outside, now! Don't stop for anything. She's going fast."

The house is on fire? The terrible commotion registered in Marie's mind as she and Rosemary stumbled from their bed. Panic beat in her breast as she watched Father pull a limp Sarah out of her bed and toss her over his shoulder. The fumes were thick and acrid, and the crackling sound grew louder. Clinging to her sister's arm, choked by fear and smoke, Marie made her way to the door, wondering if they would all get out alive.

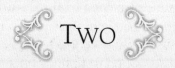

Two

There was no chance of saving the house.

"Look at that, would you?" Grandma Biggs's normally outspoken tone was subdued as she stared at the conflagration before her. "You'd think the rain might slow it down even a little."

"The rain's what's keeping everything else from going up right along with the house," Father responded, his voice dull. "There's that to be thankful for."

"And that we're all safe, William." Mother threaded her arm around Father's waist and nestled close, unmindful of his soggy, soot-blackened union suit. "That's the most important thing of all."

Father remained standing as if at attention, not giving any reply. The animals were noisy and restless, but the group of survivors huddled just inside the barn door, their panic spent, watching in silence as the fire destroyed their home and possessions. For Marie, the feelings she experienced during this night were a curious dichotomy. Though all her worldly goods perished before her eyes, she was overwhelmed with thankfulness for the gift of life itself.

Thanks to Father's alert, everyone had made it out of the house safely, and in the cold, light rain Sarah had revived at once. Harald Hamsun, awakened by the disturbance, had responded nearly immediately to their plight. He and Father and the boys had been able to make a few trips back inside to salvage some items on the ground floor, but once the flames had licked up through the ceiling and ignited the roof, they'd dared not chance more.

The heat from the burning building was incredible. Dressed in their bedclothes, soaked by the cold rain, not one of them felt anything but hot. The glow from the blaze painted their faces eerie shades of red while they stood soberly, silently, save the coughing of several sets of offended lungs.

"Hullo! William! Can I bring my team inside?" Once it was clear that everyone was safe and unharmed and that there were no efforts that could be made to save the house, Harald had returned to his home. Now he approached once again, this time leading a pair of workhorses pulling a wagon. The beasts were noticeably nervous near the heat and flames, yet he guided them with skill into the barn.

"That's it, girls. Whoa." Patting each horse, he turned toward the huddled family. "There is food and cider in the wagon," he said simply. His broad face, tinted crimson by the flames, was etched with concern. "Dry blankets if you wish."

"Thank you, Harald." Mother stepped forward to take his hand. Her smile was genuine, though stress showed in her eyes and about her mouth.

Raymond, Anthony, and Hugh wasted no time in converging upon the large covered basket in the back of Harald's wagon. Grandma Biggs was now seated on an old stool that someone had found for her, and Julia was snuggled securely in Marie's arms, her head resting on Marie's shoulder.

Marie watched with growing concern as Father stepped away from Mother's side, away from all of them, to stand by himself. He had barely spoken since they fled the house. His posture was

tense, stiff, his expression as unyielding as stone. Such uncharacteristic behavior unsettled Marie, and by the way the others
acted, she was not alone.

Only Harald seemed undaunted. He approached Father without hesitation and placed his hand on the older man's shoulder.
"You will all come to my house," he said quietly, only a trace of
his musical native accent evident in his voice.

"I can't accept such an offer," Father said through tensed jaws.
A long moment later he added, "There are ten of us. . . . I couldn't
ask it of you."

Harald waited an equally long moment before replying,
nodding slightly. "You didn't ask it, William."

Father stood, unmoving, while Harald waited patiently beside
his friend.

"Would you have us sleep in the barn, son?" Grandma asked
with only a little of her usual spunk, her voice husky from
coughing.

"Others have done it."

In Marie's arms, Julia suddenly tensed, her head snapping up
so fast it bumped the side of her older sister's face. "Mama! I
don't *want* to sleep in the barn!" she wailed, tears springing to
her eyes. "My house burning . . . and my dolly gone," she
sobbed, despite Marie's attempts to calm her, "and now I wanna
go to Mr. Hamsun's."

"Oh, it's late, my darling," Mother soothed, taking her youngest child from her eldest, "and you must be very tired. Just as
soon as your father makes a decision, we'll make you up a nice
bed. Things won't seem so bad in the light of morning." Though
she cast her husband a troubled glance, she hummed softly,
rocking the quieting child back and forth in her arms.

Maybe Mother thought things would be better by morning,
but Marie feared things might be much worse by the light of
day, especially if Father continued to behave in this peculiar

manner. Would he really insist that they all stay in the barn—
even Grandma and Julia? When the fire died down, the temperature inside the barn would fall . . . and they were all dressed in
their nightclothes.

Nightclothes.

With a downward, horrified glance she realized she was
standing before Harald Hamsun clad only in her nightdress, her
shoulders and torso covered by a damp quilt. Good heavens!
Instinctively she tightened her grip on the quilt, wishing she still
held Julia in front of her. With embarrassment she lifted her gaze
to see if he had noticed her immodest attire.

A relieved sigh escaped her when she saw that Harald's attention was still on Father. They were conversing now, voices low.
Taking a moment to study their benevolent neighbor, Marie
decided he wasn't a handsome man, not in the strictest sense of
the word. His head was a little too big, she thought, yet it matched
the rest of him. Though he stood just an inch or so under Father's
height, he seemed bigger than the taller man, probably because
his shoulders were thicker and wider.

His jaw was strong, his face clean shaven, but it was her opinion that his eyes tended to be a little on the narrow side. In fact,
she remembered once thinking that when he laughed they
seemed to crinkle up entirely out of sight. Since entering the
barn he had removed his hat and oilskin, and his light-colored
hair was plastered to his head. His clothing was wrinkled, rough,
intended for hard work. . . .

Marie stopped her musings, more than a little ashamed of
herself. Here she stood in her barn in a damp, dirty nightdress,
her own hair looking unimaginably horrid, thinking critical
thoughts of this kind man who'd come out into the rain and
offered them his assistance and virtually everything he had—his
food, his blankets, his home. He really did have a good heart.

She wondered what Chadwick would say if he could see her

in this bedraggled state. Thank goodness he never would! Her heart beat a little quicker knowing how he would doubtless be moved to great compassion to see her home burnt, her family displaced. He always spoke in such a stirring way of his great care for others, looking toward the future and conceiving of ways in which he could help his fellow man.

An enormous crash startled Marie from her thoughts. The house had just collapsed. It seemed unreal to see what little was left of their two-story frame home. Father had worked so hard just a few years ago, building a splendid addition onto the small house that had originally stood on that spot. Judging from the expressions on the others' faces, they were experiencing the same feelings. It was really true: They had nothing left but the clothes on their backs.

But we've all got our lives, thank the Lord for that.

"You all go on over to Hamsun's," Father spoke, his voice sounding flat. "I'm going to stay here and . . . and watch over things."

There was a chorus of voices volunteering to stay with him, but Father was firm in his bidding. Harald nodded, stepping toward his wagon. While Raymond and Anthony assisted their grandmother from her stool, Mother transferred Julia from her arms back to Marie's. Taking a blanket from the back of Harald's wagon, Mother wrapped it around her shoulders and went to stand next to Father.

"I'll be staying with you, William," she announced in a tone of voice that brooked no argument. "A wife's place is by her husband's side, and I'll not let you spend the night here by yourself."

Marie felt relief run through her when she saw her father's brief nod. If there was anyone who could help him, it was Mother. Many times she had marveled at how intuitive her mother was, how she just seemed to know how another person was feeling. Mother's words were always just right, too. Marie wished she could be only half as sensitive. Then she would never put her foot into her mouth ever again.

"May I take this bundle from you?"

Marie started at the sound of Harald's voice, not having noticed his approach. He smiled and held his arms out for Julia.

Goodness, they were large at this close distance. Or was it that his chest seemed so immense? And his hands were much bigger than Chadwick's. Marie knew it was rude to stare at him so, not to mention not replying immediately. But she was faced with the dilemma of standing before this neighbor man with only a bit of quilted fabric separating her body from his if she relinquished her youngest sister to him.

In the end, Julia made the decision for Marie as she unclasped her arms from around Marie's neck and lurched toward Harald. Easily cradling the three-year-old in one powerful arm, he extended his other hand toward Marie.

"Will you come to my home, Marie?"

It was as if he sensed her awkwardness and embarrassment and wanted to put things at ease between them. Nothing but kindness and concern shone from his face as he gently took her hand, enfolded it in his, and led her to the wagon. There he set Julia back in her arms and tucked a blanket around them.

"Let's go, Harald," Hugh said, his fingers already wrapped around a bridle. Raymond and Anthony waited near the row of stalls after helping Grandma Biggs take a seat between Rosemary and Sarah.

Examining his passengers with a satisfied expression, Harald set his hand on Hugh's shoulder. "Let's go, then."

The horses were only too eager to depart the uncomfortable, dangerous-smelling environment, and they took off in a brisk trot. The fire blazed with much less intensity now, giving out proportionally less heat and light. Marie watched, cold rain soaking into her hair and blanket, as Mother and Father faded into the shadows. She wondered how they would fare the night. A wave of exhaustion enveloped her as she cradled Julia's small hand within hers and, curiously enough, she found her thoughts drifting to Harald Hamsun and the way her own hand had felt in his.

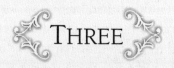

THREE

"Oh, you poor dears!" Ida Olson's unmistakable voice penetrated to the very corners of Harald Hamsun's cozy house. "I came as soon as I heard. My goodness, Helen! You look as if you've been up all night!"

From her place on the bedroom floor, Marie sat up groggily and brushed the grit out of her eyes. Oh, she smelled awful, of smoke. Glancing around, she was surprised to see she was the only person remaining in the clean, neatly furnished room. When they turned in last night, Grandma and Rosemary had shared the bed while she and Julia had made a place on the floor. How could everyone have gotten up around her while she slept on?

With a groan she pushed herself up to a sitting position, her joints aching. Gray light filtered in from the curtained window. The events of last night seemed unreal, but the stench lingering about her and the sight of her grimy nightdress confirmed the fact that their house had indeed burned to the ground. Once again she offered up a quick prayer of thanks that their lives had been spared.

Ida Olson's piercing voice continued on, grating on Marie's nerves. Once she'd asked Mother if she didn't think Mrs. Olson was nothing but a loudmouthed busybody. Mother had said no, that there were good points to be found in everyone . . . just sometimes one had to look a little harder to discover them.

". . . so Lyle and I put a few things together for you," Ida continued, having scarcely taken a breath since she'd come in the door. "We stopped by your place for a look, and there's nothing left—I mean *nothing* at all. You were lucky to escape with your lives. My gracious, those chimney fires can sure go quick. A squirrel's nest, you figure? Why, we had trouble with squirrels one year, and my Lyle . . ."

The conversation continued with Ida dominating and Mother and Grandma Biggs getting only an occasional word in edgewise. Marie pushed herself to her feet, mulling over the idea of a squirrel's nest causing a chimney fire. That made sense, she supposed; she had heard of it happening before. But since the house had burned to the ground, there was no way to be certain. What was hard to believe, though, was how fast the house had gone up in flames. A shiver ran down her spine at the thought that their entire house had been consumed in well under two hours' time.

Was this Harald's room? she wondered, looking about. She had barely taken notice of her surroundings during the night when they came in. In the gray morning light she noted that the headboard and matching dresser were made of maple. A white tatted runner sat atop the dresser, on which rested a framed photograph of a man and woman. Walking over to the dresser, she examined the pair, deciding these had to be Harald's parents. The resemblance, especially the lines and shape of the man's face, was too strong for them not to be.

Catching her reflection in the mirror above the dresser, Marie shuddered. Her oval face was smudged with soot, and her normally glossy auburn hair, though pulled back into a braid, was dull and dingy.

The small, curtained closet in the corner of the room seemed to beckon her, and somewhat guiltily she found herself pushing aside the curtain to peek inside, telling herself there might be something she could wear until she . . .

Until she what? She sighed, beginning to realize the magnitude of her family's loss. She had no clothes—none of them had any clothes—except for what they wore as they fled the fire. What were they going to do?

She took in the well-ordered row of clothing hanging in the closet, a small trunk on the shelf above the clothes rod, and two pair of shoes sitting neatly on the floor. This must be Harald's room indeed, she surmised, looking at the size of the shirts and suit coat. Only two dress shirts and a single dress suit coat hung amidst the work-grade items. She wondered how many fine suits of clothing Chadwick owned . . . and if he even had a comfortable work shirt in his possession.

Harald Hamsun was certainly a simple man, not given to fineries.

Marie started at a knock on the door and let the curtain fall back into place. "I'm awake," she said, walking with haste to the place she'd spent the night. Bending over, she busied herself with tidying the blankets.

"Good morning, dear," Mother sang out, entering the room with a basket full of folded clothing. Marie observed that her mother had washed, brushed her hair, and dressed in an unfamiliar yet worn dark blue skirt and blouse that were slightly too big for her. Fatigue showed in her features, announced by the dark circles beneath her eyes. But her manner gave away none of her weariness. "I don't know how they managed it, but Myra Leonard and Coralee McGraw were here early this morning with food and provisions and clothes—even shoes—for just about all of us. Grandma's sitting on the sofa going through some items, and I thought we could sort through this pile together. Oh, and Ida Olson just dropped some things by, too."

"I heard," Marie said dryly.

"I was pretty sure she woke you," Mother added with a tired smile, setting the basket on the bed. "I just don't understand how word got around as fast as it did."

"Maybe people haven't *heard* our news so much as they've *smelled* it." Marie wrinkled her nose, then let out a sigh. "Well, all of Decoria Township knows about the fire; I wonder how long it will take for word to reach Chadwick in Mankato?" She imagined his distress at learning of their plight, how his fine team of horses would speed south over the eight-mile distance separating them once the report reached his ears.

"Give it a couple days, dear. It often takes folks in Mankato a while to learn what goes on in the country."

Marie nodded, anticipating Chadwick's arrival, hoping it would be soon.

"Would you like to wash?" Mother asked. "There's hot water on the stove. Some oatmeal for you to eat, too. All the men are over at our place, so you can get cleaned up in the kitchen. There's sure to be something to fit you in this pile. I'd guess Coralee's about your size."

"How is Father this morning?" Marie asked cautiously. To her surprise, her mother's eyes filled with tears.

"To be honest, I don't know."

"Well, what do you think is the matter with him?"

Mother closed her eyes for a long moment. "Oh, dear. Understanding the mind of a man is often a difficult thing." Wiping her tears with the end of one rolled-up sleeve, she gave Marie a watery smile. "But I've also heard your father say a woman's mind is beyond fathom, as well. In the first place, I think he's feeling guilty for not having checked the chimney sooner. He had intended to do that this fall, but he just hadn't gotten around to it yet."

"The fire wasn't his fault."

"No one is saying it was," Mother said, shaking her head, her small hands smoothing the white blouse atop the basket of clothes. "But you can't convince him otherwise. I'm also coming to see that he has a terrible problem with accepting charity."

"But he's always been so generous," Marie said.

"Yes, dear, but giving out of your plenty and receiving in need and humility are two completely different things. It all comes down to a matter of pride, Marie. I don't find it easy to accept charity myself, but I can look at it as the Lord providing for our needs. Your father's pride is keeping him from seeing it that way, or for being thankful for anything at all. I'm so glad Harald was able to talk some sense into him last night, or we'd have all spent the night in the barn."

"Will we stay here until we rebuild?"

"Well, there's another problem," Mother said with a deep sigh. "Your father chose not to buy fire insurance, so . . ."

"So . . . now what?" Marie asked, a feeling of dread growing within her belly. "Does that mean we can't build a new house?"

"I'm not sure what it all means yet, dear, but try not to worry yourself. We own the land, free and clear, most of the crops are in, and we have some savings tucked away."

"And the animals and outbuildings made it all right, didn't they?"

"That's my girl." Mother gave her a tired but approving smile. "See how much we have? We just need to look at things from that perspective and trust that the Lord has everything under control." Pulling half the pile of clothes from the basket, she set them on the bed. "And what a neighbor we have in Harald. He insists we stay with him as long as necessary, no matter that we more than fill his house. So in answer to your question, dear, yes, I believe we will be staying here."

"That's very generous of him." Oddly touched by their neighbor's giving nature, Marie felt a lump form in her throat. She remembered the special effort he had made last night to make her feel welcome in his home, and the gentle way he had treated Julia. She had never taken the time to know him very well, but it seemed that there was more to Harald Hamsun than she had previously thought.

The next few days passed in a blur for Marie. One of the neighbors, Coralee McGraw, had taken Sarah and Julia to her home to stay for a period of time, yet it still seemed as though there were too many things to do. Cooking, cleaning, washing clothes—it never ended. Marie, Rosemary, Mother, and Grandma scarcely quit moving.

And the donations poured in. Clothing, shoes, bedding, canned goods, meat, baked items, kitchen utensils, blankets. The list of items went on and on. Just this morning Joe Kinstrup had brought a bushel of apples from his orchard, and Lawrence Pickert a smoked ham. It troubled Marie to see how difficult it was for Father to accept these goodwill offerings from others. The boys had no such problem. Last night over a late supper Anthony and Raymond joked that they ate better now than they ever had.

Harald's house was quite a bit smaller than theirs had been, and it was a challenge to make do with so many people in tighter quarters. This was most evident, of course, at mealtimes and bedtime. Poor Harald, Marie frequently thought, having his home disrupted in such a manner.

But he didn't seem to mind one bit. His disposition never wavered from calm and steady, and he truly seemed to enjoy their company. He wasn't given to long discourses or even small talk, but he was kind with his words and generous with his compliments. And as much as he could, he helped Father and the boys with their farm work and with cleaning the rubble out of the basement.

Pausing while she packed a large basket of food for the men's lunch, Marie glanced outdoors at the glorious autumn day. The clouds and cold rain of the past few days had yielded to a sunny, more temperate offering. Was it just the weather that made her spirits soar? Nothing about their circumstances had changed, yet a burst of well-being suffused her. "I'll take lunch over to the house," she offered, eager to be outdoors.

"Thank you, Marie," Mother replied from the sofa, where she sat with Grandma Biggs, altering a donated dress for slender Rosemary. "Will you also pick eggs for me? I asked Hugh to do it this morning, but I doubt he remembered."

"What do you expect, Mother? He's only twelve," Rosemary interjected. She was seated at the table peeling tart, juicy apples for pie. For some reason she had adopted a manner worthy of a bossy eldest sister, though she was the second child born to William and Helen Biggs. Grandma always said it was because Rosemary was pleased beyond reason to be fifteen minutes older than Raymond, a fact she never let him forget. Only she didn't stop at Raymond. She played mother hen to all her siblings, save Marie.

"And you were never twelve?" Marie asked with a grin, taking rare pleasure in reminding her sister that she had been fifteen to her twelve.

"You tell her, Marie," Grandma Biggs spoke from the couch, chuckling. "And if that ain't enough, I can remind her about how I used to change her—"

"All right, all right," Rosemary conceded with a laugh. "I'll

just peel apples, and Marie can pick eggs. It's better than picking a fight."

Carrying the weighty basket through the door, Marie thought
how fortunate she was to have such a good friend in her sister.
The two of them had always gotten along better than most
sisters, she suspected.

Overhead a pair of noisy blue jays cavorting among rust-hued
oak branches captured her attention. *What a perfect day to be
outdoors,* she thought, the fresh fall breeze rustling the leaves and
caressing her face and neck as she made her way down the walk
to the drive. Looking up into a sky of such dazzling blue, it was
hard to believe that anything could be wrong in the world. In
fact, this day was much like the day before their house burned,
the day she'd taken a ride through the countryside with
Chadwick. It seemed like years ago, not just days.

Why hasn't Chadwick come to call? she wondered for the
umpteenth time. News of their fire must have reached his ears
by now. She felt hurt by his failure to rush to her side. People
she scarcely knew had responded to the emergency, yet she had
seen nothing of the young man she thought she knew so well.

"Can I help you with that?"

Stopping and turning, Marie watched as Harald took long
strides to catch up with her, removing his hat as he approached.
Blue work pants, held up by suspenders, hugged his sturdy
form, and she noticed he'd rolled up his light-colored shirt
sleeves, exposing muscular forearms.

Why on earth she should notice the way the sunlight shone
upon the silky, golden hairs of those arms, she did not know . . .
yet she did.

"It's lunch," she replied inanely, feeling suddenly shy.

Harald nodded, setting his hat back on his head and taking
the heavy hamper from her arms. "Looks strange, doesn't it?" he
commented.

"What—my lunch?" Marie forgot her shyness, falling into step beside him. "You don't even know what I made."

"No, Marie, not your lunch." Harald smiled, his eyes crinkling up until they nearly disappeared. Einar Hamsun's speech had been heavily accented by his native Norwegian tongue, but only a hint of the lyrical intonation was evident in his nephew's deep voice. "See there?" he said, pointing across the lane to the copse of trees on the Biggses' property. "The empty place where your house stood."

"Oh . . . yes," Marie replied, taking in the vista—minus the farmhouse. Silently, she berated herself for her tongue-tied response. What was the matter with her? She never had any trouble holding a conversation with Chadwick. Even college-educated as he now was, he had told her more than once how much he liked talking with her.

Maybe her flustered feelings around Harald had to do with the fact that she knew he had once asked Father for permission to court her. And perhaps, also, because after the past few days she could no longer view him as a pleasant neighbor man whom she hardly ever saw. He was much more than that, she now knew.

So why, then, should she have these butterflies in her stomach as they walked along his drive, side by side? Having new knowledge of a man's depth of character most certainly should not cause one to feel agitated. And why, pray tell, did her gaze keep stealing toward him, to look him over more closely?

Pray tell.

Prayer. Why hadn't she thought of that before? In her mind she dispatched an urgent plea to the Heavenly Father that he might swiftly bring peace to this curious new anxiety that plagued her when in Harald Hamsun's presence.

"I would like to know you better, Marie."

Harald's direct words interrupted her prayer and nearly

brought her heart to her throat. She had been seeing Chadwick
Farrell off and on for the better part of four years, and he had
never once said anything so forthright. Marie thought the gravel
had never crunched so loudly beneath her shoes as it did now.
Long seconds passed while her brain frantically tried to formulate a response.

"You would?" she said, finally.

"You are a fine woman." He nodded with certainty.

A fine woman.

There was something about the way Harald said those words
that gave Marie a quiver deep down inside, and a resultant wave
of warmth spread across her cheeks. Those three short words
had conveyed appreciation and approval and manly interest all
at once. Chadwick talked a lot, certainly, and he had told her
how much he liked spending time with her, but such talk was
always flowery, or in a teasing vein. He'd never directly or
succinctly communicated any such heartfelt sentiments as she
had just heard from this simple Norwegian farmer.

Or maybe not so simple . . .

Oh, Marie, now what? Clasping her hands together, Marie
cleared her throat, missing the beginning of Harald's next
sentence.

". . . not the best circumstances right now with both of us
living under the same roof. During this time we can become
better acquainted and later, if you wish, after you've moved back
home, I will call for you."

Crunch, crunch, crunch.

On they walked, as the Indian summer sun beat down warm
and steady. Good autumn smells filling the air. Father and the
boys could now be heard easily as they worked to clear rubble
from the burned-out cellar.

"You certainly are . . . frank," Marie ventured as they walked the short jog down the lane from the Hamsun driveway to the Biggs driveway.

"Just truthful." Harald looked over at her at the same time she chanced to take a glance at him. On his broad face was an expression of sincerity and earnestness, and his bright blue gaze sought hers.

Something about his expression caused another unknown emotion to run through Marie, strong and sweet and painful, completely unfamiliar. Dropping her gaze, she studied her clasped hands. "It's good to be truthful," she managed to say, nodding perhaps too much, her words sounding faint in her own ears.

But Harald had no such problems. His voice was as warm and deep as a pot of thick golden honey, making that peculiar feeling inside her grow even stronger.

"So what do you think, Marie? Would you like to know me better, too?"

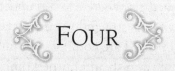

FOUR

It was a long moment before Marie found her tongue. "I . . . I . . . yes," she said, gulping, heart pounding, surprised to find that she really did want to know more about Harald Hamsun.

His only response was a smile and a nod, eyes crinkling, and he continued walking.

Staying in step beside him, Marie felt her mind whirl. The past few days at Harald's house had only whetted her curiosity about what sort of a man he was. Generous, that was more than evident. God-fearing, to be certain; he attended church regularly and read from the Scriptures in the evenings. And *truthful*—she had just learned firsthand what value he placed on honesty. She also had found him to be calm and kind and gentle and . . .

Handsome?

For as long as she could remember, Chadwick Farrell's height and lean, dark-haired looks had meant *handsome* to Marie. Harald Hamsun, with his fair coloring, moderate height and broad, powerful frame could not possibly have been more unlike that. Why, his big hands could no doubt easily . . .

Span your waist?

Now, where on earth had a thought like that come from? Marie felt her cheeks burn once again and was glad Harald's attention seemed to be occupied elsewhere. He certainly had turned this day upside down with his straightforward declaration.

"Hey, Marie and Harald are coming with lunch," Hugh called from beside a pile of rubbish and burned timbers.

"This is *my* lunch. You'll have to get your own." A grin parted Harald's lips, revealing both a sense of humor and a row of strong, white teeth. His expression of mirth, eyes crinkled up so tight she was sure he couldn't even see where he was going, brought an answering smile to Marie's lips despite her tangled feelings.

A chorus of loud cries ascended from the foundation where their house once stood as Raymond and Anthony scaled the ladder that poked up out of the ground and brushed themselves off. Marie recoiled at the sight of her brothers, soot-black from head to toe, and even in her present state of distraction she couldn't help but wonder if those clothes would ever come clean.

Lunch was a pleasant affair. Marie was glad for the congeniality and banter that her brothers provided. It presented her the opportunity to nibble on a slice of bread and sort out her thoughts. Harald fit right in with the boys, and it was obvious that they thought the world of him. Though she tried not to, she found herself watching Harald through lowered lashes as his words rang through her thoughts, over and over.

When they were nearly finished eating, Father appeared from the barn, coming over only briefly to where they sat on the damp, autumn-browned grass. Unlike the boys, his appearance was clean, if threadbare. The donated garments of one of their neighbors hung loosely on his frame, accentuating a new lean-ness. He barely said hello as he reached into the basket and took out a single apple. There was a lifelessness in his normally animated brown eyes as he muttered something about having to go to the bank. A short time later, after hitching a team of horses to the wagon, he departed for town.

The conversation took a sober turn after Father's departure. Raymond was the first to speak. "I'm more than a little worried about him. He's been like that ever since the fire."

Anthony nodded. "He hardly says anything to anyone."

"Well, he said something to me yesterday," Hugh said, hurt evident in his young voice. "All I did was drop a bucket he handed up to me—it was heavier than I thought—and he called me stupid and yelled at me like he was never going to stop." He sighed, brushing crumbs from his sooty lap. "I said I was sorry. I didn't mean to do it."

"Well, it was full of rock and mortar, and you did almost drop it on his head," Raymond said with feigned disgust.

"Your father is a good man," Harald said, nodding, "but he's carrying many burdens . . . burdens none of you have ever carried."

Hugh responded in wounded bafflement. "But aren't we just supposed to lay our burdens at the foot of the cross? Pastor Price gave a sermon on that a few weeks ago."

"Don't you remember what else he said, Hugh? He also talked about the man who laid his burdens down, only to pick them right back up again when he finished praying." Anthony's attention to and quick recall of every detail of his life never failed to impress Marie.

"Mother says he feels guilty about the fire," she said, contributing what she knew to the conversation, "and that he's having trouble accepting charity."

"What other choice do we have right now than to accept charity?" Anthony's words were spoken matter-of-factly. "And if one of our neighbors had a fire, you know Father would be there to help in any way he could."

"He would, indeed." Harald reached for an apple and took a

bite. Chewing thoughtfully, he added, "Give him some time. Acceptance is often a process."

"Well, the process is going a little too slow for me," Hugh retorted, still obviously smarting from his father's uncharacteristic temper and sharp words of the day before. "He never even apologized or—"

"Oh, Ma-riee," Raymond interrupted, drawing out the last syllable of her name on a sing-song note. "Lookie who's coming down the road."

"Chadwick the Ferret," Hugh pronounced with a snicker, recovering from his emotional ache in record time. "Grandma's right: 'Ferret' fits him better than 'skunk' because he sort of looks like a weasel . . . don't you think, Ray?"

"Well, I wouldn't say he actually *looks* like a weasel, but—"

Hugh didn't give Raymond a chance to finish his sentence before turning to Harald. "Marie wants to marry the ferret," he said with the brand of obnoxiousness only twelve-year-old boys possess, rolling his eyes in her direction. "Oh, Chadwick," he mocked, adopting an unnaturally high tone while he fluttered his hand over his heart, "come and take me away to your big fancy mansion in Mankato. I'm *madly* in love with you, and I want to—"

"Stop it, Hugh," Anthony said with annoyance. Waves of mortification billowed through Marie at their youngest brother's caricature of her. She had never once acted like that about Chadwick . . . what must Harald be thinking of her at this moment? Keeping her gaze directed downward, she busied herself packing the picnic items back into the basket.

In one motion Anthony pushed his tall, skinny body to a standing position and set his hat back on his head. "Your job is cleaning stalls this afternoon, Hugh; you'd better get to it. I would hate to think what Father might say to you if you don't have them done by the time he gets back from town."

"Come on, little brother," Raymond said somewhat reluctantly as he also stood, "you don't really want to hang around here and watch Chadwick and Marie make gooey eyes at each other, do you?"

"I am free to help you this afternoon," Harald said to appreciative noises from all three of the Biggs boys. He handed his plate and cup to Marie as Chadwick Farrell's fashionable black buggy turned into the drive, led by the paired bays. "If we work hard, we can get the cellar finished this afternoon."

Marie felt sick. For all the promise the beautiful day had held, the afternoon was turning into the stuff from which nightmares were made. Not more than a half hour ago Harald had declared his interest in her . . . and for some reason still unknown to her she had responded accordingly. Was it just the shock of his direct words that had caused the strange, potent feelings within her as they'd walked along, or was it something more?

And why today, of all days, did her brothers seem intent on humiliating her before him?

If that weren't enough, at long last here came Chadwick, his handsome face a welcome sight on any other day. He liked her, she knew, but what was truly behind the inconstant nature of his courtship—if it could even be called that? What were his real feelings for her, his intentions? Over the past years, deep down, she had allowed herself to dream of being married to Chadwick, yet he seemed content to continue on as always, spending what time they were together waxing on about his plans and dreams for the future. She knew his family—his mother, in particular— didn't approve of his spending time with her, but what perplexed her was that he made no effort to take their relationship beyond its present state, despite the fact that she strongly sensed his romantic interest.

So why, today, didn't her heart leap as his carriage approached? Where was the usual thrill that coursed through

her at the mere sight of him? Though she'd asked the Lord to
remove her anxious thoughts, it seemed they had done nothing
but multiply. Chadwick. Harald. What was she supposed to
think? What was she supposed to feel?

And what on earth was she going to do with the two of them
together?

Chancing a glance at the blond man, she saw that he studied
the advancing carriage with an unreadable expression on his
broad face. His eyes may have narrowed as he pressed big,
work-roughened hands against muscular thighs and pushed
himself to a standing position. Or it could have been just a trick
of the sunlight, Marie concluded. Harald thanked her for lunch
and went to join the boys.

"Hello, Marie," Chadwick called, bringing his horses to a halt
as he stood and surveyed the damaged landscape. A long, low
whistled note escaped him, and he gracefully alighted from the
carriage, coming to join her where she knelt over the picnic
basket. "I'd say it's true, then. I just heard today . . . she burned
right to the ground, didn't she?"

Marie nodded, more ill at ease than she could ever remember.

"But your family got out all right, didn't they?"

"We're fine." She sighed, closing the basket. There was nothing
more to pack, nothing more with which to occupy her hands. She
rose quickly, before he could offer his arm to assist her. "Except
that Father—"

"Say, I passed your father on my way out here," Chadwick
interrupted, straightening the lapels of an understated but
expensive camel-colored wool suit coat. "He must have been
a bit preoccupied; he didn't even wave.

"But I was preoccupied, too, Marie, thinking that there are
just plain too many fires," he went on, clearing his throat as he
warmed to his subject. "People lose their homes, their businesses, their belongings, and sometimes their lives. In the city,

whole blocks go up at a time. People simply need to be more widely educated on how to prevent fires. I've also been thinking about how I might someday implement a plan of public assistance to aid fire victims. . . ."

Marie nodded, thinking he looked like a politician as he spoke, hands clasped behind his back, pacing back and forth. Had he always talked so much? Thinking back, she realized that their time spent together had been largely consumed by the articulation of Chadwick's many concepts and beliefs. No wonder he liked to spend time with her; she rarely obstructed his abundant flow of words. She seldom had a chance to. With new awareness she contemplated Chadwick Farrell, drawing comparisons between his manner and Harald's.

". . . I said, where are you staying, Marie? And where did you get that dress?"

"Oh, pardon me," Marie said, pulling her attention from her thoughts to the man who stood before her, an earnest expression on his handsome features. "I've been a bit distracted . . . since the fire."

"Of course you have." Sympathy shone from his hazel eyes as he studied her appearance. "Despite your, ah, circumstances, you're looking quite lovely today. Your face seems to have a sort of radiance, a glow of its own."

"It does?" Why did he stare at her so? Marie brought her hand up to her face, thinking her cheek felt quite warm. Maybe she was really getting sick. The idea of spending a few days in bed, away from everyone and everything, suddenly had a great deal of appeal. There was just too much to think about.

"Hey, Chadwick," Hugh called, too innocently, from the ladder, "can you give us a hand down here?"

"I'd really like to," the tall, dark-haired youth replied, tucking Marie's arm in his own and strolling over to the edge of the

cellar, "but I have to be going back to town. I'm very busy today
at the bank. That looks like . . . quite dirty work down there."

The boys must have had a bet going about whether Chadwick
would help. Marie could tell from the satisfied smirk on Hugh's
face. Harald sent her a brief but questioning glance as he worked
to loosen a heavy timber that had only partially burned, his
shoulder muscles straining through his shirt.

"I must be going now," Chadwick called down. "But you'll
have to ask Marie to tell you about the plans I have for assisting
the victims of fires in the future. It's always been an idea of mine,
but after hearing today of your misfortune, it's taken root and
literally blossomed." Letting go of her arm, he gestured widely
with both his hands. "Not only do I plan to unite the community
with this effort, I will also educate the public on all possible
ways to prevent fires from occurring. It's an exciting concept,
one that I know will be of real help to all of Blue Earth County."

"Real help?" Marie heard Raymond mutter darkly, standing
just below her with his shovel in his hands. "He wouldn't know
what real help was if it bit him in the hind end."

"Well, I'm off," Chadwick called to his audience of laborers,
evidently missing Raymond's observation. He touched the brim
of his hat. "Good-bye, Marie," he said, skimming his knuckles in
a light caress down the side of her cheek. His hazel eyes studied
her face, his elegant brows lifted.

Marie cleared her throat, taken by surprise at his familiar
gesture. At the same time Hugh snorted in laughter; whether in
response to Raymond's remark or Chadwick's touch she did not
know. Quickly she stepped away from the edge of the basement,
away from Chadwick, and closed her eyes in embarrassment.

Why, today, had Chadwick chosen to touch her in such a
manner in front of her brothers—and Harald, no less? She was
never going to hear the end of it. Again she wondered what
Harald must be thinking of her.

The sick feeling inside her grew.

"Are you sure you're all right, Marie? All of a sudden you don't look so well." She heard Chadwick's voice at her side; the spicy scent of his cologne filled her nostrils. "Can I give you a lift to . . . wherever you're staying?"

"Uh, no thank you." Opening her eyes, she forced a smile. "I'll just walk."

"If you're sure . . ."

"I'm sure."

"I'll be out to see you soon," he said in a concerned voice. "Now where is it you're staying, so I can find you?"

"At the Hamsun farm, across the road," she said with a sigh, knowing he wouldn't leave until he had received that information. "But I don't know if—"

"All right, then. You can count on seeing me soon." Having said that, he hesitated, as if there were something more he wanted to say. His eyes searched her face, and she could have sworn that he looked a little nervous. He cleared his throat.

"Good-bye, Marie," he finally said, patting her arm. With a jaunty step he walked toward his carriage, leaving Marie wondering what it was he had nearly said.

FIVE

The sun was setting as Raymond, Anthony, and Hugh trooped through the kitchen doorway of the Hamsun farmhouse, their spirits high. They had washed at the pump and had changed out of their filthy clothes. Their wet hair gleamed against their heads.

"We got it all done!" Raymond announced. "The foundation needs a little work yet, but thank goodness it's stacked rock. It won't take long, and we'll be ready to build."

"Thanks to Harald," Anthony pointed out. "We never could have done it without him."

"Yeah, you never seen anyone work like him," said Hugh. "He's worth three or four fellows and six horses all in one. I can hardly wait till Father sees it."

"That's wonderful news, boys," Mother called as she set the table. "I know your father will be very pleased."

Hugh padded over to the worktable where Marie and Rosemary were putting the final touches on the evening meal. "What smells so good?" he asked, edging between them. "Mmm, fresh biscuits. How long till we eat?"

"We'll have the food on the table shortly," Mother replied, "so mind your manners until then. Say, speaking of your father, has he come back from Mankato yet?"

"Haven't seen him," Anthony replied. "Don't you think if he was just going to the bank, he should have been back hours ago?"

"He probably stopped at the lumberyard. That can take a while, as I recall," Grandma said with a snort. "Your grandpa always seemed to lose track of time whenever he went to town to look for lumber or hardware or machinery. Must run in their blood." She pushed herself up from the rocker where she sat crocheting. "Where's that Harald of mine?" she asked, making her way to the kitchen with the new walking stick he had fashioned for her the day after the fire.

Marie's heart made a funny leap when Harald's name was mentioned. All afternoon she had been looking forward to seeing him again—and dreading it, too, thinking of the way he had declared his interest in her. She had told him she wanted to know him better, too, but how was she supposed to act around him now? Maybe she had replied too hastily. Maybe she should have asked for time to think the matter over.

"*Your* Harald, Grandma?" Raymond grinned and snatched a biscuit. "He makes you a new cane, and now you've adopted him?"

"It's not a cane, it's a walking stick. You can go on and make fun of me all you like, but I'm comin' to love that young man like one of my own."

"Harald had a few things to do before he came in, and he said to go ahead without him," Anthony announced, assisting his grandmother to her chair at the crowded table. Both end leaves were extended, yet the distance between plates was minimal.

"Do you love Chadwick Farrell like one of your own, too, Grandma?" Imitating his eldest brother, Hugh light-fingered a biscuit and walked toward the table. "He came to visit Marie today, you know, and he touched her right on her face."

"What do you mean, he touched her right on her face?"

Marie felt the heat creep up her cheeks as she turned to the stove and lifted the lid on the stew. Giving the bubbling mixture in the big cast iron pot a stir, she realized Chadwick's uncharacteristic gesture had indeed been noted.

"You know, he kind of ran his hand down her face like this." Hugh demonstrated the caress in an exaggerated fashion on his own cheek, batting his eyelids and lolling his head back and forth.

"That's enough, Hugh," Mother said sternly.

Rosemary set down her spatula in exasperation and put her hand on her hip. "Oh, can't you just leave Marie alone, you little troublemaker? It's not nice to tease someone like that."

"Sure, Rosemary," he went on, "let's talk about you and Jason Gould holding hands after church last week—ouch!"

Mother had taken Hugh by the ear and now marched him out the door. Rosemary busied herself with piling biscuits in a napkin-lined basket while Grandma Biggs shook her head and pronounced, "That boy just doesn't know when to shut his mouth, does he?"

Hugh's overstated version of Chadwick's hand movement had caused more knots in Marie's stomach. Her restless thoughts shifted from Harald back to the banker's son, and why he might have chosen today to press his suit.

She had dreamed of such a moment. So where was her happiness? Her joy at Chadwick's familiar gesture? And why did thoughts of Harald keep intruding whenever her mind turned to the day's events?

After a long moment Mother reappeared, followed by an abashed Hugh, who asked his sisters' forgiveness.

"Let's eat our supper and put all this nonsense behind us," Mother said in a determined tone while the boys filed to the table. "Raymond, light that lantern over there, will you? Remember to put butter and honey on the table with the biscuits, Rosemary. And Marie, don't serve all the stew. Put some into the warming oven for your father and Harald."

Finally everyone was seated and the blessing asked. As the tasty meal was consumed, the tension fell away and the conversation turned to the day's events. Picking at her meat and vegetables, Marie found she still did not have much of an appetite.

Eventually the topic of Chadwick's visit came up again, and Grandma Biggs chuckled while Anthony gave an accounting of Chadwick's fine dress and appearance as he'd stood at the edge of the foundation, peering in at them. "You should have seen him, Grandma, going on about all the great and wonderful things he plans to do for 'fire victims' someday, yet he didn't even lift a hand when he saw a burned-out family right in front of his face."

"Hot air and horsefeathers." Grandma nodded. "I told you that boy was nothing but a pretty talker, Marie. No substance. Now take Harald—"

Marie was spared from responding as the door opened, admitting Harald and her father. Was it her imagination, or did the younger man seem to be supporting the older? Yes, Father was definitely unsteady on his feet, she noted with concern, and he looked terrible. His face was chalky—save the high color that stood in his cheeks—and his eyes were glassed over. Quickly she glanced at Mother, who wore a troubled expression on her face. The sounds of a meal being eaten dwindled away and conversation stopped.

"Did you spend the afternoon drinking, William Raymond Biggs?" Grandma's blunt question seemed to echo in the stillness of the room. "So help me, William, if you've been—"

"He hasn't been drinking; he's sick." Harald spoke quietly. "He's got a fever."

"Oh, my poor darling." Mother was out of her chair and at Father's side instantly. "You haven't been well all week, have you?"

"I didn't get the loan." Father delivered the words in a hollow monotone, casting a further pall over the room. "Herman Farrell won't loan me a cent to rebuild. He says he can't risk the credit."

"You're burning up, William. We can talk of loans another time. Harald, help me get him to bed."

"Well, why wouldn't that horse's patoot give us a loan?" Grandma Biggs demanded, outraged. "There's nothing the matter with our credit. The Biggses have always paid their debts on time, not that we've had that many of them. Help me out of this chair, Anthony." Irritation caused her voice to sharpen as she pulled herself to her diminutive height and banged her walking stick on the floor. "I smell Imogene Farrell's hand in these dirty dealings. And she calls herself a God-fearin' woman." Thumping her stick as she made her way to her son, she sputtered, "I know what this is about, William, and you should, too."

"Well, I don't know what this is about," Mother said, pulling on Father's arm, "but I know this man needs to be put to bed."

"It's a message to us, isn't it, Grandma?" Anthony glanced at Marie as he spoke, his young face solemn.

"It sure is, sonny, loud and clear. Credit risk, my eye. Herman and Imogene Farrell have enough money to burn a wet mule. This is about Marie! That wretched Imogene can't stand the thought of her boy takin' up with a country girl, and she's tryin' to make us miserable any way she can."

"Surely Herman Farrell wouldn't let his personal feelings color his business decisions, would he?" Mother was aghast at such an idea. "That can't be true, can it, William?"

"True enough that he told Lawrence Bentz over at the lumberyard not to extend me any credit, either."

Mother drew in her breath. "Lawrence told you that?"

"I don't imagine he had to," Grandma Biggs replied for her son. "I told you those Farrells were trouble from the get-go, Marie," she added, shaking her finger for emphasis. "Now don't you wish you'd listened to me?"

The tears that had gathered in Marie's eyes finally spilled down her cheeks at her grandmother's condemning words. All eyes were on her. "I . . . I . . . don't know what to say," she finally said, her voice breaking on a sob. "I'm . . . sorry."

"Marie, this isn't your fault." Harald's voice was firm and even as he entered the conversation. Bending forward, he spoke to the incensed elderly woman before him. "Please sit down and finish your supper, Mrs. Biggs. We can talk about this calmly after we get William taken care of." Concern shone in his eyes as his gaze met Marie's over her grandmother's neat gray bun.

As Harald and Mother assisted Father to the bedroom, Grandma grudgingly stepped aside. Instead of returning to the table, however, she stomped toward the stove and filled a pot with water, muttering about Imogene Farrell's wickedness and about how on earth she was supposed to make a decent fever concoction with her herbals being burned up in the fire.

Fearing she wouldn't be able to control herself from outright weeping for much longer, Marie rose and excused herself, realizing dimly it was the second time within a week she'd left the table in such a state . . . both times over the mention of Chadwick Farrell. Rosemary laid a warm hand on her arm as she walked past her, but Marie let it fall away and stepped through the door.

Giving in to her emotions, Marie allowed the tears to flow unchecked down her cheeks. How could so much have happened in less than a week? One day everything was fine, and just a few short days later absolutely *nothing* was right. Sinking to her knees on the grass near the grove of trees that lay between the barn and the stubbled cornfield, Marie cried out to God for mercy, for understanding, feeling every bit as desperate as the psalmist.

No immediate revelations came to her, no answers to the family's plight. Gradually the sobs that racked her chest abated; slowly and gently the tears stopped falling. She had no idea how much time she'd spent crying out her anguish, but twilight had long since slipped into velvety night. The moon was on the wane, allowing the points of countless stars to shine boldly in the vast sky.

How long had it been since she'd gazed at the stars? A peculiar quiet stole over her as she contemplated the beauty of the heavens, her eyes searching for and finding familiar constellations. How vast the universe, she marveled, how infinite the celestial bodies. A gentle wind stirred what few leaves remained on the branches above her and blew soothingly across her tear-ravaged face. Though the ground was damp with evening dew, the earthy smell of sod and fallen leaves mingled pleasantly, an aromatic balm for her troubled senses.

It was good to be out here by herself, alone with her thoughts. With a house full of people and activity it was all but impossible to spend private time in prayer, in contemplation. Sitting back fully on the grass, she relaxed, supposing that with all the unrest in Harald's house, no one would miss her for the time being.

God is our refuge and strength, a very present help in trouble. Therefore will not we fear. . . . Silently, she recited the Forty-sixth Psalm, reminding herself to have faith in God's power and protection, no matter what was happening. Her parents required all their children to memorize portions of Scripture, an obligation that Marie, as a child, had often fulfilled begrudgingly. Now she was thankful for her parents' firmness on the matter. Sighing deeply, she paused over the phrase *Be still and know that I am God,* resolving to spend more time simply being *still* before him.

"Marie, are you out here?" Harald stood at the back of the barn, holding a lantern aloft. A sphere of light surrounded him, illuminating the worry on his broad face. "Marie?"

"Over here, Harald," she called, knowing it would be wrong to pretend not to hear or see him. "Near the trees." Only a short time ago she would have thought Harald Hamsun to be the last person on earth she would have wanted to seek her out, but

now, curiously, she felt an unfamiliar pleasure as she watched
him approach. The lantern swung in a wide arc as he walked,
his strides sure and even, booted feet rustling the long grass.

Though the rational part of her told her it was dark and she
was being silly, her hands flew to smooth her hair and wipe
away any vestiges of tears. The pace of her heart increased the
nearer he drew, a giddy feeling settling in her chest.

"Are you all right, Marie?" His voice was gentle as he squatted
before her and set the lantern at his feet.

Squinting into the light, she nodded and attempted a smile.

"Can I walk you back to the house?"

"I . . . I'd like to stay out here a bit longer, if I'm not being
missed too much."

A smile crossed Harald's broad face, causing his eyes to crinkle in a way Marie was beginning to find very endearing. "You're
safe for the time being. Your father is in bed, your mother's got
your brothers doing the dishes, and your grandmother . . . well,
she's still all wound up."

Marie smiled shyly in return, dropping her gaze. "That's like
her." Plucking at the grass near her feet, her mind returned to
a more sober thought. "What do you think is the matter with
Father?"

He shrugged. "Hard to say. When your spirit is sick, your
body tends to follow suit."

Marie nodded, hoping nothing was seriously wrong with her
father.

Small talk out of the way, an awkward silence dropped
between them. Harald shifted on his haunches and cleared his
throat. Marie glanced up at him and quickly turned away, but
not before taking in the broadness of his chest, the size of his
powerful shoulders. The tempo of her heart accelerated even
further.

"What are you doing out here, Marie?" he asked, breaking

the quiet between them. "You were very upset when you left the house."

"You'll probably think it's silly."

"You can tell me." Something in the timbre of his voice invited her to share her thoughts with him, and before she was conscious of forming an answer, she had already replied.

"Looking at the stars . . . and praying."

"Neither is silly, Marie." On his face was an expression of sincerity and earnestness, the same one he'd worn when he'd walked down the driveway with her. "Do you mind if I sit with you?"

A thrill shot through her as she shook her head.

"You would prefer not?"

"No . . . I mean, yes . . . I mean, please sit down." She swallowed what little moisture her mouth contained and smiled ruefully. "If you still want to. I seem to have a good deal of trouble expressing myself around you."

"You express yourself just fine, Marie. That's one of the things I've always admired about you. That and your kind manner." Easing himself from his haunches, he sat cross-legged on the ground before her and blew out the lantern. In the darkness, he added, "And I would have to be blind not to notice your warm brown eyes and lovely smile. You are a beautiful woman, Marie Biggs."

His words, carried to her ears on a tender current of night wind, were both somberly spoken and deeply intimate. Even if nothing came of her acquaintance with Harald Hamsun, Marie knew she'd always remember this moment as the first in her life that she'd been genuinely courted. A part of her womanhood, until this time dormant, quickened within her, producing feelings both alien and exciting.

"Besides my . . . outward appearance, how well do you know me, Harald?" Her voice had a breathless quality when she spoke—was it from using his name?—but somehow the darkness enveloping them made it easier to speak the practical thoughts on her mind. "We've hardly had more than a passing association. Maybe I'm not the person you think I am."

His chuckle was easy. "You are. I know you from living here these past two years, from watching you in church, from sitting across from you at your family's dinner table . . . and I know a great deal of your character from your father, from the time he and I have spent together." He was quiet a moment before adding, "I've also prayed about you a great deal, Marie."

"Oh." Had she once thought his interest in courting her was due to loneliness? How wrong she'd been. Her mind worked to reconcile this new knowledge with the other mysterious elements of the night.

"What do you think about when you look at the stars?" he asked.

It was Marie's turn to clear her throat. "Well, tonight I was thinking how long it's been since I've . . . looked at the stars," she concluded limply.

"They're surely plentiful tonight," he said. "Do you know what I think when I look at the stars, Marie?"

Her eyes now adjusted to the darkness, Marie could see the outline of Harald's broad face angled up toward the heavens. "What?" She was curious to know.

"That God made each and every one of them."

"I think that, too, sometimes."

Harald was quiet for a long moment, his voice serious. "I look at the stars when I have problems to be solved."

"Do you get the answers?"

"Not usually." Marie sensed, rather than saw, Harald's smile, imagining how his eyes would be crinkled.

"Then why do you keep doing it?"

"Because it reminds me that the God who is big enough to

create the heavens and hang the stars in the sky can be trusted to carry me through whatever struggles I have here on this earth."

Lapsing into a comfortable silence, the two sat, occupied with their own thoughts while they looked at the magnificent display above them. Harald's words were food for thought for Marie, and she pondered the application of his practice, finding it sound. Now that she thought about it, she realized her mother almost never looked at the size of the problems before her— rather, she looked first to the Lord. Even with the predicaments now besetting them—the fire and destruction of all their wordly goods, Father's despondency and now illness, Herman Farrell's refusal to grant a loan . . .

The loan. Chadwick.

Marie had been so immersed in the wonder of this unex- pected interlude with Harald that she'd pushed the issue of Chadwick Farrell to the back of her thoughts. To the front he now strode, his hazel gaze peering questioningly at her in her mind's eye. What was she going to do about Chadwick and his suddenly much-more-warm feelings for her? she wondered. And what about the loan? Did he even know that his father had refused hers the money they needed to rebuild their house? There had to be something she could do to try to repair things. Maybe she could go to Mankato and talk with Mr. Farrell herself. Surely he would be sympathetic if she explained their situation. . . .

What are you doing, Marie, looking at the problem or looking to the Lord?

Gazing heavenward, she willed her anxious thoughts to stop while she viewed the countless points of light. God was in control. He would carry her—and the entire Biggs family— through whatever lay ahead. Slowly, in her mind, she recited the psalm again, thinking on its words and God's sovereignty.

Harald shifted in the darkness, his clothing rustling. It seemed her nerve endings were on fire as his knee accidentally brushed her leg. She heard him breathe in deeply, then exhale. Had the touch affected him, too?

Her peace fled.

Why hadn't he asked her about Chadwick? Surely he had to be curious about her relationship with the banker's son, particularly after Hugh had painted such an embellished portrait of their romance. In fact, "romance" was not the first word she'd use to describe her on-again, off-again association with Chadwick over the past several years.

The evening before the fire Rosemary had asked her if she was in love with Chadwick, and she had replied that she wasn't sure. The stirring feelings she'd experienced over the years thinking about him and spending time with him were pale in comparison to what Harald Hamsun was now doing to her insides.

"Are you feeling better, Marie? Would you like to go back to the house now?" Harald's voice was rich with gentleness.

"Y-yes, I think I'm ready . . . oh!" A surprised sound escaped her lips as Harald's big warm hand unerringly captured her own and pulled her to her feet.

"You have some thinking to do, *min lille benn*." The musical cadence of his native language flowed smoothly from his lips, his breath warm against her cheek.

It was a good thing Harald still held her hand, for her knees were in danger of buckling. The moment went on, sweet and terrifying all at once. Never had she stood so close to him before, her hand becoming intimately acquainted with the rugged texture of his, her senses to his unfamiliar, clean scent.

And then it was over . . . and she was disappointed.

"It's time to go back, Marie," he said, releasing her hand and bending to pick up the lantern. "There's much to be done."

Nodding, though she knew he couldn't see her, Marie fell into step beside him, thinking of the pile of problems that awaited her back at the house—and of Harald's reminder that God was indeed big enough to carry her family through their difficulties. That was true, she knew, but aside from that she wondered just how soon he could do something about the tangled-up mess she called her heart.

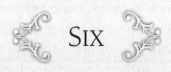

SIX

Father wasn't any better the next day, or the day after. The fever ate at him, devouring the remainder of his strength and any spare flesh it could find. Violent chills and episodes of profuse sweating visited alternately, causing him to cry out in misery. Both Mother and Grandma tried every remedy they knew, to no avail. Finally, Sunday night, Harald went to town for the doctor.

The respite of warm weather had passed, a blast of cold northerly air rushing in on its heels. It was well after nine when Harald and Dr. Camp returned, both heavily bundled against the chilly night. Dr. Camp nodded at the assembled family as Harald led him to the bedroom where Father lay. Mother had not left his side for hours.

Grandma Biggs rocked in her chair, doing more praying for her son than crocheting, Marie observed. The older woman frequently closed her eyes and let her hook rest in her lap. The rest of the family was gathered, as was the custom Sunday evenings, to take turns reading from Scripture and selected classical works, but tonight everyone seemed out of sorts.

Marie was lonesome for Sarah and Julia, but upon hearing of William's illness, Coralee McGraw had insisted on keeping the girls until he was better. She'd seen her sisters at church this morning; they seemed to be delighted with the idea of staying with Coralee's family a few days longer. They'd been having great fun playing with Annette and Bobby, Coralee had said, her children being nearly the same ages as the Biggs girls.

Marie had hardly seen Harald since their talk under the stars, and she hadn't seen Chadwick at all. With the older women spending so much time tending to William, the largest share of running the household had fallen to her and Rosemary. The boys had been busy, too, carrying on the day-to-day operations of the farm as best they could without their father's help or direction.

"What do you suppose is taking so long?" Hugh shifted impatiently.

"Patience, Hugh," Grandma Biggs replied without opening her eyes. "The doctor will be out when he's finished." Since her display of bad temper the night Father had come home sick, she had been subdued, even contrite. She had also apologized to Marie for blaming her for the family's misfortunes.

Finally Harald emerged from the bedroom, followed by Dr. Camp, who closed his bag with a sharp click. Scratching his balding head, he recited, "No injuries, no signs of infection, no rash, no pneumonia, no pain in the belly, no vomiting, no diarrhea. And no one else in the house has been ill, either." He shrugged. "I wish I could tell you what the matter is, but I can't seem to find a cause for William's illness."

"Well, something's the matter with him." Grandma sat forward in the rocker, recovering a little of her feistiness.

"Most assuredly something is the matter with him, Mrs. Biggs," the middle-aged physician agreed. "I just cannot find its cause."

"What can we do for him?" Harald asked.

"What you've been doing: Keep him comfortable as best you can and give him all the liquids he'll take. It appears he's in good hands." He started for the door and paused. "I'll be out to see him sometime Tuesday or Wednesday; by then he'll either be worse or he'll be better. Good night."

Harald thanked him for coming and accompanied him back outdoors. A helpless feeling engulfed Marie as the men exited the house, for a childish part of her had expected Dr. Camp to cure her father of whatever plagued him. For the first time she allowed herself to wonder if Father was ever going to get better. He was very ill indeed. When she'd gone in to see him just before supper, he had looked frighteningly old, much like Grandpa Biggs before he died. Tears welled in her eyes at the thought of losing him.

"What do you suppose Harald was doing all day yesterday?" Hugh asked. Sitting quietly seemed a nearly impossible undertaking for him. "He went to town early and didn't get back till late."

Grandma Biggs shushed him. "You'll learn someday, young man, the virtue of minding your own business. Harald is a grown man and isn't obliged to tell us of his whereabouts twenty-four hours a day."

Disgruntled, Hugh didn't press his point any further, but Marie had also wondered what occupied Harald's attention for an entire day. He'd acted peculiarly at church today, too, standoffish, and then had talked for a long time after the service with several men from the congregation. Perhaps he was trying to avoid her, regretting the things he'd said beneath the stars. She hadn't forgotten them, though. Not one word.

Despite her worry for her father, the things Harald had said and the memory of her hand in his burned in her mind as bright and hot as the flaming heavenly bodies that had shone down upon them that night. It seemed she had scarcely slept the past few nights for thinking of him and what the future might hold.

One thing was for certain: She could never again think of Harald
Hamsun as just a neighbor.

Marie was now very much aware of him as a man.

Morning dawned cold and clear and bright, the sky swept with
the wispy cirrus clouds country folk liked to call "horsetails."
Marie checked in on her father to find him in a deep sleep.
Mother, too, was sleeping, the upper half of her body draped
across the foot of the bed as she sat in the chair alongside.

Marie was relieved to see her parents in slumber. Softly closing the door on them, she made her way to the kitchen where
Grandma Biggs sat at the table with a cup of tea, a week-old
copy of the *Mankato Free Press*, and the Bible. The smell of
breakfast hung in the air, yet the house was quiet, save the ticking of the clock on the chest.

"Good morning, Marie. Are your daddy and mama still
asleep?"

Marie nodded, looking about. "Where is everyone?"

"Well, the boys are already doing chores, and Rosemary went
along to get the eggs. There's a pile of griddle cakes in the warming oven for you, honey." Folding her hands across the open
Bible before her, Ruth Biggs fixed her granddaughter with a keen
look. "Harald was gone even before any of the rest of us were
up." There was something in the way she said *Harald* that made
Marie wary.

Nodding noncommittally, Marie moved to the oven for her
breakfast.

"I notice we haven't seen much of him the past few days," the
older woman continued on conversationally, but Marie wasn't
fooled. Grandma was on a fishing expedition, casting her nets
wide.

"Well . . . . I'm certain he's very busy. He's got his own farm to run, plus he's helping out with ours as much as he can." Making her way back to the table, Marie sat down, spread her griddle cakes with Alice Kinstrup's fresh apple butter, and took a bite.

"I also noticed that you two spent a good deal of time outdoors together the other night."

Marie stopped chewing and met her grandmother's penetrating gaze. She swallowed. "Well, he just . . . we just . . ."

Up rose those slender, snow-white brows while a satisfied smile stole across her lips. "Yes?"

"We looked at the stars, that's all." She felt her cheeks grow warm and dropped her gaze to examine her breakfast. Why did she have the idea that Grandma was delighted—rather than concerned with propriety—to know she had been alone in the dark with Harald Hamsun?

"The stars . . . hmm . . . yes." The satisfied smile broadened into a grin as Grandma closed the Bible and reached for the newspaper, allowing her attention and one lean index finger to skim over the front-page advertisements and columns of tight print. "My, oh my, I wonder what goin's-on I missed reading about last week while our house was busy burning down. . . ." Glancing up, her expression all innocence, she encouraged, "Eat up, honey. You don't want your food to get cold."

Marie took another bite of her cakes while her grandmother read on, humming. Though she eyed the older woman with suspicion, not another word was mentioned of Harald Hamsun, or anything, for that matter. As quickly as she could, she finished her breakfast and busied herself with the dishes while Grandma took her time over the newspaper.

"What on earth is going on out there!"

Lost in her thoughts of Harald, Marie nearly dropped the heavy bowl she was wiping when her grandmother cried out. Pushing aside the dark blue calico curtain, she was startled to see a flurry of activity on the lane and at their homestead. A full dozen wagons were parked about their property, and coming down the lane were two heavily loaded lumber wagons.

"Look, Grandma—they're turning into our driveway!"

"Well, get on with you. Go on over and find out what's happening, Marie."

In a trice Marie pulled on a cloak hanging from a hook near the doorway and half walked, half ran the distance to the Biggs yard, taking no notice of the nippy temperature. The lumber wagons had been brought to a halt a short distance from the open foundation and were being unloaded by several sets of hands.

What could possibly be the meaning—

"Hello, Marie! Good morning, Marie!" Cheery greetings flew from neighbors and friends alike. Returning their hellos, Marie scanned the crowd, picking out her brothers among the men and youths busy unloading and restacking boards. She was about to make her way to them when she caught sight of Harald over near the pump with Lawrence Bentz, owner of Bentz Lumber. The two men pored over a sheaf of papers in Mr. Bentz's hands, then Harald nodded, took the papers, and wrote something across the top of them. After returning the papers to the older man, the two shook hands and rejoined the beehive of activity.

"Yoo-hoo, Marie, can you give us a hand over here?" Looking snug in a thick gray coat with a bright red kerchief tied over her curls, Nora Bromley smiled and waved from the back of her wagon. "Shoo, you kids!" she scolded, bending over her brood of well-bundled little ones. "Get back from the fire! Take a stick and go play fetch with Ace over there, away from everything. Go on, now."

The lanky mutt woofed, bounding along with his playmates as they went in the direction their mother had indicated. Cooking grates already had been set up over two large fires, and a neat stack of firewood sat ready to feed the flames throughout the day. Marie saw that many families from their church were represented: the men working over near the exposed hole in the ground where their house once stood, and the women by the wagons, preparing food and drink to sustain them all.

It was a noisy, confusing scene. Children ran and played amidst all the activity, and the sounds of delighted shrieks and laughter rose in addition to the loud clattering of lumber striking lumber. Marie walked toward Nora's wagon, more than a little bewildered, trying to take everything in.

"We need to get the coffee going," Nora chirped, handing her three large pots. "Those men'll need plenty of warming this morning. Fill these up, and when you're finished with that, you can help Vanessa and Allison put the chili together. Allison said she let the venison stew all night, so it's nice an' tender. Bess fried a mess of donuts this mornin' to go along with the coffee, an' we got more cakes and pies than Sherman's army could eat in a week." Pausing in her discourse, she asked, "Are you feeling all right, doll? You're lookin' a mite—"

"Marie! Can you believe this?" Rosemary ran up to Nora's wagon and tugged at her sister's arm, causing the large coffeepots to clank together. Her dark eyes glowed, and she was out of breath. "They're putting up our house! Harald organized everyone yesterday after church. And guess what else?" She lowered her voice and indicated with her head where Marie should look. "Jason is here!"

Pretending to admire the young man of her sister's affections, Marie tried to make sense of everything. Harald had organized all this . . . in just two days' time? If Father hadn't been granted a loan—or even credit at Bentz Lumber, then who had paid for two enormous wagons full of boards and building supplies?

The answer, she suspected, was to be found with the broad-faced man who strode across the yard with a leather apron tied about his hips. As if he felt her gaze upon him, Harald glanced in her direction and tipped his hat, smiling almost shyly, it seemed, before his attention was captured by Josh Bromley and Howard Jensen.

A delicious shiver passed through Marie, leaving a strange warmth in its wake. *Harald did this.* Her step was light as she set off toward the pump, coffeepots clunking and clanging. Rosemary had already deserted her to study Jason Gould from a better vantage point.

"Pastor Price is here!" someone shouted, as a team of horses pulled a plain carriage up the driveway.

"It looks good already—when do we eat?" the jovial middle-aged cleric called to the busy group of women. He set the carriage brake and dismounted, adding, "Joanne sends her regards; she's a little under the weather this morning. Speaking of which . . ." His eyes searched until they settled on Marie, and he walked toward her. "How is your father doing? Any better today?"

"A little, maybe. He and Mother were finally asleep, so we just let them be."

"Good! Glad to hear it. We'll keep praying, and in the meantime these good people will help you get a head start on your new house before the winter winds start flying."

Marie felt her eyes fill with tears. "I can't believe this . . . all of this . . ." she gestured.

A quiet smile stole over the pastor's face. "It's Christ's love in action, Marie."

"But how can we ever—"

"Shh, my dear. Don't trouble your heart with anxious thoughts. Here, let me help you with these big pots." His expression became animated. "We sure have a good showing, don't we? Stuart Goodrick and his boys couldn't come today, but they'll be here tomorrow. And you know how the five of them can work. . . ."

The day took on the atmosphere of a festival. Smiles and laughter came readily, despite the autumn temperature, and the busy sounds of hammering and sawing filled the air. Several times Marie tried to single out Harald, but he was in the thick of the building operations, always in the company of several others. She wanted to thank him for all this—for all he'd done—but somehow a simple thank-you didn't seem sufficient.

She wondered how Father would take this. If he had difficulty accepting such charitable items as food and clothing, what would his reaction be to a *house?* Marie offered up another prayer for his recovery, asking that he also might be gracious about receiving this outpouring of assistance from Harald, their friends, and neighbors.

By mid-morning, Ed and Coralee McGraw arrived with their two children and Sarah and Julia. Both Marie and Rosemary were overjoyed to see their younger sisters, and Rosemary took them to Harald's house to say hello to their parents and Grandma Biggs. Somewhat guiltily, Marie remembered that Grandma Biggs had asked her to go over and find out what was going on this morning . . . and she'd never returned to let her know. Oh, well, she'd know just as soon as Rosemary reached the door.

The morning passed quickly, and it wasn't until lunchtime that Marie was able to find an opportunity to speak with Harald. He had finished eating and was standing by himself at a chest-high pile of lumber, busy with a pencil and paper. Taking her bowl of chili, she walked slowly over to him, rehearsing what she would say when she reached him.

He saw her coming, though, and paused in his figuring, tucking his pencil behind his ear. "Hello, Marie." The smile on his broad face was for her alone, filled with welcome and affection and tenderness. "You've been busy this morning."

"I'd say you've been busy longer than that."

His expression became modest. "It's been no trouble."

"No trouble? Harald, you organized all this in just two days' time!" She gestured about the property with her steaming bowl of meat and beans, forgetting what she'd planned to say to him. "How can you . . . I just want you to know . . . I just want to tell you—"

He cut her off gently. "You don't have to say anything, Marie." A light wind ruffled his blond hair as he gazed at her with eyes as blue as warm summer skies. Taking the tin bowl from her hand, he set it on the stack of fragrant lumber and cupped his big, work-roughened hands around hers.

"The other day I told you I would call for you once you'd moved back home," he began seriously.

Marie nodded, a flood of emotions skittering through her breast. Excitement. Nervousness. Longing. Joy. The sounds of people and activity faded into the distance as she yielded her hands to his touch, her very self to the volumes of affection and quiet adoration she read in that brilliant blue gaze.

The sense of joy and expectancy intensified inside her as a slow smile broke across his countenance, causing his eyes to crinkle in a most delightful way. "But I've been thinking on the matter, Marie, and I want to tell you—"

"There you are! I've been looking all over the place for you!"

The moment was abruptly broken as Chadwick Farrell stalked over to where they stood, his long stride making short work of the distance between them. "What is all this? What is going on here?" His hazel eyes flashed indignation while his arm swung in a wide arc.

Marie's stomach picked itself up and turned over with a *whump* as she realized how close she was standing to Harald, and that he continued to hold her hands within his. "They're rebuilding our house," she replied in as composed a voice as she could muster, pulling her hands from Harald's and taking a step backward. "It was all a surprise. . . . Harald arranged it."

"Harald arranged it," Chadwick parroted, his gaze sharp, as if Marie's movement had just registered in his mind. "Harald arranged what, Marie?" His tone was accusing, his lips pale with anger. "I can't believe this . . . any of this." Straightening the arms of his gray-on-black pin-striped suit, he glared at the rough-clad farmer before him.

"Your father refused William a loan." In contrast to the younger man, Harald's voice was calm, his stance relaxed. He met Chadwick's glower evenly.

"So you stepped in?"

"I'm just helping where I can."

"This looks like more than help to me. In fact, it looks to me like you're trying to buy something."

"Chadwick, you don't understand—" Marie began, only to be interrupted as the elegantly dressed man reached for her arm and pulled her to his side. The spicy scent of his cologne competed with the smell of fresh-cut wood that hung in the air.

Marie looked between Chadwick and Harald, one man angrily impassioned, the other seeming almost passionless. Yet Marie knew better. Just a short time ago she'd looked into a pair of bright blue eyes filled with more passion than she'd ever imagined possible.

"He's trying to buy *you*, Marie." Chadwick's lean fingers tightened uncomfortably on her arm, and he made no pretense of politeness. "Can't you see? He's only doing this to win your affections."

Harald organized all this just to obtain my favor? It can't be true . . . can it? Surely he isn't the type to take advantage of a situation for his own gain. Marie was silent a long moment, studying the high polish of Chadwick's shoes, recalling Harald's words as he'd held her hands. *He was about to declare his feelings for you, Marie, after spending roughly a week in your company. Doesn't that seem a little sudden?*

Extricating herself from Chadwick's grasp, she sought Harald's gaze. His expression was inscrutable, though she saw him take a deep, controlled breath. "Harald's not like that," she finally said, turning to Chadwick.

Where was the confidence in her tone? The assurance?

"Who have you known longer, Marie?" Not waiting for her to reply, he continued on, bending over so his face was at the level of hers. "And what about us?" He dropped the four accusing words before her.

With that, he turned on his heel and marched off, leaving Marie and Harald with an ocean of silence between them.

What is the matter with me, Lord? she prayed earnestly, wishing she had the moment to do over again. *I know Harald isn't like what Chadwick made him out to be. Why did I hesitate? What can I do now?*

"I'd best get back to work." Harald pulled the pencil from behind his ear and reached for his paper. "Don't forget your lunch." He handed her the now-cool bowl of chili. Though his tone of voice had not changed, Marie detected the hurt in his eyes. Her failure to speak up for him had wounded him.

Just then Pastor Price, eager to swing his hammer, declared mealtime to be over.

"Good-bye, Marie," Harald said politely, formally, as the men picked up their tools and resumed their places.

"Good-bye . . ." Her voice trailed off while he walked away. She ached to do *something* to repair the damage she had caused between them, ashamed of herself for not standing up for Harald's character. He was a godly man, a man of integrity. Of that much she had become certain in the short time she had spent with him.

And just what kind of character did Chadwick display today? she asked herself. *He was mean, rude, accusing, and even . . . jealous?*

Sick at heart and not knowing which direction to turn, Marie walked to the tall grass beyond the yard and dumped out the contents of her bowl. Mother had always said that if you weren't sure what to do, you should just pray on the matter and wait.

Well, she had prayed. Now it was time to wait.

SEVEN

"Marie, I owe you an apology," Chadwick said, regret written across his handsome face. "I'm quite appalled at my actions of yesterday and can only hope you'll find it in your heart to forgive me. If you'd be so kind to grant me a few moments, I'd like to explain some things to you." He sighed and gave her a repentant glance. "If you don't wish to speak with me, I would . . . understand."

The banker's son stood outside his carriage, parked in the Hamsun driveway a good distance from Harald's house. He was wrapped in a warm wool coat, one gloved hand nervously gripping and releasing the harness on the horse nearest him. It was barely nine o'clock in the morning. Marie thought that she certainly hadn't had to wait long for something to happen, but the present hollowness in her heart told her a visit from Chadwick—even his apology—wasn't what she'd been longing for.

"What would you like to explain?"

He glanced around. "Is *he* here?"

"Do you mean Harald?" A funny pang went through her as she said Harald's name. Almost an entire day had passed since the episode, and still she hadn't been able to find an opportunity to speak with him alone. "No, he's over working on our new house." Her breath made clouds in the bright autumn morning air.

Chadwick nodded, obviously holding his tongue in check. "First of all," he began after a long pause, "I wish to tell you that I found out what happened between my father and yours, and that I had absolutely no foreknowledge of it. My father and I . . . came to an understanding on some matters, and yesterday I drove out to offer your father my apologies—and a loan. My father, for reasons he thought good, treated your father unjustly, and I wanted to make it right. When I saw all the people gathered and stacks of lumber everywhere, I realized I wasn't going to be able to . . . well, I guess I just saw red, Marie. I am very sorry," he concluded, extending his hand toward her.

Marie frowned, recalling yesterday's events. "The things you said to Harald were just plain spiteful," she said evenly. "He has been nothing but kind and generous to my entire family! Why, he took us in, Chadwick, in the middle of the night while our house burned to the ground, and he hasn't asked us *for one thing*. And as for those ulterior motives you accused him of . . . ooh!" Her voice rose as her anger spilled forth. "The last person Harald Hamsun thinks of is himself. So don't you dare slander his name within my earshot again!"

She'd failed to stand up for Harald yesterday, but today was a brand-new day, and she was determined not to repeat her mistakes.

"Marie—"

"Why don't you just tell the truth?" she interrupted. "You were angry because you saw him holding my hand." Taking a step toward the expensive carriage, she folded her arms across her chest. Then she took a deep breath, striving for a more composed tone in her voice. "I'm going to ask you to lay your cards on the table, Chadwick. What are your feelings toward me? Your intentions?"

"What? What . . . are Hamsun's?" The same note of jealousy she had detected in him yesterday was evident as he parried her questions with his own.

"I'm not talking about Harald right now; I'm talking about you. After more than four years of you coming and going as you please, I believe I am entitled to an honest answer."

A long silence hung between them. Chadwick looked uneasy, stunned, and a little sick all at once. Marie was surprised at herself, for she had never spoken so directly to him. Come to think of it, for all the talking he did, he had never spoken of personal matters in a forthright manner to her, either. But the simple act of asking for honesty, even if she didn't receive it, was oddly liberating. Her anger cooled somewhat with this discovery, and she looked past Chadwick to the brilliantly colored tree line beyond Harald's trim fields.

"Come on, Marie," came Chadwick's reply, pulling her attention back to his pleading countenance. "What do you want me to say?"

"How about the truth?"

"I . . . Marie, well, it's . . . it's a little complicated. You know I like you, Marie."

"And what of your parents' view of me? Or your father's 'good reasons' for denying our family a loan? They don't want you to see me, do they?"

"How did you . . . well, it doesn't matter anymore what they think. One of the understandings my father and I came to was that I would see whomever I wished." Chadwick seemed to recover his footing here. His voice lost the beseeching tone and regained its typical confidence.

"And I would like very much to pursue a . . . well, I would like to court you, Marie, if you would give your consent." Letting go of the harness, he stepped toward her with a handsome smile. "That's what you wanted all along, isn't it? You were just using

Hamsun to force my hand." He uttered a low chuckle as he grasped the cleverness of his logic. "Oh, Marie. You're quite a handful after all. Shall I go in and speak to your father?"

By this time the anger had left Marie, and she looked at the man before her with dispassion. Once upon a time it would have meant a great deal to her to hear Chadwick Farrell declare himself, but now her heart beat evenly within her chest, and no thrills raced through her. *I'm not in love with him,* she thought. *Was I ever?*

"No, I don't think it would be wise to speak to Father," she said.

"Oh, that's right; he's still ill, isn't he? How forgetful of me, I—"

"I don't wish to be courted by you, Chadwick."

"You . . . what?" A perplexed expression appeared on the dapper man's face. "I thought you . . ." His voice trailed off, only to resume its jealous tone. "Hamsun? You can't be serious."

Marie nodded, meeting his gaze. Something burst free within her at the admission, filling her with joy and fright all at once.

"Oh, Marie," he spat with disgust. "He's nothing but a—"

"Stop right there!" She thrust her chin out. "I told you I would not listen to your slander."

"Then this conversation is over." Stalking back to his carriage, he hooked a long leg up on the step and swung into his seat. "You're not yourself today, Marie," he called, shaking his head. "I'll give you some time to come to your senses before I call again."

Marie stepped aside as he shook the reins and went up the driveway to the turnaround, his jaw clenched. He gave her a long look as he passed by on his way out, jamming his hat on his head. He turned out onto the lane, urged the horses to reckless speed, and soon he was out of sight on the gently rolling terrain.

Marie turned back to Harald's house with a sigh, feeling both relief and trepidation. Today she had done the right thing with Chadwick, she knew, but would she be given a second chance to do right by Harald?

The new house went up faster than Marie would have ever believed. By the time Dr. Camp returned to see his patient Wednesday afternoon, its spiny framework was visible from the windows of Harald's snug home. And even better, Father was sitting up in bed having tea and toast.

His face, especially his hollow cheeks and sunken eyes, spoke of the severity of his illness, but the fever had broken more than twenty-four hours earlier. Dr. Camp was delighted to pronounce him on the mend, lecturing him on the importance of making a slow and steady convalescence.

Grandma Biggs had threatened to take her new walking stick to her son if he so much as tried to pick up a hammer and go to work, to which the doctor had nodded approvingly.

Not long after the physician's departure, Marie peeked into the bedroom where her father lay. She had been in to visit him a few times since he'd taken a turn for the better, and it seemed to her as though his despondency had lifted along with the fever. He was still weak and very tired, but she could see no evidence of the gloom that had pervaded his outlook since the fire. All the Biggses had wondered how he'd take the news of the new house, but Mother said he had just lain back on the pillow and closed his eyes, tears squeezing out from beneath the lids, when she'd told him the rebuilding was well under way.

"Hi, Father," she said softly, seeing he was awake. "Can I do anything for you?"

"Come in, Marie, come in." His voice was weak, but the old genial tone was back. "I'm about ready to crawl right up these walls with boredom, but every time I think about it, I get tired and fall asleep again." He smiled with surrender.

"You need your rest; you've been very sick." Her heart squeezed painfully to see his tousled hair and thin, dear face, and to think that she had almost lost him.

"I was more than sick, Marie," he said, his smile fading. "Come and sit in the chair here, honey. I'd like to talk to you."

"What is it?" she asked, settling herself in the chair beside the bed.

"First off, I want you to know I don't hold you responsible for Herman Farrell refusing me the loan. No one does. Your grandmother spoke out of turn that night. I hope you know she doesn't really blame you."

Marie nodded, a grin stealing across her face. "She apologized right away. Said she was just madder than a rained-on rooster to find out what Herman Farrell did to her boy."

"Her *boy*? I'm forty years old!" Father grinned back at her. "I have gray hair and seven children, and yet I'm still a boy to her."

It was good to share a laugh with her father, Marie thought, a little of her heaviness of heart melting away. She had not been able to speak to Harald alone since the other day, and that weighed on her mind. Whether he was simply too busy or deliberately sidestepping her, she could not say. Would he forgive her? she wondered. After the way she had behaved when Chadwick interrupted him, when he had been about to tell her . . .

When he had been about to tell you what? She had pondered that question many times over the past days. Countless times she had closed her eyes and recalled the way the wind blew through his hair, the slow smile that crept across his face, and the feel of his big, work-roughened hands around hers. But it was the expression in his eyes that had shaken her to the core of her very soul—and shook her still.

"I told Chadwick I didn't want him to come around any-more," she offered, meeting her father's gaze.

"On my account?"

"No." Marie shook her head. "Though he did come to apolo-gize for his father's actions. He said he didn't know anything about his father refusing you a loan until after the fact."

"That might be true enough." Father's brown gaze, perceptive as ever, searched her face. "What, then, prompted you to ask young Mr. Farrell not to visit anymore, if I may ask?"

"I don't . . . well . . ." she began and stopped, feeling self-conscious. "I just don't think my heart was right about him," she spoke up. "Besides that, his family was . . ." Mindful of her manners, she searched for a tactful way to convey her thoughts.

"I think we both know what you're trying to say, Marie. And I can't say I'm sorry not to be thinking of those folks as possi-ble in-laws." A smile flickered across his face, and he directed his attention to adjusting the covers around him. "Would there be anyone else in your heart right now?" he asked in a seem-ingly offhand manner.

"Do you mean besides you?" she replied with more cheek than she felt, as warmth spread across her face. She knew her grandmother suspected her growing feelings for Harald, but to save Chadwick, she hadn't admitted those feelings to a soul. With her emotions so unsettled, she hoped Father wouldn't pursue this line of questioning.

"Listen to you, shamelessly charming your sick old father. Yes, I mean besides me. But if you don't want to talk about it right now, that's fine." Wrestling a pillow into position behind his shoulder blades, he lay back and waxed philosophical. "The heart can be a mighty troubling place at times, can't it? It's seldom a man has so much time to lie around and reflect on things," he continued, not waiting for an answer, "but I've had more time in bed these past days than I can ever recall. None of it by my choice."

"But you were—"

Holding his fingers to his lips, he gestured for her to be quiet and listen. "I was sick, all right, sicker than I can ever recall. But it took nearly dying for the Lord to get my attention—and break my pride—about the way I'd been behaving about the house burning . . . and show me what was really important in life. I hope you—all of you—can forgive me."

"Of course." Tears welled in Marie's eyes as she leaned forward and laid her head against her father's chest. His hands stroked her hair as he went on speaking, the sound of his voice rumbling in her ear.

"I'm not ashamed to say I've learned a great deal about humility from Harald Hamsun through these trials. He might be young, but he's got more wisdom and maturity than most men twice his age. You just don't run across many men in life like him, Marie."

No, I've never run across a man like Harald Hamsun, she silently agreed. A bittersweet pang pierced her chest, causing her tears to brim forth as she wondered if she would be given another chance with him. Listening to the steady thudding of her father's heart, Marie let her head rest fully against him, knowing he had done more than extol Harald's virtues.

He had just given her his blessing.

The moment went on, sweet and tender, until Grandma Biggs appeared in the doorway and cleared her throat. "Time for your daddy to get some rest, Marie. 'Sides, we need some more wood brought in, and everyone else is over at the house."

"Love you, Marie," Father whispered before he let her go. "Take heart. I have a feeling everything is going to work out for the best."

The wind was cold against Marie's face when she stepped

outdoors for the wood. Intent on loading the split logs into the little cart and getting back inside as quickly as possible, she didn't hear Harald approach.

"Let me help you with that, Marie. I've been wanting to talk with you."

Startled, Marie turned to look up into a pair of sky-blue eyes. At the sight, she felt as though her lungs had collapsed upon themselves. All the things she'd been meaning to say to him flew right out of her head while she let the log in her arms fall into the cart with the others.

Lord above, he was *handsome*. Well-built, strong, and handsome. How could she have lived across the road from him for two long years and never noticed that? The broadness of his shoulders was evident through the work-grade red-and-black-plaid coat he wore, and Marie knew a well-muscled pair of arms joined with those shoulders. *What would it be like to be held in those arms?* she wondered. To lay her head against that chest?

Somehow she managed to breathe.

But where was his smile? The crinkles around his eyes? He seemed at ease, and his expression was kind as he gazed at her, but she had a feeling she wasn't going to like what he was going to say.

"Marie, I made an error in judgment about you," he began, confirming her worst fears and shattering her heart into tiny pieces with his words.

She no longer felt the cold bite of the wind against her face as numbness washed over her. Nodding, she dropped her gaze to the ground, wishing the earth could swallow her whole.

EIGHT

"I made an error in judgment, but I take the blame for it." Harald's rich voice was filled with regret. "With both of us living here, it just wasn't proper for me to . . . well, Marie, I need to apologize to you for putting the burden of my affections on you."

Burden? He thought his affections were a burden? In an instant the cold wind whisked away her numbness; hope leapt afresh within her breast. Was it possible he still cared for her? Was there a spark yet of that bone-melting warmth to be found in his gaze? Gathering her courage, Marie looked him full in the face, only to be disappointed.

It was Harald's turn to study the frozen ground beneath their feet. "You've been seeing Farrell for some time, I know—"

"But I—" she tried to interrupt.

"Let me speak, please, Marie. This is important for me to say." He cleared his throat. "I didn't keep my word to you, and that is why I need to ask your forgiveness."

"Didn't keep your word? What are you talking about, Harald?" she asked, puzzled.

"I told you I wouldn't call for you until you moved back to your own house," he said, lifting his gaze to meet hers. "In my . . . impatience, Marie, I rushed you. You have every right to wonder about the things Farrell said, but I hope, in time, you will come to believe they are not true."

Instead of the glowing warmth she had hoped to find, Marie read genuine distress in his eyes. Sorrow and compassion rose within her, and she ached with the need to relieve his suffering—pain he had endured on her account.

"Harald," she began, pulling off the battered, oversized leather mitts she had donned for her task. Tucking them under her arm, she stepped toward him and reached for his hand. His fingers were bare and icy cold, extending from the cut-away tips of the woolen gloves he wore. Warming them between her hands, she felt the roughness of his skin against hers and nearly wept at its sad state. Chapped. Cracked. A fresh, angry gash arced across his middle knuckle, while smaller nicks and cuts laced his thumb and other fingers.

This was the hand of a man who was trying to buy her affections?

What nonsense. She thought of Chadwick's smooth hands and long, lean fingers. His fine clothes and fancy carriage. Of all the intellectual prattle, eloquent speeches, and altruistic ideals she had listened to over the years. Chadwick's goals and generosity, she realized, extended only far enough to serve himself. Why had she never seen that before? And, worse yet, how could she ever have dreamed of marriage to a man like that?

Tears gathered in her eyes as she thought of Harald's selfless, giving nature. Of his care for others, his consideration for each member of her family. Of his integrity and character. His candor. Heavens, was it possible that she loved him already?

Swallowing past the lump in her throat, she saw that he was waiting for her to speak. "It's I who owe you an apology, Harald. I know you aren't . . . you aren't any of those awful things Chadwick said about you, and I'm sorry for not standing up for you when I should have. You're the most upright man I know."

A single tear traced its way down her cheek while the cold wind carried a sprinkling of the season's first snowflakes. "Can you forgive me?" she whispered, her hands seeking to cradle his.

"Min skatt," he murmured, bringing her hands to his cheek while the distress in his eyes dissolved into liquid blue heat. Softly, he slid her fingers over his mouth and pressed a soft kiss against her skin before releasing her hands. Ever so gently, then, he wiped the tear from her face, the rasp of his rough skin—or was it his touch?—setting Marie's nerve endings on fire. Feelings she had never known raced through her, potent and sweet.

"Min scott? Wh-what does that mean?" Her words were breathy, her heart slamming against her chest.

"It means . . ." he said in a honey-rich voice, taking a half-step forward and closing the distance between them. His big hands cupped her shoulders, then slid down her upper arms. "It means I want to kiss you in the worst way, Marie."

"Oh . . . that's the . . . literal? . . ." Unexpectedly, a silvery ball of laughter escaped from her throat before the wild beating of her heart recommenced. "I don't think you're telling me the truth, Harald."

An answering grin lit the broad face so near hers, causing his eyes to crinkle in the way she would never tire of seeing. His nearness, combined with the fiery feelings coursing through her, made her next words husky and unimaginably forward.

"Then how do you say, 'I want to kiss you back'?"

"Jeg vil kysse deg tilbake," he answered lyrically, his words ending in something like a groan as he closed his eyes. His grip on her arms grew tighter before he released her, taking a giant step backward. His hands balled into fists and released once, twice, three times before he opened his eyes again.

"Marie," he began, his voice taut with an emotion she wasn't certain she could define. Had she displeased him with her shameless admission? Offended him?

His next words dispelled those fears, the passion in his gaze nearly singeing her with its intensity. "To be honest, I would like nothing better than for you to kiss me back, Marie. All day. All night. For the rest of my life. If you only knew how long . . ." he said, his words trailing off. With visible effort, he banked the blue flames in his eyes. "But for your sake, I want to do this properly. I will court you, Marie, when you've moved back home."

"But—" Though Harald's interest in her was unmistakable, disappointment shot through Marie at his timetable. He wouldn't court her till she'd moved back home? That could be weeks, maybe months!

"It's for the best, *kj're* Marie. Until then we will wait."

Marie nodded, joy and impatience warring within her. "How fast can you build a house?" she asked with impertinence, rapidly becoming acquainted with a heady sense of feminine power as she saw the resultant blaze of emotion in Harald's steady gaze.

"Faster than you're gathering this wood. Now in the house with you! I'll finish this."

With a last, long yearning look at the man vigorously tossing logs into the cart, Marie slipped on her leather mitts and began walking back to the house, hardly feeling her feet touch the ground. The snow was coming down at a quicker rate, filling the air with its frosty beauty and collecting in lacy white ridges against the irregular texture of the brown, frozen earth.

Being courted by Harald.

Spending the rest of her life with Harald?

I'm falling in love with him, she thought with a sense of awe. How on earth was she ever going to be able to wait for their house to be finished? It was like being six years old and thinking that Christmas would never come, only much, much worse. Surely the coming days and weeks would never pass.

❄ ❄ ❄

But pass they did, and the work progressed steadily on the new house. A soft blanket of white covered the countryside, a quiet harbinger of the deep snows and bitter winds for which Minnesota winters were known. The geese and songbirds had long since departed for warmer climates, leaving behind their hardier kin: sparrows, jays, cardinals, dark-eyed juncos.

Father had recovered from his illness, his spirit as well as his body restored. Once again his easy laugh rang out, and his dark eyes brimmed with vigor. The younger girls had rejoined the family some time ago, and all the Biggs children, save Marie and three-year-old Julia, had returned to school. The boys had pleaded a strong case for staying out of school even longer so as to continue helping with the construction of their new house, but Father was insistent: to school they would go.

At the beginning of the day and again at the end, Harald's small home teemed with people and activity, yet he still seemed not to mind the disruption of his formerly quiet life. With his parents both gone and his only sister and her family living four hundred miles away, he said he considered it a blessing to share his house with the Biggs family.

As Christmas drew nearer, the notion grew in Marie's mind that perhaps the snow-sprinkled autumn afternoon with Harald had never happened . . . that his caressing voice and smoldering blue eyes had been a figment of her imagination. *Maybe it was nothing but a daydream, Marie,* she thought with increasing impatience and uncertainty, for since that day Harald had behaved no differently toward her than he did toward Rosemary or Grandma . . . or even little Julia.

She'd prayed for patience, she really had. But she'd never before known such feelings!

And how could Harald act so . . . so . . . *normal,* she

wondered, when she did nothing but ache to spend a little time alone with him, to know more about him. How she yearned for the touch of his hand, to hear the intimate deepening in his rich voice as he spoke her name, gazing at her with enough warmth to melt every drift and flake of snow for miles around.

Chadwick had called for her twice before Thanksgiving. Both times she had politely but firmly turned him away, still somewhat amazed that his presence had no effect on her whatsoever. The last time he visited, he verbalized his unhappiness and disbelief that she had thrown him over for a simple Norwegian farmer. "I'm very disappointed in you, Marie," he had said before driving back to his fine home and position in Mankato. "You could have had a lot better than what you're settling for."

Settling for? Oh, but you're quite wrong about that, Chadwick. I feel anything but settled when it comes to Harald. . . .

"Isn't it exciting, Marie?" Her mother's animated words broke in on her thoughts. "Your father thinks we'll be able to move back home by Christmas. There will still be plenty of finish work to do, but at least we'll be home." She smoothed the boughs of fragrant, fresh-cut pine Anthony had brought in. "That being the case, I think we should make two advent wreaths instead of one. Then we can leave one here for Harald. Bring me in some extra wire, Anthony," she called, as her lanky second-eldest son prepared to step back out the door. "And tell everyone to come in for supper soon. We'll make the wreaths when we're finished eating."

The aroma of pot roast filled the cozy house, mingling with the yeasty tang of the bread Mother had baked earlier. Sarah and Rosemary set the table while Julia sat at the foot of Grandma's rocking chair, playing with her paper dolls.

"Marie, would you mix up a batch of sugar cookies for tonight, please? We'll bake them when the roast comes out. I've got a sack of white sugar there in the cupboard. Julia, my darling, will you come help Mama put this evergreen in a box? Then we need to find some candles."

"Do you suppose Harald ever had an advent wreath before, Marie?" Grandma Biggs asked, peering up from her crocheting.

"I . . . I couldn't say," she replied, striving for a nonchalant tone, though her heart had begun a rapid throb within her chest at the mention of his name. Why would Grandma ask her such a question?

"Einar's place has been without a woman's touch for a long time." She chuckled to herself. "Now he's got six women livin' under his roof. Yes, indeed. That's more than he needs. Just one ought to do him fine." She picked up her hook and work-in-progress. "Don't you think, Marie?"

Marie felt the heat begin in her cheeks. Did Grandma know something? She hadn't revealed her secret feelings for Harald to anyone—except Chadwick. She supposed it was humorous, really, that her erstwhile suitor should be the only person to whom she'd spoken of the state of her heart.

"You know what I think, Grandma?" nine-year-old Sarah piped, sparing Marie from having to answer. She set the last of the forks in place on the hopelessly crowded table. "I think Harald needs to have his own wife. He's going to be lonely when we go back home." Turning toward her eldest sister, she added in a loud whisper, "He's nice, Marie. I like him an awful lot better than I liked Chadwick."

"Me, too," Rosemary agreed. "I can't say I'll miss Chadwick Farrell."

"Amen to that, child," Grandma responded tartly. "I never did like that boy. Drivin' around in that fancy carriage of his, thinkin' he's so wonderful, his big head all swoll up like a kraut barrel. God willing, we've seen the last of him around these parts. I'm still tryin' to come to terms with his daddy refusin' us the loan, but I got plenty a'more prayin' ahead of me before I can do the forgivin'."

"Did Harald pay all the money for our new house?" Intense curiosity caused Sarah's young voice to drop in pitch. "He must be richer than Chadwick."

"I've been wondering about that, too," Rosemary declared with a grin, "only I didn't think it was polite to ask."

"Well, it certainly *isn't* polite to ask, and I would hope I've raised you better than that." Mother leveled a stern look at her adolescent daughter before softening. "But I can't see any harm in telling you that Harald did pay for the lumber and building supplies. He had some money put by from when his father died, which he was only too happy to pull out of Herman Farrell's bank. Your father and I consider it a loan, and we intend to pay him back every cent."

"But why do you need a loan? I thought you and Father had some money saved up." Rosemary's dark eyes were quizzical.

"We do, my dear, but we also have an entire household to furnish. Harald insisted we spend our money on that, and pay him back for the house at a later time."

"Thank the Almighty for Harald," Grandma exclaimed as the rocker ceased its motion. "Ain't many men like him, 'cept the ones I raised."

"You mean Daddy, don't you, Grandma?" Sarah said with a giggle. "You're bragging 'cause you were his mama."

"Of course I am, honey. I raised up your daddy and his brothers to be fine men."

Mother moved through the kitchen, a secret, knowing smile curving her lips. "And don't forget all our good friends and neighbors," she reminded her mother-in-law. "Without them, we'd be nowhere near as far along as we are."

The rocking chair resumed its steady rhythm, the crochet hook in the gnarled fingers flashing silver in the fading light.

"Well, I still say men like Harald are few and far between. He's going to make some woman a dandy husband someday . . . don't you think, Marie?"

Really! Would Grandma never let the subject drop? Marie looked up from creaming the butter and sugar together, fruitlessly searching for some article of conversation so as to change the subject—only to see all eyes upon her. "What are you all looking at?" she snapped as a burst of giggles erupted around her. "Harald's got no time to pursue such nonsense."

There was fear in that admission, deep-down dread that perhaps Harald had changed his mind about things. About her.

And if he *hadn't,* well . . . she didn't know whether to admire him or throttle him for being such a man of his word. *I will court you, Marie, when you've moved back home. . . . Until then, we will wait.* The memory of his gaze made her stomach quiver. *I would like nothing better than for you to kiss me back, Marie . . . all day, all night, for the rest of my life.*

"Nonsense?" Grandma Biggs's gaze was keen from where she sat in the far corner of the room. "If you say so, Marie. If you say so."

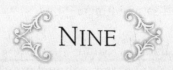

NINE

"Cut me a small piece of that red ribbon there, will you, Sarah? We'll give this little fellow a spot of color." Rosemary's slender fingers fashioned a tiny bird out of a pine cone and soft feathers.

"Where did you ever come up with an idea like that?" Father spoke with admiration as he leaned over her shoulder, obviously delighted with the craft his daughter's hands had wrought.

"Oh, it's not my idea. I learned it from Betsy Lira. She said her Aunt Mary Jo taught it to her when she came to visit from St. Paul last time."

"Well, I've never seen anything like it."

After a pleasant supper, the Biggses and their host had gathered again around the table, now spread with aromatic pine boughs, small branches of dried bittersweet, ribbons, buttons, thread, and snips of colorful fabric.

Harald sat next to Raymond, weaving greens into the wire forms he and Father had constructed. "You people make some handsome advent wreaths," he said. "I don't believe we ever put so much into it when I was growing up."

"We *always* make the *best* wreaths," Sarah averred. "Every year before Advent we have a party and make a wreath, and Mama gives us cookies and tea out of . . ." Her voice trailed off, only to resume thick with disappointment. "I guess we won't have tea this year, will we?"

"Of course we'll have tea, Sarah. Marie's already put the water on." Mother's voice was soothing, though touched with wistfulness. "We just don't have Grandma Perry's tea set anymore."

"It got burnded up," Julia added importantly, slipping down from Anthony's lap and padding over to Harald's side. She tugged on his sleeve. "Our house had a fire, and *everything* got burnded up."

"Yes, it did, little one. But we're still going to have tea, and we've almost got a nice, new house all ready for you . . . and that makes me very happy." Was it Marie's imagination, or did Harald's rich voice deepen with hidden meaning as he spoke to her sister?

Twisting the dishcloth in her hands, she paced back and forth between the stove and the worktable, waiting for the last pan of sugar cookies to finish baking. Then she'd have no reason to continue avoiding the happy gathering at the table. The large pot of water on the stove had almost reached a boil; a well-washed kettle, its bottom filled with loose black tea, stood ready to receive the steaming liquid. The kettle, plus a mishmash of mugs and cups, would serve this year in place of her maternal grandmother's blue-and-white china tea set.

Marie sighed. She'd also had a sentimental attachment to the dainty collection, but it wasn't only the tea set that had her heavyhearted. In fact, it mostly *wasn't* the tea set . . . it was Harald.

He was a man of honesty, a man of his word. That she knew. And he had been very plainspoken about his intentions that snowy afternoon last month. But her spirits had been low ever since before dinner, when she'd been the object of her family's good-natured kidding about him. How could they all be so certain that she was right for Harald when *she* wasn't even

certain any longer? Her intellect battled with the doubt that
gnawed holes in the fabric of her faith.

I can't live like this much longer, Lord, she prayed, sliding the
pan of lightly browned cookies from the oven. *I love him, I know
I do, yet I'm miserable.*

"Mama, Harald's hand is bleeding! Look, right by his thumb!"
Julia cried, prompting a flurry of movement and exclamations
from the gathered Biggses.

"It's nothing, really," he protested, holding up his hand. "Just
a few pricks from the pine."

Grandma Biggs stood and edged her way through her younger
grandchildren to stand before Harald and examine his hand in
an imperial manner. "Young man, your hands are in a sorrier
state than my husband's ever were," she declared, turning them
over, "and I thought his were the rawest I'd ever seen. I must've
spent half our marriage applying salve to that man's cracked
skin. Now you come on over to the kitchen and let me take care
of this." Her tone brooked no argument, and she marched to the
pantry. "I've got a little can of ointment all mixed up for such
things."

Marie watched as Harald rose from his chair and stepped
toward her, wearing a half-comical, half-uncomfortable expression on his face that said he was only doing this for Grandma
Biggs's sake. He smiled as he passed her, nodding and lifting his
eyebrows at the neat rows of cooling cookies.

See, Marie? He's more interested in the cookies than he is in you.

Work—and conversation—quickly resumed at the table.
Anthony slid into Harald's chair and finished the last bit of weaving on the nearly completed wreath, while Raymond had already
passed his neat-looking work on to the girls for decoration.

"Give me those paws, Harald," Grandma Biggs ordered,
balancing her walking stick against the pantry and working open
the lid of the tin with some difficulty. Taking a generous finger

full of the puce-colored unguent, she applied it to the angry, chapped skin.

As she slid the cookies off the sheet with a shiny spatula, Marie covertly watched Harald's profile. What a man he was, she thought, her heart besieged with both yearning and discomfiture. How would it be, she wondered, to be held—

"Oh, my!" Grandma drew in a quick breath, as if in pain. "Marie, my rheumatism is acting up something fierce. Come on over here."

Marie started at her grandmother's request but moved obediently in her direction.

"Let me help you sit down, Mrs. Biggs." Harald spoke with concern, his hands glazed with Grandma's ugly colored concoction. He stood helplessly before the older woman, wanting to help but not knowing how.

"No, stay put; it's just these old thumbs of mine . . . they don't work so well anymore. I'll wipe off and maybe go rock a spell while Marie finishes up for me." In a twinkling she had removed the salve from her hands with her apron, even before her granddaughter reached her side. "Now, Marie," she instructed, audaciously taking the younger woman's hands and setting them over Harald's. "This needs to be *thoroughly* rubbed in. And mind you pay extra attention to the badly chapped areas," she added sternly, her tone of voice belying the merriment in her keen brown eyes as she looked back and forth at the pair. "Now rub!"

Marie felt as if she had fallen into a trance the instant her hands covered Harald's.

Warmth.

Incredible warmth. That was the only thought on her mind as she began to move her fingers over the work-damaged skin. The emollient already had begun to soften the rough surface of the hands beneath hers, and Marie felt as though she were being drawn into a sumptuous tub of sleek, rich oils as well. But though her arms and legs grew languorous, her insides felt anything but.

Please, Lord, she appealed, *I can wait for as long as you say, but I just need a little reassurance.*

Her prayers were swiftly answered as, in a quick motion, his big hands closed around hers, nearly stopping her heart. Did his breathing sound a little irregular? Ragged, even?

"Marie," he said in a low voice, moving nearer, his fingers beginning a stirring caress of their own. *"Min kj'restet . . . min elskede.* Once again I find my honorable intentions flying out the window."

Holding her breath with both wonder and hope, Marie slowly looked up from those strong hands, up past the broad, muscular chest, into his face.

"Jeg elsker deg, Marie. I love you."

"I love you, too, Harald," she whispered in reply, pure joy pouring into her soul. "I was so worried you'd changed your mind."

"Never." A slow, certain smile curved his lips, filled with secret, unspoken promises, his eyes crinkling tenderly.

"Look! Marie and Harald are holding hands!" Hugh crowed from the table. "Hoo-hoo! And they're looking at each other all funny." He laughed with the innate hilarity of a boy straddling adolescence. His mother and sisters attempted in vain to hush him, unable to hide their own smiles.

"Well, it's about time someone got the ball rolling," Grandma Biggs muttered from the rocker, her flying crochet hook glinting in the lamplight. "Those two have been purely miserable for weeks on end!"

A burst of laughter rose from the assembled Biggses while Harald's hands tightened reassuringly around Marie's. With the smile continuing to crease his broad face, he turned his gaze toward Father. "I love Marie," Harald declared, "and it is my hope that—"

The older man interrupted, a pleased look on his countenance. "If you're asking for my blessing, Harald, you had it long ago."

"Does this mean Marie is going to marry Harald?" Sarah piped innocently.

An explosion of exclamations, conversation, and delighted laughter burst out in the snug house while Harald pressed his lips against Marie's ear and asked her to wait in the kitchen.

Helen and Rosemary sprang from their chairs to embrace Marie while Harald wiped his hands on a towel, handed the cloth to Marie and disappeared into his bedroom. A few moments later he returned with the small trunk she had once noticed high on the shelf of his closet.

"Don't pour that water yet," he cautioned the women in the kitchen, setting the trunk on the table and whetting everyone's curiosity. "I have something here Marie may want."

"What is it?" Julia asked with wonder while her family gathered around. Marie's heart beat with excitement as she was all but whisked to the table by her mother and sister.

"It was something of my mother's . . . something I remember with great fondness."

Crisp, yellowed tissue paper. A half-dozen slim, leather-bound volumes bearing foreign text. A neatly folded, daintily woven woolen shawl of red and white. As Harald removed the items, one by one, the air of expectation around the table grew.

At the bottom of the trunk sat an oddly shaped bundle, wrapped with a plain ivory-colored towel.

"What's that?" Sarah asked, her voice filled with intense curiosity.

"It's Marie's, if she would like to have it." Harald's gaze met hers, drawing her to his side. "Open it, *min kj'rlighet,*" he urged.

Marie's fingers hesitated over the soft cloth as she tried to guess at the gift Harald offered. Finally, she unwrapped the towel to discover an exquisite china teapot with six matching cups and saucers. "Oh . . . Harald," she whispered, tears filling her eyes. The Biggs women crowded closer, each straining for a glimpse of the fragile, beautifully decorated vessels.

"May I serve you tea?"

Nodding somewhat dumbfoundedly to Harald's tenderly spoken query, Marie found herself being assisted into a chair at the table while many hands made short work of clearing away the residue of the wreath construction. Anthony arranged the two laurels side by side in the center of the table, ten tall candles standing at attention amidst a profusion of lush greens. He gave her a shy smile and a pleased wink as he stepped back.

It seemed only a moment before Harald, Mother, and Rose- mary returned from the kitchen bearing the tea and a tray of cookies. Setting a dainty saucer and cup before her, Harald paused with the teapot in his hands.

If his expression weren't so earnest, devotion shining from his brilliant blue eyes, Marie might have laughed at the incongruity of the fragile porcelain container in his wide, weather-beaten hands.

"There's one more thing of my mother's, Marie," he said, nodding toward her cup. "It's yours, as well . . . if you will accept it." He smiled then, his eyes crinkling delightfully.

A hush fell upon the room as Marie slowly reached for the cup, her fingers beginning to tremble when a small clink reached her ears.

"There's a *ring* in Marie's cup!" Sarah cried.

"Oh," was all she could say, pulling the cup toward her, seeing for herself that Sarah's words were true. The delicate band of gold gleamed with quiet elegance, its feel smooth against her probing fingertip. Looking up, she met Harald's gaze and silently dispatched a prayer of gratitude to her heavenly Father for the great treasure he had given her. Love—and thanks—welled up inside her as the troublesome tears began once again.

"Well, Marie?" Grandma Biggs queried. "Our tea's going to get cold if you don't stop your dillydallying and give him an answer."

"I'd be honored to accept your mother's ring, Harald." Marie smiled through the wetness tracing its way down her cheeks.

The room exploded in cheers while Harald set down the pot, took her face in his hands, and tenderly wiped her tears.

And then he poured her tea.

RECITE

This recipe was given to me by my friend's mother, who was Norwegian to the bone. These cookies have always delighted me because of their rich yet delicate flavor. You won't be able to stop at one!

Sugar Cookies

Cream together:
1 cup powdered sugar
1 cup oil
1 cup sugar
1 tsp. vanilla
1 cup butter
2 eggs

Sift:
4½ cups flour
1 tsp. soda
1 tsp. salt
1 tsp. cream of tartar

Blend dry ingredients into the first mixture. Roll into balls, place on ungreased cookie sheet, and flatten each ball with the bottom of a glass dipped in sugar. Bake at 350 degrees for 9–10 minutes. Makes 6 to 7 dozen.

Crosses and Losses

For all the Mary Roses I have known

ONE

St. Paul, Minnesota; December 1880

"Mama? How long till Daddy comes home? Four minutes?"

Joyce Colburn knelt to stroke her daughter's cheek, delighting in its downy smoothness. Two neat braids contained the child's fine, nutmeg-colored tresses, each decorated with a violet bow to match the ivory-and-violet dress she wore. "I don't know how many minutes it will be until Daddy comes home, Audrey," she replied to the three-and-a-half-year-old, who so badly wanted to be four that she used the beloved number in her speech as often as possible. "But he sent word that he would be home for dinner tonight."

Muffling a sigh, Joyce wondered if there had been any change in her husband since she'd last seen him. He had been away on business for more than a month. Given their situation at home, she suspected that he deliberately chose the traveling assignments that so often kept him away weeks at a time. Even when he was in town, he kept long hours at his office in the city.

"Mama? I like you. Do you like me?" Audrey melted against her, and Joyce enfolded the petite child in her arms, carrying her to the plush armchair nestled near the library's bay of windows. "Of course I like you . . . and I love you, too." Settling into the chair with her daughter on her lap, she breathed deeply of the essence of little girl, her lips seeking the downy-soft cheek. "Nanny certainly has you looking smart this afternoon. Did you pick out this dress for Daddy?"

"Yes." Audrey nodded and was silent a long moment. "Mama, does Daddy like me?" she finally said in her piping voice, turning to look into her mother's eyes.

"Why, yes, of course your daddy likes you—and loves you, too. I'm sure he can hardly wait to be home and give you a great big kiss." The declaration rang false in her own ears, but she felt Audrey relax against her. "Does Nanny know you're down here, pumpkin?"

"No. Kathryn was waking up from her nap, and I just runned down to see if Daddy was home yet."

"I see. And what are Lynelle and Bobby doing?" Despite the approach of Christmas, the older children, ages eleven and nine, had become more somber with each day that passed. Did the loss of their baby sister two Christmases past still grieve them so deeply? Or were they more aware than she suspected about the gulf between their mother and father? This sigh that escaped couldn't be disguised.

Audrey wriggled off her lap. "I'd better go back upstairs. Nell and Bobby are back from skating, and I don't want Nanny to be cross with me." She started to run off and caught herself, slowing to a walk. At the doorway she turned, extending her index finger with importance. "Mama? Remember to tell me when Daddy comes home."

"Of course, Audrey."

"Maybe it will be in four minutes." A pair of index fingers now pointed toward her. "Or four hours."

"Yes, sweetheart, no doubt it will be somewhere between four minutes and four hours."

Satisfied, the youngster blew her a kiss and retreated. With a third sigh, Joyce settled back into the chair, alone with her worries and thoughts. *Mama, does Daddy like me?* Did even little Audrey sense the troubles that strained the fabric of her family? Things had gotten to the point where Joyce wasn't sure Samuel even liked—or loved—*her* anymore. And certainly, there would be no kisses shared between them. Perhaps a formal brush of his lips against her cheek. No closeness, no embrace.

Glancing around the library, she took in her home's lovely furnishings and the elaborate holiday decorations she'd painstakingly placed. So many material blessings. Across the room, a small blue spruce bore an elegant profusion of ornaments, bows and candles. Swags of fragrant pine graced the mantel. And wafting through the house were the aromas of many good foods being prepared in honor of Samuel's homecoming. For days she'd thrown herself into adorning their home in St. Paul's fashionable Irvine Park neighborhood, as if by creating a perfect environment she could create the illusion of a perfect family.

But an impeccably adorned home could not bring life to a marriage that was all but dead. Who was she fooling? The household staff was aware of the ever-widening chasm between her and her husband. The children, with whatever level of understanding, also knew things weren't right. Once their overgrown but grand playmate, their father was now a distant stranger. And he barely acknowledged little Kathryn, soon to be two.

Something inside Samuel had withered when Kathryn's twin sister, Mary Rose, had succumbed shortly after her birth. At first Joyce was secure in thinking time would heal her husband's wounded heart, but almost two years had passed with nothing and no one being able to breach its woody cords and ligaments.

She stood and walked to the window, staring at the snowy neighborhood. Dusk approached. As she watched a sleigh and team of horses pass down the street, she allowed herself to hope that this homecoming would be different. That a miracle had been worked in her husband's absence. She had prayed without ceasing for him to accept the Lord's comfort, but he seemed to have walked as far away from his faith as he had from his family. Never could she have traveled through such a valley of despair if not for the daily mercies of her Savior.

With a bittersweet stab, she allowed her thoughts to dwell on Mary Rose. Both Joyce and her physician had suspected that Joyce carried twins when she'd gotten large well ahead of her time, new mother's marks multiplying on top of the old. She and Samuel were delighted with this turn of events, chuckling and speculating at what bountiful fruit her womb might contain. But nearly two months before the end of her confinement, her waters had burst and labor was upon her like a galloping horse.

Mary Rose had arrived before Dr. Pfeiffer. The silver-haired gentleman scarcely had time to remove his jacket and roll up his sleeves before Kathryn joined her sister. Babies died, she knew, but she'd always had such easy births and healthy children that she secretly believed she would forever be preserved from such calamity. Her anxiety at delivering prematurely accelerated to gut-wrenching fear when Dr. Pfeiffer sat down and told her how slim were the girls' chances of survival.

He was correct on Mary Rose's account. Born plump and as red as a tomato, she took her last breaths only a few hours after her birth. But scrawny, pale Kathryn clung tenaciously to life, refusing to give up the battle. Even so many months later, tears burned behind Joyce's lids, and she released a deep, shuddering sigh as she recalled the raw emotions of that endless night. One baby dead, the other near death. Waiting. Wondering.

Samuel had tried to be strong for her, but the intensity of that time had proven to be too much for him. He'd always warned her that he didn't do well with death. Even before Mary Rose was gone, he'd fled the room with a choked apology. Two years later he was still running—from her, from their family, and from little Kathryn. It broke her heart to know that he had only the barest acquaintance with their surviving youngest daughter.

The survivor. That's how Joyce thought of tousle-headed Kathryn Cecilia. Quiet determination was readily visible in her character, tempered by a winning smile and expressive hazel eyes. Just like Samuel's eyes . . . used to be.

Letting the curtain fall back into place, she glanced at the needlework she'd set aside upon Audrey's escape from Nanny's watchful eye. The crewel still life was a promising piece, but she absolutely could not sit down and place one more stitch. As Samuel's arrival drew ever closer, the more unnerved she became.

The plush Oriental carpet absorbed the sound of her footsteps as she walked from the library to the hallway, her silk skirt swishing gently. Soft laughter and the clink of china drifted from beyond the closed doorway of the dining room, telling her that Carol and Ida were setting the table for this evening's meal. The two young domestics were good-natured and hardworking, and Joyce knew she was fortunate to have such wonderful household help. Ida lived in, while Carol came three days a week. Gertrude, their live-in cook, had been with them for the past seven years.

The house was as clean and shining as she'd ever seen it, as if the servants also thought that by putting things in order amidst the wonder and hope of the Christmas season, she and Samuel might somehow be set to rights.

If only it could be so.

Climbing the carpeted curved staircase, she continued down the second-story hallway to the staircase that rose to the third story. This was the children's area and also where Nanny, Ida, and Gertrude slept. From above, the reassuring voice of Margaret Murray could be heard, no doubt treating the children to one of her wonderful stories. As often as not, Nanny's tales came from her childhood in Scotland or wealth of imagination rather than the pages of a book. Many times had Joyce paused, listening outside the nursery door, enthralled.

Instead of going upstairs, however, she turned and walked toward her and Samuel's bedchamber. Why had she visited the room so many times today, making certain everything looked as warm and inviting as possible? Each time she'd also checked her appearance in the tall mirror near her wardrobe, satisfied that the blue silk suited her rounded figure and pale complexion, yet unsatisfied at some intangible thing about it all. Her hand closed on the knob, the well-oiled hinges of the door making not a sound as it swung open. She was at a loss to control her restlessness this afternoon, at a loss to—

She was brought up short at the sight of her husband. With his back to her, he unpacked his luggage, having not yet noticed her presence. With love and longing, her gaze drank in the details of his appearance. His hair, the color of lakeshore sand, appeared to have just been trimmed. Did he still have his mustache? His hat and suit coat had been tossed across the end of the bed, and the way the fabric of his shirt strained across his shoulders as he worked did not escape her notice.

An ache—almost like a physical pain—began in her chest as she thought about what their marriage had become: a cohabitation of strangers. How she longed to feel his arms around her again, to press her face against the warmth of his neck . . . to whisper the deepest feelings of her heart into his ear during the dark of the night. Prayer and patience had been her sustenance these two years past, but she didn't know how much longer she could go on this way. While he was home, he spent more nights in his sitting room than he did in here. She was losing him; they were all losing him.

"Welcome home, Samuel," she spoke with a tentative smile, not wanting to startle him or be caught staring. Why had he come in so quietly? Did he have a surprise for her? Her heart throbbed against her ribs as he turned, and she hoped with all her might that in his gaze she would find peace and joy.

But the hazel eyes of the stranger blinked once, twice, taking in her presence; his head inclined politely at her greeting. "Hello, Joyce. You're looking well." With that, he returned to his unpacking, as if dismissing her.

A mixture of potent feelings surged inside her, anger not the least among them. What had happened to Samuel, her husband? The man she thought she knew so well? Did he think he could keep his grief in check forever? And didn't he know that by doing so, he'd abandoned her to her bereavement? She opened her mouth to speak, but before she could utter a word, a flurry of footsteps sounded behind her.

"I heared Daddy! Daddy! Daddy!"

A chorus of whoops and shouts and footfalls carried into the room as Audrey pushed past Joyce's skirt and ran to her father. "I heared you come in, Daddy!" she cried, wheeling on her older brother and sister. "I told you I heared him. He sneaked in as quiet as a mouse up the back stairs, but you didn't believe me."

Lynelle and Bobby stood just outside the doorway, tentative about entering, their faces eager nonetheless.

"Why should we believe you?" Bobby spoke with the superiority of a much-older brother. "You're only three."

"Merciful heavens, children! Such manners!" came Nanny's unmistakable voice. "And Master Robert. Is that any way to speak to your sister?" Slowed by her arthritic knee as well as by Kathryn's halting descent, she did not reach the second-story landing until well after the older children, her admonitions competing with the toddler's insistent cries of "Da-dee! Da-dee!"

Joyce swung her gaze from Samuel to Nanny and the children, then back to where Audrey stood before Samuel, her breath catching in her throat as the seconds drew out. Samuel had not outright rejected the children before, but he looked as though he wanted to repack his items and be gone. She saw his gaze flick past her to Kathryn, now borne in Nanny's sturdy arms. Now quiet, their youngest child's wide hazel gaze was fixed on her father.

Unaccustomed to receiving her father's attention, Kathryn snuggled deeper into Nanny's bosom. Her thumb disappeared into her mouth, but she continued to hold Samuel's gaze until Audrey tugged several times on his trouser leg.

"Daddy, are you happy?" the three-year-old asked. "You don't look happy. Are you sick? I was sick one day when you were gone, and my tummy hurted. Is your tummy hurting? Nanny can give you a dose of castor oil and make you—"

"Audrey, darling," Joyce interrupted in the nick of time. "Your poor daddy has barely gotten in the door. Think of how fatigued he must be from his travels. Let's all give him some time to collect himself; then we can have a nice visit."

"Indeed, lass," Nanny seconded in a no-nonsense tone that thirty years' experience had perfected. "Come along."

With grudging obedience, Audrey walked toward the door. "I'm going to be four, Daddy," she persisted over her shoulder. "In Febillary. But Kathryn has the next birthday. Do you remember? She's going to be two. And so is Mary Rose, up in heaven. But I'm bigger. Four is bigger than—"

"That's enough, Audrey." Samuel spoke for the first time since the children had assembled, his expression having gone rigid at the mention of Mary Rose. "Go with Nanny, all of you." His voice was stern yet flat, his hazel gaze lacking the indulgent light with which it once shone.

Joyce stood in the doorway after Nanny and the children's hasty departure, her protectiveness toward her children sparking maternal, righteous anger at this father who would spurn their affections. Yet at the same time she was troubled by the subtle signs of suffering she read in his appearance. Faint, dark hollows encircled his eyes, and his cheekbones seemed to indicate a new leanness.

"Samuel," she said, at a loss to know the right feelings, the right words for this moment. *Patience, Joyce,* she told herself, taking a breath. Trying to remove any stain of censure from her voice, she went on. "The children have been so looking forward to your return." Extending her arm, she walked toward the bed in an attempt to engage him as gently as possible. "Please don't be angry at Audrey for mentioning Mary Rose. With Kathryn's birthday coming up, it's only natural that she would remember her, too." She fingered the corner of the leather bag on the bed. "We all remember her."

A long, controlled sigh sounded from the man next to her. "I'll be downstairs in half an hour." Keeping his back toward her, he walked to his wardrobe.

Tears blurred Joyce's vision as she walked from the bed-chamber and pulled the door shut tight. Taking a long moment to compose herself, she prayed, *Dear Lord, I hurt so deeply at times that I don't think I can bear it. Why does he continue to reject us? If you can do such things as part a sea and place a babe in a virgin's womb, won't you please do a miracle in Samuel's heart? In this season of hope, I ask for your grace and healing for this family.*

With one last dab at her eyes with her delicate handkerchief, she set off down the stairs to the library for her Bible. Surely the Lord would provide some passage or verse that spoke to the pain and desolation that washed through her like an icy current.

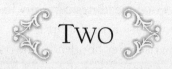

TWO

The moment Samuel heard the door click quietly closed, the air left his lungs in a long, slow breath. Shoulders sagging, he leaned against the wardrobe for support. Waves of weariness coursed through his body, the urge to crumple to his knees nearly over-whelming.

How much longer could he continue battling the weakness that threatened to level him? It was a mistake to have come home for the holidays; maintaining a stalwart frame of mind was all but impossible around Joyce and the children.

He had nearly succeeded in not thinking of the night of the twins' birth until Audrey had brought up Mary Rose. In a trice, memories of that terrifying night had rushed forth from the neat compartments in which he'd stored them. Joyce, moaning and writhing with pain. Mary Rose, sliding into his shaking hands. Dr. Pfeiffer's arrival; his grave expression. The cradle near the foot of the bed. His miniature newborn daughters gasping for breath. And Joyce again, pale and weak, shivering despite a mound of covers, crying an endless stream of tears.

How powerless he'd felt. How helpless. How out of control. There wasn't anything he could do for Joyce or the babies except pray, and his ineffectual pleadings certainly hadn't been enough to alter the course of Mary Rose's short life.

Laid out in the parlor after her death, she'd looked like a beautiful little doll. A child-size patchwork quilt of cranberry and green and white, made by his elderly aunt Millie in the southern part of the state, swaddled her still form. A second quilt of another design had arrived at their home some weeks later, also fashioned by Millie's arthritic hands, once she heard their tragic news.

Stepping away from the wardrobe, he pinched the bridge of his nose between his thumb and forefinger in an effort to halt the sudden sting of tears. *Concentrate, Samuel. Don't think about it. You can't do anything to change the past, but you know how to prevent such a tragedy from happening again. Be strong and go on from here.*

He knew his rejection of Joyce caused her pain. It caused him pain, too. Today she had looked so beautiful standing in the doorway that his resolve had nearly crumbled. In her arms he knew he would find sweet solace from the burdens he carried. He remembered how her fingers would stroke his hair and rub the knots from the back of his neck. . . .

For so long now he'd discouraged any contact between them that she no longer ventured to make such gestures. But she had to understand it was for her own good. Never again would there be a chance of a baby—or losing one—because if he lived to be a hundred, he would never forget Mary Rose's eyes.

He remembered leaning over the cradle to look at the girls while speaking to Dr. Pfeiffer, Mary Rose's gaze fixing upon him the instant she'd heard his voice. There had been something unearthly about her eyes, the color of her irises so dark as to appear bottomless. Yet, there was trust to be read there, as well. Like a slow-spreading stain, panic had begun in his vitals, radiating outward to his limbs. What could he do for this wee, gasping child who stared at him, silently pleaded with him, looked to him for something he couldn't give? And Joyce, sobbing for God to spare her babies?

Panic overcoming him, he'd bolted from the room, learning a few hours later that Mary Rose had died. For nearly two years he'd carried the shame of his weakness, having failed both his wife and daughter in their time of need. Never again would he be weak, he'd vowed, for his family deserved better. They deserved a man they could respect.

Taking his hand away from his face, he walked to the mirror and willed himself to collect his wits. Good. He'd managed to forestall any emasculating tears. A washcloth to his face and a stiff brush through his hair ought to put his appearance in order. Steeling himself to endure time with his family, he turned away from the mirror, not liking the grim man he saw reflected in the glass.

❋ ❋ ❋

"I dinna ken whar that mon's brains are at!" Nanny muttered, her Sutherland brogue intensifying with her aroused sense of justice. "An' Audrey, dearie, I'm thinkin' you're absolutely correct aboot a healthy dose of castor oil bein' just the thing to poot 'im to rights. Indeed!"

Back upstairs in the third-floor nursery, Lynelle and Bobby watched their gray-haired caretaker settle into her cushioned rocking chair near the stove. Neither Audrey nor Kathryn wasted any time clambering into her lap, snuggling in and awaiting a story.

"An' why stop a' castor oil?" she continued in an undertone, rocking her two young charges, "when jalap or calomel would do the job e'er so mooch better?"

"Nanny?" Lynelle queried with a meaningful glance at her brother. "Do you mind if Bobby and I write some letters while you tell the girls a story? We'll just be at the table by the window."

"Certainly not, young miss," came a most proper reply, the inflection of the older woman's speech changing remarkably. "'Twould be most beneficial for you to keep up your penmanship while on your holiday recess."

"Thank you, Nanny." Tugging Bobby's arm in an urgent, disguised manner, Lynelle pulled him over to the table on the opposite side of the large open room, several feet from where the others sat.

"Ouch! Let go of my arm! What do you think you're doing?" Bobby knew enough to keep his voice low, but his irritation was plain to hear.

"Nanny just gave me the most wonderful idea," she whispered in reply, elation coursing through her. Forcing her actions to be unhurried, she walked to the shelf and took down paper, pens, and ink. With a smile and a nod at Nanny, who had launched into the Tale of the Laird of Logie, she returned to the table, where Bobby waited.

"Well, what is it? What's your idea?" he asked before she had fully taken her seat.

"Castor oil."

"Castor oil? What are you talking about?"

"Giving Daddy castor oil, silly. A great big dose." Waiting for him to grasp her logic, she uncorked the ink bottle and dipped her pen. It was a marvelous scheme, really. So romantic.

"You're calling me silly?" His expression was both incredulous and scornful. "At least I haven't taken leave of my senses. Why on earth would you want to give Daddy a big dose of castor oil?"

"So he would need Mother to take care of him . . . ," she drew out, raising her eyebrows meaningfully.

"Ohhh." The sandy-haired boy was quiet a moment, thinking.

He scratched his nose with puzzlement. "You mean to poison him, then."

"Poison! Castor oil's not poison."

"If you say so." Bobby's hazel gaze spoke his disbelief. "And just how do you think Daddy's going to drink a big dose of castor oil without knowing it?" A shudder racked his thin shoulders. "I can taste it in anything."

"You have a point." Doodling against the plain white paper, Lynelle leaned closer to her brother. "But did you hear Nanny mention jalap and calomel? Those are even stronger than castor oil, and I know where Gertrude keeps a bottle of calomel." Excitement growing, the petite, dark-haired girl made an effort to keep her voice down. "We can put it in his pudding. You know how he always likes a dish of pudding in the evening. He'll be so sick that he'll think of Mother as an angel of mercy attending to him, and he'll fall in love with her all over again."

"She *is* awfully good to us when we're sick, isn't she? Do you really think it'll work?"

She nodded, a ripple of pain undulating across her heart. "We've got to do something, Bobby, and soon. Things between them are getting worse all the time. I'm afraid . . . I'm so afraid . . ." Her throat grew thick, and she wasn't able to continue.

"Aw, Nell, don't cry." Bobby's expression was sober as he awkwardly patted her arm. "Tonight we'll doctor the pudding and see what happens."

An impressive ham, scored neatly in a pattern of diamonds, sat on a platter at the head of the table near Samuel's right hand. Studded with cloves and glazed with brown sugar and honey, the roast put forth a sumptuous fragrance, mingling with other tantalizing aromas of Gertrude's finest work.

Joyce watched her husband as he focused his attention on

carving the meat. After offering the briefest of thanksgiving prayers, he had not spoken another word. Glancing across the table at her eldest children, she gave them an encouraging smile. She had hoped to prevent this homecoming dinner from becoming a stilted affair by asking Lynelle and Bobby to be present for the entire meal rather than having the children join them only for dessert, as was customary when Samuel was home. Many nights while he was away, she and the children dined together informally in the kitchen.

She could see how much this opportunity meant to them, noticing the pains they'd taken with their appearance. Lynelle, on the brink of adolescence, already fussed with her hair and clothing a great deal. Her dress of yellow velvet set off her dark hair and eyes in a striking way, presenting a glimpse of the lovely young woman she would become. Next year she would move down from her partitioned area of the nursery into her own room on the second story.

Bobby, who most days couldn't care less about the state of his dress, had selected his finest clothing for the occasion. His sandy hair lay in place, and telltale dampness near his temples gave evidence of a recent face washing. In itself, that was remarkable. His countenance was solemn while he waited for his meal, and it struck Joyce how much more he resembled Samuel with each passing year.

The meat was sliced and plates were passed without a word. It broke her heart to know that these good, dear children were so hungry—not for food, but for their father's attention. He was feeding them, indeed providing for them in a generous manner, but not nourishing them in the ways they needed most. *O Lord, these children need their daddy back,* she prayed silently. *The grinning, rough-and-tumble man with whom they used to play for countless hours on the nursery floor.* Audrey was too young to remember her father during her first year of her life, and little Kathryn had never known Samuel in such a way.

"How was skating this afternoon?" she asked, hoping Samuel might be drawn into the conversation with the children. "It looked like a nice day to be outdoors."

"Peter Christiansen got a bloody nose when we played crack the whip," Bobby offered, eyes brightening.

Lynelle glanced at her brother with disapproval. "Lawrence Sayles and Paul Robinson and some of the big boys got the whip going way too fast, and poor Peter was on the end. I think they let him go just to be mean."

"Oh, my. Is he badly injured?"

"He's fine, Mother," Bobby reassured, spearing a bite of ham and glancing toward his father. "By the time I walked him home he wasn't bleeding no more."

"*Anymore*," Lynelle corrected while sampling the spiced gooseberries. "But his coat was a mess."

Bobby nodded eagerly. "It was. The blood poured out of his nose just like someone turned on the faucet—"

"I hardly think this is a subject for the dinner table." Samuel's voice was curt, and he did not look up from his meal.

"Oh . . . sorry." The animation left his son's face. Lowering his gaze, he stirred his whipped potatoes with his fork.

After a long, uncomfortable silence, Lynelle and Joyce started to speak at the same time. "Pardon me, Mother. Please go ahead." Though only eleven years of age, Lynelle's manners were impeccable. Margaret Murray was a kind and loving caregiver, yet her standards for the children's behavior were high.

Joyce managed a warm smile despite her disappointment at how the meal was progressing. "I was going to say that we should enjoy Gertrude's holiday cookies in the library this evening. We can light a nice fire and have Margaret bring down Audrey and Kathryn."

"Do the little ones have to come?" Bobby sighed and made a face. "Audrey talks so much that she makes my ears want to fall asleep, and Kathryn just gets into everything."

"Hmmm." Joyce laid her forefinger against the side of her cheek. It was awkward conversing with the children with Samuel's troubled presence at the head of the table, but she was determined to give it her best. "I seem to remember an adorable little boy who never tired of asking questions *and* who used to get into everything—"

"Aw, Mother, please don't tell any 'adorable little boy' stories tonight. I'm sorry I said that about the girls. I'll be patient with them, I promise."

Samuel cleared his throat. "Did Gertrude make me any pudding? That's the one thing I've missed, being away. You can't get a decent bowl of creamy chocolate pudding anywhere."

Pudding? He cared only about his pudding? Joyce watched a look pass between the children while hurt and anger conflicted within her. Had it struck the children, too, that what their father seemed to miss the most while traveling was his nightly bowl of Gertrude's pudding? What about his wife? His children? Not trusting herself to speak, she took a small bite of ham and counted to ten while she chewed and swallowed.

"Yes, Samuel, Gertrude made you your chocolate pudding." Again she noted a meaningful glance pass between Lynelle and Bobby before both children became suddenly very busy with their dinners.

"I hope you find it as satisfying as you remember."

THREE

"Hurry up, Nell! Ida's going to be back for the tray any minute."

Bobby's voice was low and urgent, making her nervous hands tremble all the more. Having pilfered from a high shelf in the pantry a small bottle labeled "Calomel," Lynelle tried to figure how much of a teaspoon the recommended dosage of one-tenth to twenty grains might be. A quarter? Half? Oh, why weren't the conversions coming to mind? She reread the small print on the label, willing more information to be there than was.

A plate bearing an assortment of Gertrude's cookies waited atop a tray on the wooden table in the center of the kitchen. Gingerbread men, pfeffernuesse, lemon snaps, and nutmeg logs were arranged in a concentric pattern on the round dish. And next to the cookie plate was the lovely glass bowl holding their father's beloved chocolate pudding.

A few pans remained soaking, but most of the dishes had already been washed, dried and put away by Ida and Carol. The stout cook had retired to her room an hour before, having earned a well-deserved respite from her duties. Carol, too, had hung up her apron and let herself out the side door. Lynelle and Bobby had been waiting on the back staircase for Ida to take the

tea into the library, knowing they would have only a few
minutes during which to accomplish their task.

Now, huddled over the pudding bowl, the air between them
was electrified. Neither one of them was tempted by the delicious-
smelling cookies on display. Bobby looked as though he might
begin wringing his hands as Lynelle tapped a small measure of
white powder onto the spoon. *Hydrargyri Chloridum Mite. Dosage:
One-tenth grain to twenty grains.* One-tenth to twenty grains! Why
such a wide range?

"That little bit isn't going to do anything," Bobby insisted.
"Fill up the spoon, just to be sure."

"Aren't you the one who was concerned about us poisoning
him?" she whispered in return, feeling her heart pound against
her ribs. Nanny had implied the potency of this medication—
and a grain was a small measurement. "Half a teaspoon should
be plenty," she countered, tapping out a little more. Quickly, she
stirred the powder into the still-warm, thickened milk and corn-
starch mixture and did her best to smooth the surface of the
pudding.

No sooner had she tucked the bottle into her pocket and
whirled back from laying the spoon into the sink when the door
swung open, admitting Ida. The short, slender young housemaid
regarded them with amused tolerance. "Snitching cookies, are
you? Seems a little silly when I'm about to serve them to you in
the library."

"We haven't taken any cookies, Ida," Bobby responded with
wide-eyed innocence. "See? None are missing. We just came to
see if we could help you carry anything."

"Mm-hmm," she responded with suspicion, eyeing the plate.
"Well, if you took any, you did a fine job of straightening the
others. Off with you now, and no one's the wiser."

Up the steep, narrow servant's staircase they ran, peering into
the hallway when they reached the second story. Empty. Their

footfalls were nearly noiseless on the thick carpet as they rounded the corner and ran to the opposite end of the hall. Breathing hard, they were nearly to the top of the third-story staircase when the nursery door opened.

"Come away, wee yins," Margaret spoke to the little girls. "'Tis a wonderful treat to have cookies in the library wi' yer father and mother—" She broke off when she spied her two older charges coming up the stairs. "An' jist whar have the two of you been?" she queried, the gentle quality of her voice assuming its familiar no-nonsense tone.

"Oh . . . Bobby had a spot of gravy on his shirt. I helped him get it out," Lynelle replied while her brother nodded his head. Being winded from her exertion and the excitement of their conspiracy gave her words a breathless quality. One untruth uttered, she hoped she'd be forgiven for a second. "We were hurrying back so we could all go downstairs together."

"Aye, then. Come on, all of you. Maybe the grand meal has been just the thing to set this home to rights again."

"Daddy? Do you want to see Miss Hillary? She's my doll, and she's four years old. Did you remember that I'm going to be four on my next birthday?"

"Yes, Audrey, I remember that you're nearly four," Samuel replied in a tolerant tone before finishing the last few bites of his pudding. He had made the most of his treat, consuming the chocolate concoction slowly over the past half hour. Folding the newspaper he'd been reading, he set the dish and spoon on the small table next to his chair. "Bring Miss Hillary over, will you? I'd like to have a look at her."

The breath caught in Joyce's throat, and she nearly pricked her finger at her husband's agreeable tone. Securing the needle in an unworked section of her crewel piece, she watched with misting eyes as Audrey carried her dolly toward Samuel. What a good idea this had been, having the family gather together in the library for cookies and tea. Perhaps things were going to work out this Christmas, after all.

"Daddy, can Kathryn come by you, too?" Without waiting for his reply, she pulled her younger sister down from the chair where she sat nibbling a rich nutmeg log. Together, they approached their father. "We like you, Daddy, and we miss-ed you," she went on, the inflection of her suffixes often forming their own distinct syllable. "Me an' Kathryn, we'll be good girls, I promise. We won't talk about anything—Kathryn!" she interrupted herself. "Don't suck your thumb. Remember? You'll get butt teeth."

"*Buck* teeth. Like the deer." Bobby corrected from across the room, his patience with his garrulous little sister never very great. The entire time they'd been in the library, he and Lynelle had been huddled together whispering at the small table set farthest away from where the rest of the family sat, their private conversation interspersed with several glances at their father. Owing to their miserable dinner experience, Joyce did not correct their poor display of manners but instead allowed them to be off by themselves.

Modern gas lighting shone from frosted-glass wall sconces, and a merry fire burned in the grate, its gentle glow adding to the rich texture of the library's wine-colored fleur-de-lis wall coverings. The Christmas tree and holiday decorations set off the room to perfection. In years past, countless cozy family evenings and lazy Sunday afternoons had been spent in this room; dare she hope this gathering place would see many more such happy times?

Samuel made a great show of admiring Miss Hillary's hair and clothing while Kathryn looked on with wide eyes, thumb firmly planted in her mouth. He had not yet addressed her or the older children, but Joyce's spirits soared as she watched him interact with Audrey. Could something so simple as a bowl of favorite pudding have warmed his heart so?

Watching the light strike the planes and angles of his face as he spoke to Audrey, she allowed herself to realize the full measure of how much she'd missed his companionship, his tenderness, his smile. His friendship. Sometimes she thought the loss of her husband, though he still lived and breathed, hurt even more than losing Mary Rose.

"Are ye bairns ready for your good-night story? Wee Robin Redbreast, the finest singer in all of Scotland, has set off to see the king and queen on their golden thrones. Will he make it, I wonder?"

"An' the bad, bad cat tries to eat him!" Audrey cried with delight.

"Hush, wee yin. We canna tell the tale till faces are washed and teeth are brushed. Now bid your father good night and along ye come."

Nanny's entrance couldn't have been better timed. Taking advantage of the distraction of the children filing past, Joyce dabbed her eyes with her handkerchief. "I'll be up for kisses shortly," she managed to call out.

A long moment of silence passed.

"We're invited to a holiday ball at the Forepaughs' this Wednesday evening," she remarked, referring to their neighbors on the other side of the park. A successful entrepreneur, dark-mustached Joseph Forepaugh had established the largest whole-sale dry goods house in the Midwest. "And just two days after that is Christmas Eve already," she added, hesitant to mention Kathryn's birthday, which fell between those two dates on the twenty-third.

"I can't believe how the children have grown." Samuel's gaze was upon her, an inscrutable expression on his handsome face.

A log snapped in the fire, followed by the sound of setting wood. "They're fine children, Joyce. You're doing a wonderful job with them."

"Why . . . thank you, Samuel. They are getting big, aren't they?" Her pleasure at his compliment, however, was momentary. Taking up her needle, she began working a flurry of stitches.

Why the sudden discomfort in speaking a few sentences of conversation with her husband? What was the matter with her? Wasn't this the new beginning she had been hoping for? Once again the troublesome moisture gathered in the corners of her eyes. "I'd best go up and kiss the children good-night," she managed to say, rising from her chair. As much as she'd longed for such an opportunity, it was proving to be too difficult for her emotions to handle.

"And Joyce?" Samuel added, reaching for the paper at his side, his hazel gaze lingering on her. "Kiss them again for me."

Nodding, she exited the library without daring another glance at this man who caused such disturbance inside her.

❊ ❊ ❊

"You said Daddy had to go to work 'smorning, Mama," Audrey spoke between bites of oatmeal. "But he's not gone. I heared him upstairs, talking."

Talking? That was one word for it, Joyce thought, still smarting from her husband's ill-tempered words. "Your daddy is feeling unwell this morning, Audrey," she replied, "so you and Kathryn must do your best to play quietly today."

"What's the matter with Daddy?" Lynelle asked, eyes wide. Both she and Bobby had stopped eating, their spoons coming to rest in their bowls.

Hastening to put their fears to rest, she explained, "He woke with some griping pains in his belly earlier this morning. He's not feverish, so I'm sure it's nothing serious. Please don't worry, my darlings."

"Oh . . . but doesn't he need you to take care of him?" Glancing at Bobby, Lynelle continued to look alarmed despite the reassurance she'd given. "I mean, when we get sick, Mama, you care so kindly for us."

"I would love nothing more than to attend to your father," she replied truthfully, "but he prefers to be alone in his misery. Now eat before your breakfast gets cold."

A wry, sad smile curved her lips as she recalled waking to dull light filtering into the bedroom. As troubled and confused as she'd been last evening, sleep had been a long time in coming. When she'd returned to the library after tucking in the children, Samuel had wished her a more amicable good-night than he had in months, yet had made no move to put down his paper. Alone, she'd climbed the stairs one more time.

What an odd mix of sentiments he had displayed since his return home. Irritability. Gruffness. Wanting to be left alone, yet displaying the first glimpses of softening any of them had seen in many, many months. She knew that hidden behind all these things were unplumbed depths of grief and sadness. Why he was unable to move forward, to let his family help him, she did not understand.

Her first waking thought this morning had been to wonder whether or not he had come to bed. Since the birth of the twins, he spent more than half his nights on the sofa in his study. Leaning up on one elbow, she'd checked the bedcovers next to her and seen that his side of the bed was mussed.

He'd been there.

Oh, Lord, was there a reason to hope the tide was turning, even a small bit? As she began to mull things over in her mind, the door to the water closet adjoining their room had opened, and Samuel had shuffled toward the bed, holding his abdomen.

"Are you ill, Samuel?" she'd asked, alarmed by his disheveled appearance.

With a groan, he'd sunk onto the bed and curled tightly on his side, facing away from her.

"Samuel?" she'd tried again, laying her hand on his shoulder. Through his nightclothes, his skin was damp but not hot.

"Are *you* sick?" he'd snapped, albeit weakly.

"No, I feel . . . fine."

"The children?"

"I haven't heard a thing from upstairs. I'm sure Nanny would have woken me if they were ailing."

"Well, I wonder what I could have eaten to give me such a bellyache? If no one else is sick, I have to wonder about that pudding. Maybe Gertrude used spoiled milk . . . or she poisoned me with bad eggs. She hasn't been very friendly toward me for quite some time now."

And no wonder, she'd thought. He and Gertrude used to have such fun kidding one another, but nearly two years had passed since he'd given any of their help more than a brusque hello. "Samuel, you know Gert would never do such a thing," she had spoken with gentle reproach. "She uses only the freshest ingredients to prepare our foods. Any spoiled milk or eggs would have been sent straight out the door."

"Aahh." He'd half sighed, half moaned as his belly rumbled loudly. "My middle is twisted up in knots." Groaning again, he'd rolled his head toward her, wearing a vexed expression on his pale features. His hair, usually so neat, was as tousled as she might find Bobby's on any given day. How she'd longed to smooth her fingers through the sandy-brown strands and lay her palm against the lean plane of his cheek, a motion her hands used to make as naturally as her lungs drew breath.

"Can I bring you something?" she'd asked, her heart turning over at his distress. "Mush? Tea and toast?"

"Nothing," he'd snapped. "I want nothing but to be left alone. No mush, no tea and toast, no doting wives, no company, no *nothing*."

"Mama?" Audrey broke in on Joyce's thoughts, pulling her mind back to breakfast at the kitchen table. "Are you happy? I eated four more bites of my oatmeal, and it's all gone. See? I'm being a good girl, amn't I?"

"Eat!" Kathryn exclaimed with shining hazel eyes, wearing as much oatmeal on her face and bib as she had in her stomach. Pearly-white baby teeth gleamed in a messy but beatific smile. "Wuv you, Mama."

Quiet joy flooded her soul as she gazed around the table at her four children. How a heart so heavy could simultaneously know such gladness was a mystery she would never comprehend. Much the same was the bittersweet stab she experienced whenever she thought of Mary Rose, gone from this earth but alive with Christ in the heavenlies. *Suffer little children, and forbid them not, to come unto me; for of such is the kingdom of heaven.* No matter how her heart might ache for her daughter, Jesus' words in the Gospel of Matthew never failed to bring her comfort and courage.

And so should she have the same faith as she suffered in this situation with Samuel. Together, before the Lord, they had made this marriage covenant for better or worse. This morning she would meditate upon verses extolling God's mercy and his mighty power.

And upon the virtue of hope.

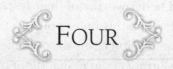

FOUR

Food poisoning. He was sure of it. The only other time Samuel
had felt this miserable was when he'd eaten tainted chicken salad
as a youth. The intestinal griping continued throughout the
morning and early afternoon, leaving him weak as a pup. When
he could, he dozed, having fitful dreams of being sick . . . only
to awaken in the darkened bedchamber, sick.

Beyond the walls and door of his sickroom, he heard the
ongoing routines of his household. Ida's and Carol's hushed
voices carried to him as they went about their tasks, and from
above were sounds of his children's movements and laughter.
From time to time he heard Joyce speak, but he hadn't seen her
since he'd sent her away earlier in the morning.

Remorse for his uncivil words scuttled his already low spirits.
He hadn't meant to be so short-tempered; he knew she had only
wanted to help. The loving warmth of her hand upon his shoulder had also unsettled him, bringing with it the full realization of
his emptiness and longing for human touch.

He didn't deserve such a wife, such faithful children. If only
things could have been different—if only Mary Rose had
survived, then his cowardly weakness would have never been
brought to light and his family forced to suffer a double loss.
They had not only lost a precious and innocent child, they had

lost a husband and father worthy of their respect. What dishonor he'd brought upon this household.

It was best he was leaving again so soon after the holidays. Architects from his firm were in demand not only in St. Paul but also in many other cities. Joyce obviously had things well in hand at home, and the children were healthy and strong and full of life. He knew the Good Book had been her source of strength and comfort since the twins' birth. He'd been a believer once, and he supposed he still was, but the verses and teachings he recalled didn't speak to the burdens he carried.

A strong cramp gripped him, drawing his belly so tight that he was forced to pull his knees upward. He'd thought the worst of this sickness over, but maybe he was wrong. Finally, the spasm released its clutch, leaving him depleted and ready to fall into more disturbed slumber.

How much time passed until he awakened, he did not know, but the sounds from the nursery above had stilled. Murky, overcast light stole in around the drawn drapes, signaling twilight's early approach. His belly had quieted, he noticed, and for the first time since he'd been stricken ill, he thought a bit of tea and toast had appeal.

Rolling carefully from his side to his back, his shoulder blade came to rest upon a hard, cold object. What on earth? With some difficulty, he pushed himself to a semisitting position. Grogginess clouded his mind as his hand reached back and closed over the offending item.

The textures of springy hair and soft fabric confused him until he pulled Miss Hillary before him, her lovely hat and clothing in disarray from his inadvertent ill treatment of her. How had . . . Audrey. A curl of warmth began in his chest at the thought of his willful daughter tucked into her bed for her afternoon nap, plotting to sneak away and pay him a visit.

Quiet as a whisper, she must have stolen in while he slept, leaving her beloved doll to keep him company. Resting back against the pillow, he gazed at his daughter's porcelain treasure until his eyes blurred. It wasn't good to get too sentimental, he told himself, carefully laying the doll on Joyce's pillow beside him. Closing his lids, he longed for the oblivion of dreamless slumber to carry him away from the mess he had made of his life.

"It didn't work, Lynelle," Bobby said in an accusing tone, bringing up the subject they'd avoided all day. His breath formed white clouds in the late afternoon air as they neared home, skates slung over their shoulders. "All he did was stay in his room all day, and Mama didn't even go up there again after breakfast."

"Well, you never know . . . she could have tended to him while we were gone this afternoon."

"Do you really believe that?"

"No," she said, sighing with discouragement, wishing things had gone differently. "No, I don't."

Quietly, they entered the side door of the house and removed their boots. Gertrude labored in the kitchen, a dour expression pinching her ordinarily pleasant features. Thinking the better of asking for hot chocolate, Lynelle hooked Bobby's arm and pulled him up the servant's stairs.

"And would ye look at those rosy cheeks." Nanny greeted them with quiet tones as they entered the nursery. "Reminds me of bein' a lass back in Rogart, wi' the biting winds whirling off the North Sea." She sat alone in the rocker, a book opened across her lap. "Shh, now, the pair of ye. The wains are still asleep, as well as yer father down below. Hang up yer coats, an' come sit here beside the stove and take off yer chill."

"How is he?" Lynelle asked, moving farther into the room. The dread she'd been carrying throughout the day swelled into fear at Nanny's mention of her father. She hadn't meant to do serious harm with the calomel, but what if she and Bobby *had* poisoned him? What if he died? Catching her brother's gaze, she saw the same dread reflected there.

"I've heard Gertrude has made him some tea an' toast, so he must be feeling better."

"Oh . . . good!" Lynelle's relief rushed forth with her exclamation, making her knees weak. Taking a seat before the radiant heat of the small stove, she extended her chilly toes and fingers, wondering why it always felt as though the ice-cold parts of her were burning as they began to warm.

"Were ye so worried, lass?" Nanny inquired, rocking in a slow, steady tempo.

Flustered, she didn't know how to reply. "Well . . . it's just that Daddy is hardly ever ill . . . and . . ."

"Och, 'twas not a serious matter," the middle-aged widow replied, continuing on in an undertone as she was often wont to do. Her eyebrows went up in an expressive manner, and her short legs pushed the chair back and forth with more gusto. "Leastwise, not till word came down that he'd accused the cook of preparin' spoiled foods."

"He thinks Gertrude gave him rotten food?" Bobby asked, scratching the side of his nose. "Whoo! I bet she's mad! No wonder she was stomping all over the kitchen."

"Aye, she's in fine fettle over the matter. If not for the sake of yer kind mother, I believe she would have packed her bags an' been gone. She was insulted!"

"Oh, dear," Lynelle said quietly, filled with fresh anxiety. Things were getting worse all the time. Daddy hadn't wanted Mother to attend to him at all, and now their cook had been blamed for something she hadn't done. "What do you think is going to happen?" she asked in a quavering voice.

"I bet Gertrude will *really* poison him now!" Bobby interjected with a snicker. "He'd better check his tea."

"Bobby! This is serious!" How could he make a joke while the future of the Colburn family hung in the balance? If something didn't change soon, she was afraid their father would leave for one of his business trips and never come back.

"Hoot! A wee sma' bit o' gripin' in 'is belly an ye'd think the world had come to an end." Nanny shook her graying head and rocked harder. "The mon's gone daft wi' his grief," she muttered, setting her jaw. "Aye, Meg, I say to meself, life is hard. Yer own womb barren an' yer man lyin' in 'is grave. But ye ken fine well the Guid Laird has 'is own plans for yer life, an' ye still go on.

"'Tis true the wee wain Mary Rose died, boot canna the mister see the glorious treasure he 'as before 'im? Four bonnie bairns an' a fair an' gentle wife, but nay, he will na look beyond the end o' his nose. God forbid it would take somethin' happenin' to 'is family to pull 'im out o' the bog he's mired 'imself into."

Lynelle feared her mouth had dropped open. One glance at Bobby confirmed that he was as shocked as she by Nanny's discourse. Never before had their caretaker spoken such a portion of her mind.

"Whisht! Pit yer eyes back in yer heads, dearies, and dinna mind a grieved old *cailleach* an' her loose tongue." Margaret Murray's intense expression faded, and her face melted into a tender smile. Picking up her book, she added, "I love ye so, all of ye. Keep to yer prayin', for the Laird Jesus 'as a special fondness for the prayers of 'is wee bairnies. Perhaps there's a miracle yet to be done this Christmas."

Dinner was a quiet affair. As at breakfast and lunch, they gathered around the kitchen table for the evening meal, a simple fare of oyster stew, crackers, and spiced pears. Mother did her best to keep up a brave and gracious front, but Lynelle could see the strain the day had taken on her. Though they had many of their dinners in the kitchen while Daddy was away, a strange hollowness persisted in her middle while the family ate. Was it the

knowledge that he was home yet apart from them and that
things were very, very wrong?

Dejected, she continued to ponder their situation while she
and Bobby played checkers in the library that evening. How
different last night had been with the whole family gathered,
a fire crackling in the hearth. Daddy had clearly enjoyed his
pudding, and he'd even smiled when Audrey had showed him
Miss Hillary. How she longed for the kind father she remembered, the one who had always made her feel so special.

A fire burned in the grate, but tonight the atmosphere of the
comfortable room was devoid of warmth. Nanny had come for
Audrey and Kathryn right after dinner, and Mother was in her
own world while she sat in her chair and stitched. From time to
time she dabbed her eyes with her handkerchief. Was she also
comparing the hopeful tone of last evening to the dismalness of
this one?

"King me," Bobby spoke in a morose tone, having jumped
three of her checkers in one move.

Hope, she thought, dutifully stacking a second red checker on
the piece invading her back row. *That's what's missing tonight.*

Last evening things had been promising. Though she and
Bobby had no doubt transgressed by putting calomel in Daddy's
pudding, they had been buoyed by the anticipation of Mother
and Daddy coming together again.

What they needed was another plan. Something more reliable—something that would surely reunite their parents.
Nanny's words from this afternoon came back to her, igniting
one thought after another. Of course! How could she have over-
looked something so very obvious?

"Bobby?" she whispered, leaning toward him over the checker-
board. Her lips twitched as she tried suppressing her excitement.
"You'll never believe it! I just got the most wonderful idea."

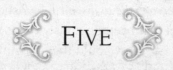

FIVE

A sprinkling of stars shone above winter-barren branches. The heavy odor of burning coal carried on the breeze, commingled with the more pleasant tang of wood smoke. In the distance, a chorus of dogs barked. Snow crunched underfoot as Samuel and Joyce walked along Irvine Park Drive to the Forepaugh residence on Exchange Street. The mercury hovered near twenty degrees, mild for a Minnesota winter's evening.

"Is your stomach still a little tender? I noticed you didn't eat much at dinner tonight," Joyce commented, trying to make conversation with the taciturn man beside her. After being laid up all of Tuesday, he had risen early and gone to the office today. "We don't have to go if you're not up to it. I'm sure Joseph and Mary would understand."

"I'm fine," he replied in a distracted tone, taking her elbow to guide her around a patch of slick ice. Once past the hazard, he abruptly let go of her arm.

Thank goodness it's only a bit farther, Joyce thought with hurt and confusion, wondering what thoughts were contained inside her husband's head. Until just two years ago, she would have said she knew his mind as well as her own. Now he was like a stranger, one whose mind she didn't know—nor one whose heart she could claim.

And what of tomorrow, the twins' birthday? she wondered with foreboding. Samuel had been obviously upset when Audrey had mentioned Mary Rose. How could they possibly celebrate Kathryn's birthday without remembering her twin sister? There wasn't a day that had passed since December 23, 1878, that Joyce hadn't thought of her beloved little one and wondered what life would have been like if she'd lived. And the children, especially, liked to talk about their little sister in heaven.

Though Kathryn and Mary Rose had been so different in appearance, Dr. Pfeiffer believed they were identical twins. In her mind's eyes flashed the picture of a pair of sweet, tousle-curled toddlers—two sets of expressive hazel eyes looking to her and calling her "Mama."

Whatever would she do if something happened to Kathryn? Outspoken little Audrey? Or Bobby or Lynelle? The pain of losing a child was something on which she had never reckoned. Living through it had been nearly unbearable. What if God decided to take another?

"Hello, neighbors!" John Matheis called, owner of the Carpet Emporium bearing his name. He walked toward the Forepaughs' from his home on Walnut Street. While Samuel answered, Joyce cleared her throat and blinked back a dam of moisture, wondering in a rather detached way—almost as if she were an observer looking at someone else—at the intensity of pain in her chest.

How long until this hurting stopped? It seemed like every time she stopped to take stock of life and notice that she had gone a day—or even a week—without shedding tears over the loss of her baby, the heartache would return with the force of a hard, unexpected clap on the back. Samuel's aunt Millie had written several letters to her during the past two years, exhorting and encouraging her to continue on, that time and the Lord would indeed heal all wounds. "Perhaps not in the way or at the speed you'd like," she'd penned, "but upon self-examination, I found that progress had been made upon each anniversary of my children's deaths."

"Well, here we are," Mr. Matheis announced, turning up the walk to the elegant, three-story Victorian home. The strains of festive music carried to them as they climbed the steps of the many-columned porch, and Joyce realized she must make an effort to shake the melancholic turn of her thoughts. Thick garlands of fragrant balsam swagged the entrance, and even before they could knock, dark-haired Joseph Forepaugh threw wide the front door, exclaiming, "Come in, come in!"

The parlor contained an assortment of refined merrymakers as well as a five-piece wind and string ensemble. Pulling one hand from her satin muff, Joyce untied the matching, quilted hood and handed both novelties to the Forepaughs' straight-postured manservant. She remembered the day when Samuel would have helped her out of her coat, but he had already moved from the foyer into the parlor. Several acquaintances greeted him, and he was quickly drawn into conversation by a knot of men.

"Good evening, Joyce." Mary Forepaugh smiled kindly. "We're so glad Samuel was home and that you both could come. Please come this way; I don't believe you've ever met . . ."

An hour passed, then two, while Joyce made conversation with neighbors she knew and strangers to whom she was intro-duced. Several couples danced in the lavishly decorated parlor, swirling and turning beneath the glittering chandelier. Once upon a time she and Samuel would have been one of those laughing pairs. Throughout the evening he did not approach her, but once, glancing up, she found the weight of his stare upon her. His expression, once again, was unfathomable.

"Did you read in the *Evening Dispatch* about the expenses of the president's mansion?" Virginia Rollins queried, giving her bonnet a pat. Ostrich tips and silver ornaments bobbed with the matriarch's movement. Stifling a yawn, Joyce longed to be home, kissing her children good-night. With effort, she refocused her attention on the conversation at hand.

"Why, the president's salary alone is fifty thousand, and the upkeep of the public grounds nears eighty thousand dollars! I don't understand why . . ." On and on the older woman talked, calling the White House's items and expenses to mind as effortlessly as if she'd committed them to memory. Which she probably had, Joyce thought, finding her mind wandering once more.

"We need to leave, Joyce." She hadn't noticed Samuel's approach, but his voice was in her ear, low and urgent. "Right away."

"What is it?" Turning with surprise, she saw worry etched on her husband's features.

He swallowed hard. "Ida just came with a message that the children are violently ill."

"Oh, Samuel," she breathed, reaching for his arm. "Which of the children?"

"She didn't tell me . . . she just said that Nanny wants us home immediately."

"Joyce, Dr. Pfeiffer is right over there," Mrs. Rollins interjected, her ears every bit as sharp as her tongue was purported to be. "Sherman," she summoned, pointing to the silver-haired gentleman helping himself from a tray of candies. Her imperious voice carried without difficulty over the music. "There's trouble over at the Colburns'. They're going to need you to go along home with them. The children are ill."

"Be right there," the physician called evenly, popping a candy into his mouth. If he was perturbed at being pulled away from the party, it didn't show. The crowd parted, allowing the three of them passage to the foyer. Towing Joyce through the midst was Samuel, his strong fingers laced through hers. Panic raced throughout every part of her body as he threw on his overcoat and helped her into hers. Never one to be caught without his necessary instruments and supplies, Dr. Pfeiffer claimed his black bag along with his hat and overgarment.

Please, Lord, she pleaded in a silent prayer, hastening down the steps and front walk, *don't take any more of my babies from me. In your wisdom, you know what measure of sorrows each heart can bear . . . O Jesus, please be merciful . . .*

The two blocks' distance home was covered in record time. Samuel shared the details of his illness of the day before with the physician, as well as his suspicion that he'd been served tainted food. Joyce wasn't sure how she knew, but a sense of womanly intuition told her that their comestibles were not the problem. The thought of diphtheria, every mother's dread, coated her heart with a thick, oily layer of fear.

Ida waited for them, peering around the heavy wooden door with wide, frightened eyes. "Oh, good, you've got the doctor. Hurry, they're making a terrible noise up there," she cried out, opening the door to admit them. "Such awful pains. We don't know what they've got."

Indeed, from above came piteous moaning and wailing. Taking the carpeted risers two at a time, Samuel sprinted up the staircase without bothering to remove his hat or coat. Ida hurriedly helped Joyce and Dr. Pfeiffer from their outerwear, filling them in on as many details as she knew.

"There's been no vomiting or diarrhea, leastwise not yet," she addressed the physician. "One minute they were fine, and the next they were like this!" The young servant's words tumbled one over another. "Poor Meg's beside herself, runnin' from one bed to the next. Of the four, Kathryn, the baby, seems to be fine . . . just bewildered at all the goings on. Gertrude's taken her down to her room for the time being."

"Is there a fever?" the physician inquired as they climbed the stairs. "Catarrh? Did the pains come on suddenly, in the back and limbs?"

"Oh, sir," Ida breathed, out of breath with exertion and emotion. "Are you thinking . . . are you thinking it's . . . diphtheria then?"

Joyce's heart raced beneath her bodice of heavy stamped velvet. Oh, her babies. God help her sweet little ones. Lynelle, Bobby, little Audrey. She couldn't lose them, she just couldn't. Every year the dreaded disease claimed the lives of countless little ones.

"A rash, you say, miss? Big red spots?" Dr. Pfeiffer stopped at the landing before ascending the second flight of stairs, wearing a quizzical expression beneath his silvered mane. "Sudden, concurrent onset of pain in three children, accompanied by the appearance of swift-spreading erythema *circinatum*. How curious."

Pouring down from above, in addition to the children's anguished cries, was Samuel's deep voice and a torrent of Scottish brogue. Oh, what was happening to her family? Joyce wondered with despair. Just when she had thought things couldn't get any worse, her troubles had multiplied.

"Mrs. Colburn, I'm going to ask you and your husband to wait outside while I examine the children. Your presence may only upset them more while I do so," the physician explained, shifting his heavy bag from one hand to the other. "Mrs. Murray can assist me while she tells me what she knows of this intriguing illness."

A moment later Samuel exited the nursery and trudged down the stairs, joining her in the hallway of the second story. On his face was an expression of such wretchedness that she was moved to comfort him. Or was it he who comforted her? Into his strong arms she melted, and for what seemed like an eternity, her tears soaked the lapel of his coat while she cried out her sadness, her grief, her fears.

Her husband's embrace was a warm and comfortable haven, making her think of one of the opening verses of the Ninety-first

Psalm: *He shall cover thee with his feathers, and under his wings shalt thou trust.* The mental image of being nestled under the wing of the Lord was one that had sustained her through many black hours and days after Mary Rose's death, especially as Samuel grew more and more distant.

"Try not to . . . worry so, Joyce," Samuel comforted with halting words, his fingers tracing the contours of her upswept hair. The familiar fragrance of his shaving lotion wafted to her nostrils, warm and spicy. "If anyone can . . . Doc Pfeiffer is . . . one of the best." What remained unspoken was that despite Dr. Pfeiffer's skill, one of their daughters now lay in her grave. Were more of their children to follow?

Suddenly, Joyce realized that the noises upstairs had ceased. Only a moment after that awareness struck her, the nursery door opened and Dr. Pfeiffer called out, "Mrs. Colburn? Would you please come up here?"

"What's happening?" Samuel demanded to know, his arms stiffening around her. "What's happened?"

"Things are quite all right," the physician reassured. "We'll call for you in a short time, Samuel."

Things were all right. Oh, thank you, Lord. Relief flooded her eyes with fresh tears, and taking a deep, shaking breath, she disentangled herself from her husband's arms and met his gaze. "Thank you," she spoke aloud, offering him a smile into which she poured the essence of her feelings. *How I love you,* she added silently, still uncertain of her standing with him.

"Oh, Joyce. I wish . . ." He sighed heavily while studying her face with hazel eyes full of emotion. "I just want you to know—"

"Mrs. Colburn?" the physician repeated.

"Excuse me," she spoke softly, torn between her desire to prolong this long-awaited moment with her spouse, yet needing to see with her own eyes that their children were fine. With another whispered apology, she hurried up the staircase and into

the nursery, where she was met by Dr. Pfeiffer just inside the
door.

"I'm afraid there is a problem," he began in low tones. "Let's
step over this way." He indicated the opposite side of the nursery
from the children's partitioned sleep areas. "Mrs. Murray is with
them, which will give us a few minutes to talk."

"A problem? But I thought you said they were all right." Like
a fountain, fear quickly bubbled up inside her.

"The children are fine," he reassured with a gentle smile. "I
fear they will not be so fine, however, a short time from now."

"What . . . what do you mean?"

"Well," he began, stroking his chin. "Let's just say that their
pains desisted the moment I discovered their spots could be
removed with a damp cloth."

"What?"

"Red watercolor, I'm afraid."

"Oh." She was quiet a long moment, digesting this news.

"You see, Joyce, they falsified their illness to bring you and
your husband home from the party in an attempt to . . . ah,
reunite the two of you. They also hoped this scheme of theirs
would vindicate your cook, whom, I understand, was accused
by your husband of serving tainted food." He cleared his throat,
a deep noise that sounded suspiciously like a chuckle. "If the
dear woman hasn't missed her calomel yet—"

She interrupted the physician with a gasp. "Calomel! Don't
tell me they . . . oh no!"

"Calomel," he confirmed, nodding. "Oh yes, indeed. Once the
confessions began, they rather rapidly poured forth. The drug
was in your husband's pudding, night before last."

"Are they so angry with him then?"

The tender interlude downstairs only moments ago had done
nothing to change the fact that her and Samuel's problems were
very real . . . and very large. As hard as she'd tried to shield the

children from the farce their marriage had become—as well as play the roles of both mother and father—it was now painfully obvious she'd failed.

But had she done such a poor job of things that she'd unwittingly turned the children against their father? She'd never meant for that to happen. To the contrary, she'd always tried to portray him in the best possible light. Thinking of the sad state of affairs their family life had become, her knees grew weak, and she sought a chair.

"No, my dear, they're not angry," the kindly physician clarified, drawing up the chair across from her and patting her hand. "They're not angry at all. They're just frightened of what the future may hold, frightened that their father may walk out the door and never come back. They only wanted to put their family back together again, Joyce. And in not an entirely irrational line of reasoning, they thought that if they made your husband ill, he would need you to take care of him."

"I tried, and he all but threw me out on my ear."

"Yes, well, you know what men can be like in the sickroom." A smile creased his face before his expression grew serious. "I didn't realize how grave your situation was here, my dear. Is there anything I can do to help? Speak to Samuel, perhaps?"

"No . . . I don't think . . ." Sighing, she shrugged her shoulders in a slight, bereft movement. "I don't know what you could say to him. He puts more distance between himself and the children with every passing month."

"And you, too." The words were phrased not as a question, but as a statement.

She nodded, unable to answer. Her children's greatest fear was also her own: that Samuel's remoteness would one day become such that he would simply not come home.

"Mama?" Audrey's voice piped from across the room. "Can you wash me? After Nanny put us to bed, Nell and Bobby painted me,

Mama, and they said I had to scream and yell like I was being
eaten by cannonballs or they wouldn't like me anymore. That was
very, *very* bad, wasn't it, Mama?"

"*Cannibals,* not cannonballs," came Bobby's exasperated retort.
"Can't you remember anything?"

"Not another word out of ye, Master Robert. An' you, Audrey,
come on back here. Aye, you were all naughty little wains this
nicht. Trickin' everyone the way ye did . . ." The weight in
Nanny's voice gave testimony to her fatigue and low spirits. "Let
yer mother finish talkin' with the good doctor in peace, now,
whilst I wash off yer paint."

"Wash off whose paint?" came Samuel's grim voice. His shoes
struck hard notes against the smooth, wide-planked floor as he
strode into the nursery, the sound deadening once he stepped
upon the oilcloth rug and came to a halt. "And what kind of
tricks have been played?" he called out into the large room that
had suddenly grown as hushed and still as a snow-covered
cemetery. "Someone had better give me an answer, and soon."

Lynelle's quiet weeping broke the silence as Joyce stood, her
insides quavering. Gone was her husband's loving tenderness;
the stony stranger now stood before her. "Samuel, please come
sit with us," she entreated. "Dr. Pfeiffer was just explaining—"

"I'd like to hear an explanation from the children themselves,
if you don't mind." Turning to the right, he disappeared into the
sleeping area. "You're excused for the night, Mrs. Murray," he
growled.

With a sad, apologetic expression, the children's caretaker withdrew from the room. Dr. Pfeiffer's gentle hand stayed Joyce's
impulse to be at her children's side as well as her instinct to
defend their reasons for their actions. "Let him hear it from the
children himself," the doctor spoke softly, as two other young
voices joined their elder sister's in remorse for their wrongdoings.

Dampness flowed down her cheeks at her children's tearful disclo-
sures, followed by her husband's censorious words.

"I am the head of this household. I will leave when I wish, and
I will come home when I wish. No one will tell me what to do or
when to do it, nor will I be manipulated by my children. It takes
a man of *strength* to lead his family, and tonight I see the results of
being long neglectful in disciplining your unruly ways."

"It's all my fault, Daddy, not Bobby's or Audrey's," Lynelle
blurted. "Please don't punish them. I'm so sorry . . . I just
thought—"

"You do not have permission to speak right now, Lynelle. And
I will do whatever I see fit to correct this reprehensible behavior."

"Oh, Daddy, please don't . . . spank . . . me," Audrey cried,
sobbing. "I like you, Daddy, an' I just want you to like me, an' I
won't . . . an' I won't be . . . bad no more . . . I promise, Daddy."

A long silence took place, punctuated only by muffled whim-
pering. "You will keep to the nursery until Christmas Eve," he
finally spoke, sounding more weary than angry. "All of you. You
older children will write letters of apology to everyone affected
by your actions. And nothing of this sort had better happen ever
again."

Sparing only a cursory glance at Joyce, standing next to their
family physician, he departed the nursery.

"The children have need of your love and reassurance now,"
Dr. Pfeiffer spoke. "And I will leave you to that. My good
woman, I have no doubt that you—and most assuredly your
children—have tried just about every means under the sun to
soften your husband's heart. It has been my experience that
sometimes, however, such accomplishments can be made only
by the Lord above."

"What am I to do in the meanwhile?" she whispered in anguish.
"And just how long are these children supposed to wait for their
father to give them a scrap of his attention? They've been so good

and patient . . . and he will hardly even look at them. Do you
know, Dr. Pfeiffer," she added, righteous indignation sparking all
through her and stiffening her spine, "If I were they, I would have
acted up long before now."

The benevolent gentleman nodded, as if deep in thought.
"You have to submit this situation to the Father's capable hands,
Joyce," he said slowly. "Not part of it and not most of it; all of it."

"But I've done that, over and over again. Nothing changes,
except to get worse. I don't know how much longer I can go on
like this. I'm getting so tired and so weak . . . I'm just about to
the end of myself."

He continued to nod. "Yes . . . good. The end of yourself is
the place where Christ can begin his real work. Continue in your
prayers, offering him your weakness, and we shall see what
happens."

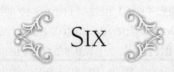

SIX

The ticking of the travel clock in the darkened room seemed as loud as the inner workings of Big Ben. Samuel fidgeted on the couch in his sitting room, causing the undersized wool blanket to fall off his shoulder. With an exasperated sigh, he tried to tuck himself back in, only to pull the cover too high, exposing his lower legs to the chilly air. It would take only a few minutes to get up and build a fire in the small stove across the room, but even that everyday task seemed insurmountable.

Peace would not come. Sleep would not come. Even numbness would not come. Bone-aching fatigue engulfed his body and mind, yet the respite of unconsciousness lay just beyond his grasp. Over and over he studied the shadows of his desk, his bookshelf, his drawing table, remembering how this room had once been a delightful sanctuary.

Tonight these four walls had the feel of a prison cell closing in on him, a dark, echoing chamber in which resounded the pain-filled cries of his children. Not their initial wailing and moaning, during which time he'd been so frightened of their contorted and red-spotted appearance that he'd been nearly out of his mind with worry over losing them.

No, the cries that tortured him were the things they'd said

later. Terrible things. True things. Things to which no one had
ever given voice. Not that Joyce hadn't tried, in her gentle way,
to draw him out with her love. But since failing both her and
Mary Rose, he'd felt so unworthy and unlovable that it had been
easiest to fall away from the family and allow the distance to
grow, all the while pretending nothing was the matter. He'd told
himself that he'd get matters straightened out one day, but that
day had not yet come.

Now what was he to do? The children had cried out his failings
and transgressions for all to hear. Their conviction had shamed
him worse than his own guilt, but what awful thing lay inside
him, preventing him from giving them reassurance of his love?
For he did love them—and Joyce—more than his own life itself.

With an anguished sigh, he threw aside the blanket and sat
up, fumbling for a match. After lighting the kerosene lamp on
the table beside the couch, he arose and silently padded from
the sitting room. The house had been quiet for hours. Up the
stairs to the third story he rose, entering the nursery quietly on
stocking feet.

To each bed he went, his heart wrenching as he gazed down,
one at a time, upon his sleeping children. Lynelle, on the brink of
womanhood, her face soft and smooth and beautiful. She lay
curled on her side, her covers drawn neatly to her chin. Bobby,
sprawled on his back, blankets in disarray at his knees. Pulling the
covers back over his only son, a near replica of himself as a boy,
he allowed his fingers to caress the already strong line of his jaw.

Audrey, finally quiet in slumber, with only a hint of baby
roundness remaining in her cheeks. When had she changed
from a toddler to a young girl? *I'm going to be four, Daddy . . . in
Febillary . . . do you remember?* With a sigh he moved to Kathryn,
whose second birthday was this very day. Before his youngest
daughter he paused the longest, drinking in the details of her
angelic appearance. Like her eldest sister, she slept on her side,

the small quilt his aunt Millie had sent tucked in around her. As he continued gazing upon her, he noticed that each exhaled breath fanned the soft curls framing her little face.

Would Mary Rose have looked as sweet? he wondered, remembering her round, red face and trusting, dark gaze . . . and her tiny chest, working so hard to draw breath.

Unwelcome memories of that night rushed to the forefront of his mind, filling his eyes with tears. How could he have abandoned his own daughter? The least he could have done was to pick her up and hold her, giving her what comfort he could. But instead he'd acted the coward, running away from his fears.

And still he ran.

Just like you ran away from your mother's deathbed, an inner voice accused. *Remember? Shame on you, Samuel. You were ten years old—more than old enough to walk in and say your farewells. But you were so scared that you ran away. And when you came back, Ma was already gone—no more chances.*

Tears ran down his face as he relived the past, his father's harsh words still burning inside him. *I'm ashamed to say you're my son, Samuel. The world's got no place for sissies, especially weak-livered little cowards who can't even look death in the eye. Death's a part of life, boy, and the sooner you learn that, the better. If you want to get anywhere in this world, you've got to be strong. Now get in there and pay your respects to your mother. Pity you couldn't have done it last night when she was still alive.*

Since then, he'd striven to be strong and successful in everything he did, if for no other reason than to show his father that he wasn't a failure. And still he labored for his father's approval, though John Colburn had lived only ten years beyond his wife, dying suddenly of an unknown ailment. Never had the matter been discussed again, and never had Samuel been granted his father's forgiveness.

Shoulders sagging, he returned to the cold sitting room. If his own father couldn't even forgive him for his weakness, how could his wife, his children? How could God? How *could* God, indeed? Anger surged inside him as he wondered how a good and loving God could take a mother from a ten-year-old boy. Or an infant girl from a couple who had waited with delight to welcome her to their family?

He had always believed in God but had never been quite as assured of his character as Joyce. While his wife looked toward the Lord as the source of her strength and comfort, he was just as certain that there was something to be said for a man's own hard work and vigor. He remembered Joyce speaking of taking up the cross of Christ daily and following him.

Well, right there, that seemed to indicate some sort of strength was needed. Blowing out the lamp, he settled himself on the couch and arranged the blanket evenly over his legs and torso. Strength. More strength would take care of the problems in his life. In a short prayer, he asked the Lord to grant him the strength he needed to put his life in order.

Closing his eyes, he finally found sleep.

About the best thing Joyce could say for Kathryn's birthday was that she got through it. Samuel had worked a long day yesterday, returning home well after the household had retired. Though the children had been restricted to the nursery, she had hoped to make as cheerful a celebration as possible in honor of her youngest daughter.

The affair had been dismal, at best. Samuel's umbrage—and his absence—hung over the third story like a pall. Kathryn was too little to understand what had transpired, but she sensed something was the matter and spent much of the day with her thumb in her mouth.

Nanny, too, was uncharacteristically quiet, and Lynelle and

Bobby had moped while composing their letters of apology. Audrey had been fretful, asking incessant questions about Mary Rose until Joyce had gone downstairs to fetch the carved wooden box she kept in the back corner of her wardrobe.

She doubted Samuel knew of its existence. And until yesterday, the children hadn't either. With somber faces they'd gathered around as she'd lifted the lid and shown them, one by one, the few humble yet priceless treasures contained in its depths.

A lock of whisper-fine hair, held fast by a knotted thread, tucked lovingly into a small envelope. Tiny footprints of ink, forever preserved upon a sheet of her finest stationery. One ordinary baby blanket, the first in which Mary Rose had been wrapped. During the past two years, it had been unfolded and refolded countless times, its soft weave absorbing a hundred thousand mother's tears.

At the bottom of the box lay the baby quilt Samuel's aunt Millie had sent during her confinement. Each block contained a pattern of triangles and squares known as "Crosses and Losses," only slightly different from the familiar "Anvil." In death, Mary Rose had been laid upon her great-aunt's work of love. Once again Joyce had marveled that the elderly woman's arthritic fingers were still able to turn out such perfect stitches.

Remembering how her lifeless daughter had looked against the backdrop of white, evergreen, and cranberry calico, Joyce's eyes had filled with tears. A moment later Nanny had joined her in sorrow for the "poor wee wain," and then the children, too, had wept. What she'd intended to be a day of celebration had turned out to be a gloomy gathering, indeed.

And today, Christmas Eve, was thus far no better for the Colburns. Samuel had gone into work again without having spoken a word to her since the evening of the Forepaughs' party. Would he be home for the sumptuous dinner she had planned? For their traditional after-dinner gathering in the library?

Sighing, she walked into the flurry of activity taking place in the kitchen. The temperature in here was warmer than any other room in the house, and a distinctive, sweet smell hung in the air.

"The gizzard took three hours to simmer tender yesterday, so if I add an hour's time to that, the bird should roast for four." Gertrude, her good humor restored, spoke her calculations more to herself than anyone else as she tied trussing cords around the plump turkey she'd just stuffed with oyster dressing. "Ida, check on the almond macaroons, will you? As soon as they're finished, we'll need to stoke up the fire for Mister Tom."

"Oh, hello, Mrs. Colburn," Ida greeted, taking her hands from the sink and wiping them dry on her apron. "I know I told you this yesterday, but I'm sure glad to know the children are well. I was scared out of my wits the other night." She shook her head and smiled, a dimple peeping from the corner of her mouth. "The note they sent down to me was so dear."

"So was the one they sent me, but I still can't believe they had the gumption to put calomel in Mr. Colburn's pudding," Gertrude exclaimed, hoisting the turkey into place on the roasting rack. She nodded, meeting Joyce's gaze. "Your husband apologized to me real early yesterday morning on his way out. Said he was sorry for accusing me of what he had and how much he appreciated my years of service to the family."

"Well, I'm so . . . glad," Joyce replied, both pleased and surprised at the resolution of at least one unpleasant matter.

"We're going to put on the finest meal you've ever had," the cook went on, arranging a folded cheesecloth over the poultry, "and I predict that this will be your family's most wonderful Christmas yet."

"Thank you, Gertrude," she spoke softly. "I hope you're right." Walking from the kitchen, she stopped in the dining room and checked her decorations. Running her hand over the smooth, dark wood of a chair back, she remembered Christmas dinners past. Excitement, joy, and laughter once filled this room—as well as every other room in the house—on the commemoration of the Christ child's birth. But for the past two years, the holiday had been as bleak and barren as the landscape of her husband's heart.

Perhaps tonight, as Gertrude predicted, would be the turning point. If Christmas wasn't a time for hope, she didn't know what was. Oh, how she'd prayed since that heartbreaking scene in the nursery. Dr. Pfeiffer's words about submitting the entire situation into the Lord's hands had not left her mind for a moment, and with every prayer she uttered, she asked him to take control of their plight.

On through the rest of the first story she walked, tying a bow here, adjusting a decoration there. In the library she paused a long moment, gazing from the pine-graced mantel to the perfectly adorned spruce across the room. Exquisite. Nothing could be improved. Their lovely home stood in impeccable readiness for the holiday celebration that would soon be upon them.

But would it be a celebration? she wondered, searching her mind for something else, anything else, that she could do to bring healing to her fractured family—for the children if for no other reason. Her love just hadn't been enough.

Even through the blackest hours of grief, she had lavished every last ounce of her love upon her marriage and family. Samuel hadn't responded, but the children had. Still, she and the children, minus Samuel, weren't complete. She owed it to them to keep trying.

When was the last time she'd told Samuel she loved him? she asked herself, unable to remember when she'd had the courage to utter the words she used to speak so freely. After Mary Rose had died, she'd told him several times, but he'd only continued moving farther away from her and the family. Eventually, she stopped trying to tell him what he didn't seem to want to hear.

Tonight, she decided with quavering insides, she would tell
Samuel of her love for him. Even if he didn't respond in kind,
she was long overdue in reassuring him of her feelings. Their
embrace, two nights past, made her long afresh for the easy relationship they used to have, as well as being held tenderly in his
arms. Yes, she resolved, tonight she would tell Samuel of her
love for him.

If he came home.

SEVEN

"Nanny, why doesn't my daddy like us?" Audrey asked in a plaintive voice, edging her way from the sleeping area to where her caretaker sat near the fire. "He didn't come home for Kathryn's birthday an' that made us very, very sad, didn't it? We cried . . . remember? Are we going to cry on my birthday, too?"

"Hush, dearie, an' come here. There will na be cryin' on yer birthday," Nanny reassured, setting her book aside and opening her arms in invitation. "'Twill be a grand day in February, indeed, when we celebrate the fourth anniversary of yer birth. We were a wee bit sad to be missin' yer sister Mary Rose yesterday, is all. 'Twould have been her birthday, as well."

"An' she's dead, Nanny, isn't she?" Audrey replied, clambering into the haven of her nursemaid's lap. "She lives up in heaven with Jesus. Am I going to live in heaven with Jesus pretty soon, too?"

"Och, I pray yer mother forgives me for yer not havin' a nap this afternoon," Nanny muttered before answering. Holding the child close, she stroked her silky hair. "The Laird Jesus took yer sister to himself because he knew her body wasn't strong enough for this world. Now, you've a fine, strong body, lassie. I should think ye'll be on this earth for many years to come, but ye must always be ready for his call."

"But why did he call Mary Rose first? I'm bigger. I'm going to be four."

"We know," Bobby spoke under his breath to Lynelle. Chafing at their second day of confinement, the pair played an indolent game of cat's cradle at the table near the window.

"Shh, quiet," Lynelle retorted, using her pinkies to quickly pull the string crisscross from her brother's hands, wanting to hear what Nanny had to say. Her glimpse yesterday into their mother's secret box—as well as into the private depths of Mama's sorrow—had evoked a mysterious, more kindred type of grief inside her young breast. It was as if a new place in her heart had opened, expanding wider as each item came out of the box.

Such love Mama had for all of them. Would she love her own children so dearly? Lynelle wondered with a foreign anxiety. Until yesterday, her mind had not conceived of such thoughts. Was this what growing up was about? Thoughts and concepts wonderful and terrifying at the same time?

"The Laird's takin' of Mary Rose was an act of his mercy an' love," Nanny continued, rocking at a steady pace, "just as surely as was his leavin' Kathryn behind to help with the heartache."

The three-year-old was quiet a long moment before asking, "Nanny, does my Daddy have a heartache?"

"Aye, child." The middle-aged woman sighed. "I'd say his heart be achin' most of all."

"More than Mama's?"

"Aye."

"More than Nell's an' Bobby's?"

"Aye."

"More than mine? More than Kathryn's?"

"Aye, dearie."

"But Mama cries and cries, an' I never seen Daddy cry. He doesn't talk, neither."

"Yer father was once a talkin' man, but he's long past due

facin' the tragedy of his wee Mary Rose. Imagine him to be a boilin' pot o' water, lassie, wi' a roastin' fire below. What steam is bein' made canna be released, for he's holdin' the lid jammed on so verra tightly."

"Is he going to spill over someday? That happened to our mush one morning, an' it stinked, an' Gertrude had a big, big mess to clean up."

"A clever wain you are, Miss Audrey, indeed. Aye, we've been seein' wee puny sputters here an' there, but a churnin' eruption is on its way, mark my words."

"What kind of eruption? What do you think is going to happen?" Cat's cradle forgotten, Lynelle toyed nervously with the loop of string in her hands. Glancing at her brother, she read the same uneasy expression on his face as was certainly on her own.

"Dinna fash yerself, lass," Nanny replied. "To worrit an' fret only invites the de'il to come make mischief. The good Laird will take care of yer father in his own way. Ours is to be faithful to our prayin'."

Bobby stood suddenly, his chair clattering with the force of his movement. His face had grown red, and moisture glinted in his eyes. "I've said a million prayers! They don't work! They don't keep him home! Why is he gone all the time? How is he supposed to face something he never sees? Mary Rose is dead, but we're still here. He doesn't even look at us anymore!"

An answering anguish arose inside Lynelle as her brother sprinted from the table to the privacy of the sleep area. At the sound of the choking sobs he tried to disguise, tears flooded her eyes as well.

"Here now, lass," Nanny spoke, rising from her rocker. Holding Audrey's hand, the older woman and the younger walked to the table to comfort her. "Take heart. Our Laird works in weal and woe."

"Oh, don't cry, Nell," Audrey consoled, letting loose Nanny's grasp and wriggling into her sister's lap. Small fingers stroked her face. "Jesus will fix Daddy's heartache an' clean up his mush when it spills."

"I'll see to Master Robert, if ye don't mind. A good dose of fresh air would no doubt do ye both a world of good. I'm thinkin' that ye've fulfilled the punishment yer father set forth. 'Keep to the nursery till Christmas Eve,' he said. And Christmas Eve it is. Whisht! Outdoors wi' ye, now, for just a short while. I'll send yer brother right along."

"Thank you, Nanny." Wiping her tears, Lynelle smiled and wound her arms around her sister. "Let's get our coats."

"Do you mean me, Nell? I get to come with you?" Her features showed amazement at being included with her older siblings on an afternoon outing, and she cupped Lynelle's face between her small hands. "Me? Audrey?"

"Yes, I mean you, silly. We'll walk to the park."

"Not too long, now," Nanny admonished, on to her next task of soothing Bobby's distress. She spoke over her shoulder, "It'll soon be time to be gettin' dressed for yer fine dinner. Roast turkey and all the trimmin's, I hear. 'Twill be a miracle if Kathryn hasn't been wakened by all this ballyhoo. A half a nap between the pair of ye wee yins won't do at all. At least ye'll be sound asleep by the time St. Nicholas makes his way through the city."

"Did you know I'm going to stay awake till St. Nich'las comes?" the three-year-old chattered, hopping down from Lynelle's lap and tugging her hand. "Bobby told me we could set a trap for him, an' then we could get all his toys—"

"Hush, Audrey," Lynelle interrupted, feeling a solemn weight pressing on her young shoulders. "Christmas isn't about laying traps for St. Nicholas and stealing his toys. It's about God sending the Christ child to us. Remember what Mama read from the Bible last night? The angel told the shepherds, 'Fear not . . . I bring you good tidings of great joy . . . Ye shall find the babe wrapped in swaddling clothes, lying in a manger.'"

"That means baby Jesus!"

"Yes, Audrey. Baby Jesus, the Savior of this whole world. Isn't it amazing to think that one tiny little baby, wrapped in a blanket, was born to heal the hurts of all men?"

Audrey nodded, suddenly pensive as she pulled her coat from the peg near the door.

Though Lynelle didn't find her younger sister's nonstop jabbering as irritating as Bobby did, she was relieved that this concept had finally given Audrey's voice pause. Reaching for her own coat, she wondered what this year's Christmas would bring . . . and if the Christ child could bring healing to even her father's heart.

❄ ❄ ❄

Three-thirty. Checking the time for the fifth time in as many minutes, Samuel pushed back his chair and rubbed first his eyes, then the back of his neck. He'd been working hard these past two days getting preliminary drawings completed for a local congregation wishing to build a new church. Projects stood stacked elbow deep on his desk, proof of the great demand for talented draftsmen and architects in the Twin Cities. Frequent requests from other cities came to his firm, as well, and he and his three partners had all they could do to keep up with the workload.

Once upon a time he had struck a balance between his home life and his work time. This equilibrium had foundered with his baby daughter's death to the degree that he could say that he was almost completely immersed in his work.

Almost.

There was still a part of him that could not forget the pleasant and satisfying years of matrimony and fatherhood. Nor could he

imagine his present life without Joyce or the children. It was just
that things had deteriorated to such an extent that he didn't
know what to do anymore. His vibrant and affectionate wife had
become timorous. Lynelle and Bobby had not only poisoned him
but employed artifice in their attempt to rectify wrongs of which
they were innocent. Audrey begged for his attention every
chance she got. And Kathryn just sucked her thumb when in his
presence, watching him with wary hazel eyes.

"Hey, Sam, when are you going to call it a day?"

"I'm just about finished," he answered automatically, glancing
up to see friend and colleague Charles Young in the doorway,
already dressed in his overcoat. Instead of moving along, Young
continued to regard him with a concerned expression, tapping
his hat against his chest.

"You . . . are going home, aren't you?"

"Yes, I'm going home, Charley. Why do you ask?" Nettled,
Samuel's reply was clipped. The already tense muscles in the
back of his neck stiffened beneath his starched collar.

"You've been putting in some long days since you've been
back," Charles spoke, undaunted, "and I wonder how much
Joyce and the children have seen of you. Go home, Samuel. It's
Christmas Eve. The work will still be here next week."

"Thank you for the reminder," he ground out, thinking of the
family dinner and Scripture reading that lay ahead of him this
evening. Burdened as he was by the sorry state of his family life,
how was he supposed to hold up under hours and hours
together with them? He felt so powerless and ineffectual that he
could barely hold himself together. In a show of almost vicious
force, he kneaded the trail of knotted muscles leading downward
from his neck to his shoulders.

"I'm concerned about you, Sam. You just haven't been yourself in a long time."

"I'm fine," he lied, his hand dropping away from his shoulder, limp. Physical and mental exhaustion nearly overwhelmed him. Forcing his features into what he hoped was a semblance of a smile, he added, "I was just leaving, myself."

"Well, good." His friend's serious brown gaze studied his face, and he nodded. "I'll wait and walk out with you, then."

Left with no other option, Samuel slowly rose from his chair and took his hat and coat from the rack standing in the corner.

EIGHT

"What's for dessert, Mother?" Bobby asked in his most polite voice, wiping his mouth on his napkin and returning the cloth to his lap. His manners and those of his sisters had been impeccable throughout the entire meal.

This was the first time the Colburns had been together as a family since the night of the children's feigned illness, and, despite Joyce's worries to the contrary, dinner had not gone badly. Samuel had been home from the office early, disappearing for a long bath before joining them at the table. His mien this evening was polite but remote, as if nothing had happened.

"Gertrude made charlotte russe," Joyce replied with an encouraging smile, knowing the rich, creamy cold dessert was a favorite of her husband and son alike. Her smile faded when she gazed upon her husband. Though his hair and clothing were as neat as ever, she was disturbed by his lackluster hazel gaze and the drawn appearance of his face. Also, his plate remained more than half filled.

"And you will enjoy the almond macaroons, my darling," she spoke to Kathryn, seated in a high chair at her left. Her heart ached for the man at the head of their table. What could she possibly do to help him? During the past two years she'd tried everything she could think of. Would telling him she loved him be as futile as pouring a thimbleful of water on an acre of parched ground?

"Daddy?" Audrey spoke, having restrained her garrulous tongue admirably through the meal. Thanks to a talking-to first by Nanny, then a second by Joyce, all the Colburn children had been on their best behavior. "Daddy?" she repeated. "Did you know that the baby wrapped in the blanket can heal the hurts of all men?"

"Yes, Audrey, I know," he spoke with a deep sigh. "Happy Christmas."

An awkward silence passed. "Mama?" Audrey spoke in a loud whisper, setting down her fork. "Mama, I need to go upstairs. I have to—"

"Shh, darling," Joyce admonished in a gentle tone. "Just excuse yourself from the table. Would you like me or Lynelle to come with you?"

"No, I can go all by myself," the three-year-old replied with a liberal amount of disdain.

"All right, then. We'll wait on dessert until you return."

"Aww-dree," Bobby expressed his impatience at having to wait for his beloved serving of ladyfingers and rich Bavarian cream. "Why didn't you 'go all by yourself' before dinner?"

Having slid from the side of her armless chair, the second-youngest Colburn straightened her lovely holiday dress and walked to where her brother sat. "Just hold yer horses, laddie," she declared in a perfect imitation of their nursemaid, extending her index finger toward him, "I'll be back in four months. . . . I mean, four minutes."

"You don't even know what a minute is," he retorted, his irritation replaced by a glint of mischievousness just a second later. "Hey, Audrey," he challenged, "what were you wearing the day before tomorrow?"

Audrey paused, raising her eyebrows in a lofty manner. "You can't trick me. Lynelle taught me to say, 'What I'm wearing right now.' So there."

Watching her audacious youngster sashay from the dining room, Joyce disguised her smile by dabbing her mouth with her napkin. A quick glance at Samuel showed him seemingly unaffected by his children's raillery. This, to her, was doubly sad, for her husband used to be the instigator of much jesting and horseplay.

Once Audrey returned, the dishes were cleared, dessert was served, and finally the meal was over. While they'd finished eating, Ida had built a snapping blaze in the library's fireplace and lit the ivory-colored candles on the tree. From atop the spruce, the angel garbed in flowing ruby robes smiled her mysterious, faint smile, one hand outstretched as if to bid them entrance.

The library had never looked better, Joyce thought as they retired to its welcoming milieu. Samuel sought the comfort of his chair, looking a bit aggrieved at the prospect of no newspaper within sight. Indeed, the only volume on the table next to his chair was the leather-covered family Bible. Ida's devout faith had apparently precluded the presence of such secular reading material the eve of the Christ child's birth.

"Daddy, are you going to read the story of the baby in the blanket now? The baby that brings healing to all men?" Audrey ran to sit at his feet. "I'm ready. Are you ready?"

Taking her cue, Kathryn, Lynelle, and Bobby took places near the foot of their father's chair. Joyce settled into her chair, her throat growing thick at the sight of the children gathered before Samuel. *O Jesus,* she fervently prayed, *please let this be the night you bring your healing to this man. Please restore him to us—and to yourself.*

Clearing his throat, Samuel picked up the Bible and slowly

turned its pages until he found the place he desired. "'And it came to pass in those days,'" he began, "'that there went out a decree from Caesar Augustus . . .'"

Her husband's rich voice washed over her, bringing memories of happy Christmas Eves past as well as mental images of Lynelle and Bobby as infants, toddlers, and growing children. Of Audrey, sticky-fingered and wobbly-legged, bringing delightful chaos to her first Christmas Eve celebration. Since she and Samuel had become parents, it had been a tradition for the family to gather in this room after dinner as well as for Samuel to read the Christmas story from the second chapter of Luke's Gospel. Later, they'd make popcorn, and she would play carols on the piano. . . .

"'And this shall be a sign unto you; ye shall find the babe wrapped in swaddling clothes, lying in a manger. And suddenly there was with the angel—'"

"The baby!" Audrey cried, leaping to her feet.

"Sit down," Bobby whispered loudly as she used his shoulder to steady herself. "He's not done yet."

"Daddy, I have a surprise for you," Audrey averred, tugging at Samuel's trousers.

"A surprise? What kind of surprise?" Setting the open Bible on the table, he studied the excited youngster before him with bemusement.

"Your father wasn't finished reading, Audrey." Joyce leaned forward to correct her impulsive daughter. "You know what poor manners it is to interrupt someone."

"But Mama, I have a wonnerful surprise for Daddy!" she entreated, wriggling in her enthusiasm. "Please, Mama? Please? Please?" Without waiting for a reply, she turned back to her father. "Daddy," she instructed, holding her finger out like a teacher's pointer, "you have to close your eyes and sit very, very still like a mouse. You can't open your eyes, not till I say so."

Instead of showing disapproval, Samuel seemed to brighten at his daughter's directions. With a smile, he reached out to stroke her glossy hair. "All right, Audrey," he granted, "I will close my eyes and wait for my wonderful surprise."

"No peeking," she iterated, scrutinizing Samuel's face to be sure his eyes were indeed tightly closed.

"No peeking," he confirmed.

Joyce's heart filled with hope at this delicate interchange, and she watched her daughter drop to her knees and reach beneath the long table skirt beside Samuel's chair. Grasping a small object between her thumb and forefinger, she climbed into her father's lap and brushed her hand against his cheek.

"Can you guess what this is, Daddy? Don't open your eyes!"

Everyone leaned closer to see what tiny, mysterious item Audrey held. "What is it, Audrey?" Bobby asked, craning his neck for a better view.

Samuel's face broke into a gentle smile while he obediently held his eyes shut. "Hmm, it tickles. Did you find a feather for me, Audrey? That would be a nice surprise in the middle of winter."

"No, Daddy, it's not a feather. You guessed wrong." A giggle accompanied her words. "Now wait. No, no, no! Don't open your eyes! I have 'nother surprise for you."

Nimble as a monkey, she vaulted from Samuel's lap and retrieved another item from her hiding place. The air caught in Joyce's lungs as she watched Audrey pull Miss Hillary from beneath the table and place the doll in her father's arms.

Wrapped around Miss Hillary was the baby quilt used to lay out Mary Rose.

Lynelle and Bobby turned frantic gazes to her while Kathryn chortled, "Ba-by!" Half rising from her chair, Joyce felt her perfect, hope-filled Christmas Eve celebration crash down upon her. "Audrey—," she began helplessly.

"Now you can open your eyes, Daddy," spoke the child, who paid not a whit of attention to her mother.

"You're giving me your doll?" Samuel queried, examining the porcelain face nestled within the folds of the quilt. A chuckle escaped his throat. "I seem to remember her coming to pay a call the other day. . . . Miss Hillary, isn't it? Audrey, dear, you don't have to—"

Stopping midsentence, he pulled a corner of the covering away from the doll. His fair complexion reddened, and his movements grew jerky as he struggled to balance his daughter, hold the doll, and unwrap the quilt.

"I know what this is." Though his voice was strangled, Joyce read open hostility in the gaze he flashed toward her.

"Yes, Daddy, it's Mary Rose's blanket. Mama saved it in a special, special place, an' she saved her hair, too." Unaware of the emotional storm brewing in the man on whose lap she perched, Audrey opened her palm to reveal the tiny bunch of gossamer strands. "I tickled your face so you could feel her touch you." With wide eyes and a sober expression, the three-year-old went on. "Nanny an' Lynelle said the baby in the blanket can heal the hurts of all men, an' they said your heart hurted the most about Mary Rose going to heaven to live with Jesus. So, Daddy, we can pretend Miss Hillary is Mary Rose, an' you can hold her all night long. I don't want your heart to hurt anymore, Daddy, an' I don't want you to spill over and get mush everywhere."

The crackling of the fire was the only sound in the room for what seemed like an endless time. Hurt and confusion were written on Audrey's face as her father pushed doll, blanket, and child from his lap and stood.

"You put her up to this." The accusation shot to Joyce like lead from a rifle.

"No, Samuel, I didn't know—"

Cutting her off, he railed, "I don't need you reminding me of my failures. Any of you!" Steadily, his voice grew in volume. "All these stunts and tricks . . . and Mary Rose's hair? Why don't you just say what you think, Joyce, and be done with it?"

"Wh-what do you mean?" Never had Joyce seen her husband so angry. The children had scuttled to the far side of the room with their father's outburst, the older two protectively holding their younger siblings. On their faces was reflected the fear in their young hearts.

Instead of quaking, Joyce was aware of a queer paralysis creeping over her—a dreamy, floating sensation similar to being in a dream. None of this could possibly be happening. Things like this didn't happen to families like theirs, did they?

"What more do you want?" he shouted, the cords on his neck standing out. "Why don't you just come out with it and tell me you wish you'd never married me?" Samuel's nostrils flared, his chest heaving with emotion.

Wish she'd never married him? Had he really said that? There was nothing farther from the truth. Her arms and legs felt funny, tingly, and it was hard to draw a deep breath. She loved him . . . oh, yes . . . that's what she was going to tell him tonight—that she loved him. On the mantel, candles flickered, creating a halo of light around her husband's head and shoulders.

"Samuel," she began, her voice sounding strange in her ears, "I don't think any of those things, and I . . . I only want to tell you . . . that I love you. We all love you."

There. She'd said it. Whatever happened next was in the Lord's hands.

"You love me?" he spat, sudden moisture shining in his eyes. "How could you? How could you possibly?" He stood silent a long moment, during which Joyce dared not breathe.

"I can't do this anymore," he finally said in a spiritless voice, a single tear tracing its way down his cheek. "I can't." Shaking his head, he turned stiffly and walked from the room. A minute later the front door opened and closed.

"Mrs. Colburn?" Ida whispered from the doorway. Huddled behind her were Nanny and Gertrude. "Mrs. Colburn, what's happened? We were having our dinner in the kitchen and heard the shouting. . . ."

"Mr. Colburn has . . . left." Joyce was surprised at the calmness of her tone. Where were the tears? The weakness? The hysteria? Her husband had just walked out the door, maybe never to return. From where had such buoying strength come?

"Please go back and finish your dinner. I'd like to be alone with the children. Oh, and Meg, I'll be putting them to bed tonight. You may have the rest of the evening off."

"Aye, ma'am," the nursemaid said with a nod. "Ye know where to find me if ye'll be needin' anything."

"Oh, Mama," Lynelle cried once the servants had cleared the doorway. "Does this mean Daddy's never coming back?" In her arms whimpered Audrey, holding fast to both Miss Hillary and the colorful baby quilt.

"Hush, my darlings," she spoke, walking over and kneeling before them. "Do you see what happens when we take matters into our own hands? This is God's place to work, not ours, and we need to give your father over to him right this minute. I've been as guilty as you by quietly trying to fix things, trying not to cause trouble, trying to make a beautiful home—"

"But those aren't bad things, Mama, not like the naughty things we did." Lynelle sniffed and wiped her eyes with the back of her hand.

"No, they might not seem bad, but my reasons behind them were to accomplish the same thing you children set out to do— bring Daddy back to us. We need to tell the Lord we're sorry for trying to take over for him, and ask him to take good care of our daddy."

"But what if—"

"No more what-ifs, Robert. We either trust in our Savior, or we do not. Do you remember how the eleventh chapter of Hebrews begins?"

"I remember, Mama." Lynelle's voice quavered. "'Now faith is the substance of things hoped for—'"

"And 'the evidence of things not seen,'" Bobby finished.

"Very good, children. If we trust completely in the Lord, our faith is built only stronger during such times as these. Now, I cannot imagine how God can solve a problem so large, so troublesome, so complex as the one plaguing our family. I only know that he can, and that we cannot. Shall we finally tell him so?"

Heads bowed and hands clasped, Joyce led them all in a brief prayer, one in which she asked forgiveness for their lack of trust. "We also give Samuel over to you, totally and completely," she continued, her voice finally breaking. "You know the desire in our hearts to have him restored to us, Father, but he is yours to do with what you will. We pray this in the name of your Son, our Savior, the Lord Jesus, whose birth we celebrate and thank you for this night. Amen."

A soft chorus of amens arose from the children as they engulfed her with tearful hugs and kisses. How very blessed she was, indeed, to have four such healthy, beautiful, and loving children. As difficult as it would be if Samuel never came back, this would be enough, she decided, her heart overflowing with a sudden wash of tranquillity.

Yes, it could be enough.

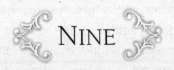

NINE

Block after block Samuel walked, the rigid control he had worked so hard to maintain over his life slipping from his grasp. How much did Joyce and the children want from him? What did they expect? There wasn't a thing he could do to change the past. He couldn't bring back the dead.

His anger grew when he thought of his family and their manipulations. How could he go back home after what they'd done tonight? Joyce and the children had simply pushed him too far. He might have been able to forgive the calomel-laced pudding and the children's counterfeit illnesses this week, but this evening's stunt was beyond what he could abide.

I tickled your face so you could feel her touch you.

Reflexively, he rubbed his cheek where Audrey had brushed her baby sister's tiny curl. He hadn't even noticed whether or not Mary Rose had had hair. What he remembered was her laborious breathing, the struggle to draw air into her little body. And those dark eyes, fixing on him, seeking from him.

Fresh pain assaulted him, fueling his anger and grief. He'd tried his hardest to be a good husband and father, a good provider. And he *had* been all of those things . . . until . . .

Unbidden, the memory of rolling over on Miss Hillary

intruded into the storm of his fury. Audrey, his intrepid and ever-talkative daughter, smiled at him in his mind's eye. Somehow the clever three-year-old had escaped Nanny's watchful care the afternoon he'd experienced the ill effects of Lynelle and Bobby's attempt to repair his relationship with Joyce, tucking her precious doll beside him for comfort.

That meant Joyce's denial was probably true, that she didn't have foreknowledge of Audrey's impulsive deed this evening. But what was this business of keeping Mary Rose's hair? Her blanket? Wasn't that unhealthy? Ghoulish, even?

What about your mother's brooch? The image of his mother's cameo pin, tucked deep inside the top desk drawer in his sitting room, came to mind. From time to time he unwrapped the inexpensive but treasured item, remembering the happier days of his childhood before she had fallen ill. Surely it wasn't unnatural for him to keep a small memento by which to remember and honor her memory.

In her brief life, what else did Mary Rose have to offer?

Tears welled in his eyes, and he slowed his pace, for the first time noticing the snowfall. Taking in the fresh, pristine mantle covering the city, he realized his anger had somehow, mysteriously evaporated. In its place were left only pain and weakness, his familiar adversaries.

Hadn't he worked hard enough to overcome his childhood ineptitude and deficiencies? What more was required of him? Hadn't thirteen years of marriage and the establishment of a prosperous career been enough to mature the frightened boy deep inside him to manhood?

A fresh wave of longing washed through him, making him realize how badly he desired reconciliation with Joyce and the children. His family, his life. How he loved them. Over the years they'd built a household of love and laughter until—until the twins had been born.

Until he'd failed them.

Samuel . . . I love you . . . we all love you.

Joyce's stricken words in the library came back to him. She loved him . . . she *still* loved him? How could she, after what he'd done? He was weak, unworthy.

He realized he'd stopped walking. The snow had grown thicker, causing a hush to fall over the city. Where was he? To his right, in the yard of a small church, was an outdoor crèche. Glancing across the street, he recognized the row of businesses. It hardly seemed possible that he'd covered two miles since walking out his front door.

Now what?

Now where?

He sighed, looking upward. No answer there, just an infinite, dizzying pattern of snowflakes. Aware of frigid hardness pressing against his leg, he glanced down to find himself in contact with the wrought iron fence in front of the church.

He was about to step away when something about the manger scene drew his attention. What was it? The illumination of the corner gaslight barely reached the white-cowled figures. Mary, Joseph. The wise men, the shepherds, the animals. He found it curious that this small house of worship had spared no expense in setting up such an elaborate Christmas display.

At the center of the grouping was a rough wooden cradle stuffed with hay. Still, lonely, and cold lay the white-layered babe upon his crude pallet, the small form all too reminiscent of another motionless child. Samuel shivered in his misery, realizing he had grown chilled while standing.

My strength is made perfect in weakness.

Where had that thought come from? No doubt some Bible verse from long ago. There was nothing perfect about weakness; his own father had taught him that. Why else had he worked so hard, for so long, to be strong?

Thinking of his labor, his trials, his exertion, he sighed with weariness. What good had any of it been? He was on the verge of losing his wife and family. Exhaustion, guilt, and worry had become his constant companions. He just couldn't go on any longer. Shoulders slumping, he leaned forward into the fence, allowing the bars to bear his weight.

A gentle stillness fell upon his spirit as he pondered the helpless infant Christ child in the yard before him, trying to reconcile this Jesus with that of the omnipotent Savior. King of kings. Lord of lords.

Lamb that was slain.

My strength is made perfect in weakness.

The longer he stood contemplating these holy mysteries, the more aware he became of the inner quietness creeping over him, a strange but wonderful weightlessness of being. The sensations of cold and desolation slipped away until he was aware only of peace . . . such peace he had never before known.

A sermon he'd heard shortly after Mary Rose's death came to mind, one in which the pastor had spoken of the power that was found in weakness—weakness submitted to the Almighty. It was a sermon he'd rejected, dismissed as utter ridiculousness. But tonight the words came back with crystalline recall, making him wonder if they were true after all.

And if they were . . . *O Lord, how could I have been so wrong?*

"Please forgive me," he whispered, bowing his head, his beliefs of strength and manliness crumbling beneath the purity of the truth offered him. The enormity of his sin loomed, came sharply into focus, faded and was gone.

Forgiven.

And Samuel Colburn knelt on the snowy sidewalk, surrendering himself and his fears to the one who loved him beyond all imagining.

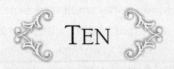

TEN

"Mama, do we get to stay here all night?" Audrey whispered, her small fingers running over Mary Rose's quilt, then caressing her sister's curls. "Look, Mama, Kathryn and Miss Hillary are already sleeping like a bug in a rug. I wanna sleep in your bed, too." Closing her eyes, she collapsed back against the pillows, feigning slumber.

"Faker. Anyway, two people are 'bugs in rugs,'" Bobby scoffed. "Don't you know anything about pluralizing?"

"*Pearl*izing? What are you talking about?" Audrey's night-gown-clad body nearly jackknifed in reaction when he tickled her foot, and she covered her mouth to muffle her giggles.

And Kathryn dreamed on, her thumb tucked securely between her lips.

Despite their earnest prayer in the library, the evening had fallen flat after they'd popped popcorn and drunk hot chocolate. Singing carols just wasn't the same without Samuel's rich bari-tone to anchor their voices. Where Joyce had gotten the idea to invite all the children to her bedchamber she didn't know, but their countenances had brightened immediately at the prospect. The race was on to wash faces, brush teeth, don night wear, and jump into the large carriage bed.

The light burned low, and a small wood fire crackled behind the screen. A cozy hour had passed, during which they'd shared stories and reminiscences. No one asked when Daddy was going to be back—or *if* Daddy was going to be back; it was as if an unspoken understanding had passed between them downstairs this evening: Daddy was in God's hands.

"Tell me the story of when I was born, Mama," Audrey entreated, wriggling her way beneath the covers. "Were you so happy?"

"I was delighted, Audrey," Joyce confirmed with a smile. "You joined our family on the snowiest February day imaginable. My goodness, such a storm was raging."

"Was the snow taller than the roof?"

"No, not quite that high, but it was very deep. Do you remember how excited both of you were to meet your new sister?" she inquired of Bobby and Lynelle, who shared a quilt at the foot of the bed. "All Lynelle wanted to do was hold you," she said to the enthralled nearly four-year-old, "and your brother couldn't wait to teach you how to walk and talk."

"He teached me how to walk? And *talk?* Bobby? He teached me a very lot, didn't he, Mama?"

"Too much!" Bobby covered his face with his hands, shaking his head, while Joyce and Lynelle shared a round of quiet laughter.

All interest lost in the story of Audrey's birth, the children continued their banter. As she adjusted the covers and leaned over to press a kiss against Kathryn's temple, a faint noise caught her attention, a soft sound such as someone quietly closing the front door. Had Samuel come home? she wondered, her heart leaping—only to falter. Maybe it was only Ida, checking the lock.

Or if it *was* Samuel, how did she know he had come home to stay? Perhaps he had only returned to gather his things—in which case, he would be further aggrieved to find all five of them in his bedchamber.

Her gaze flew to the six-panel door when she heard quiet

footsteps on the stair. Pulse quickening, she then took in the four beautiful children she and Samuel had created, trying to impress upon her mind a permanent image of them at this moment. So full of life, so trusting, so precious. No matter what happened, whatever their situation was to be, God was sovereign, she told herself, promising never to forsake her.

"I think Daddy's home," whispered Lynelle, head cocked, breaking off her words with her siblings. She turned worried eyes to her mother. "Will he be angry to find us in here? What should we do, Mama?"

"I know . . . let's hide!" Audrey exclaimed, pulling the covers over her head.

"We don't need to hide," Joyce spoke with more reassurance than she felt, reaching over Kathryn and Miss Hillary to pull the coverlet back down, the friction causing Audrey's fine hair to fly all directions.

Despite the tension in the room, a snicker escaped Bobby. "You should see your hair—it's sticking out everywhere! You look like a wild dog, Audrey."

"Wild da-awg?" she replied with a giggle. "I should bite you, then!" Extricating herself from beneath the covers, she leaped at her brother.

"Audrey! Bobby!" Joyce called, just as Samuel opened the bedroom door. He stopped just inside the opening, taking in the scene before him.

"What's going on in here?" he asked sternly, folding his arms across his chest.

"Daddy, Bobby just called me a wild dog," Audrey tattled, pulling herself off her brother and sitting up primly. The three children sat at attention, moving not a muscle.

"And why would he do such a thing?"

"He said my hair was sticking out everywhere."

Walking to the bed, his features softening into a gentle smile,

Samuel reached out and smoothed the flyaway strands. "Your hair is sticking out everywhere. Come here, pumpkin," he invited, opening his arms.

Needing no urging, Audrey flew into her father's embrace. Joyce let out the breath she didn't know she was holding and blinked away sudden tears. Samuel. Something had happened to him; she could see it in his expression, his carriage, his smile. Gone was the distant stranger; back was her husband, the father of her children.

"I need to ask your forgiveness, Audrey," he said humbly, taking a seat on the bed. Shifting her to the center of his lap, he spread his arms once more. "Lynelle, Bobby?"

Without hesitation, the older children sought their father's closeness, vying for position. "This includes you, too, little Kathryn," he added, emotion choking his voice, gazing at her sleeping form with an expression of love and longing.

Joy and gratitude flowed through Joyce, her peace made perfect when a hazel gaze brimming with emotion sought her own. "I love you," he whispered, "all of you. And I can only tell you how sorry I am for the way I've treated you." Clearing his throat, he paused before continuing, his voice gaining strength. "You were right, Audrey. My heart was hurting because of Mary Rose dying . . . and because I was trying to be strong on my own. How foolish I was."

"Nanny said your heartache was going to boil over and make a big, big mess," Audrey offered, cupping her father's face in her hands.

Joyce winced at her daughter's words but relaxed when she saw her husband's mouth twitch into a smile.

"A big, big mess? Yes, well . . . Nanny was right. Do you think you can forgive me for making such a big, big mess of things?"

"I forgive you, Daddy," Lynelle cried, nestled in his left arm. "But can you forgive me for putting calomel in your pudding—"

"And calling you home from your party?" Bobby finished, hanging his head.

"And I tickled you with Mary Rose's hair. I wasn't s'posed to sneak in Mama's wardrobe, but I did," Audrey confessed.

"And will you forgive me, as well, Samuel?" Joyce asked, seeing his gaze focus on her with surprise.

"For what? It was I who wronged you."

"I tried too hard to hold on to you, tried to manage things on my own. I didn't allow God much room to work."

"Nor did I," he replied. "But that's changed. You'd never believe . . ." He shook his head, an incredulous smile breaking over his face like a sunrise upon a long-darkened land. Pressing a kiss upon the head of each child he held, he raised his head and looked at her. "Let me just say that I have the most amazing story to tell you tonight . . . later."

Joyce smiled, her gaze locking with that of her husband's. He was back. Peace shone from his countenance, and in his eyes shone that special warmth reserved for her alone. Joy and completeness swelled within her, pushing aside the painful memories the past two years had held.

"Da-dee?" came a sleepy voice from the head of the bed. "Da-dee home?"

"Yes, Kathryn," she replied, reaching out to take the warm, strong hand her husband offered. "Our daddy is home."

Paths Briefly Crossing

Too many of you have passed through my hands
    Over the years,
Passing, pausing, paths briefly crossing
    On your way from here to there.
Your brief little lives woven together for a purpose
    Only our Creator shall know
And we can only guess at—
    If we can see past the pain to do any guessing at all.
But I know, sweet little ones, your lives did have purpose
    As did your deaths;
I rest in that; I trust in that—
    All the while tears stream down my face.
And I, too, ask,
    "Why must this be so?"
So I pause for a time to hold you, to admire you,
    To love you for a moment as if you were my own.
I press a little kiss upon your brow
    And say a prayer,
Filled with sorrow for how your family will miss you
    And how the world will never know you.
"Enough!" I tell myself.
    "Don't do this anymore!"
But I will,
    Yes, I must
Because, amidst the suffering
    There is a peace—
A calm, hushed stillness
    That I cannot explain.
Slowly and gently my troubled heart is soothed
    Until I am restored
And I am ready
    For the next one of you to pass through my hands.

PEGGY STOKS, R.N.

 RECIPE

I've made this recipe many times since my girlhood. Rich and flavorful, these cookies are made even better with the addition of freshly grated nutmeg. A small investment (less than five dollars) in a spice grater will more than pay for itself as your family and friends marvel at the exquisite taste of your baked goods.

Nutmeg Logs

1 cup butter
2 tsp. vanilla extract
2 tsp. rum-flavored extract
¾ cup sugar
1 egg
3 cups flour
½ tsp. salt
1 tsp. nutmeg

Cream together butter and sugar. Add egg, vanilla, and rum-flavored extract; beat well. Add flour, salt, and nutmeg; mix thoroughly. Shape dough on sugared board into long rolls, ½ inch in diameter, then cut into 3-inch pieces (logs). Bake at 350 degrees for 12–14 minutes. Cool, then ice. Sprinkle with freshly grated nutmeg before the icing dries.

For icing, mix together:
1 cup powdered sugar
pinch of salt
1 tbsp. butter
½ tsp. vanilla extract
½ tsp. rum-flavored extract
1–2 tbsp. milk

P.S. I almost chose my Grandma Hughs's homemade chocolate pudding recipe to share, but I thought better of it. . . .

A Note from the Author

Dear reader,

Ideas and inspiration for this story came from many places, and I will never forget the evening my ten-year-old daughter, Allison, and I sat down with a pile of quilting books to decide on a title for this novella. Together we compiled a long list of contenders, the name of nearly every quilt pattern evoking a wealth of plotting possibilities. Our search was over when Allison discovered "Crosses and Losses," and thus the story was born.

About the origin of the pattern name I know very little. *Maggie Malone's Classic American Patchwork Quilt Patterns* (Drake Publishers, Inc., 1977) gives brief mention to the pattern, which is also known as "Fox and Geese" or "Double X and X." Forty-two blocks make up a full-sized quilt, each block containing a bold, colorful mix of squares and triangles. It's just the sort of quilt that would look right at home in my family room—if I ever had a few spare moments to devote to one more project!

So whether you're an expert quilter, a sewing machine hack quilter (like yours truly), or have never sewn a stitch in your life, I pray that this unique collection of Christmas stories blesses your life in some special way this holiday season. Merry Christmas.

Warmly,
Peggy Stoks

The Beauty
of the Season

For my mom, Judy.
Your courage in the face of adversity has been
one of my life's greatest lessons.

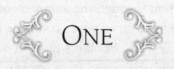

"Now, Eli, if I'd known there were so many lovely women in Maple Grove, I never would have wasted all those years at veterinary college down in Ames."

A face of wrinkled brown leather split into a delighted smile while matching, corrugated hands pulled the team and wagon to a halt. "Maybe you got some good sense after all, Clark. You mighta just spared yourself some special Iowa sayin's I been savin' up," the thin, elderly man called down to the younger.

"You haven't heard the last of our Minnesota sayings, either." A deep-throated laugh escaped the other man, whose hair and beard were the color of a rusty nail. He stood on the well-worn dirt in front of Eli Woodman's barn, in his hands a large, shiny black bag and a wide-brimmed hat that had seen better days. His eyes lit with interest on the young woman seated next to Eli.

"I been tellin' him all about you, Rebecca," Eli Woodman whispered to his grandniece before making what he considered to be a proper introduction. "Miss Rebecca Belanger of Minneapolis, I'd like you to meet this new fellow here, Hugh Clark. He ain't a farrier, but a full-schooled veterinarian just moved up to the area from Iowa." He cleared his throat and nodded after drawing out the last syllable of the state, pronouncing it *weigh*.

"We been usin' him through the summer for differ'nt things an' he been doin' a fair job, I s'pose. Today he thinks he's gonna fix up our new horse." He shook his head in disgust. "Ain't had her three months and she's dead lame already."

"I'll give her my best, Eli." The veterinarian laughed again, a warm and pleasant sound. "With such praise and confidence in my skills, it's a wonder I've gotten any other work in these parts." His gaze shifted briefly from Rebecca to her uncle, then back again. A welcoming smile curved his lips in a most handsome way. "Good afternoon."

"Pleased to meet you," Rebecca managed to state, feeling heat rise up from beneath the high collar of her blouse. Instinctively, she lowered her gaze and turned her face toward the left. At the same time she tucked her left hand into the folds of her skirt, even though she wore a concealing pair of gloves.

Lovely, he had said? His eyes must not work the same as everyone else's. Yet, all the same, his words brought a quick rush of pleasure amidst Rebecca's discomfiture.

"It's a pleasure to meet you as well, Miss Belanger." To her dismay, the veterinarian's voice was much nearer her ear than before. Before thinking, she swung her head to see that he was practically standing at her elbow, extending his hand to her. "May I help you down?"

"That would be right kind of you," Eli replied, unmindful of Rebecca's embarrassment. "Saves this old back a little wear and tear." He swung down from his perch and landed in the dirt, spry as ever for a man just past his sixty-fifth year. Heading toward the house, he called over his shoulder. "I'll tell Jo we're home, Bell; then we'll put your things in the cottage."

Left with no reasonable choice but to give Hugh Clark her hands, Rebecca took a deep breath and murmured her thanks. It was too late; he'd already seen her face and the enormous purple birthmark encompassing its left hemisphere. Accustomed to twenty years of people's reactions to her port-wine stain, she waited for the shock to reflect in his eyes. Or pity. Or disgust.

"Did he just call you 'Bell'?" Nothing more than puzzlement showed in his brown-flecked gaze. "I thought he introduced you as Rebecca."

As she was assisted to the ground, Rebecca turned her attention to a stand of maples just beginning their autumn turn from green to what she knew would become magnificent shades of orange, red, and yellow. Puzzlement echoed through her mind, as well. Why didn't this man react like others? Whenever she met new people, she steeled herself to their various reactions, saving her feelings of hurt and rejection until later when she was alone. Consequently, she kept the world in which she circulated quite small.

Her next-door neighbor and best friend Jane Eberley had always tried to change that, but now Jane was married and expecting a baby, her time and thoughts occupied by the many concerns of being a new wife and mother-to-be. In June she had moved to her new home with her husband, leaving Rebecca happy for her and bereft all at once. With all the changes that had taken place, the two miles that separated them often felt like two thousand.

Rebecca was her parents' only child, and she lived with them yet in their comfortable Minneapolis home. In an unspoken manner, they also seemed to encourage her isolation from society. She would get a better education at home than at public school, they had decided for her when she was quite young. That didn't mean they weren't loving—for they were, and they had not spared any expense in engaging the finest tutors for her education. In the back of her mind, though, lurked the thought that once they had seen the disfigured infant they had created, they had not dared bring any more children into the world.

And that they were ashamed of her.

It was only at Uncle Eli and Auntie Jo's farm that her feelings of unworthiness melted away. Perhaps it was the exposure to the beauty and grandeur of God's creation, to the harmony and rhythms of making a living from the land. Or maybe it came from Eli and Jo themselves, the childless pair who had lavished their love and attention on her all through her childhood and growing-up years.

With her father's parents back east and her mother's parents long-ago deceased, Eli and Jo were the closest thing to grandparents Rebecca had ever known. Sometimes it seemed impossible that only twenty miles separated the modern city life of Minneapolis from this idyllic piece of nature . . . as well as from a life of self-consciousness to one in which she sometimes went days without thinking about her markings.

"Uncle Eli always called me 'Beckybell' when I was young," she found herself replying, recalling countless sunlit mornings and afternoons she'd trailed behind her uncle as he tended to his work, "and somehow over the years it just dropped down to 'Bell.'" Chancing a glance at him, she saw once again the handsome smile.

"Ah, yes. Bell. I'm learning that your uncle can be quite clever with words when he wants to be."

"You think shortening 'Beckybell' to 'Bell' is so very clever, then?" She failed to see his point, the challenging contradiction escaping her lips before she thought the better of speaking. Perhaps Uncle Eli had been a bit premature in boasting of Dr. Clark's college education. Openly, she studied his face, noticing that the arrangement of his features caused a curious feeling in the base of her stomach. Or was it a slight hunger for air?

A gust of wind ruffled her hat and threatened to knock his from its perch atop his bag, so he walked over to retrieve the battered piece of leather. Placing it atop his head, his grin became mischievous. "Quite so if you speak French, *belle*."

Her breath caught in her throat at the combination of wind, sun, handsome man, and outrageous flirtation. *Belle*, indeed. She had studied the Romance languages. This wooing was just the sort of thing that happened to the heroines in the novels Jane used to smuggle into her bedroom. Yet for a moment, she gave herself over to the feeling, a giddy, glowing, floating sort of feeling, that had been oh-so-inadequately described in the stories she'd read.

No man had ever called her beautiful before.

But scarcely before it had begun, reality grounded her soaring flight of fancy. No man would be likely to comment favorably on her appearance, ever again. Beautiful was one thing she wasn't— her birthmark had seen to that.

"Je ne crois pas qu'Oncle Eli parle Français du tout," she replied in a clipped tone, turning the marked side of her face away from him. Tears that she was normally able to keep at bay threatened to spill from her eyes.

Was Hugh Clark nothing but a scoundrel, toying with her emotions? Her first impression was that he was a kind and friendly man. Her second was . . . what? To dare hope that such a nice-looking man might be interested in her? *Not likely, Rebecca,* she told herself. *You know that courtship and marriage are out of the question for you. Who in his right mind would dare take the chance of producing burgundy-splotched children? Remember, you learned long ago that the worst cruelty often comes from the most unexpected people.*

"Your grasp of the language is much better than mine, but I think you just told me that your uncle doesn't know French."

"I'm sure of it. Now, if you'll excuse me—" She turned on her heel, blinking back the itchy hotness behind her eyelids.

"Wait," he called, taking a half-dozen rapid steps to close the ground between them. "Please wait." In place of the grin was a contrite expression. "I can see I've offended you." He was so near that she could smell the soap from his clothing . . . or was it the man himself? It was both foreign and pleasant, and she marveled that a man who likely spent much of his time in barns did not smell like one.

"With the rigors of schooling and setting up a practice, I must plead ignorance in the matters of male conduct in the presence of the fair sex. I beg your forgiveness, Miss Belanger. I hope you might give me another chance . . . your uncle speaks so highly of you."

"Just what has my uncle said about me?" With each word of Dr. Clark's heartfelt speech, Rebecca's confusion mounted.

"Oh, he mostly says things about the brightness you bring to their lives. That you're thoughtful and kind and compassionate and loving as the day is long. He also says you can be full of mischief and give back every bit of rascality he dishes out."

The curious feeling returned to her stomach while Hugh spoke. If his friendliness was sincere and did not spring from impure motivation, then why had he asked for another chance? What kind of man was he? she wondered. She'd never met anyone quite like him.

"Maybe you want to know a little about me," he offered, as if he followed the direction of her thoughts. "I grew up on a farm outside of Ames and always loved tending to animals. Getting through veterinary college was always my aim, if you'll pardon the pun, and now that I've done that, here I am in Maple Grove starting my practice. A few other things happened here and there along the way, but I figure we ought to leave some things for the sake of future conversation." His grin was infectious.

Hinges squeaked and Uncle Eli reappeared from the house. For just a moment as he came down the porch stairs he looked old and tired. But then, squaring his shoulders, he walked across the yard to join them, the spring back in his step.

"How is she?" Rebecca asked, sudden shame washing over

her. The reason she'd come to the farm, after all, was to help out during Auntie Jo's recuperation from a broken hip. But with the veterinarian's flattering words flowing as deep as the Mississippi River, she'd been entirely distracted from her original purpose.

"Snoozin' away," her uncle replied. "Be a good time to get you settled in the cottage. Since her tumble down the steps, neighbors and church folks have been takin' turns seein' to Jo durin' the day." His voice softened with tenderness. "I see her through the nights."

"Are you sure you wouldn't rather have me stay in the house, Uncle Eli? I can help at night as well as during the day."

"I'll see my darlin' through the nights, Bell. You'll have plenty to do with the harvest comin' in. 'Sides, we know how much you like the cottage."

Reflexively, all three heads turned toward the small, wooden structure tucked just inside the nearest stand of maples. Situated a good forty yards away from their present house, the cottage was Eli and Jo's original Maple Grove dwelling. Rebecca's dauntless great-aunt forbade Eli to tear it down while she had breath in her body, declaring that their first Minnesota home held too many memories to be turned into kindling.

So that was how Eli had come to add the duties of maintaining the cottage to his already busy life of farming. Once shingled with bark, the small dwelling now boasted a proper roof. Thirty years of changing seasons had weathered the split-log siding to gray, adding only to the cottage's charm, in Rebecca's opinion. The once-sagging front porch had been replaced with a new one, and the flower box beneath the small front window was never without foliage or pine boughs, depending on the time of year.

Auntie Jo kept the indoors of the cottage as tidy as she did their newer, larger frame home. Already Rebecca could picture herself waking in the cozy, homemade bed beneath a pile of her aunt's sunshine-dried quilts. The rustle of leaves and calls of birds scarcely known in the city were as splendid a symphony as she could ever imagine. The cottage had always been a wondrous place to her, a private sanctuary that she could pretend was her very own.

But it stood second only to the warmth of Eli and Jo's home. Auntie Jo always had an enormous eight o'clock breakfast waiting for her and Eli—sausages, bacon, flapjacks, eggs. The town had been aptly named for its many groves of maple trees, and delicious syrup was made by many of the local residents.

Dr. Clark was the first to break the silence, speaking in a professional tone. "Well, I came to tend a hoof, and I'd best get to it. Thank you, Eli, for the introduction to your most remarkable niece. She is indeed everything you said and speaks French like a Parisian, to boot." A hint of the previous grin played about his mouth.

"Speaks French? Now why in tarnation would you two be talkin' in French?" He shook his head. "I can't understand a word of it. *Oui, oui, oui* . . . sounds like hog-callin', if you ask me."

Rebecca couldn't resist meeting Hugh's amused gaze, her brows lifting a scant quarter inch at her uncle's admission. *Told you so,* she communicated.

". . . entirely too much book learnin' between the two of you," Eli went on, though pride was evident in his voice. "Bell here gots herself a pile of learnin', but better'n that is her heart. Solid gold—just like Jo's."

"You've got a good woman," the veterinarian seconded in all seriousness. "Please give your wife my best when she wakes and tell her she's in my daily prayers for a swift recovery."

"She'll be sorry she missed you, Clark. She always enjoys your visits."

Though his reply seemed to be to her uncle, Rebecca's impudence vanished when, a moment later, the brown-flecked gaze sought her own. "You might mention to her that I'll be by tomorrow." With long strides he retrieved his bag, then was swallowed up by the shadows of the barn.

"Speakin' French? If that don't beat all." Eli chuckled, a twinkle evident in his blue eyes. "Oh my, yes, Bell, it's good to have you back with us again. Come on, honey. Let's get you settled before Jo wakes up."

Settled? With Hugh Clark coming by again tomorrow? Rebecca knew she would fit back into her relatives' lives like a hand in a glove, but after this afternoon's extraordinary meeting, "settled" was one thing she doubted she would be for a long time to come.

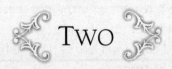

TWO

"Those weren't the best eggs I ever ate, but they weren't the worst, neither."

"I know, I know," Rebecca replied to her uncle with mock weariness. "I'll just have to keep practicing until I get them right." Sunshine streamed in the east windows of the kitchen, illuminating the breakfast table and Eli's grizzled head. Taking a bite of her flapjack, she watched her uncle wipe the remaining egg yolk, syrup, and melted butter from his plate with the last slice of bacon.

"Not bad," he commented, chewing thoughtfully, "but tomorrow you could fry the bacon a tad more crisp."

Auntie Jo interrupted her husband's ritual teasing from her bed in the next room. "Eli Woodman! Just be thankful Bell put a hot breakfast before you this morning, you old rascal."

Rebecca giggled. "He thinks I don't know he's trying to trick me into making more food for him. It's the same old carrot he dangles whenever I make molasses cookies. 'They're not half bad, Bell, but you'd better try again tomorrow,'" she mimicked in a gruff tone. Leveling her fork toward her uncle, she lifted her brows. "I'll never make the best cookies you ever ate, will I, Uncle Eli?"

"That," he replied, reaching for the peg that held his hat, "is something you will never know unless you keep trying." A self-satisfied grin played about his lips as he rose from his chair and headed toward the bedroom.

"Pay him no mind, Bell," Auntie Jo directed. "He's always been a scoundrel in the kitchen."

"Among other places," he remarked, silencing Auntie Jo's whoop of surprise with a loud kiss.

Rebecca smiled at the older couple's exchange. Unlike her parents, who rarely touched, Eli's and Jo's love was plain for all to see. *What would it be like to have such an affectionate and devoted husband?* she wondered, thinking of Auntie Jo's radiance whenever Eli was near. Face tilted upward expectantly, lips curved into an indulgent smile, the older woman's fine-wrinkled cheeks bloomed like wild roses as often as not. Rebecca often thought her aunt's bright blue eyes and expression held the sparkle of a young girl's.

With a sigh, she stacked her plate on Eli's. The wine-colored birthmark that stained her face had also, to a lesser degree, mottled, blotched, and whorled its way down her left arm to her fingers. With her sleeves rolled up a few turns, the discoloration was stark against the white of Auntie Jo's china plates.

"Leave those dishes, Bell," her aunt called, "and come sit. Martha Denning said she'd come by later this morning and do whatever needed doing."

"Hope she don't get a notion to bring more chowchow," Eli muttered, walking through the kitchen. "I was eatin' on that for days after last time she was here, an' it wasn't even good." He made a face as he put his arms into his coat. "Too sweet."

"You mind your complaints and count your blessings, Eli Woodman! If not for the generosity of our neighbors, you'd be staring at an empty table."

"Ain't your hearin' ever gonna go, woman?" In a quick movement, he put on his hat and turned, with a rueful expression, toward Rebecca. "Hears like an elephant, smells like a bloodhound, an' has eyes sharper'n a hawk. A fellow ain't got half a chance when his wife's senses are more animal than human."

As Jo's quiet laughter filtered toward them, Rebecca was overwhelmed with the love she felt for this unique couple. Married over forty years and they still chortled and joked like youngsters. Yet she knew things hadn't always been easy for them.

Not long after they'd come from Vermont as newlyweds, Uncle Eli had enlisted to fight in the War Between the States, leaving Auntie Jo on her own to battle the Midwest frontier on their fledgling farm. More difficult than that, though, was the fact that the older woman had never been able to carry a babe in her womb past seven months; one small stone back East and three markers in Rush Creek Cemetery gave testimony to their crushed dream to bring forth new life.

For some people, such great loss would be reason enough to welter in bitterness, but somehow Jo and Eli had persevered through each demise, emerging with quiet, strong faith that Rebecca imagined could indeed move a mountain.

"Would you like another cup of tea, Auntie Jo?" Rebecca asked, entering the generous-sized bedroom. Against the opposite wall sat a handsome bed of maple, next to which stood a bedside table. Completing the room's furnishings were a dresser, mirror, wardrobe, two chairs, and a sewing machine. Lacy curtains had been drawn back to admit the morning light.

"You made a good breakfast, Bell, but I'll wait on more tea till later." Propped on two pillows, the stockinged sole of her greataunt's foot hailed her, toes waggling in greeting. "The more I drink, the more I'll have to trouble you for the pan."

"You know it's no trouble."

"Maybe not for you, but hoisting this old body up and down plumb wears me out!"

"Josephine Woodman worn out? I've never heard such talk." This was the closest thing to complaining she'd ever heard from her aunt, yet Rebecca saw traces of suffering around the blue eyes she loved so well. These past two weeks had to have been difficult for Jo and Eli both.

"I wish you would have called for me right away," she said with gentle reproach, slipping into the chair at the bedside. "I would have been on my way in the time it took to pack a bag."

"I know that, honey, but for a week we didn't have any idea I'd broken anything. I took to bed after the fall, thinking I'd be fine in a day or two, but when the soreness only got worse, I figured I must have done myself some serious damage."

"How's the pain?" She took the hand her aunt offered, warm and strong and small. How many tasks had these hardworking fingers accomplished in sixty-two years? she wondered. This confinement had to be something near to torture for Jo, a farmwife who rarely ever stopped moving.

"It doesn't hurt so bad today. At first I used some of the opium Dr. Janery left me, but it locked me up something fierce, if you know what I mean." The face she made was at odds with the elegant silver hair framing her features. "That's about the last thing I need on top of everything else."

"Uncle Eli said it may be some time till you're up and around."

"The doctor figures I fractured the neck of my thighbone when I fell and says I'll need to keep to bed for a few months. After that, I'll walk with crutches . . . maybe always."

Rebecca's other hand came up to clasp her aunt's hand. Her eyes grew moist. "I'll stay as long as you need me . . . . even always."

"Oh, Bell." Jo's eyes closed for a long moment, and when they opened, their azure depths glistened with tears. "What would we do without you?"

"I don't know what I would do without you," she whispered, quite honestly, in reply. "I love you and Eli so much, Auntie Jo."

"As we do you, sweet Bell."

A gust of autumn wind rattled the windows while beyond, a noisy flock of grackles gathered in the trees. Motes of dust performed a slow waltz on the morning sunbeams. The moment stretched on, sweet and painful, until Rebecca noticed fatigue growing on her beloved aunt's face.

"Oh dear, you're tired and I'm keeping you from a nap." With a final squeeze, she withdrew her hands and stood.

"I don't know why I've been sleeping so much," Jo replied, almost irritably.

"Your body's working on knitting those bones back together so you can toss a few more forkfuls of hay before you depart this earth."

The choleric cast of the older woman's lips gave way to a grin. "You're remembering back aways. I haven't forked hay in quite a few years now." Changing the subject, she asked, "What did you think of our new veterinarian, Bell?"

"He was—" Rebecca felt her face warm, remembering the things Hugh Clark had said to her . . . the way he had said *belle*. "He seemed like a good man."

"Yes. He's only been here since July, but Eli and I think highly of him. As far as we know, he's a bachelor." Her snowy brows lifted, her voice turning speculative. "And I heard you two got on quite well."

"I . . . I only made his acquaintance."

"In French?" The blue eyes twinkled.

"I . . . he . . . oh!" Rebecca's tongue seemed wont to trip over itself before she regained control of the unruly organ. "He made a comment about my name."

"Really?"

"He . . . wondered why I was called Bell, so I told him."

"And what was his comment?" Jo persisted, looking remarkably alert now.

The flustered feelings she'd felt the afternoon before returned full force. She also remembered Hugh Clark's smile. "He said Eli was clever for naming me Bell."

"Because . . . ?" Jo supplied.

"Because in French, *belle* means . . . 'beautiful,'" she finished miserably.

"Well, he's absolutely correct—you are beautiful." Jo nodded, a smile playing about her lips. "I knew he had intelligence. Pull that cover up over my leg, Bell, will you? I believe I'll take my nap now." Closing her eyes, the older woman settled back into her pillow. She let out a deep breath. "And mind you don't let me sleep through Dr. Clark's visit today."

At precisely noon, Hugh Clark turned down Territorial Road, the long dirt lane that would bring him to the Woodman farm. The stray dog he'd taken in and named Lucky rode beside him, the mongrel's paws disheveling the small bouquet of asters he'd placed on the seat. The abscessed hoof he'd tended did not require a following-day visit—two would be more like it, but he had the matter of Miss Rebecca Belanger to attend to.

Allowing for the sixth-grade crush he'd had on Emily Tessier, he'd never given himself over to the pursuit of courtship. Science and animals had been his passions for as long as he could remember; whatever spare time he'd had after chores was spent learning about one or the other. This interest was strongly encouraged by his father, a gentle-hearted man who shared his love for animals.

Hugh's acceptance to the Ames Veterinary College was a cause of great celebration in his family, second only to the jubilation caused by his graduation. Owing to the number of veterinarians in the Ames area, however, he knew the feasibility of setting up practice in his nearby hometown was poor. His sister, Deborah, who had moved to Minneapolis with her husband in '86, suggested he move north and try Hennepin County. The city itself held no appeal, but upon visiting some of its outlying areas, Hugh's heart had been captured by Maple Grove, a land of gentle, rolling hills dotted with small lakes and majestic stands of hardwood.

After renting a modest house, he'd set to advertising his specialty in the local paper. Eli Woodman had been the first to use his services, making no bones about the fact that he would personally run him out of the area if he wasn't what he said he was. His care of Woodman's colicky cow was efficient, however, and the older man had done him a great service by word-of-mouth endorsement.

Hugh had immediately taken to the dry, wisecracking farmer and his sprightly wife. It hadn't taken long for him to witness their deep faith in the Lord as well as their uncommon love for one another. Eli Woodman was a born talker, his favorite topic being persons near and dear to his heart. Next came farming, local residents and events, and if he was allowed to wax on unchecked, eventually would come precise recountings of the months he'd spent on Tennessee soil during his time in the volunteer infantry.

It was during these long, lazy dissertations he'd learned of Rebecca. So skillfully did Eli paint descriptions of both appearance and character with his speech that Hugh felt as though he knew the persons of whom the older man spoke. All summer and into fall, the old farmer had shared accounts of his grand-niece from Minneapolis, stirring a place within Hugh that had not been seriously affected since the days of Emily Tessier.

He'd been wanting to meet Rebecca Belanger for some time, but what he couldn't understand was why he'd been so brash and forward upon their introduction. True, he might feel as though he knew her, but she didn't know the first thing about him. No wonder he'd drawn the reaction he had.

Eli hadn't exaggerated, either, about her sensitivity regarding her birthmark. She had visibly shrunken from him upon their introduction, turning the affected side of her face away. Perhaps he had tried too hard to let her know he didn't care one whit about the stain on her skin. "Careful there!" he admonished Lucky, glancing at the rapidly deteriorating bunch of flowers. "Or my second impression will be worse than my first."

Tail thumping, the multicolored canine received the advisement with gratitude, assuming that any words his new master spoke were words of praise. Unable to resist the tilted head and expressive brown eyes, Hugh reached over and gave his pet a good scratching behind the ears. A blissful yawn escaped Lucky's jaws, and he lay down upon the upholstered bench.

The scenery rolling by the carriage was peaceful, tranquil, utterly pastoral. His family and roots were in Iowa, but he was beginning to think Minnesota had quite a charm of its own. He chuckled, remembering Eli's response to his expression of such thoughts. "You might want to reserve judgment there, son, till you been through one of our winters. More than a few faint-hearted folks have packed up an' tore back south at first thaw."

Hugh's smile faded when he passed by the Scruggs place, a small, forlorn home standing amidst a collection of ramshackle outbuildings. Eli's lips thinned when he spoke of Barter Scruggs, a man whom Hugh had not yet met. It was commonly believed that Scruggs made and sold liquor illegally, and he was reputed by many to be a mean drunk.

Standing in sharp contrast to the surrounding beauty of so many neatly tended farms, the Scruggs property looked seedy. Weeds sprang forth from the driveway and yard; no smoke rose from the chimney. A family dwelled in this sad place, he

thought, shaking his head and realizing how fortunate he was
to have been raised by the parents he had.

Catching sight of the edge of the Woodman property, his
mind turned again toward Rebecca. Was it foolishness on his
part to think so much of a woman he, in all actuality, barely
knew? Just what was it about Woodman's grandniece that had
so captivated his attention? he rather sternly asked himself.

It was her heart, he decided only a second later, remembering
the common threads of Eli's recountings. Rebecca sounded so
much like Jo, fun and selfless and giving. That the young woman
held a special place in Eli's affections was plain to see. Hugh
sighed and readjusted his hat. Maybe this attraction to Rebecca
had something to do with watching Eli and Jo together and longing for a woman with whom to share such a relationship.

Could mere foolishness explain the quickening in his chest as
he directed the team of bays down the Woodman drive? Lucky
seemed to sense his anticipation, awkwardly pushing himself to a
sitting position and mangling several more blooms in the process.

"Thank you kindly. I'm sure Miss Belanger will be delighted
to receive these flowers you have so thoughtfully crushed."

Sometimes Hugh was certain animals smiled. Grinned, even.
Tongue lolling, Lucky turned his head toward his master and
seemed to lift an eyebrow.

He couldn't resist a chuckle. "You'd do well to be on your best
behavior today, dog. I'm already on unstable ground."

Something between a grunt and a second yawn escaped
Lucky. Regarding his master a moment longer, the canine turned
his attention forward. The crystal song of a cardinal sounded
from a nearby tree, carrying clearly on the sun-warmed autumn
air. "Tell me, Lucky, how do I go about convincing this young
woman I couldn't care less about a big old birthmark?" he
mused. "People's insides count for a whole lot more than their
outsides—it's a fact your kind knows much better than mine."

The thumping of the white, black, and brown tail was the end of the asters. Hugh shook his head and fingered what had been a simple but attractive bunch. "No flowers. Now I'll have to rely on my charming personality . . . and that didn't get me very far yesterday." Though his words were light, he contemplated what he would say to Rebecca . . . . Bell . . . *belle.*

She was a lovely woman. He remembered how her glossy dark hair had peeked out from beneath her stylish traveling hat, framing a face filled with graceful planes and angles. Her eyes were dark, snapping with fire when she'd spat that snappy line of French at him. There were no thoughts in her mind of her birthmark at that moment, he'd wager.

A slow smile curved his lips. Yes, Rebecca Belanger was a very interesting woman. If he wasn't mistaken, Eli was not-so-subtly maneuvering the two of them together, the old rascal. How Rebecca felt about that—or even if she was aware of it—he didn't know, but he imagined that once Eli Woodman set his mind to something it was as good as done.

"All right, Lord," he spoke aloud with a brief glance overhead, "between you and Eli I've fallen half in love with her. But knowing someone by proxy and knowing her in person are two different things. I'm ready and willing to go the other half of the way, but you've got to give me some help. I think you know what I mean. Amen."

Satisfied, he brought the bays to a halt in the Woodman yard. "Lucky, you stay put," he ordered, eyeing first the dog, then the flowers. "I've had enough help from you already today."

THREE

Rebecca's hands were submerged in dishwater when, out of the corner of her eye, she saw Hugh Clark's carriage turn into the drive. Quickly, she dried her hands and smoothed the apron she wore over her blouse and skirt, her heart thumping at the sight of the veterinarian sitting tall in his seat. Though she would never admit it to another soul, her eye had been drawn to the window all morning.

"Looks like you got company," Martha Denning remarked as she mashed a heap of boiled potatoes. The energetic, middle-aged woman had arrived a little before nine and in that time had not only swept and dusted the entire house, but had put together such a fried chicken dinner as to make the angels weep. Adding another splash of milk to the potatoes, she stirred with even more vigor, her voice a little breathless. "It's that new fellow, if I'm not mistaken. People are talking about him . . . saying mighty good things. Rebecca, dear, why don't you set another place, and we'll invite him to stay for dinner."

"Is that Hugh Clark you're talking about?" Auntie Jo's voice called. "You'd best not let him get away without feeding him, Mart. You never know what those bachelors are eating on their own."

"Isn't that the truth! You know my neighbor, Mr. Harbaugh?

He makes himself nothing but fried eggs every morning, noon, and night. I don't believe he's ever washed the pan, either." All morning Martha had been conversing with Jo from whatever room she happened to be in, just as naturally as if they'd been facing one another across a table.

"I've seen worse." There was no satisfaction in Jo's voice.

"You're meaning the Scruggs place, I reckon. What were you ever doing inside those walls?"

"Oh, I've brought a few baskets down. Bread, jam, things from the garden. It'd like to break your heart to see how those people live."

Rebecca listened carefully as she added another place setting to the table. She was acquainted with some of her aunt and uncle's neighbors, but of the mysterious Scruggs family living in the dilapidated house down the road she'd heard little.

"I'm not sure Mrs. Scruggs is right in the head," Jo continued. "She can be looking square at you, and it's as if she doesn't even see you."

"It can't be good for a person to be shut away like that. And what of the little ones? I couldn't even tell you how many there are."

"Just two . . . that I know of, anyway, but they're always kept out of sight. I'd like to do more for Lavinia, their mother, but their father hangs so close that I can barely say half a dozen words without him telling me it's time to go home. If not for the food, I'm sure he wouldn't let me on his place."

"Barter Scruggs is a dangerous man. . . ."

Rebecca's heart went out to Mrs. Scruggs and her children as the older women talked, the stir she'd felt at Hugh Clark's arrival taking a backseat to her compassion. It did not surprise her in the least to learn of Jo's charity toward the least fortunate of her neighbors. But the thumping of boots on the wooden steps outdoors a moment later brought the conversation to a close and Rebecca's concerns about the veterinarian back to the forefront.

"How do, Miz Denning? Forgot to tell you ladies there'd be two more for lunch," Eli called, entering. "Arthur and Jake are hired on through the harvest."

Rebecca had met both men in the past, hardworking locals. They greeted her and Martha politely as they came in, their hands and faces damp from washing. Bringing up the rear was russet-haired Hugh Clark.

Eli sought Rebecca's gaze and winked. "Best make it three. S'pose we'll have to let the new fellow sample your cookin' as long as he showed up right at mealtime." Cocking his head toward the veterinarian, he added conspiratorially, "In my courtin' days I was treated to several fine meals by Jo an' her mama by takin' such a tack."

Hugh threw back his head and laughed. "I wasn't expecting a meal, but I won't turn it down . . . especially since I smell fried chicken."

White teeth gleamed in the reddish-brown beard, and Rebecca was both dismayed and overjoyed to see that Hugh Clark was every bit as nice-looking as she remembered. His gaze sought hers, his broad smile reaching all the way to his eyes.

"Good day, Miss Belanger," he spoke warmly as she busied herself with setting two more places. "I hope having me will be no trouble."

"No trouble at all," Eli answered, clapping the veterinarian's shoulder while Rebecca's inner voice shouted that the man's presence would indeed trouble her nerves a great deal. "Sit down, everyone, and load up your plates while I see to my bride."

Rebecca helped Martha dish up while Eli made a brief visit to Jo and the men settled around the table. Self-consciousness made her movements seem unnatural. How was she going to manage sharing a table with him? Worse yet, what might he say in front of all the others?

"Is that for your aunt? Let me." Shivers shot down her legs at the sound of his voice near her ear. Taking the plate she was fixing for Jo at the stove, he added a biscuit to the chicken, potatoes, and baked squash. "I owe her a visit, so I'll have my meal with her." With that, he set the plate on the tray, took his own, and disappeared around the corner.

Though Rebecca had been hungry after a morning of vigorous housework, her appetite had fled with the appearance of the hazel-eyed man. She picked at the meal, her stomach tied in knots. Much laughter came from Jo's bedchamber; she and her noontime guest seemed to be having a wonderful time.

Several times last night Rebecca had awakened, thinking of Dr. Clark's parting remark . . . *You might mention to her that I'll be by tomorrow.* After what had transpired between them yesterday, had she been mistaken to read double meaning into his message? She had thought his words spoke to her as well, but it seemed as though she was mistaken.

Why was she so disappointed?

The buttered squash tasted terrible in her mouth, and she set down her fork. Martha ate as heartily as the men. Jo's laughter pealed yet again, followed by Hugh's, causing Eli's eyes to crinkle with pleasure.

Thick wedges of warm apple pie, accompanied by steaming cups of strong coffee, capped off the dinner and were fairly gobbled down by the men before Eli announced it was time to return to the fields. Rebecca sighed while they departed, studying her uneaten food . . . listening to the happy sounds of Auntie Jo's and Hugh's conversation.

"You can consider it done," came Hugh's voice, preceding his appearance in the kitchen by just a moment. He handed his and Jo's dishes to Martha. "If your niece agrees, that is."

Looking up, she saw the hazel gaze seeking hers. Feeling suddenly silly to be sitting alone at the table before a plate of barely touched food, she pushed back her chair and began piling plates. "If I agree to what?" she asked, focusing her attention on the task at hand.

"Pick grapes!"

"Pick grapes? What are you talking about?"

"Your aunt tells me she's sick about missing the wild grapes, and she wonders if we would be so kind as to take some buckets and see what the birds have left." His eyebrows rose entreatingly. "Grape jelly is my favorite."

"I . . . we? I . . . I'm not certain if I remember where to look," she hedged, knowing exactly where wild grapevines grew in profusion. She and Auntie Jo had been there many times over the years, their visits ultimately culminating in clouds of grape-scented steam pouring from the bubbling jelly pot.

"I'm willing to make it an adventure then. Why don't you get directions while I see to that hoof? It just so happens that I have the next few hours free."

"But I—"

"No buts," Martha interrupted firmly, whisking the stack of dishes from beneath Rebecca's hands. "You go on and find Jo some grapes, and while you're at it, enjoy this lovely weather for the rest of us. You've already scrubbed up the worst of the pots, so I'll just wash the rest."

"Your escape on a purple platter, Miss Belanger." Hugh's grin was infectious; Rebecca felt the beginning of an answering smile tugging at the corners of her mouth. "How about you produce two buckets and meet me outside in ten minutes?"

"Ten minutes," she found herself agreeing, feeling very much like a small leaf that had just been swept aloft by a surprising gust of wind.

❄ ❄ ❄

The grapes were a disappointment after all, puckered and leathery on the vine. Down the hill and deeper into the woods, Rush

Creek flowed at a lazy pace within its winding banks. The sun shone warm upon their shoulders, but the breeze carried with it the promise of cooler temperatures. Lucky trotted beside the pair, his gait both peculiar and efficient, as they walked on the gravel road back to the Woodman farm.

"It's amazing how he keeps up so well." Rebecca had been astounded when the three-legged dog had jumped from the veterinarian's carriage, tail wagging. As if Lucky understood she was speaking about him, he turned his head and regarded her in a friendly manner. "I keep wondering what happened to the poor thing."

"We'll never know. He was near dead when I found him." Hugh swung the empty bucket he carried, shaking his head. "I don't understand how some people can treat animals so cruelly . . . or people," he added softly, after a pause.

Rebecca's heart thundered at the gentle words spoken by the man beside her. Beneath the close-cropped beard she could see the strong set of his jaw. His form was as fine as any she could imagine, his height exceeding her own by five or six inches. What she liked best about him, though, was the kindness that shone from his brown-flecked eyes. Laughter, tenderness, and empathy seemed to be stored in his gaze, free for the dispensation.

He should have been claimed by some beautiful young woman long ago.

She couldn't understand why he had chosen to spend this afternoon with her, engaging in pleasant conversation and seeking to tickle her rib with his funny stories, making her feel as though he truly enjoyed being with her. *And what would he know of the cruelty of others?* she wondered. He was . . . normal.

"People would say terrible things about my father. Snicker . . . stare . . . whisper," he continued in a ruminant tone.

Answering grief rose inside Rebecca, for he had just described her entire existence. Tears blurred the colorful countryside before her.

"He never let on that it bothered him, but I wonder, deep down, if it did. It bothered me, though, an awful lot."

"What . . . why would people treat your father so?" she asked, finally trusting her voice enough to speak.

"Because of his scars. He was burned in a barn fire when he tried to rescue the stock."

"Oh."

"I was too young to remember anything, but my mother told me he nearly died." Strong teeth flashed amidst the copper glints in his beard. "I'm sure glad he didn't, though, because if not for him I doubt I'd be where I am today."

"Where? In Maple Grove, Minnesota, not picking grapes?"

He threw back his head and laughed. "Your tongue is quick in any language, *belle*. It's good to become acquainted with the lady Eli told me about."

"Just how much talking has my uncle done?" She strove to make her words casual, but inside, a thrill threatened this disguise of her emotions.

"Enough to spark a healthy interest in spending time with you."

The glow of excitement left her in a rush, and she dropped her head. "You can't mean that."

"I can't? Pray tell me why not."

"Because I . . . because of . . ." Tears threatened yet again. Oh, why had she thrown aside her caution and agreed to walk with this man? A courtship like Jane Eberly's was just not possible for her. "Because," she averred, studying the dirt at her feet.

"Because of a little dab of color on your cheek?" His voice was a smooth caress on the autumn air.

"We both know there's more than a 'little dab of color' on my cheek. Why don't you just say it—I'm ugly." Rebecca stopped walking, hot wetness spilling over the area in question. "Ugly," she whispered angrily, her fist coming up in a quick, jerky motion to wipe her tears.

Hugh stopped in the road also, allowing a respectful distance between them. Lucky sat on the side of the road, head cocked, glancing first at his master then at the anguished woman.

"Please just leave me alone." Anguish and defeat welled up inside her, and she dropped the bucket in the weeds at the side of the lane. How many afternoons had she spent curled up on her bed at home, in tears over her disfigurement?

"Oh, but then I couldn't be a gentleman." Reaching in his coat, he pulled out an ironed square of linen. "My mother told me to carry a clean wiper for just this situation. 'You never know when you'll meet a damsel in distress,' she told me when I left for college. Besides reminding me to say my prayers and brush my teeth, I believe that was the only advice she gave me." He held the handkerchief aloft for a moment before closing the distance between them. "You're my first damsel in distress," he said gently, pressing the soft fabric into her hands.

Accepting the cloth, she wiped her eyes.

"Do you really believe that little dab of color prevents me from seeing your lovely dark eyes?" he asked, guiding her chin upward with a light touch of his knuckles.

Rebecca's heart seemed to skid to a stop at the contact of his fingers. With a shaking breath, she met the steady hazel gaze. The warm fingers traced upward, grazing her cheek, the soft hairline just above her ear.

"*Belle*," he asserted, "I see before me a woman with a beautiful oval face, whose hair and skin are silkier than anything I've ever before imagined. She smells a little like fried chicken, but underneath that is something mysterious and flowery that makes me want to keep smelling and smelling. Her mouth is—" She was powerless to move as his head bent toward hers. Stopping just short of a kiss, he touched two fingers to his mouth before brushing her lips with them in a featherlight caress.

He'd nearly kissed her. She swallowed in shock.

Taking a step back, he smiled wryly. "Rebecca, do you believe your aunt and uncle would love you more if you had no marks on your skin?"

"I believe my parents would." Finding her tongue, she was surprised at the contentious words that had escaped.

"Ah, but I asked you about Eli and Jo. Give me the truth. Do you believe they would care more for you without this birthmark?"

"No," she replied after a long pause, lowering her gaze.

"Is it possible, then, that others might feel the same?"

"I . . . I . . . you don't understand—"

"I think I have some understanding, *belle*. Will you answer just one more question for me?" The soothing timbre of his voice was such that she could imagine sick and injured animals lying down in surrender before him.

"What is it?" With a deep sigh, she looked back up into the earnest features of the man before her.

"Do you believe God is good?"

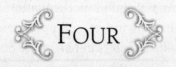

FOUR

More so than his demonstration of his feelings, Hugh Clark's question burned within Rebecca the remainder of the day and all through the evening. Did she believe God is good? Why had he asked such a thing? *Did* she believe God is good?

Jo, as if she sensed a matter weighing on her niece's mind, had handed her a stack of letters after the supper hour. "I've been looking through these today. Why don't you take them with you out to the cottage?"

To her questioning look, her aunt had replied, "They're the letters Eli wrote me from his enlistment."

"From the war? Why do you want me to read them?"

"There's a pressure on my heart to give them to you tonight, Bell." The blue eyes had shone as bright as a midsummer sky, gentle and warm. "You've not been courted before, and I expect your feelings must be running somewhat out of order."

"My feelings? . . . Who says I'm being courted?"

"*I* say so, dear, for two reasons." A winsome smile had curved Jo's lips, melting years from her features. "The first is observation. The second is because a certain young man asked if I thought you would be amenable to being called upon."

"Oh . . ."

"Already knowing Eli's mind on the matter, I was pleased to tell Dr. Clark that he may indeed call upon you."

Holding the bundle of letters in her lap, Rebecca had sat quiet a long time. "I don't know what to think. I've always loved staying with you because it's . . . safe here. But this time everything seems all wrong. You're hurt, and I worry so about you, and I don't know what to think about this man who looks at me like—"

"He looks at you that way, Rebecca Belanger, because you are a beautiful young woman," had come Auntie Jo's forceful words, "inside *and* out. I know I should hold my tongue, but I've got to say I've never had a minute's time for the way your mother and father have kept you squirreled away from the world. You need to get out and live!"

"If this is what 'living' feels like, I'm not sure I like it."

"Yes, it can be mighty strange and even frightening at times— painful, too—but there's no doubt it's all worthwhile."

"Auntie Jo . . . do you believe God is good?"

"Yes, child, I do."

"Even when bad things happen?"

"That all depends on who's deciding what's bad, I reckon. God's ways are often a mystery to his children."

"Well, what about falling and breaking your hip? Or . . . not being able to have children?"

"Or being born with a birthmark?" The gentle blue gaze held fast upon her. "Bell, you need only open the Scriptures to be affirmed of the Father's love for you. What you have to decide for yourself is if God—who loves you so much that he sent his only Son to die for your sins—is for you or against you."

Outside the cottage the wind gusted, breaking Rebecca's reverie as it rattled the window on the small structure's south side. Braiding her hair into a thick plait, she readied herself for bed, thinking that now she had not one question to ponder but two.

The small fire she'd built had taken the chill out of the air, and she settled into the well-worn rocker with a quilt and the letters Auntie Jo had pressed upon her. The reason Jo had given them to her still wasn't clear in Rebecca's mind, but perhaps reading them would distract her from her cumbersome thoughts.

Thumbing through the stack, she noted various postmarks and Eli's distinctive script. Beginning with what seemed to be the first missive, dated September 24, 1864, she read of her great-uncle's sadness to be separated from his wife and home. Rebecca couldn't help but think that the more formal style of his written word stood in contrast with his colloquial speech.

> . . . *Just before we got to St. Paul a little girl came out and stood by the gate and waved her handkerchief and cried. I don't know if she had any friends in the troop or not, but I felt like crying along with her. An old woman also came out and waved her bonnet and said, "God bless you boys. May you live to come back."*
>
> *After the boat started, I could not help but think of you and wonder when—if ever—I shall see you again. . . .*

Immediately engrossed in a story of which she'd only heard bits and pieces over the years, Rebecca realized she was most likely sitting in the same place, before the same stove, that Jo had sat reading these letters some twenty-six years before. How difficult it must have been for Jo to be alone, managing the farm on her own. And for Eli, journeying through adverse conditions to a fate unknown. A letter dated October described his travels.

> *Rain, rain, rain. I never seen so much of the blame stuff in my life. We been marching. . . . I was never so happy to lay on the soft side of a brick floor as I was when we finally got through Indianapolis. Many of our rations are stale. . . .*

Through both tears and smiles she read through the next
several letters. Even in the face of such hardship, Eli's and Jo's
love for one another radiated from these pages written over a
quarter-century ago. Her uncle often gave voice to his con-
science, as well, as advice for Jo's management of their farm.

> *My dearest wife,*
>   *Perhaps I write too often, but I am impatient to hear from you.*
> *I keep your picture with me and gaze often at your face, missing*
> *you. . . . I feel badly that so much has fallen to you while I am*
> *away, but I do not doubt our home is in capable hands. . . . We*
> *have landed in Tennessee. . . . Several of us have had the jaundice*
> *and I am feeling sore. All day today and yesterday we heard*
> *cannons. I am saddened to think of the fellows who have been sent*
> *to their Maker, leaving widows and orphans beyond any reckoning*
> *I care to do. . . . Don't let Harlan Loucks take down those trees on*
> *the east side of that clearing till a line is run. If they're on my side,*
> *I want them. If not, I don't care what he does.*

The fire burned low, no longer keeping pace with the cold
radiating from the walls. Shivering, Rebecca glanced up at the
clock and was shocked to see the hour. A busy day of cleaning
the cellar awaited her on the morrow, and here it was past
eleven o'clock. With longing, she eyed the remainder of the
letters, knowing it would be best to save them for later.

Yawning, she felt weariness both physical and mental.
Looking around the shadowed interior of the cottage, she
thought of the good life Eli and Jo had made here in Maple
Grove. Eli had come home from the war uninjured, their farm
had prospered, and their love for each other had grown stronger
each year.

What, in her twenty years' experience, could remotely
compare to the richness of their lives? She could barely conceive

of encountering such challenging circumstances, let alone knowing such love. A nervous flutter danced across her ribs when she thought of Hugh Clark and the idea that he wished to court her.

If things were to . . . progress, would they realize such love as Eli and Jo? she wondered. What adventures lay in their future, or did a peaceful destiny await them? Would there be children?

No! She couldn't let herself think of such things. No man would dare sire children with a woman such as she. Some years ago, her parents had taken her to Dr. Neibling, a St. Paul physician specializing in skin diseases. She had overheard the serious-eyed doctor telling her parents it wasn't likely she would pass on the extensive *naevus vascularis* to any children she might bear, but that one could never be certain.

Though she'd never spoken of it to another soul, a dream had died inside her that day. From that point on she had never allowed herself to think of becoming a wife or mother. And now Hugh Clark with his kind hazel eyes had burst upon her life, daring to challenge her way of thinking . . . daring to call her *belle*. Beautiful.

Daring to ask her if she believed God is good.

Troubled, she added another log to the fire, blew out the lamp, and climbed into bed. "Just think about it," he'd urged after she'd first fumbled for an answer, then grown incensed at her failure to find a smooth reply.

For the most part, things had been on an even keel by the time they'd walked back to the farm with their empty buckets. Turning down Eli's invitation to stay for supper, the veterinarian had parted with a warm smile and the promise of joining them the following evening.

Tomorrow. He was coming again tomorrow . . . courting her . . . asking her questions she couldn't answer. The wind gusted again, sounding frigid and mournful. Between the cold sheets Rebecca tried to pray but soon gave up, feeling ashamed. She had always loved Jesus, but what if she did indeed doubt the Father's character?

Then what?

All of a sudden her life had taken a turn she had never anticipated, and she was finding it all too much to take in at once. Even the familiar milieu of the cabin failed to soothe her frayed feelings. Her mind continued to whirl while she sought one position after another, to no avail.

Sleep was a long time in coming.

With a fresh bouquet of asters tucked safely out of harm's way, Hugh drove to the Woodman farm at twilight. Had he pushed Rebecca too hard by asking her about God yesterday? he wondered. It had just popped out of his mouth before he knew it. What about nearly kissing her? Would she even be glad to see him this evening?

By her demeanor, it was plain to see when she was thinking about her birthmark and when she wasn't. Perhaps he was too impatient about wanting her to believe he didn't care about the color of her skin, but he found the Rebecca who wasn't thinking about her markings an absolutely captivating young woman. Saucy, bright-eyed, witty, quick to smile. In his ardor he had pressed his fingers to those lovely lips, unprepared for the tender, protective feelings that had surged through him.

Rebecca. *Belle*. She was so beautiful, and it pained him to know she regarded herself as ugly. His father had been a grown man when his tragedy occurred, so the unkindnesses of others did not penetrate as deeply into his interior as they apparently had into Rebecca's.

Eli hailed him as he pulled in the drive. "Take your team on into the barn," he directed, "and come wash up. Bell's got supper just about ready."

After he'd seen to his horses, Hugh reached for the asters. "At least I can give her these tonight," he said aloud.

"Hoo-eeh! Flowers an' all!" Eli came up alongside the carriage. "You talkin' to yourself in here? Practicin' what you're gonna say?"

"No, but maybe I should," he said reflectively. "Things have been coming out my mouth lately that I have no intention of saying."

"It's been my experience that women manage to have a way of jumblin' a man's tongue," the older man agreed, chuckling. "That Bell, she's somethin', ain't she?"

"She is, indeed."

"Pretty, too, only she don't think much of her looks." Eli grew serious. "Over the years, Jo an' I have come to think of Rebecca as the granddaughter we never had. Stiff as a board, she was, when she first started coming to visit as a little tyke, but she soon loosened up an' became herself. It's funny, she's almost like two differ'nt people at times."

"You mean when she's thinking about her face and when she isn't?"

Eli gave him an assessing look in the lantern light. "You've got a quick understandin', young fellow. Don't let her shake you off."

"I'm not one to be easily shaken off," he replied with the beginnings of a grin. "But she's given it her best effort a time or two."

The older man sighed in agreement. "If you knew the things people have said to her face . . . about her face, well, you could see where a bit of defensiveness comes out when she meets strangers. After a while, once she figures they ain't gonna go on about her face, she settles back down an' is herself. I been prayin' she'll take a shine to you."

"Me too," Hugh replied, holding aloft the asters. "My father always knew how to bring a smile to my mother's face. I figured it couldn't hurt."

"Yep. Flowers. That'll get 'em every time." Eli nodded knowingly. "Come on inside now an' let's have some of that Eye-talian macaroni she's been talkin' about this afternoon. I don't recall eatin' such a dish before, but if it ain't no good, I know she's made a pile of molasses cookies for dessert. An' they're better'n good. Have I ever mentioned what a fine cook Bell is? Jo's taught her just about all she knows, an' . . ."

Hugh let the farmer talk as they walked to the house, wondering if he—and his bouquet of flowers—would be a welcome sight to the dark-eyed girl whose inner wounds he longed to heal.

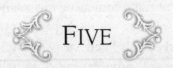

FIVE

"I don't believe I've ever eaten such tasty macaroni before. What do you think, Eli?"

"Not half bad," the older man replied to the younger, "but a bit heavy on the cheese."

"That's just what I like about it," replied the auburn-haired veterinarian, taking a large forkful of tender beef, noodles, and cheese coated with well-seasoned tomato sauce. "Your niece is skilled in the kitchen."

"Jo's turned her into a fair cook," Eli commented with a wink, "but don't swell up her head with too much sweet talk an' flattery."

"Yes, that's probably wise," Rebecca dished back, "considering what happened with those poor molasses cookies this afternoon. Pity . . ."

Her day of cellar cleaning and reorganization had been blessedly shortened by the arrival of Addie Unsell, a woman of impressive strength and work ethic whom Rebecca had known for years. Together they had scrubbed and disinfected the storage area beneath the house, removing every questionable food item and restocking the shelves with fruits and vegetables to last the winter.

Of course, Jo kept that room as tidy as every other and had
already gotten a good start on putting away produce from her
garden. Crocks and barrels lined the walls on a system of well-
constructed shelves and supports, while bunches of herbs hung
from hooks in the ceiling.

Rebecca couldn't explain how her short night of sleep had
given her sufficient energy for her tasks, but when she had
awakened she'd felt well rested and alert. The sharpness of the
disquieting emotions she had experienced the evening before
had dulled, leaving her state of mind contemplative rather than
frantic.

Through the day, she had thought a great deal about Hugh's
question—and Jo's, as well. And if she had forgotten, last
evening, to turn her attention to the startling display of interest
the handsome veterinarian had pressed on her lips, she had
more than made up for it today. Thrice, the kindly Mrs. Unsell
had teased her about woolgathering.

After their work in the cellar was finished, Rebecca had
returned to the cottage to shed her dirty clothes. Washing from
head to toe, she paused to inspect her face in the glass. The
birthmark hadn't changed, of course, but she studied her lips,
her eyes, her hair, pretending to see them as a stranger might.
Her brows rose like elegant wings above nut-brown eyes, matching the lustrous locks framing her face. If she turned her head
three-quarters to the left, she imagined someone might find her
features . . . fair.

"What about 'em?" Eli's words brought her back from her
thoughts as he strained to look over Hugh's shoulder, first
toward the counter, then the pie safe. "Where's those cookies?"

She shrugged, feigning wide-eyed innocence. "Oh, Uncle Eli,
they spread more than usual on the pan, so I thought it best not
to serve them to company. You understand, I'm sure, since you
always seem to find them lacking in some way. Thank goodness

the batch didn't go to waste. Mrs. Unsell said her boys wouldn't mind if their cookies were flat or not."

"Dad blame! You went an' gave the whole batch to Mrs. Unsell?"

From the bedroom came delighted chuckling. "You've been had, you old rascal! Bell hid them in here, and if you don't stop making mischief about her cooking, I just might not tell you where they are."

"I got ways of makin' you talk, Missus Woodman." Eli's grin was roguish as he pushed his chair back from the table. "An' I'm comin' to find me some cookies!"

"I can see why you like it here," Hugh said through his laughter, his hazel gaze falling warm upon her. "I've never met a pair quite like these two."

Rebecca's heart came to another curious standstill as she studied Hugh's face over the supper table, remembering how his fingers had touched her cheek, her ear, her hair. And then how his lips had hovered over hers for just a second. The touch of his fingers on her lips had been warm and startling, and she wondered how his beard would have felt against her cheek. . . .

"A penny for your thoughts, *belle.*"

Dropping her gaze as quickly as she would a hot potato, she felt such a furious blush arise that she was sure her birthmark was indistinguishable from her unblemished skin. Quickly she stood and began gathering dishes, the pounding of her heart more than making up for its seeming cessation a few moments earlier.

His hand stayed hers. "I'd like to talk with you again. If I help you with dishes, will you take a ride with me?"

"I don't know if . . . I . . . where?"

"Just down the road aways. The moon is nearly full and orange as a pumpkin. I'll ask your uncle's permission . . . that is, if you'd like to go."

Nodding, Rebecca couldn't suppress the joyful smile that

curved her lips. Of course she would like to go! For heaven's sake, she was being courted! Actually, truly, really courted. Happiness made her voice clear and strong as she lifted her gaze.

"Do you prefer to wash or dry, Dr. Clark?"

A sheer veil of clouds had come up to mute the moon's vivid coloring. The wind blew from the northwest, tugging dried leaves from branches overhead and scattering them at will to the countryside below. The temperature was low enough to chill the end of Rebecca's nose and transform her breath into puffs of steam, but she found it refreshing.

Or was it simply being in Hugh Clark's company she found refreshing?

A mile passed while they alternately shared the details of their day and slipped into companionable silences. Hugh's grip on the reins was loose as the horses clopped along the gravel road at a slow, steady pace.

"Thank you for coming out with me tonight," he said, glancing over at her. "I wasn't sure if you wanted to spend time with me after the way I seem to blurt out what's on my mind. I must seem insufferably forward."

"You *are* a bit forward."

He sighed, shaking his head. "I fear I've acted like Lucky where you're concerned, bounding too far ahead for my own good. I'll try and slow down some."

"Actually, I've never been courted before, so I don't know the difference," she quipped, trying to lighten the heaviness she heard in his voice.

"We're even, then, because I've never called on anyone, either."

"You can't be telling the truth!" Rebecca was astonished at this revelation.

"I can't? Why not?"

"Because you're so . . ."

"Because I'm so?" The familiar grin reappeared, and he cocked his head toward her. "Because I'm so what?"

"Intelligent. Funny. Nice-looking." She all but whispered her disclosure. "I never thought any man would look at me twice."

"Well, you're selling yourself short, *belle*. I've looked at you more than twice and I plan to keep looking."

The gleam in his eye backed up his words, and Rebecca once more experienced the breathless, heart-stopping feeling with which she had recently become acquainted.

"I've never had the time nor inclination for courting," he said in a more serious tone. "I knew it was a financial strain for my parents to send me to veterinary college, and along with that came courses in medicine, surgery, chemistry, zoology, histology, ophthalmology, pathology, and any other 'ology' you can think of. Heifers were the closest things to girls I saw for the better part of three years."

"But . . . did you leave a girl back home?"

"Yes, I must confess I left Emily Tessier—"

At his reply, Rebecca's bubble of happiness burst. She should have known Hugh Clark's calling on her was too good to be true. Undoubtedly Miss Emily Whoever had the milkiest white complexion in all of Iowa—

"—back when I was eleven or twelve years old. She never did like me much, and I heard she married Tom Stratton a few years ago. So I come to you unencumbered by romantic entanglements. Excluding the heifers, of course."

He was teasing her. Without thinking, she raised her muffler and whapped the fluffy accessory soundly against his arm.

His deep-throated laughter filled the air. "Had you worried, did I?"

"Not a bit," she replied primly, finding it difficult not to succumb to his merriment.

"I've been thinking about something," he said, pulling the horses to a halt. "I know you're here to help your aunt, but next month I'm invited to spend a few days with my sister Deborah in Minneapolis—she's throwing a big party for her husband's thirtieth birthday. If Eli thinks he can spare you, well, I'd be honored to have you accompany me."

"I can't." Every trace of joy, gaiety and anticipation was swept away by an icy current of dread. She knew about the people of Minneapolis . . . how they whispered . . . and pointed . . . and stared.

"As my parents are so far away, I was hoping you might like to meet my sister." She heard the question in his voice but was powerless against the tide of self-disparaging thoughts rushing through her mind.

She felt his touch through the sleeve of her coat. "Rebecca, you look as though you're about to cry. Please tell me what you're thinking."

"I . . . I can't."

"Yet another 'I can't'? Does this have anything to do with what we talked about yesterday?"

She shrugged, fighting back the tears.

"Well, just for the sake of continuing this conversation, I'll assume that little dab of color on your face is the reason you won't consider going to Minneapolis with me."

"Oooh! You and your 'little dab of color'! Did you ever consider that I might know something about Minneapolis—after all, I *live* there!"

"Oh, of course. I'll have to speak to my sister, then, about how she treated you."

"You know I've never met your sister!" she cried in frustration, trying to make him understand why she had to protect herself. A sob choked her voice. "Every so often my friend Jane would talk me into going out in public, to the library, to a concert. My parents frowned on it, but she kept after me. 'Come on, Becky, it'll be fun. This time it's going to be different.' Well, it was *never* different."

Short of breath, she gulped in a lungful of cold air before continuing. "The only place I ever went was to church, and that wasn't much better. Only there I was known as 'John and Henrietta's poor daughter.' Maybe those don't sound like very good reasons for not going out in public, Dr. Hugh Clark, but they're good enough for me."

Two strong arms engulfed her shaking frame, pulling her toward a solid, manly torso. The dampness of her cheeks was absorbed by the coarse fibers of his wool coat, while gentle fingers untied her hat ribbons and stroked her upswept hair.

"Rebecca," his deep voice rumbled in her ear, "if I could take this pain from you, I would. You know all people aren't unkind or insensitive. Think of Eli, Jo, their fine neighbors . . . think of me. How about we do some reasoning together, *belle?*"

Reasoning! What could he possibly say that would stop the flood of unworthiness flowing through her?

"Remember what I asked you the other day?"

"Yes," came her grudging whisper.

"Well, I have another question for you: In whose image were you created, Rebecca Belanger?" His arms steadied her as she struggled to sit up. Reaching inside his coat, he produced a neat square of white linen and handed it to her.

"I suppose you're going to tell me God has a great big birth-mark on his face." She accepted his handkerchief but not his words, dabbing her eyes and blowing her nose in a most unlady-like manner.

"No . . . but I've heard his Son has a few scars."

"You shouldn't joke about God like that! It's just not . . . respectful."

"I'm not joking." Urgency showed in both his tone and

expression, and he took her hands into his. "Think about it, *belle*. How much respect does it give the Almighty to declare that his creation is ugly?"

"What . . . what do you mean?" Rebecca's emotions were a jumble; his concepts struck her ears as both confusing and complex.

"I mean that the Good Book tells us we were created out of God's love—*in his image*—and because of that fact, we are good. Very good, the book of Genesis tells us. Rebecca, our dignity as persons rests in the fact that we are unique, beloved creations of the Creator. When I was younger, I used to take it to heart when people would say cruel things about my father. His burns were extensive—and so are his scars—and more than once I was sent home from school for using my fists to try and shut the mouths of the boys who taunted me for how my father looked. Yesterday you called yourself ugly." His voice dropped. "What was hardest to hear was the certainty in your voice."

"But—"

With a squeeze of his hand, he stopped her protest. "Let me ask you one more question: Do you think your life would be perfect if you didn't have a birthmark?"

"No," she whispered to her lap after a long silence, his syllogism crystallizing into perfect clarity.

"I realize I have known you only a few days, but I would like to know you many more, Rebecca . . . if you'll give me the chance. I'd like to make you a promise, too, if you'll make me one in return."

Taking a shuddering breath, she lifted her gaze to his.

"I promise I won't railroad you into doing anything you don't feel you can do, if . . ."

"If what?" she replied, feeling both weariness and hope course through her. Even in the near-darkness, she could see kindness, acceptance, and conviction shining from his countenance.

"If you promise to never again say you're ugly. You are a lovely young woman, and I want you to repeat that ten times each day." His lips twitched with the beginnings of a grin.

"Only if you promise to limit yourself to asking me one question per day. I don't think I can cope with any more than that."

His laughter rang to the treetops. "I did just tell you I was going to stop blurting out what was on my mind, didn't I?" With a final squeeze of her hands, he shook the reins and set the horses back to walking, regaling her with a tale from his days of veterinary college.

Though traces of dampness lingered on her cheeks, a curious lightness of heart stole over her while she listened to his deep voice. What manner of man was Hugh Clark? She had never met—nor ever imagined—anyone like him. She knew she had much thinking to do about the things he had said, and she might even consider telling herself ten times a day that she was a lovely young woman.

But one thing was for certain: She wasn't going to his sister's party in Minneapolis.

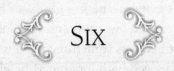

SIX

Autumn dug in its heels, spitting northerly winds from leaden skies. Skeletal branches emerged from trees previously decked in carmine glory, and nightly coats of frost covered the land, freezing the topsoil and turning the creek edges into sharp, delicate lace. For the most part, the *clackety-clack* of threshing machines had fallen quiet. The harvest was in, and winter would soon spread its white cloak over the land.

Hugh Clark knew both joy and sadness as he thought of Rebecca. She had come a long way out of her shell in the weeks they had been seeing one another, yet there was a part of her that he couldn't seem to reach, no matter how hard he tried. When she was at ease, she was a charming and often witty conversationalist, as well as the most empathetic of listeners. As Eli had once said, her heart was pure gold.

She had been deeply moved by the missives her uncle had written home from the war and had shared excerpts and sometimes whole letters with him. After adorning the outside of Jo and Eli's house in anticipation of the upcoming holiday season and the first real snow, she had also placed fresh pine boughs in the window boxes of the cottage. Her delight in having a domicile of her own was evident, the few glimpses he'd had of the interior revealing feminine warmth and hominess.

That womanly touch was something from which he could benefit, he acknowledged with longing as he glanced around his plain bachelor surroundings. Licking his finger, he tested the iron. Not quite hot enough. He sighed, wondering what the Lord had in store for him as far as Rebecca Belanger was concerned. If he was halfway in love before he'd even met her, he was at least three-fourths of the way there now.

As he had come to know her better, he discovered her earnest spirit of wanting to do the right thing. That she had faith in God he did not doubt, but years and years of believing something so wrong about herself—and the Lord—had built roadblocks to her having a vital and growing relationship with him. But what could be done to help her? Worse, her life experiences had only reinforced the falsehood. Jo and Eli had provided a loving sanctuary for her over the years, but only to a limited degree. It was impossible to completely shield Rebecca from the unkindness of others.

His love he offered freely, but even that wasn't enough. What had to change was something inside her, and that was up to God and Rebecca. For now, he must practice patience.

This time the iron sizzled when he touched his wet finger against its surface. Laying a starched white handkerchief across the ironing board, he smoothed its wrinkles and began the series of movements that were becoming second nature the longer he kept house. Fold, press, fold, press. A grin tugged at his lips as he guessed that his *belle* was responsible for approximately half of his soiled hankies.

She hadn't changed her mind about accompanying him to Minneapolis to attend Deborah's party, nor was the topic open for discussion. Whenever he broached the subject, she archly reminded him of his promise not to railroad her into anything she wasn't ready to do. Of course, in return he made her recite a full decade of "I am a lovely young woman."

Much laughter usually ensued such an episode, for she would roll her eyes and pull horrid faces while repeating the phrase. Deep down, though, sadness lingered inside him as he waited for her to truly believe the words she spoke.

Later today he would depart for Minneapolis—alone. But first he would drive out to the Woodman farm, for Rebecca had offered to care for Lucky while he spent the few days away. Who knew? Maybe she had changed her mind about going with him since he'd seen her yesterday. Fold, press, fold, press. Lucky dozed on his rug in the corner, opening one eye from time to time to observe his master's strange movements.

If you don't have hope, you don't have anything.

An oft-quoted saying of his mother's popped into mind as he set aside a handkerchief and reached for another. Perhaps Rebecca was packing right this minute, planning to surprise him. He had written both his parents and his sister about her, asking for their prayers.

He guessed he was just an optimist at heart. With God, anything could happen—anything at all.

And in just a short time from now, he would know if anything had happened.

Watching the light and expectation leave the hazel eyes she had come to find so dear felt a little like dying, Rebecca discovered. She felt sick at heart for refusing to accompany him to meet his family, for no one had ever brought such joy into her life as Hugh Clark.

Over tea with Auntie Jo just a few days past, she allowed that she was falling in love with him. Whether or not he loved her in return she couldn't say for certain, but Jo was convinced he did.

Eli, too. Uneasiness filled Rebecca as she wondered if she wasn't being horribly selfish about this whole situation.

"You're sure, then?"

"Yes."

"Well, then . . . I guess I'll be off."

"I'll take good care of Lucky for you," she called, reaching down to pet the tail-wagging mongrel sitting at her feet. She wished she could say more . . . she wanted to, but couldn't.

"I'm sure you will. So long, Rebecca. I'll be back for him when I return." His shoulders were stiff as he climbed into the carriage, his voice strained. With a nod, he shook the reins and was off.

He said he'd be back for the dog, but would he be back for her?

Lucky started after his master, but she held fast to his collar while the carriage departed. Smart dog—she should have the same inclination. If she valued her relationship with Hugh at all, why didn't she just shout his name? It would be so simple to tell him she'd reconsidered . . . tell him she'd go.

But she didn't.

Smaller and smaller the coach appeared, until it was swallowed by a distant bend in the road. With a deep, sad sigh, she walked up the path to the steps, Lucky trailing behind her. "I don't know how Auntie Jo will feel about having you in the house, but we'll give it a try," she spoke to the canine.

As it turned out, Jo welcomed Lucky's presence in her sickroom. "As long as he behaves himself," she admonished. Obediently, he lay down on the scatter rug next to her bed and closed his eyes.

"Goodness, Bell, you look as though you lost your last friend." The sharp blue eyes swept over her appearance, not missing a thing.

"I think I just did."

"Did you quarrel with Hugh?"

"No, but maybe it would have been better if we had. I know I hurt him by not going . . . only he was too polite to tell me so."

"I see."

She heard no condemnation in her great-aunt's voice, yet Rebecca felt ashamed before her. She shook her head. "I should have gone."

"You could still go, Bell. Eli would take you to the train . . . or heavens, take you all the way to Minneapolis, if you wanted. We'll make out fine here without you for a few days. I can eat on that roast you've got in the oven from now till next week."

Meeting Hugh's sister wasn't what brought up the old, familiar feelings of dread. It was the thought of facing a roomful of staring strangers, enduring the discomfort that would certainly follow.

Is that too great a price to pay for being Hugh Clark's friend? Think of what kind of friend he's been to you . . .

"Auntie Jo, would you excuse me? I need to get out . . . take a walk."

"Mercy, Bell! It's heading on towards dark, and the mercury's dropping like a stone. You don't want to be out there. Why don't you just go out to the cottage for a spell?"

"I need to walk," she persisted, the urge to move—to get away—running high. Her emotions were agitated and comfortless, and she was sure the elements couldn't make her feel any worse than she already felt. "I'll take Lucky with me, and I'll be back to make gravy before you know it." Forcing a smile as she arose from the chair, she called the dog and left the bedroom before the gathering tears spilled from her eyes.

❄ ❄ ❄

Forgetting her gloves was a blunder she sorely regretted. Not immediately, for at first her distressing thoughts overrode all tactile sensations. It was when she turned to walk back to the farm, a good mile down the road, that she felt the cutting edge of the north wind. She also became aware that darkness had almost completely fallen, its descent accelerated by the gray, forbidding skies. A fine mist stung her cheeks.

Shivering, she pulled her hands more deeply into the sleeves of her coat. "Sorry you have to share my misery, Lucky," she said, noticing that the dog headed into the wind with his nose pointed to the ground. He stopped midstride to look up at her, cocking his head with what appeared to be sympathy. His tail beat back and forth like a brush.

"You're such a good dog," she said with a sigh, wondering why animals could display more virtuous traits, oftentimes, than humans. "Hugh sure found himself a champion when he— Lucky!" Her compliment ended in an outcry as the multicolored dog suddenly growled and streaked from the road to the dried underbrush, his missing limb not seeming to hamper his progress whatsoever.

"Lucky! Come back here! Lucky!" she cried again and again, quickly losing sight of him. He barked once, twice, then fell silent. The crashing of branches and leaves grew more faint until the only thing sounding in her ears was the bluster of the wind.

"Now what?" she spoke aloud, pacing back and forth. The mist had changed to tiny, sharp grains of sleet. "Lucky!" she tried again several more times to no avail. They were still a mile from the farm, and his flight had taken him even farther away.

What was she going to do? Worse yet, how could she tell Hugh she'd lost his dog? He had entrusted Lucky to her care, and she had disappointed him in even that simple thing. The sleet grew more forceful, hissing as it hit the trees and ground. "Lucky!" she called again, her cries swallowed by the inclement weather.

She eyed the underbrush and woods with indecision, not knowing the wisest course of action. Not a soul was in sight, nor did she see any houses or lights. Returning to the farm to enlist Eli's help would be futile . . . full darkness would be upon her before she traveled even half the distance. Too, upon returning, how could she be sure of the exact place where Lucky had disappeared?

Her decision was made when she thought again of Hugh, of the hurt and sadness she'd seen in his eyes when he'd departed. She'd wounded him with her refusal to go to his sister's party; she couldn't hurt him again. Into the underbrush she hastened, her skirt catching on spiky stems and branches.

"Lucky!" she tried again, the crisp tangle of low-growing vegetation finally yielding to a stand of hardwood. Here the ground was easier to traverse, but large, dark trunks and branches blotted out what little light there was. Her eyes strained in the gloom. "Oh, Lord," she half prayed, half sobbed, "please help me find this dog. I know what Lucky means to Hugh, and I just can't let him down again."

Bewilderment set in as she looked first to the right, then to the left, trying to discern in which direction to begin searching. "Lucky!" she called, stepping forward, only to trip over a good-sized branch buried by leaves.

"Ooh!" she cried, the heels of her hands stinging from the sudden impact. Dampness soaked her skirt and chilled her knees, intensifying her icy state. Her shoes and socks were sodden.

"Come on, boy," she entreated, picking herself up and moving ahead. "Please, Lucky!" Her progress was slow on the slick forest floor, its relative flatness soon giving way to a significant downward slope. She realized the creek would be ahead of her. Fresh worry filled her. What if Lucky, on his three legs, had tripped or fallen down the hill . . .

Had she just heard a voice? She stopped, grabbing hold of a sapling for support on the slippery incline, while she strained to listen. Again she heard something and very nearly shouted her position, but there was a quality to the sound that raised a chill having nothing to do with the weather.

Instinctively she knew it was evil.

Physical discomforts forgotten, Rebecca shrunk against the trunk of the sapling, wishing it were big enough to hide behind. The voice was louder now, more distinct, its owner clearly in a rage. Filthy words and dreadful threats spewed from his mouth, directed toward the person he was searching for.

Scarcely breathing, she held fast to the tree, guessing that the dangerous-sounding man was sweeping the creek bottom. The dual cover of storm and darkness suddenly became her friend, and amidst her prayer for deliverance, she thanked God for the disguise he'd provided.

After what seemed like endless hours, the man's voice grew faint. Waiting until she no longer heard anything but the hiss of the storm, she collapsed at the base of the tree. Muffled, hacking sobs escaped from her throat as she realized the direness of her situation. Not only was Lucky lost, but she was lost as well.

Tears spent, she resolved to try and find her way out of the forest. If she walked directly up the hill in the direction from which she'd come, perhaps she would eventually make her way back to the road. The danger came in losing her direction once she reached level ground. Too, fear of the snarling man kept her from crying out for help. What if she was trespassing on his land? He'd made no secret of the fact that he was more than willing to do bodily harm. . . .

A branch cracked behind her. With a gasp she spun her head while trying to maintain her hold on the sapling. Fresh fear made her arms and legs rubbery, inefficient, putting her in danger of falling down the bank. Heart flopping within her chest, she tried to speak, to let the terrifying man know she was simply lost, that she meant no harm.

But the point of something thrust suddenly into the small of her back cut off the appeal lodged in her throat.

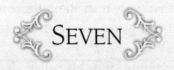

SEVEN

The familiar muzzle was insistent, pressing again and again into her back, her side. Relief washed over her, making her limbs weak and her quivering heart thump in hasty tempo. "Lucky!" she breathed, turning to enfold the dog in her arms. But he would have nothing to do with her embrace.

"You scared the wits out of me," she scolded in a low voice, mindful that the violent-sounding man might still be near. "What are you—ow! . . . Lucky!" she exclaimed as he dug his nose harder into her ribs.

"All right, I'm getting up. Let's get out of here and go home. You *can* get us out of here, can't you?" Her skirt sodden and heavy, she struggled to rise. "Come on, boy," she whispered, climbing a few steps up the hill. Reaching behind her, she felt for his wet coat, her hand swishing nothing but air.

"Lucky, where are you?" Squinting, she could just make out his silhouette, still beside the sapling. "Come *on,* Lucky. Let's go home."

He didn't move.

Exasperated, she step-slid back to the tree, determined to take him by the collar. "I mean it, dog. We're leaving. You dragged me out here in the middle of these woods on this wild chase and made me listen to that scary man shout those awful things that would scald my ears if I weren't so cold. It's storming, in case you haven't noticed!"

As her icy fingers fumbled for his collar, she realized she was babbling. "Come," she commanded in the sternest voice she could muster. But Lucky didn't budge, countering his weight against her tug. Instead, he whined, an urgent, plaintive sound.

"You're hurt!" Realization dawned upon her, redoubling her anxieties. Even if she could make her way out of the woods, she doubted she could carry the good-sized dog the entire way home. She groaned, sinking down beside him. "Oh no, boy, what are we going to do?"

With another whine, he vaulted from her, heading neither up nor down the hill, but sideways. "Ooh!" she cried, lurching to her feet. "You'd better not be hurt, because when I get ahold of you, you're going to think about changing your name!"

Onward they went, perhaps thirty yards, with Lucky whining and staying just out of her reach. Several times she fell, once striking her side hard against a leaf-buried stone. "Lucky," she pleaded through the lancing pain in her ribs. "I don't understand what you're . . . I can't do this anymore. I have to . . . stop." Sinking down upon her haunches, she bowed her head in surrender, utterly lost.

Lucky whined again before returning to her side, nudging the outside of her arm with his snout. "I can't play this game with you," she wept, noticing that the darkness was all but complete. "We're lost, you fool dog, and no one knows where we are."

With another mournful whimper, Lucky bounded from her.

"I'm not following you—," she started to say, her blood running colder than the night when she heard a child's voice.

"Doggy? Is that you again?"

Rebecca shook her head incredulously, wondering if she were imagining things.

"Oh, Doggy, I'm so glad you came back," the child spoke again, the voice coming from just ahead. "I think Pa's gone now. I don't hear him no more."

"Hello?" Rebecca ventured, the pain in her side forgotten. "Is there someone out here?"

Silence.

God in heaven, there was a small child out in this storm. A shudder of horror coursed through her as she realized this little one was most likely the object of the man's pursuit. "That nice doggy is with me," Rebecca called, her voice quavering with both cold and emotion. "His name is Lucky."

More silence.

Having little experience with children, she didn't know what to say to draw the youngster out. "He brought me out here to find you because he knew you were cold," she attempted. "I mean you no harm."

Several long seconds passed before a reply was forthcoming. "Do y'have any food?"

"I don't have any with me, but I know where we can get a nice, warm dinner. Where are you, sweetheart?"

"B'hind a tree."

"Can I come to you?"

Again there was a long pause. "I'll come out, but you have t'tell me where you're at. I cain't see nothin'."

"Lucky will help you find me," she suggested, scrabbling along the hillside toward the sound of the child's voice. "What's your name?"

"Hannah."

"Hannah? What a . . . lovely name." Exertion and distress caused her breath to come in puffs. "Do you know . . . Hannah from the Bible?"

"No." The child's voice was near now, just ahead. Sleet continued to hurtle from black skies, grainy and frigid.

"I'm in . . . front of you now, Hannah. If you keep walking, you'll come right to me."

"What's your name?"

"Rebecca."

"I get whopped for talkin' to strangers."

"Well, we're not strangers any longer. I know your name and you know mine." Her fingers closed around a tiny, thin wrist. Like hers, the hand was bare. Rebecca's heart clenched when she pulled the child close and discovered she wore no coat. Without a thought, she began unbuttoning hers. "We're going to sit by this tree for a spell, Hannah," she said, "and help each other warm up."

"I *was* gettin' cold."

"Why, in this weather, I'm certain you were!" she exclaimed, her nose protesting at the unwashed odors arising from the girl. Bracing her back against a tree, she enfolded the bony child in her arms and lapped the front edges of the overgarment about her. "See? We both fit."

"Oohh!" Hannah breathed as they made a clumsy pitch to the ground. Lucky pressed himself close beside them. "It feels good to be out of the wind."

"Are you lost, Hannah?" she began, not knowing how to ask the youngster about her troubles. The ravings of the girl's father had left Rebecca still feeling weak in the knees. No one, least of all a child, deserved such treatment.

"Not if it wasn't night. I come out here a lot when my pa gets nettled. I go back in the mornin', when he's sleepin'."

She stayed outdoors all night? Rebecca swallowed, judging that the child couldn't be more than seven years old. "Do you have a mother?"

"Yes."

"Well . . ." Her thoughts raced as she searched for words. "What does she do when your father becomes . . . angry?"

"Nothin'. She don't talk much." The child sighed, snuggling more closely. "You smell good. Where does the other Hannah live?"

"I don't *know* the other Hannah because she lived a long time ago."

"Was she nice like you?"

"She was very nice, and she loved God with all her heart. Have you . . . do you know about God?"

The thin shoulders shrugged against her breast. "Pa says mean things 'bout him."

"Sometimes people get the wrong idea about God and believe things about him that aren't true. But God is good, Hannah, very, very good." Holding this neglected child in her arms, Rebecca felt the truth of those words penetrate deep into her heart. What would have happened to this little lamb tonight if Lucky had not brought them together? Was it possible that the Lord had woven together this mysterious set of circumstances to rescue Hannah's life? Her voice broke as she added, "Not only is he good, but he loves you with his whole heart."

"No one loves me." The words were so quiet that she might easily have missed them.

"Oh, Hannah, that's not true," she countered. "It's because of God's love for you that he made you . . . and he knows you better than anyone—inside and out. Why else do you think he sent Lucky and me along tonight? He knew you needed some help and that you were hungry and cold."

"I been hungry other times. Why din't you come then?"

A deep sigh escaped Rebecca, and she wrapped her arms more tightly around the child. "I don't know. I wish I could have come the very first time you were hungry or cold, but for some reason the Lord wanted me to come tonight."

A small hand came up and touched her benumbed cheek.

"You're nice. My Aunt Sharlit, she's nice, too, but Pa don't let her come over no more."

"How about you come over to my house tonight, Hannah? The first thing we'll do is get warm, and then we'll eat a lovely dinner of roast beef and potatoes and gravy. I have a nice, soft bed with lots of covers, and I'm going to tuck you right in the middle of it."

"Is that where Doggy sleeps?"

She couldn't suppress the chuckle that burst from inside her. "I think Doggy can sleep just about anywhere he pleases tonight."

"I like your laugh." The little voice became wistful. "You're lucky. You're big. You got everything an' you know everything, even 'bout God. You're always happy, ain't you?"

"Oh, Hannah, I don't—"

"An' I bet you're a beautiful, beautiful lady. Like a princess."

If you only knew.

Her discomfiture at the youngster's words made the toll of the past hour too much to bear. As soon as they got home—if they got home—Hannah was going to see her face. What would she think of her beautiful princess then?

"I'd say it's time to go have our dinner," Rebecca announced with false brightness. "We'll have to travel a little ways, but I'm going to wrap you as snug as can be in my coat, so you'll stay warm."

"What about you?"

"I'll be just fine, sweetheart. Remember? I'm big."

Her words were a lie . . . all her words were lies. Could she honestly profess the kind of faith she'd presented to this girl? Hugh Clark had made short work of slicing through the tangled ball of falsehoods surrounding her heart, but she still didn't have the kind of faith it took to walk through life with her mottled face, blessing God at every turn.

The frenzy of the sleet and wind striking her was worse than she'd anticipated without her coat, nearly unbearable. As the three made their awkward ascent up the bank, Rebecca prayed aloud the words of Psalm 23, hoping that God in his mercy was indeed with them.

And that if they made it safely from this place, he would lead her in the path of righteousness, for his name's sake.

Eli picked them up a half mile from the farm.

As Lucky had guided Rebecca to Hannah, he led them both from the woods to the road. Without the relative shelter of the trees, the wind was a dreadful thing. Staggering down the road with the weak, exhausted child in her arms more often than not, Rebecca felt as if she must be in the midst of a dream.

But then she saw a light in the distance and heard her uncle's voice calling her name over and over. Never had she seen him look as old as he did when he finally reached them. Without a word, he loaded child, woman, and dog into the box of his wagon, covered them with horse blankets, and turned his team into the wind.

After what seemed like an eternity, they were safely in the barn and the doors had been swung shut. The sound of the storm was subdued but echoing in the tall structure.

"What's your name, sweet pea?" he asked the ragged youngster. Burrowing her head in Rebecca's chest, the girl didn't answer.

"You can talk to Eli, honey," Rebecca assured the child. "He's my uncle, and he's taken us to his home. You'll be safe here, and well cared for." Though they'd been out of the wind a short time, her face was still numb, her words sounding as though they were too carefully formed.

"Can we eat?"

"That's the first thing we'll do once we get into some warm, dry clothes." Over the girl's head she spoke to Eli. "Her name is Hannah. Lucky led me to her in the woods . . . her father was . . . after her."

"Am I right in guessin' you'd be a Scruggs, darlin'?" Eli's weathered face was set in a grim cast.

Against her chest, Hannah nodded.

"She says yes."

"S'what I thought. Think you can manage things, Bell? I've got a call to pay before the weather gets worse."

He intended to go back out into the night? In her opinion, the weather could hardly get worse. "But Uncle Eli—," she protested, fearing for his safety. She fell silent at the fire blazing from the blue eyes beneath the brim of his hat.

"Go on in the house, Bell, and take care of the child. I'll be back when I'm finished."

EIGHT

Once warmed, fed, and bathed, little Hannah Scruggs gave an account of her home life that brought tears of sadness and outrage to Rebecca's eyes. If she lived to be a hundred, she knew the things she learned from this child would never leave her memory.

Hannah and her brother Howie had been forced to hide during Jo's visits to their farm, but the girl recognized Rebecca's kindly aunt and took to her immediately. When Eli opened the back door some two hours after he had rescued them from the elements, Hannah was curled up next to Jo on the bed, sound asleep.

The lamp in the bedroom burned low, and Jo and Rebecca had long since finished their tea. The storm had lessened, bursts of sleet hitting the side of the house only infrequently. Neither of them had voiced their worry about Eli's safety, but Rebecca saw that Jo's relief at his return was as great, if not greater, than her own.

"Aw," he said, coming to the doorway and viewing the scene before him. Deep red suffused his cheeks exposed to the cold and wind, and he reached in his pocket for his handkerchief. "Poor little tyke. I bet she's never been warm an' dry an' all tucked in."

"Just where have you been, Eli?" Jo asked in a quiet voice, glancing at the sleeping child beside her.

"Don't worry, woman, I didn't go chargin' right into the Scruggs place, if that's what you're thinkin'."

Jo's expression said more than any word she could have spoken.

"First I went to see Chet Evans, an' then we got the constable." Eli stepped into the room and pulled up a chair beside Rebecca. She had heard of C. E. Evans, the justice of the peace living down the road.

"And then?" Jo persisted.

"An' *then* we went chargin' into the Scruggs place. Only Barter was out cold from whatever poison he pours down his hatch. The missus jus' sat there starin' at the wall, but their boy—he's about nine—was only too happy to leave. Constable Owens took Scruggs away to lock him up, an' Evans took the woman an' her son to spend the night. Apparently there's an aunt who's wanted the children for some time." He shook his head. "It's my guess she'll get 'em now."

"Aunt Charlotte. Hannah told me about her," Rebecca said softly.

"As soon as the weather clears, Chet's holding an inquest." Eli looked gravely at his niece. "You'll be asked to testify before a jury."

Testify . . . before a jury? With all eyes trained on her? She hadn't had anything like this in mind when she'd scooped up Hannah and taken her home. But before she could protest, he went on.

"Chet suspects this'll be a criminal matter, so you'll most likely be testifyin' again before a Hennepin County jury when the trial comes up."

"I . . . I don't . . . I can't!" she burst out.

Hannah stirred but did not awaken, and Jo gazed at her with

tenderness before turning those expressive blue eyes toward her niece. "Take one thing at a time, Bell," she said. "The most important thing is that you saved this child and her brother from further maltreatment. We'll stand beside you with whatever comes next."

Eli buried his head in his hands. "I could just kick myself for not doin' anything before now. I knew things weren't right at the Scruggses', an' I did nothin'."

Jo sighed. "I stand just as guilty, but neither of us had any proof beyond what we suspected. Thank the Lord for moving his hand of justice tonight by puttin' Bell where he did. I have confidence that Barter Scruggs will get his due."

Eli shrugged. "Maybe."

"Let's all get to bed and have a good night's sleep," Jo suggested. "Perhaps things won't look quite so glum in the morning. Bell, why don't you stay in the house tonight?"

"As long as Hannah's asleep, I think I'll go out to the cottage," she replied, rising, feeling the exhaustion seeping from deep within her bones. Auntie Jo's broken hip . . . handsome Hugh Clark and all his challenges . . . a neglected child driven out into a storm . . . the specter of testifying before not one jury but two.

Why had all these things happened to her since her arrival in Maple Grove? she silently questioned, feeling all thoughts of peace spin wildly away from her. Eli and Jo's farm had always been a sanctuary, a haven from the many adversities of life. The cottage, especially, had always been a retreat where she found joy and renewal.

Why now, she asked the Lord, had her place of peace become home to a host of hardships?

❄ ❄ ❄

Humming, Hugh Clark drove out Territorial Road toward the Woodman farm. The sun shone from a sky of glazed sapphire, and a brisk wind threatened to yank his hat from his head. The evidence of the ice storm that had struck the area had melted, leaving the Saturday morning countryside looking much as it had before he left.

It had been wonderful to see Deborah and her family in Minneapolis, and the time away had given him fresh perspective about his relationship with Rebecca. He looked forward to sharing the details of the party and of his visit, hoping that she would one day soon be willing to meet his sister . . . and his parents.

Only a twinge of hurt remained when he thought of her refusal to accompany him. It had occurred to him that he had only had a few weeks to combat what had been, for her, a lifetime of hurts. If his instincts could be trusted, he suspected she was as interested in him as he was in her. Once the issue of her birthmark was laid to rest, they would be free to pursue whatever the Lord might have in mind for them.

He smiled, thinking ahead to that day.

Lucky was good medicine for whatever ailed a person. His bouncy, optimistic nature and soulful eyes could melt the heart of even the most cantankerous curmudgeon. Hopefully the canine had been able to provide Rebecca with his special brand of comfort.

Sunlight struck the shingles of the Woodman farm, making short work of the morning frost. He didn't have much time to spend with his *belle* today, but perhaps they could make plans for Thanksgiving . . . even Christmas.

To his disappointment, she did not answer his knock at the house. Strange, Lucky wasn't to be seen or heard either. He was ready to turn and seek Eli in the barn when he heard Jo's faint, "Hugh Clark, come in!"

"Hello?" he called, opening the door.

The older woman's voice was urgent. "I saw you coming up the drive. Bell's not here, but the inquest is being held over at the schoolhouse. If you hurry, you can still make it."

Had she said *inquest?* In heaven's name, what had happened

in the few short days he'd been away? Alarm tripped his senses and sent him toward the bedroom with long strides. "Pardon my boots on your floor, Mrs. Woodman, but just what is going on? Why in heaven's name is Rebecca involved with an inquest?"

Five short minutes later he had a summary of the facts and was speeding toward the schoolhouse. If Rebecca had been fearful of going to a mere party, how was she going to handle giving such important testimony before the company of a justice of the peace, a jury . . .

And especially the accused?

The school yard was filled with horses, wagons, and carriages. Hastening up the wide clapboard structure's front steps, Hugh heard an indistinguishable but commanding voice say something, followed by a woman's soft reply.

Trying to make as quiet an entrance as possible, he slipped through the door and took the nearest chair. His heart clenched at the sight of Rebecca seated at the front of the room, giving her answer to the white-bearded, distinguished gentleman occupying the teacher's desk. In his hand was a pen; as Rebecca spoke he made notations in a good-sized ledger.

Approximately fifty student seats faced forward, a full half of them occupied by persons who had long since outgrown their dimensions. On the front and side walls of the room hung blackboards and an assortment of maps. Six large, curtained windows lit the room, beside one of which stood two men.

"I see, I see." The justice of the peace paused after Rebecca's response, stroking his beard. "While you were in the woods, you heard Mr. Scruggs say some things. Would you tell the jury what you heard?"

Rebecca visibly shrunk. "I . . . I couldn't repeat that kind of language."

"For the record, Miss Belanger, you must tell us what you heard."

She closed her eyes, nodded, and took a breath. Upon opening her eyes, she fixed her gaze toward the back of the room, starting slightly when she noticed Hugh. "He said . . ."

If Hugh had been shocked at Jo Woodman's brief account of things, he was sickened as Rebecca recounted the terrifying, vile threats Barter Scruggs had bellowed out to his young daughter. On top of that, the man had chased his own seven-year-old child out into the woods, during a storm . . . apparently not caring if she returned home or not.

"Can you think of anything else?" Justice of the Peace Evans queried after Rebecca had finished.

"She didn't even have a coat," Rebecca added, her voice choking. "A defenseless little—"

"More like a willful, disobedient little brat!" a raspy, sardonic voice interrupted. "And where did you come up with this . . . this *woman* here? Why, I've seen boils on my backside better lookin' than she is!"

Three times the gavel struck the desk. "Mr. Scruggs, I must warn you again not to—"

"Well, look at her!" Scruggs persisted, rising from his chair to face the jury. "All blotched up an' ugly! Are you going to believe a person stained with . . . such devil's marks? She's a witch, a spawn of Satan, doin' his—"

Fury boiled inside Hugh as he watched his beloved endure the unkempt man's verbal blows, and he found himself on his feet, heading toward the front of the room. He noticed Eli had risen from the front row as well, body tight and fists clenched.

"Order!" shouted Evans, banging his gavel furiously. He nodded to the two men near the window, who came forth to subdue the offensive man. The room erupted in a clamor while Evans continued to strike the wooden mallet against the desk.

Through this, Rebecca continued to sit woodenly in her chair, her head bowed in resignation. She wore a dress Hugh had not seen before, a finely tailored blue and gray garment that showed the beauty of her feminine form in a tasteful, elegant way. Her hair gleamed in its upswept arrangement. He imagined she had selected her finest clothing for this ordeal, carefully preparing for the worst yet praying to God it wouldn't happen.

Finally, some semblance of order was restored to the proceedings. "I have heard enough," Evans proclaimed, setting down his gavel in a manner that spoke of his displeasure, "to render judgment in this examination. Besides hearing Miss Belanger's sworn testimony, I have also heard much from both young Scruggs children regarding their home environment." He leveled his gaze at Scruggs. "And I have, with my own eyes, witnessed their home environment. By law and fact, sufficient evidence has been presented to warrant this case a criminal matter, and I hereby judge and determine that the accused, Barter Scruggs, will be tried at Hennepin Country District Court for the neglect and endangerment of his children. He will be detained—"

The remainder of Evans's judgment was lost in the ensuing hubbub, as the two constables forcibly removed Scruggs from the schoolroom. Eli was the first to reach his niece, throwing a protective arm about her. But she did not raise her head, keeping it bowed, as if in shame.

"Rebecca!" Hugh called, pushing past the jurors rising from their chairs. "Rebecca . . . *belle!*"

At that, her head lifted. "Don't call me that anymore," she said, regarding him with hollow eyes. "And if you have another one of your 'questions' for me today, Dr. Clark, I don't believe I've got an answer."

Eli shot Hugh a helpless, sympathetic look as she rose stiffly from the chair and walked toward the door without a backward glance.

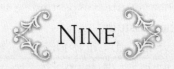

NINE

Finding little for which to be grateful, Rebecca passed Thanksgiving week miserably. Over and over Barter Scruggs's vicious words ran through her mind. All she could think of was that sometime early in the coming year she would have to endure the judicial process—and his malevolence—all over again.

The only bright spot in this entire matter was that Hannah and her brother had been removed to their Aunt Charlotte's home in Dayton. Mrs. Smith had been contacted and had come for her niece and nephew just before the inquest. Her manner was both gentle and kind, and Rebecca trusted that the maltreated children would soon thrive under her loving care. Mrs. Scruggs, her sister, had been taken to the state hospital in St. Peter for treatment of her insanity.

Curiously, not once during the time Hannah had spent with Rebecca had the girl said anything about her face. While the youngster was saying good-bye to Lucky, Rebecca had impulsively offered for her to take the dog until she was settled in. Eyes glowing, the girl had wrapped her arms first around Lucky's neck and then had flown into Rebecca's arms. With laughter, Mrs. Smith declared that Lucky would be set a place at the head of the table for all he had done. Rebecca hoped Hugh would approve of her gesture, suspecting he would have done the same thing in her position.

She need not have feared. Uncle Eli conveyed to her that Dr. Clark was pleased with her decision. He also wished to meet with her at her earliest convenience, Eli had passed on, not able to keep himself from expressing his opinion that she should do so at once.

But November slid into December and she continued to avoid Hugh Clark, and to a large degree, God, as well. From the cottage each night she cried out sad and angry prayers, expecting no replies. It wasn't fair that she'd been born with the curse of such a birthmark, not fair at all. She scoured the Scriptures, reread each of Eli's letters to Jo, finding consolation nowhere. Throughout her days she tended her aunt and moved from one chore to the next, consumed with dread at the upcoming trial.

The wind soughed about the cottage, sounding to her as mournful as her frame of mind. She eyed the bed, knowing sleep was far off. With a sigh, she picked up the stack of her uncle's letters and selected one at random.

February 13, 1865

South Tunnell

    . . . *What you wrote about waking up crying made me feel the most helpless and homesick I have been since leaving Maple Grove. What a tragedy it is that our newest daughter also rests in her grave rather than in your arms. Dearest Jo, please do not lose heart in this battle of life. Remember what cannot be cured must be endured. With the help of our heavenly father . . .*

What cannot be cured must be endured? Her eyes flicked back over that particular phrase, and she wondered how she had missed it in earlier readings. Tears came to her eyes as she imagined Auntie Jo sitting in this same place during the dead of winter, grieving the loss of her children with no sympathy or encouragement save a packet of letters written by a far-off husband whose fate was also uncertain. How had she ever managed?

Just then came a brisk knock at the cottage door, causing Rebecca to start violently. "Who is it?" she called, feeling as though her heart had come to rest somewhere near her tonsils.

"Hugh Clark, Rebecca."

Hugh? What was he doing here at this time of night?

"I spoke to your uncle. We saw that your lamp was still lit. He gave me permission to call on you, but he's standing out on the porch counting off five minutes and not a second longer."

"Just a moment," she called, not doubting for an instant that her great-uncle had said such a thing. In some form or manner he managed to mention Hugh Clark in every third sentence he spoke.

A burst of cold air swept into the cottage when she opened the door, and she noticed a light snow had begun since she'd left the big house. A white dusting covered the russet hair and broad shoulders of the man standing on her threshold. He held his battered brown hat in his hands.

"May I come in?" His breath rose in so many clouds, disappearing into the night. "The mercury's dropped since I left home."

Nodding, she opened the door to allow him entrance. Anxiety knotted her stomach as her thoughts raced one way, then another, trying to devise an explanation—or excuse?—for avoiding him. With her distress also came twin waves of longing and remorse, much stronger than she'd ever expected.

What kind of fool had she been to cut off all contact with a man whose heart contained so much goodness? Her eyes drank in the sight of his familiar form while he stamped the snow from his boots and hung his hat and coat on the peg next to hers. She recalled the sunny fall day they'd met, remembering how he'd all but swept her off her feet with his bold, wooing words. Such romance she had never expected in an entire lifetime.

And then there was his courtship of her in the ensuing weeks. Seeing Hugh Clark tonight brought back every wonderful emotion of the autumn, all the hope and expectancy, every flutter of burgeoning love.

"I hear the Scruggs children are doing well. Best of all, their father is locked up until the trial," he commented, pulling a straight-backed chair up before the stove. Rubbing his hands together, he held them near the radiant heat. "Ahh, much better. Aren't you going to join me where it's not so cold?"

At the mention of Barter Scruggs, Rebecca recoiled inside. The words the evil man had spoken about her appearance slithered through her soul with the coldness of a serpent. *All blotched up an' ugly . . . stained with the devil's marks . . . spawn of Satan . . .*

"Eli was telling me about the letter Mr. Evans got from their aunt this week," he went on, "thanking all of you for what you did for Hannah and her brother. Just think, Rebecca, if not for you . . . who knows what might have happened?"

"It could have been anyone," she said stiffly, dragging her feet toward the warmth of the fire and the pair of hazel eyes regarding her. "Anyway, Lucky found her—he's the real hero."

"Hmm, and you just happened to be in the right place at the right time to meet up with her, during a storm, deep in the woods? And let's not forget who carried the little one to safety. A dog would have been hard-pressed to do that, or for that matter give his legal testimony, *belle.*"

Belle? How could he say that? She was the furthest thing possible from beautiful. Molten anger sparked when she thought of her birthmark and of all the things she had suffered on account of it. Hands on her hips, she found herself unable to take her seat. "I thought I asked you never to call me that again," she challenged. "And what really brings you here tonight? I'm sure it wasn't to talk about Hannah Scruggs."

"Well," he said, his grin cautious, "I did have it in mind to ask you to the Dennings' Christmas party on Saturday night. Martha stopped me one day and—"

She shook her head and held up a hand. "We need to clear the air about some things, Dr. Clark."

"I agree, *belle*," he asserted, also taking to his feet, "and I *will* call you that because I *do* believe you are beautiful." Frustration colored his expression. "Rebecca, I thought for a time that you might have feelings for me. Was I mistaken? Was it only my imagination that you trembled when I touched your face that day out on the road?" He dragged his hand through his hair. "Do you realize how close I came to kissing you that day? I think you do, and what's more, I think you wanted me to."

Rebecca swallowed, remembering through her anger the wild mix of emotions she'd experienced that sun-gilded afternoon.

"*Belle,* I've wanted to kiss you a thousand times since then—no, make that *ten* thousand times—but I've held back, not wanting you to have the wrong idea about me." He held his palms upward in supplication. "Is it too much to hope that you might feel the same about me? I think I've fallen—"

"Stop. Don't say it," she interrupted through the tears spilling from her eyes. Her voice sounded brittle in her ears. "I've been thinking about you, too—"

The tension left Hugh's face and he lowered his arms. A joyous smile turned up the corners of his mouth.

"—and can't help but wonder if you're confusing l-love with sympathy."

There. She'd finally given voice to the terrible suspicion weighing on her mind.

"Are you telling me I've been courting you only because I feel sorry for you?" Gone was the smile, the hopeful expression. Passion burned in his gaze, threatening to incinerate her where she stood.

Years of collective pain and unworthiness caused her to lash out. "Well, look at your father . . . look at me . . . look at your *dog*, for heaven's sake! I'm just one more cripple you've taken under your wing!"

The silence following her angry declaration was broken only by the doleful sound of the wind.

When he finally spoke, his words were so quiet she had to strain to hear them. "I know your life's been hard, Rebecca, and I don't disbelieve anything you've told me. What happened during the inquest . . . well, that was the evil of a sinful man warring with the ugly truths you brought to light. You did a good thing that day; you did the right thing, and such sacrifice always comes with a price. If it makes you feel any better, I wanted to cry for what you endured . . . and for every other painful thing you've endured your whole life long. If I said, 'There's more to a person than how she looks,' I know you would be the first to agree. You know your Scriptures, and you know that God looks on a person's heart."

His next words were choked, delivered in a whisper. "The sweetness that comes from inside you is what I love most about you, Rebecca."

Tears blinded her vision, and she reached the post of the rocker to steady herself.

"But there comes a time, *belle,* when a person has to make a choice about how he's going to live his life. It's when times get hard that you most need to remember whose child you are and what's really important. I can give you more time, more understanding . . . but if I give you as much as you think you need, I know you'll slip away from me. You already are . . . I can feel it happening."

"Hugh—," she began, longing for the shelter of his strong arms and at the same time wishing she could hide for shame at the pain she'd caused him.

"Your birthmark stands between us only because you let it, *belle*. I couldn't care less if your face were orange or pink or blue. It's *you* I love—all of you."

He loved her? "Oh, Hugh," she whispered.

"Can we build from here?" he asked, a hopeful thread running through his voice. "Start again with the understanding that people are going to sometimes treat you badly on account of your birthmark? We both know it's inevitable. But the difference, from now on, will come from in here. From the truth." His fingers tapped against the left side of his chest.

"But . . . it's so . . . hard . . . to . . . be . . . me," she sobbed. "I'll never be . . . normal."

"Pshaw! What's normal? Normal looking? Normal acting? Common? Usual? Ordinary? You're unique, *belle*, and when you're not thinking about your face, you're the most delightful and refreshing person I know. What you need to tell yourself— and believe—is that you are the way you are because God chose to make you that way. You please him, Rebecca."

"But I'm not pleased with the way he made me!"

"Have you ever told him so?"

"Oh, right! And just how would I do that?"

"By laying out your heart before him and telling him everything." A slow, tender smile curved his lips. "Do you really think you're keeping such a monumental secret? After all, he is God. I don't think you'll be telling him anything he doesn't already know. Surrender all your anger and pain to him, *belle*, and I promise he will do a wonderful and beautiful work in your heart."

"But not my face . . . or my arm or my leg, or any of the other places in between!" Once the bitter words had left her mouth, she blushed with embarrassment, realizing she had spoken immodestly. Dropping her gaze, she studied the rug beneath her feet.

"I didn't need any of my anatomy courses to know that the only place that counts lies just beneath your ribs." He paused, clearing his throat. "I'll leave now, but before I go, I want to give you one more thing to think about."

"What?" she finally asked, looking up. If she had thought her heart heavy before, its weight now was insupportable.

Stepping across the distance separating them, he cupped her face in his hands. Gently, slowly, he brought his lips to hers. Instead of being fleeting, however, his kiss was warm and lingering, a promise of glorious things to come. His right hand moved from her face to clasp her hand, and as he lifted his lips, he gazed deeply into her eyes and raised her hand to the hard expanse of his chest. "Feel that, *belle?* I may be a doctor of veterinary medicine, but I don't think what my heart is doing right now has anything to do with sympathy."

Rebecca's breath caught at the strong thudding of his pulse beneath her fingers. His brown-flecked eyes continued to gaze into hers, piercing her, while his warm breath fanned her face. Lord above, how could a person experience such great measures of agony and gladness at the same time?

"Come to the dance with me," he urged. "What's the worst thing that can happen?"

"Someone will make fun of my face."

"So let them. You're going to have a new heart."

"I don't know . . ." she whispered, stepping backward from his embrace. All her old fears and feelings of unworthiness threatened to rise up and choke her. Taking a panicked breath, she blurted out, "I can't . . . I just don't think I can."

Hugh's expression was patient, his gaze steady. "I have faith in you, Rebecca, and I have faith in our God. Give yourself over to him and let him work." With a final nod of encouragement, he retrieved his hat and coat and disappeared into the night.

She didn't know how long she stood staring at the closed door after he left. She wanted the things he had spoken of—and she wanted Hugh Clark, as well. Ever since her childhood she had said her prayers and believed in God, but Hugh's unique perspectives of the Almighty gave her pause.

Give herself over to the Lord? How was she supposed to do that? As far as she understood, she was already his. And even if she knew exactly what Hugh meant, what would be the result of such abandon?

The russet-haired man had outdone himself this time. In only five minutes he had given her more to think about than could be contemplated in five lifetimes.

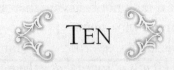

Ten

"Bell, you look as though you have more troubles than Job had boils."

Auntie Jo, who had advanced from strict bed rest to sitting up twice daily, readjusted her roomy yellow wrapper while occupying the comfortable, cushioned chair Eli had carried from the living room to the bedroom. Her affected leg was extended before her, supported by a footstool and two plump, soft pillows. Afternoon sunlight bathed the room in bright hues.

"I know that inquest was a wretched experience for you," she went on, her blue eyes filled with concern. "But Mr. Evans told Eli that if not for what you did, those poor children would still be suffering. I'm sure you're dreading the trial; how could you not? I wish you'd talk to me, honey, and tell me what's going on inside your head." She paused a moment, as if weighing her next words. "Especially about Dr. Clark."

"There's nothing to say," Rebecca spoke in a low voice. "There are just too many problems."

"Are those his words?"

Rebecca was silent as she finished changing the sheets. Since Hugh's visit earlier in the week she had thought a great deal about the things he'd said, not believing that she could live a life untroubled by her port-wine stain.

He also told you he loved you, Rebecca, her inner voice spoke, *and what you felt in his kiss affirmed that a thousand times. You know you love him, too. What are you going to do about that?*

Since that night she'd been thinking about returning to Minneapolis to await the trial. Dr. Janery was pleased with Auntie Jo's progress and had hinted at his last visit that she might soon be up on crutches. With her aunt on the mend, Rebecca's presence in the home wouldn't be as crucial as it had been when the older woman had been strictly bedridden.

It would be for the best if you just pulled out of his life. What he really deserves is an uncomplicated, unmarked woman who won't subject him to a life filled with problems.

"I've been wondering if it isn't time for me to go home," she announced, tucking the blanket at the foot of the bed with a series of efficient movements.

"Yes, I suppose playing nursemaid to an old woman can't be much fun for a young person."

"Oh, it's not that, Auntie Jo," she said quickly, stopping her work to convince the older woman of the truth. "I love being here."

"Do you? Eli and I have noticed that you've seemed most unhappy over the past month or so."

"It's not you, really. It's just . . . well . . ."

"Hugh Clark," the white-haired woman supplied with a knowing expression. She nodded. "You know, Bell, when Eli's courtship turned serious, I wanted to bolt like a jackrabbit into tall grass."

"You did? How come you told me you loved him when you were a young girl—even before he started courting you?"

"Because I did love him back then. It was when he started making noises about settling down that I got scared." With a half smile, she let her head rest against the back of the chair. "Goodness, that was a long time ago."

"But you married him . . ."

"I did, indeed, after doing some wrestling with the Lord."

Rebecca took a seat at the end of the bed. "*You* wrestled with the Lord? I don't know anyone with stronger faith than you."

The ticking of the clock was the only sound in the room for a long moment. "Faith isn't always an easy process, Bell," Jo finally answered. "Time and many painful experiences go toward its building, and I've come to realize that the greatest gains are made through times of greatest adversity. To be honest, I wrestled with the Lord about getting married, moving to Minnesota from Vermont, losing each baby, and sending Eli off to war. After many unhappy years I finally quit my wrestling because I realized God was going to have his way no matter what kind of fuss I put up, and that it was a whole lot easier on all concerned if I just went along with as thankful and cheerful a heart as I could."

Rebecca was quiet, trying to reconcile the woman she'd just heard described with the great-aunt she'd known from her childhood.

"Did you get a chance to read through Eli's letters, honey?" Jo asked.

She nodded, answering slowly. "The one Uncle Eli wrote you from South Tunnell, where he urged you not to lose heart after your baby . . . well . . . was that a time you were wrestling?"

"It was a time I wished more often to be dead than alive."

"Oh . . ." Rebecca was speechless at this disclosure.

"Burying our third baby while Eli was off to war was the blackest moment of my life. The day I gave you the letters, Bell, I challenged you to decide whether God was for you or against you. I'll confess to you now that during the winter of '65 I believed he'd set his face against me."

Rebecca tried imagining such despair. They had dared much, Eli and Jo. Moving halfway across the country, far from family and friends, staking a claim and settling the land. Conceiving child after child, only to lay each one in the ground. Shouldering the burdens of the oppressed and believing in that cause so deeply that Eli had enlisted in the Union Army.

And yet through all this they'd loved, and continued moving forward, and grown in their faith. When she thought of such bravery and conviction, Rebecca felt very small indeed. What was the pain of a birthmark compared to all that?

Auntie Jo picked up her Bible and went on. "While I waited and hoped for Eli's return, I chose to read Job, of all things . . . maybe because I thought I could identify a bit with him. Do you recall the last chapters of the book, where God speaks?"

"When he tells Job to gird up his loins like a man because he wants to ask him some questions?"

"It's more than that, dear. The Almighty Creator challenges Job, a mere man, to give him the *answers* to unanswerable questions . . . beginning with 'Where wast thou when I laid the foundations of the earth?' Day after day I read those chapters and wondered how I would reply if I were in Job's place. One day my hardness of heart broke and my cry to God was the same as Job's: 'I know that thou canst do every thing, and that no thought can be withholden from thee.' From the depths of my despair I repented, Bell, and the Lord heard me. He restored my faith, making it stronger than it had ever been before." The Bible lay on her lap, unopened, while a single tear traced down the wrinkled cheek.

Was that what Hugh had been talking about? In her mind, she heard her beloved's words from the cottage. *After all, he is God. I don't think you'll be telling him anything he doesn't already know. Surrender all your anger and pain . . . I promise he will do a wonderful and beautiful work in your heart.*

Moisture gathered in Rebecca's eyes as she longed for the same release. She felt so weak, so tired, so unworthy. Her shoulders slumped and she hung her head in misery.

"Honey, I know that birthmark has made your life painful." Auntie Jo's voice was tender. "But there is one who is greater than all that, one who promises that his yoke is easy and his burden light. I know of your love for Jesus, child, but there is a kingdomful of treasures that are yours for the taking. To claim them you must walk in victory, not defeat."

"How?" she sobbed, dropping her head to her lap. "I want that more than anything."

"Then we won't wait a moment longer. Come over here, my love, and kneel beside me. The one who calls you knows of your suffering, Bell. He suffered much himself. . . ."

Her limbs felt leaden as she moved. "But what do I *do?* I just don't know what to do."

Her aunt's hand was warm upon her head as she knelt before her. "Just speak to him as plainly as you would me, child. Tell him of your sorrows, your fears, your longings. Confess the error of your ways. Tell him of your desire to live as he wants you to—in joyful freedom."

"Father," she began in a whisper, her mind and spirit in turmoil, "my faith in you is weak." Fresh tears fell. "I haven't been very good about accepting the way you made me, and I think I've blamed you for all my unhappiness. I'm . . . so very sorry, and I beg your forgiveness. Instead of wishing I was different all these years, I should have been asking for your help to live as you wanted me to. Hugh and Auntie Jo have helped me see how much you love me—and my part in rescuing Hannah shows me how dearly you care for each one of us. And that you would send a man like Hugh into my life—"

The thought of such undeserved love caused her to weep at length, all the while her aunt's gentle fingers stroked her hair.

"Please help me see myself as you see me," she finally spoke, "and live as you want me to live. Amen. Oh—and if Hugh Clark is still willing to court me, I would be grateful for another chance in that area as well. Amen."

"Oh, honey, you're going to be just fine," the older woman whispered, wiping her eyes with her other hand.

"For the first time, I have to agree with you." In her heart dwelt a smoothness, a peace she had never before known.

"Now what is to be done with our handsome veterinarian?"

"I . . . I don't know. He invited me to the Dennings' party tonight. He also told me he loved me, Auntie Jo," she confided. "I . . . just don't know how—"

"Hold on! Is this the old Rebecca talking, or the new Rebecca?"

Rebecca felt a chagrined smile steal across her lips while her aunt went on. "Martha told me the Rand Trio will be providing the music at her party. Eli and I have tapped our toes to their tunes many a time. Now, mind you, this is just my opinion, but I think you look particularly fetching in that dark pink dress with the cream stripes."

"Are you saying I should go to the party?"

"Absolutely." The blue eyes twinkled with glee. "And just maybe we'll be having ourselves another type of celebration before too long."

Instead of pushing aside the wave of joy and hope that rose inside her at her aunt's words, Rebecca allowed the marvelous feelings of anticipation to wash over her. With that came the memory of the lingering kiss in the cottage . . . the feel of Hugh Clark's heart beating beneath her fingertips . . .

She glanced at the clock and froze.

"How am I going to get ready in time?" she burst out. "What am I going to do with my hair? Oh, no! How will I get word to him that I've changed my mind?"

Jo chuckled. "Don't fret. Eli will drive you over to the

Dennings', and you can just tell Dr. Clark you've changed your mind—in person."

A scant hour later, Rebecca was ready for the party. Eli whistled when she appeared in the kitchen, his wrinkled face lighting with pleasure. "I declare, Bell, I never seen you lookin' so lovely! That young fellow won't be able to take his eyes off you."

"Do you really think so?" The last rays of the setting sun shone through the window, catching her in the face as she twirled around.

"I know so. Now let's get you over there! Can you hold down the place for a while, Mrs. Woodman?" he called.

"Take your time, Eli. Have a cup of eggnog for me while you're at it. And Bell, remember that you're walking in victory, dear. I'll want to hear about your evening the minute you get home. Promise you'll wake me up?"

"I promise."

The horses were eager to stretch their legs in the frosty twilight, and the trip to the Dennings' took scarcely a quarter hour. Recalling the events of the stormy night last month, Rebecca felt a shiver as they passed by the darkened Scruggs place. What wickedness those children had suffered! Thinking of Barter Scruggs brought another chill and the memory of his words during the inquest.

Many of Jo and Eli's neighbors she knew, but there would no doubt be many there at the party she didn't. Once again she would have to endure the stares, the snickering, the whispers. In her excitement to surprise Hugh, how had she forgotten what her life used to be like? *Remember you're walking in victory . . . there is a kingdomful of treasures that are yours for the taking . . .*

Did God have Hugh Clark in mind as one of those treasures?

"Looks like there's quite a crowd," Eli commented as they turned in the drive. Warm yellow light spilled from every window of the Dennings' two-story structure, and horses and conveyances of every type were parked about their yard. Eli caught the tune of the cheerful carol being carried on the crisp night air and began humming "O Come All Ye Faithful" while the all-too-familiar apprehension began building inside Rebecca. Could she really walk into a crowd with her head held high?

As if Eli read her mind, he broke off from the chorus and turned his head. "I expect you're gettin' cold feet right about now."

"How did you know?"

"I been around a few years, Bell, an' been through a few things myself. Times like this is when we gotta let the Holy Ghost lead us on."

Rebecca smiled at her uncle's earnest expression. "Don't worry; I'm not going to bolt. I figure the worst that can happen is that someone will make fun of me."

"That's right, honey—sticks an' stones."

However, her nervousness mounted as Martha Denning warmly swept them into the house. A full three dozen adults had assembled, and Eli made his greetings as he led her through the throng. Rebecca tried not to worry about what people might be thinking of her face, but it was difficult. A fine mist of perspiration broke out on her forehead and dampened her back. If Hugh wasn't here, she reasoned, she would have Eli take her back home at once.

The musical trio played before the window in the Dennings' large sitting room; the room was lit with several wall lamps and the lovely glow of candles. Catching sight of Hugh across the room, Rebecca felt the tension drain from her like water from a pipe. An enormous grin split his face when he saw her, and he raised his arm in greeting just as "Deck the Halls" came to its drawn-out conclusion.

"Look at that lady, Mama!" cried a little boy with a loud voice. He stood before Rebecca, pointing toward her cheek. The relative quiet left in the wake of the carol became dead silence as people glanced at one another with stricken expressions. "Would you look at her face! She looks just like a purple Holstein!"

But instead of hurt, a mysterious and joyful laughter bubbled up from inside her. Kneeling down, she smiled at the youth. "Why, I've often thought the same thing myself. I guess it pleased the Lord to make me with a few dabs of color."

"What does it feel like? Can I touch it?" he asked, stepping forward. His mother, nearly apoplectic with embarrassment, failed to reach him before his fingers swept across Rebecca's cheek.

"Hey, it doesn't feel any different at all," he said, disappointment evident in his voice.

"Mind your manners, Monty. This is the lady who put Barter Scruggs away," an older youth said from behind the boy. His nod toward her was respectful, serious. " 'Member what Pa said . . . she's got more guts than you can hang on a fence."

"I'll second that. I was in the jury along with your pa," a deep voice warranted. "Miss, you done the bravest thing I think I ever saw."

Before she knew what was happening, the room erupted with whoops, cheers, and an abundance of applause. One of the fiddlers elbowed the banjo player, and the trio launched into a lively rendition of "For He's a Jolly Good Fellow." Person after person moved forward to shake her hand, offering her congratulations and welcome.

And from across the room, a pair of hazel eyes beamed their love and approval.

Epilogue

In the pale moonlight outside the cottage, Hugh enfolded Rebecca in his arms and chuckled. "I'd say you just gave 'the belle of the ball' a whole new meaning tonight, Miss Belanger. That was some party." His tone became mischievous. "Remember the day we met . . . how you took me to task over by the barn there? You spit out that French so fast and hard I could barely understand what you said."

Rebecca smiled and gazed up into the face of her beloved. "I must confess to wondering at your intelligence . . . and being more than a bit bowled over by your forwardness."

"Well, that was really Eli's fault. Thanks to him and all his talk, I was halfway in love with you before I helped you down from the wagon—only you didn't know it yet." He pressed a kiss against her forehead. "I doubt I'll ever be fluent, but I must tell you I've been brushing up on my French. I thought it only fitting."

"Fitting for what?"

"For this." He knelt on the packed snow outside the threshold. "I spoke to your uncle tonight, and I intend to speak to your father, as well . . . but I can't wait, *belle*. *Je t'aime*, Rebecca. *Acceptes-tu d'être ma femme?*"

"Marry you! Are you . . . do you really . . ." Words failed her as she realized this moment was really, truly happening. A gentle wind blew through the trees overhead, its sound as familiar and comforting as the Voice in her heart.

"Yes, Hugh Clark, I'll marry you," she said with confidence and joy, taking hold of the hand he extended. "I love you, too," she managed to add just before she was engulfed in his embrace.

Somehow, she could imagine no better life than the one she was living.

Best Ever Molasses Cookies

1 cup sugar
1 egg
¾ cup shortening
2 tbsp. molasses
2 cups flour
1 tsp. cloves
¼ tsp. salt
1 tsp. cinnamon
1½ tsp. soda
1 tsp. ginger

Cream shortening and sugar. Add egg and molasses; beat well.
Mix in spices and dry ingredients. Shape into approximately
one-inch balls, roll in sugar. (During the holiday season, I often
use red or green decorating sugar.) Bake at 350 degrees for 9–10
minutes.

A Note from the Author

Dear reader,

Even though an author thinks she might know at a story's outset how the tale will end, many surprising things often occur while writing everything between page 1 and the end. In this case, a box of musty treasures led to many twists and turns in *The Beauty of the Season* that I never expected when I wrote the proposal.

I was casually acquainted with the materials my grandmother, Ivy Evans Tasler, had collected as a genealogist and amateur historian. Maple Grove, Minnesota, is a real town that was settled, in part, by her grandparents—Chester and Helen Eddy Evans. Many of Eli's letters from the Civil War were patterned after Evans's letters home to his wife. I must tell you that the initial paragraph of the first letter Rebecca read in chapter 4 was taken verbatim from Chester's first letter home to Helen. I felt it captured the sadness and emotion of the troops' departure in a way fiction could not improve.

C. E. "Chet" Evans indeed served as justice of the peace of Maple Grove from 1875 to 1891. The justice logbook is a fascinating account of many civil and minor criminal offenses committed throughout its thirty-plus years of recording.

It was a pleasure to discover that my great-great-grandfather was a gifted writer. His letters and essays were well written, touching, and often insightful. He was also a man of faith, who clearly trusted in God's providence. As a tribute to him, I would like to share with you the poem he wrote Helen on their fiftieth wedding anniversary:

Fifty Years

Full fifty years of wedded life
Dear wife we've spent together
We've seen adversities, dark clouds,
And love's bright sunny weather.

We've had sad days and joyous ones
And laughed at fate's hard measure:
We've filled the cup of life with love
And quaffed it off together.

We've lived the lonely frontier life
And heard war's bugle call,
We've thanked God for the victories
That proclaimed peace for all.

We have kind friends and children dear
To fill our earthly measure
And when we drain the cup of life,
May we pass on together.

C. E. EVANS
December 25, 1910

May the peace and joy of this holiday season be yours, and may your life be blessed with the richness of a deeper relationship with our risen Savior, Christ Jesus the King.

In him,
Peggy Stoks

Wishful Thinking

To Jane

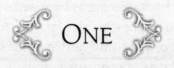

ONE

"Howdy-do . . . Miss Wilcox?"

"Afternoon," Elizabeth Wilcox replied after a pause, looking over the smiling, nattily dressed gentleman who had walked up the drive along the south side of her modest house.

The fellow's appearance was neat to a fault. Even in the wilting August morning, his suit and shirt were well pressed, and a fine serge hat sat at a jaunty angle upon his head. Though the wind stirred up a fine dust from the road, it appeared as though none had dared settle upon his dapper clothing. As he drew close to the porch, she noticed he held his left hand behind his body.

This spruce man must be the widower who had made the 150-mile move from Minneapolis, slightly north and a good ways east of Marshall, Minnesota. Hattie Crabtree had heard from Jane Pruitt, who had heard it first from Emma Graham, who had it on good authority from Irvetta Auerbach, that a Mr. Determan of the Twin Cities had purchased the house and twenty acres next to Betsy's property. The news had set a full two-thirds of the Marshall Ladies' Sewing Circle buzzing like so many bees.

"Elmore Determan's the name," the bewhiskered gentleman announced, extending the nosegay of orange coneflowers he had hidden behind his back. "Seeing as how we're going to be neighbors, ma'am, I brought these daisies for you. And might I say, while it's true the Lord's earthly garden holds such a variety of radiant flowers, all pale in comparison to your delicate beauty."

Struck dumb by his flattering words, Betsy's hand stilled on the handle of the barrel churn she had been steadily turning. For a few moments the liquid inside continued sloshing, then it too fell silent, overtaken by the sibilant sounds of innumerable insects and conjoined twitters of robin, meadowlark, and bobolink.

Radiant flowers? Delicate beauty?

What nonsense.

"Rudbeckia," she responded, throwing out the first thing that came to her mind. "Rudbeckia is the proper name for those flowers, Mr. Determan. You picked them down near my ditch, didn't you?"

His smile grew only wider, creasing his face in a most pleasant way. "Yes, ma'am, I did."

She noticed that his eyes were every bit as blue as the summer sky behind him. How did a man full grown manage to have about him the air of a carefree, impenitent little boy? she wondered. Extending the bouquet toward her, he lifted his eyebrows. A green inchworm and two black spiders adorned his offering, each crawling its own direction across the profusion of petals. Lord only knew what other insects his posy contained.

"Will you take them? Please?"

Gesturing toward the stairs, she sputtered, "You can set them there. I have to get this butter churned."

"I'd be happy to give you a hand." A second later, his jacket lay next to the flowers on the wooden steps, and he rolled up his sleeves. His arms were strong for a city man, she noticed, and sun-browned. His shoulders, too, appeared to be the sort that had managed their fair share of work over the years.

He chuckled. "Surely you don't eat all this butter yourself,

Miss Wilcox. Why, you'd be fat as a little tusker if you did. Move on over now, ma'am, and let me have a go at this."

Under his capable hand, the crank turned smoothly and the rhythmic, sloshing sound resumed. If Betsy was flabbergasted to have had to slide quickly down the bench as her new neighbor made himself at home, she was even more shocked when his voice lifted in song.

"Shall we gather at the river,
Where bright angel feet have trod,
With its crystal tide forever
Flowing by the throne of God?
Yes, we'll gather at the riv—"

"I most certainly do not eat all this butter myself, Mr. Determan," she said, finally finding her tongue and interrupting the spiraling chorus. "I keep a small amount for myself and sell the rest," she replied, shooting her new neighbor her most disapproving expression.

"Is it good?"

"Why, most certainly!"

"I might buy some if it's good." His twinkling gaze lit upon her, disarming the tart response on the tip of her tongue. For heaven's sake, Mr. Elmore Determan had a *dimple* right in the middle of his cheek.

What manner of man brought flowers to an utter stranger of the opposite sex, took over her chores, and had the indecorous manners to sing one of those newfangled gospel songs at the top of his lungs? The fatuous type who frequented camp meetings and tent revivals, no doubt. Why, the old fool had to be seventy years if he was a day.

You're no spring chicken yourself, Elizabeth Wilcox.

Glancing down at her own knuckles that had grown more knotty with each passing year, she realized she had passed her sixty-eighth birthday in May. With her only sister and both parents having passed into the hereafter, there was no longer anyone to make an occasion of the Ides of May, as her father had always referred to the day of her birth.

For over thirty years she had taught school. Teaching had been a good vocation, and her savings had enabled her to purchase this modest homestead and acreage where she had spent the past ten years of her life. There had been a time when she had grieved over the realization that marriage and motherhood had indeed passed her by, but all in all, she considered herself richly blessed by the many pupils she'd had the occasion to teach. Some of her former students wrote to her still.

And even though she had retired from the schoolroom, every Sunday morning she led twenty-three students, ages seven to twelve, in ninety minutes' instruction of Bible teachings, Christian living, and, for good measure, a sprinkling of the virtues of convention and etiquette. Today's youth were simply not being raised with the same values that had been instilled a generation earlier.

She glanced askance at her new neighbor, whose white beard waggled as he whistled the remainder of his tune. With what kind of manners had he been raised? she wondered. Did he suffer from a lack of instruction, or had he cast aside a proper upbringing in favor of living so impetuously? What had his wife been like?

Gracious, why did she care?

"What do *you* think heaven will be like, Miss Wilcox?" Mr. Determan inquired in a cheery tone. "Do you expect we'll gather at the beautiful, silver river with all the saints?"

"I'm sure I don't know."

"But you believe Christ died for your sins, don't you? That the Son of God came to give hope and peace to fallen mankind?"

"Yes, good sir, I am well aware of my catechism."

"Well, praise the Lord for that! Hallelujah!"

Even as she wondered at the intrusive and highly personal nature of his subject matter, he continued speaking.

"Yessiree, I used to think all the Jesus-dying-for-my-sins business was all a bunch of fiddledy-hoo, until I met the man."

Betsy felt her face draw into a prunish expression. "You've met Jesus Christ?"

Elmore Determan's blue eyes twinkled, and a merry smile creased the tanned, wrinkled face. "Oh yes, I have. I met him at a revival back in '75, and he's been at my side ever since."

Betsy cleared her throat and lifted her brows. "You have no way of knowing I taught school for thirty-four years, Mr. Determan, nor that my greatest vexation with students was caused by careless, imprecise speech. Now, there's only you and me on this bench. I do not see the Lord. Perhaps what you meant to say was that you experienced some sort of religious fancy, or that after years of dissolute living you repented of your wicked ways and decided to follow the path of righteousness?"

"No, I meant what I said." His hand stilled on the churn while his expression waxed gleeful . . . and if she wasn't mistaken, just a bit mischievous. "I take it maybe you haven't met him up close, then. Perhaps one day I can introduce the two of you."

She was right: he *was* one of those religious extremists. How otherwise perfectly sensible people could get caught up in such mania was beyond her. Church was church, and religion was religion. It was only seemly to follow the customs and heritage set forth by the noble men and women who had gone before them. Talking about the Lord as if he were sitting right on this bench? That was . . . what was the word he had used? *Fiddledy-hoo.* She allowed herself the pleasure of a slight, disdainful sniff at his outrageous comments.

"I make it a habit of introducing him around, on the off chance a person might not be acquainted with the great Jehovah. I won't be on this green earth forever, but I aim to spread the

Good News as far and wide as I can before I go. Yessiree, this old ticker of mine could give out any minute," the white-haired gentleman went on, winking broadly as he patted his chest. "And then, as I always say, it'll be 'no more Elmore.'"

His laughter was booming, genuine and infectious, causing her pursed lips to loosen a little. *No more Elmore.* How much mileage had he gotten out of that particular witticism over the years? she wondered, watching him in his merriment. His features were pleasantly arranged, she decided, noticing his chin, his nose, the shape of his brow. And as hale and spry as he appeared, she would not be surprised if his heart should beat another full score of years.

"This may be wishful thinking on my part, Miss Wilcox," he said, raising snow-white brows and gazing into her face with those lively blue eyes. "But as we're going to be neighbors, it seems only right that we should become better acquainted. I was wondering if I might bring over a few ears of sweet corn around suppertime? If you were to supply the butter and salt, we could have ourselves a feast of grain. See, that way, too, I could gauge whether your butter's any good—"

"I'll have you know my butter is excellent, Mr. Determan. You will find none better in these parts." As she fired off her retort, she realized she had just provided tacit consent for the wily old man to enjoy his sweet corn at her dinner table. Oh, why had she taken his bait? It was a well-known fact that single men and widowers were ever in pursuit of a woman's good cooking.

Her neighbor stood and stretched his long legs. "Well, then. I look forward to sampling your fresh, good butter, Miss Wilcox. You have a big pot of water boiling, and I'll shuck the corn before I come. See you about five?"

Betsy could think of nothing to say as he paused at the bottom of the stairs, favoring her with another of his winning smiles. Nor was she able to formulate a suitable response as he tipped his hat and strolled past the hollyhocks. Only when he reached the dirt drive and lifted his arm in a confident wave did she shake her head in disbelief at what had transpired.

For all her elocutionary skills, she'd just been rendered speechless.

Returning to her original position on the bench, she set her hand on the metal handle of the churn and stared after her new neighbor. She may have been outmaneuvered this time, but as sure as the dawn, she would not allow such a thing to happen again. She would be well prepared when Elmore Determan returned with his ebullient faith, his jovial manner, and however many ears of husked sweet corn.

Yes, Elizabeth. You'd best be prepared.

Giving the crank a halfhearted turn, she experienced a strange, winded feeling as she recalled her neighbor's blue gaze. Heaven above, was it possible for a person to be thrown completely askew by a pair of eyes? a dimple? a sprightly grin? Or had she simply become muzzy-headed from the heat?

Turning hard on the crank, she was surprised to find herself humming the very tune to which she had, a short while ago, taken exception.

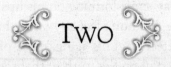

TWO

Elmore whistled as the pile of cornhusks at his feet grew larger. It was too hot to be indoors or even sit on the front porch, so he'd moved his cane rocker from beneath the eaves out to the yard, where he rocked contentedly in the welcoming shade of an elm tree.

For all the years he'd spent living in the city, he had not forgotten the uniqueness of a late August afternoon on the prairie. Wide open and windy, yet sultry, rich, and heavy. Something about this month was peculiar from all others, he mused, perhaps due to the gentle yet persistent welling up from the earth and its growing things, a ripening into maturity that stippled the air and piqued the memory.

He closed his eyes and recalled Augusts gone by—Augusts he had spent living on the plains rather than in the noisiness of the city. Some of the prairie years he had spent coopering; others he had farmed. He couldn't complain about his years of city work or city living, but he preferred the sight of the spreading land, the tall waving grasses, the freedom of the wind.

He could no longer deny he was slowing down. In a few weeks' time, he would celebrate his seventieth birthday. His mouth formed the word: *seventy*. How could that be? he wondered, a faraway smile forming on his lips. Where had the years flown? Inside, he didn't feel any older than he did as a young man of nineteen, but his aging, more-often-than-not-aching body insisted upon the truth in that seemingly unbelievable concept: he would soon begin his eighth decade of life.

Was it in the Lord's plan that he would live until ninety? a hundred? He chuckled. Ah, such things were not for him to know. With the wind in his ears and the weight of a succulent ear of corn between his hands, he raised his face and gave silent thanks to the Creator for giving him life and for allowing him to return to the prairie he had always loved. *This* was where he wanted to live out the remainder of his earthly years, however many there may be.

Opening his eyes, he glanced at the modest property he had purchased. A house with three rooms. Pasture on either side of the small barn out back. An empty chicken coop. He didn't need more. As the previous owner, an aging widow, had done, he would rent most of his twenty acres to the farmer living north of him. Upon making the real estate transaction, he had learned that James Pennington, the farmer, also rented farmland from other neighbors . . . among them, Miss Elizabeth Wilcox.

A pleased expression settled upon his face as he thought of the intriguing, exacting woman he had met today. He didn't know what had possessed him to stop and gather a bouquet of daisies—*rudbeckia*—he amended, recalling the crisp yet lilting sound of her voice, nor what had inspired him to use such embellished speech upon making her acquaintance. He only knew that with each response she gave, he found himself enjoying her company all the more. And to tell the truth, he had rather enjoyed making mischief with the very proper Miss Wilcox. He imagined she had endured enough naughty schoolboys over the years for his rascality to be of too much consequence.

Setting down the husked ear of corn, he reached for another

and paused to examine the tuft of silk protruding from the end. It had dried to a crispy brown, indicating its readiness. Margaret, his wife, had been in her prime when he'd lost her to childbed twenty-four years ago, along with his only son and namesake. His smile faded. Meg had been thirteen years younger than he, filled with life—and plenty of sparks and fire to go along with all her vivacity.

The pain of losing her had faded over the years, yet sometimes . . . he sighed.

Sometimes, when he really stopped and thought, he was aware of his loneliness. Most times, it did not trouble him. After Meg's passing there had been plenty to keep him occupied. Raising his daughter, Clarice, keeping food on the table, and, of course, spreading news of the Savior wherever he could. A gentleman at his church back in Minneapolis had exclaimed some years ago, "Determan, it seems as though your objective is to distress the comfortable and comfort the distressed!"

He had never forgotten those words, nor had he quite known in what manner the fellow had rendered them. But if that was what his plain talk about Jesus had accomplished over the years, then perhaps his outspokenness wasn't an entirely bad thing.

He thought of Clarice and sighed again. Clarice and her husband lived in New Ulm, a thriving town situated approximately halfway between Marshall and Minneapolis. No doubt, as soon as her schedule permitted, she would be traveling westward on the Number Eighty-One to inspect her father's domicile and cluck her tongue.

Allowing his thoughts to amble, he found himself wondering how Clarice and Miss Wilcox would get on. One eyebrow went up as he decided most likely, not well at all. Thankfully, there would be no occasion for them to meet. Humming an even livelier rendition of the gospel he had sung for his gingery neighbor this morning, he began shucking the ear of corn in his hands.

Yessiree, taking his supper next door tonight would be just the
thing. In fact, he rather hoped their conversation would continue on the same note on which it had left off.

"Rudbeckia," he said aloud when he had closed the chorus,
trying to mimic the exact precision of speech and depth of
reproach she had uttered in that single word. Ribbons of green
cornhusk and whitish yellow silk fell to the ground while he
sought just the right diction. "Rud*beck*ia. Rud*beck*-ia." There.
That was it—"Rud*beck*-ia."

"Rud*beck*-ia," he repeated in falsetto, delighted that he had
captured the essence of her articulation. Genuine laughter
bubbled up from inside him, and he again realized how very
much he was looking forward to spending more time in the
company of Miss Elizabeth Wilcox.

Many times Betsy had appreciated the amount of trouble to
which the settler of this humble prairie homestead had gone by
culling dozens of cottonwood saplings from the edges of nearby
Lake Marshall and transplanting them onto the property. Now
well established, several of the trees topped fifty feet in height.
Today the ever-present prairie wind rustled pleasantly through
countless green, triangular-shaped leaves, and in the relative
shelter of the grove of cottonwoods on the west side of her
home, Betsy set up her outdoor table with great care . . . and
determination.

Mr. Elmore Determan might have inveigled himself to dinner,
but she would not play hostess to any sort of impropriety: they
would take their meal outdoors.

A crisp white cloth went down first. Armed with a miniature
hammer and several brads, she tacked the fabric into place
beneath the rough tabletop. For this open-air meal she had
decided in favor of her everyday plates rather than the few pieces

of fine china she owned. These she lifted from the seat of her chair and set on the spread with a decisive thump. The artful old gentleman would have to be content with what he got. What nerve he possessed . . . first challenging the quality of her butter, then inviting himself over to try some.

To be truthful, his departure this morning had left her in a curious frame of mind. Foremost, of course, she retained a degree of irritation caused by his presumptuous manner and outlandish claims. And adding insult to injury was that catchy, unbefitting song he had burst out singing while churning her butter. No matter how many times she had tried ridding her mind of its first verse and refrain, one or the other would steal back like a thief in the night, causing her no little consternation.

But as she laid a knife and a cup by each plate, she realized that something like a challenge also stirred within her. She was actually looking *forward* to seeing her new neighbor again. How could that be? Especially since he irritated her so?

Perhaps she was merely experiencing a feeling similar to the one she used to have when faced with a particularly vexing student. She was proud to recollect that in all her years of teaching, she had never been bested by a pupil. It may have taken some time to establish the rules and boundaries, but she had found that stern discipline tempered by fairness and small amounts of clemency had served her in an excellent fashion. But before she could think of how she might apply a similar strategy to her new neighbor, his voice gave her a start.

"Are you nailing down the plates so they won't blow away, or are you worried I might abscond with your dishes?"

Whirling about, she was confounded to see the very gentleman about whom she had been preoccupied for hours. How had he sneaked up on her? She'd been glancing toward the lane every few minutes to spot his arrival. With a sack—presumably filled with corn—he gestured toward the hammer and nails lying near one of the plates. His blue eyes sparkled while he waited for her reply.

Caught off guard yet again, Betsy could not seem to manage a clever retort, or for that matter, any sort of retort at all. Of their own accord, her hands flew to her apron and smoothed away its creases. *Why did you do that?* she immediately chided herself. *He's going to think you're overly concerned with your appearance— or even preening, of all things. Irvetta Auerbach might still be trying to catch herself a man, but she hasn't got the sense to know she's too old for such foolishness.*

"I'm not ready for you yet," she finally sputtered, gathering up the hammer and brads and sliding them into her roomy apron pocket. Feeling hot and snappish and slightly winded, she was dismayed to find herself once again taking notice of her neighbor's smart appearance and arresting features. He was as neat and crisp as he had been earlier in the day, while she felt as wilted as an uprooted weed.

His lips twitched, and it struck her that along with his burlap sack, he carried with him an air of suppressed amusement. Fifty years ago she might have cared to engage in happy-go-lucky banter with a member of the opposite sex, but such departures from conventional conversation were simply not seemly for persons of their age and maturity. Surely he must realize that . . . *if* he possessed any of the latter.

Reaching deep into her inner well of fortitude and experience, she found the composure to acknowledge his ridiculous greeting. This morning he may not have realized that she did not care to be trifled with, but she must set forth that line of demarcation without any further delay. "For your information, Mr. Determan," she began in a no-nonsense tone, "I have no intention of nailing down my plates—which would no doubt shatter if I were to attempt such a thing, nor do I host any real suspicion that you wish to flee with my dishes. If your curiosity must be satisfied, I used these implements to fasten the tablecloth to the underside of the table."

"Yes, ma'am." He nodded, waiting as though he sensed she had more to say. She might even have believed he was earnestly considering her words if not for the glint of mischief she detected in his gaze.

Lifting her chin in a way that had never failed to let her pupils know she meant business, she went on. "I would also appreciate, sir, if you would cease and desist addressing me in such a colloquial manner. I am not the sort of woman who cares to be trifled with."

Her neighbor puckered his lips and let forth a low, admiring whistle while shifting the bag of corn from one hand to the other. "I'll bet you turned out some right fine students over the years, Miss Wilcox. Some real big talkers."

Irritation with her new neighbor pricked her even more strongly than before. "Did you hear what I said, Mr. Determan? I do not wish to be spoken to in a playful manner, handled idly, indulged, mocked, ridiculed, or anything else of that ilk. Nor do I care for flirtation or coy remarks. Certainly I make myself clear."

Up went the snowy brows. "Certainly! I heard you loud and clear, Miss Wilcox. We both did." His face creased into an outright grin. "Me and you-know-who. Now where would you like me to put the corn?"

Betsy couldn't help the frustrated *ooh* that escaped her as she gestured abruptly toward the porch. With an obliging nod, he turned and started for the house, leaving her staring at his back and hotly aware that he had once again tied her tongue in knots. Half of her wanted to call out that he could just march himself straight back home, while the other half wanted him to stay long enough so she could give him a proper dressing-down.

As if he'd read her mind, he looked over his shoulder and

grinned. *What an exasperating man,* she thought, trying to formulate what she might next say to him. Moments later he reached
the foot of the porch steps. "Why don't I have myself a seat on
this perch you have up here," he called, turning a second time,
"and wait out-of-doors till you ring the dinner bell. You but say
the word, Miss Wilcox, and I'll carry our meal to your winsome
little table." She thought he may have even winked, but with the
way the late-afternoon sun struck his face, it was impossible to
say. She'd known him only half a day, but she wouldn't put it
past him.

"It would also be my pleasure to help you with the dishes
after our alfresco repast." He sounded out of breath after he'd
climbed the three stairs and settled his frame onto the bench. He
set the corn at his feet. "You're very kind . . . go to such trouble
. . . least I can do." His playful manner had vanished, and his last
words had been spoken in a gentle, gracious manner.

"It's . . . no trouble," she found herself replying, helplessly
studying the bewhiskered gentleman who had doffed his hat,
closed his eyes, and leaned his head back against the side of her
house. How could it be that a few minutes ago she was ready to
give him a swift rebuke but now felt her anger dissipating in the
face of his disarming appearance?

"I'll just take this and go inside," she muttered, bending to
retrieve the corn. Not waiting for a reply, she hurried into the
kitchen. The water she'd set on the stove was boiling at a good
clip, creating what she supposed must be a tropical climate
inside the already sweltering room.

Fresh perspiration moistened her neck and back, but she
knew it wasn't just the temperature of the kitchen that unsettled
her so. What *was* it about Elmore Determan that kept her as
ruffled and rattled as . . . . as she didn't know what? she asked
herself, setting the bag of corn on the table. There was simply no
word to describe how she felt.

In the short course of a single day, this solitary man had unbalanced her to a degree that thirty-four years' worth of schoolroom students, school boards, and superintendents had never managed. Withdrawing the hammer and nails from her apron, she shook her head at all of Mr. Determan's silly repartee. But when she thought of him, what appeared in her mind were not his merry blue eyes or his impish smile but the unguarded, almost defenseless expression upon his face as he'd closed his eyes and reclined in her porch seat. Something about that picture twisted her heart in an uncomfortable, unfamiliar way.

She put the corn on, then opened the icebox and removed the butter crock. What was she doing having supper with such a . . . such an unusual man? she wondered with no small amount of anxiety. Her movements were choppy and hurried, not calm and deliberate as they usually were.

What did she have in common with Elmore Determan except for shared residence in Lyon County? What would they talk about over their meal? Another thought struck her. What if he had fallen asleep on her front porch? How would she wake him? *Should* she even awaken him?

Nothing in her life had prepared her for such a predicament, and she almost wished he had never come over. Yet, if she was honest with herself, there was a part of her that was the tiniest bit glad for a change in the sameness of her days.

THREE

"You don't say, Betsy! He fell asleep right on your porch?" Hattie Crabtree's mouth formed a perfect *O* and her swiftly basting hands came to a complete halt as she looked around at the assembled members of the Marshall Ladies' Sewing Circle. Even the *clackety-clack* of Jane Pruitt's sewing machine treadle had fallen silent.

Aware of all eyes upon her, Betsy regretted saying anything about her new neighbor having come to supper. But as Irvetta Auerbach had progressed from broad hints to outright nosiness about the Twin Cities widower who had moved next door to Betsy, Elizabeth had ended up giving a brief synopsis of Mr. Determan's visitation earlier in the week.

This week the Marshall Ladies' Sewing Circle was meeting in the Pruitts' handsome sitting room in downtown Marshall, while the group continued their goodwilled efforts making warm winter clothing for the less fortunate souls of Lyon County. Fourteen of the group's twenty-one members were present this warm and muggy afternoon—eleven busy with various implements of stitchery, the other three knitting caps and mittens.

"Oh my, whatever did you do?" Emma Graham exclaimed, dashing Betsy's fervent hope of someone introducing another topic.

"Well, I woke him up, of course," she answered more sharply than she intended, but seeing the deliciously intrigued expression on Irvetta's face irked her.

Miss Irvetta Auerbach was far too fanciful and impulsive for a woman of her fifty-some years, Betsy had decided a good while ago. Though her appearance was in no way unpleasant—plain features tending a bit toward pudginess, clear hazel eyes, and dark hair, which in the past several years had taken on an admirable shade of gray—she had never married. Perhaps that was why the woman was an enthusiastic and incurable romantic, working tirelessly at promoting the matrimonial state in whatever way she could.

"Did you *still* take your meal together?" Irvetta persisted. "Did he like your butter?"

"He seemed to," Betsy answered evasively, distinctly recalling that in tandem with the basket of bread she'd set alongside the corn, Mr. Determan had all but emptied her butter crock. What she didn't reveal was that he had heaped lavish amounts of praise upon her throughout the meal—for her bread, her buttermaking, her hospitality—and once he'd even commented on the rare color of her eyes . . . as if brown eyes were unusual. What nonsense. A lesser woman might easily have been swept away by such flattery.

"I heard he *lived* in these parts for a time, back in the seventies," Irvetta was saying.

"He did? I do not recall ever making his acquaintance," Jane commented, puzzled. An elegant woman in her midfifties, she was considered one of the pillars of the rapidly growing town of Marshall.

"I didn't know him in the early days, but he turned up at church last Sunday," Mabel Dunn contributed, nodding her approval. The eldest member of the circle at eighty-one years of age, Mabel looked like a tiny, fragile, snow-white bird. She

raised her right hand for emphasis, thimbles glittering on her
third and fourth fingers. Her voice possessed that precarious
tremor peculiar to persons of her maturity. "He sang louder than
the choir and congregation combined."

"He was quite inappropriate." Anna Dilley's already flushed
cheeks became the color of cherries. "The way he shouted 'hallelujah' and 'amen' throughout Reverend's sermon—why, my children scarcely behaved themselves for wanting to snicker all
during the service. And what's more," she grumbled, clearly
outraged, "he wasn't the least bit embarrassed. He seemed to be
enjoying himself!"

Elmore Determan singing at the top of his lungs in church?
Betsy wasn't at all surprised by Anna's remarks about her new
neighbor. What amazed her, however, was the number of circle
members who responded to Anna's commentary with amusement.
Did none of them have proper respect for Sunday worship?

"I believe I'll come to your church next week!" Emma
declared to a fresh round of laughter, her eyes crinkling with
merriment. "If the Second Coming were to occur right in the
middle of our service, I have often wondered how many would
be awake to notice."

"Has Mr. Determan joined your congregation, Anna, or will
he be visiting around?"

"If he's making the rounds, it sounds as if we need to prepare
for him!"

Questions and comments flew riotously about the room until
Mrs. Dilley spoke over the assemblage. "I sincerely hope this
man has made his first and last visit to our evangelical association," the red-cheeked matron concluded, stabbing the needle
back through her cloth. "And I don't find any of this amusing,
ladies. Elizabeth, what do you have to say?"

Finding herself once again at the center of attention, Betsy
hesitated. With everything inside her she agreed with the youn-

ger matron's assessment of Mr. Determan's lacking social graces, yet she was shocked to find herself experiencing a flicker of loyalty toward the dapper gentleman who had sat at her table and asked her about herself.

"I wonder if he's looking for a new *wife?*" Irvetta postulated, drawing the gazes of thirteen sets of eyes. "I heard that his wife died years and years ago, but you know a man's never too old to be looking. And for that matter, we aren't either."

"Well, I'm not looking at any man," Hattie announced with vinegar in her tone, silencing the titters that had begun at Irvetta's last remark. "But widowers? If you ask me, they're all looking. Since John died, you would not believe the number of old gallants who've come out of the woodwork, thinking I'd be overjoyed to say 'I do' and begin starching their shirts."

"Not *all* widowers are like that," Irvetta objected, gesturing toward Betsy. "Why, I'm sure Mr. *Determan* is nothing of the sort, *is* he?"

"How could I say? I hardly know him."

Irvetta, having yielded herself to the rapture of her fertile fancy, did not heed the stern look Elizabeth directed her way. "Well, you can *never* tell what will happen," she trilled. "Think of it, Betsy! Maybe Mr. Determan's falling asleep on your porch was his way of choosing you! Like Ruth slept before Boaz, only in reverse. Remember three years ago when Stanley Foley proposed to Grace Emery? Now who would have ever thought those two would make a pair? But look at them today, happy as larks. And then there's Mr. Forbes and Ada Kinmore, and do you remember Florence Johns—"

"We remember, 'Vetta," Emma interrupted patiently. "But I think you're a bit premature in linking Mr. Determan's name with our Elizabeth's. They have only shared a single, neighborly, get-acquainted meal. That hardly puts them in the same alliance as some of these other couples."

Couples? Betsy quelled a most unladylike urge to snort. Who said anything about her and Mr. Determan being a couple?

Gazing directly at Betsy, Minnie Bernhard spoke up from the far corner of the room, her knitting needles having resumed their blurring speed. "I met your Mr. Determan the other day in town. Came around a corner and there he was. My, Elizabeth, did you notice his eyes? I thought them arresting. Or maybe it was the way his face lit when he smiled—"

"Pardon me for interrupting, but did any of you hear that a Mr. Haney of Minneapolis is going to buy out Wakeman's Drugstore?" Emma flashed a sympathetic glance toward Betsy as if to say she was sorry this applesauce about Elmore Determan had gone on as long as it had. "I hear he wants to put in a soda fountain, and he's also planning to—"

"Mr. Haney! Oh, how could I have forgotten? I *did* hear about him!" Irvetta interjected, looking as though she might explode. "And listen to this: he's *never* been married. Just think, next month we will have yet *another* eligible bachelor in town."

Thankfully, the conversation turned completely to the newcomer, a graduate of the University of Minnesota's pharmacy department. Betsy tried listening with interest as Irvetta relayed each piece of information she had learned, but as she worked at setting the sleeve into the girl's nightgown in her lap, she couldn't keep her thoughts from her unusual new neighbor, the man with the bright blue eyes and ready smile who trumpeted his praises of the Son of God for all to hear.

The man who had thought to bring her a spray of rudbeckia.

"Do you ever find yourself at all lonely, Miss Wilcox?"

"Lonely?" Betsy reflected on Mr. Determan's question, slightly less wary of him than she had been upon first making his acquaintance. However, he possessed a mysterious quality that continued leaving her off-kilter more often than not. They had now shared three meals in less than two weeks, and this evening they sat side by side on her porch seat—with as much space between them as she could manage—sipping lemonade.

"Are you asking if I am lonely, as in *desolate* and *forlorn?* I should say not." She sniffed. "With my friends, the various works in progress in the Marshall Ladies' Sewing Circle, and the large number of pupils in my Sunday school class, I am really quite preserved from loneliness."

"Yes, of course," he replied thoughtfully. After taking a sip of his beverage, he sighed with contentment and gestured toward the western sky, where the setting sun illuminated a bank of fleecy clouds. "Would you take a look at that? Who could ever dream up such furious, glorious beauty? In fact, such a sight makes me want to fall to my knees and—"

"Yes, yes," she interjected, quite afraid he might do just that . . . and ask her to join him. "What made you ask if I was lonely?" She couldn't stop herself from inquiring, a defensive feeling having risen in her breast while replying to his initial question. Gripping her glass more tightly, she forced herself to take an unhurried sip before asking, "Do I *appear* to you to be lonely?"

His blue gaze fastened upon her with an expression she couldn't quite fathom, while a half smile played about his lips. In all her days she had never met such a person as Elmore Determan. That first day she had wanted to dismiss him without so much as a fare-thee-well, but during their meal beneath the cottonwoods she had become aware of a secret sense of enjoyment while in his company. Certainly Irvetta Auerbach must *never* be privy to such information.

"Yes indeedy, you appear to have your life in quite efficient order, Miss Wilcox," he replied, nodding.

"I 'appear' to . . . what do you . . . well! I hear you are visiting

churches all over Marshall. Are *you* lonely, Mr. Determan?" she
sputtered, wishing at once she hadn't recklessly turned tables
and asked such a personal question of this unsettling gentleman.
Only the Almighty knew how he might answer. But before she
could moderate her reply, he chuckled and slapped his hand on
his thigh.

"Am I lonely? I don't think I can count the number of women
who have tried chasing me down over the years, believing they
were doing their Christian duty to preserve me from loneliness."

Chasing him down? What arrogance! Oh, heavens, surely he
didn't think she was.

Betsy didn't allow herself to finish the ludicrous thought.
Despite the evening's coolness, she felt her face heat. In all her
born years, she had never made a fool of herself by pursuing any
man. That wasn't to say that in her prime she hadn't had a few
fellows come courting. Things had just never . . . worked out.
And after so many years, there was nothing romantic left inside
her—and certainly not inside Mr. Determan, either.

"After Meg passed . . ." He surprised her by sighing and growing reflective. "After she was gone, I didn't feel called to take
another wife, even though it might have been easier on Clarice
to be raised with a woman's gentle touch in the home."

"Clarice?" she exclaimed, setting aside her discomfiture at the
information he had divulged. "You have a daughter?"

"Oh yes, I have a daughter," he replied in an enigmatic tone.

A silence settled between them, and they each sipped their
lemonade. It shouldn't surprise her that he had a daughter, she
told herself sensibly; it was just that she had not thought of him
as a father. Where *was* this daughter? she mused. On the other
side of the country? Abroad? Didn't she care that her father was
alone in a southwest Minnesota prairie community amongst
strangers? And what of Meg? she wondered not for the first time.
When had she died? Of what? Were there other children?

"I figure you're probably burning with curiosity down at the southern hemisphere of this bench there but are far too polite to ask, so you're hoping and praying I'll tell you more."

"Really, Mr. Determan!" she objected with a *tsk*ing sound. How could a person stir such a tender emotion inside her one second and exasperation in the next? "You needn't feel obligated on my account."

"Not in the least," he replied with a grin. "I can tell how badly you want to know."

"*Hardly*," she replied with a sniff. "If you were to walk off into the sunset without saying another word, I should not care one whit."

His booming laughter rang out, scattering a cluster of grackles that had settled in the yard below. "But, Miss Wilcox, what if my old ticker should give out while I am in the process of disappearing into that magnificent, resplendent sunset?" Winking, he patted his chest. "You would never know what you wish to know about me, and then, as I always say, it'll be no more—"

"Oh, you and your japery! The only thing the matter with your ticker, as you call it, Mr. Determan, is that it is filled with wisecracks and tomfoolery. I declare, you ought to call yourself '*go*-more Elmore,' for you appear more robust than all of my church elders combined."

"Why, Miss Wilcox, I had no idea you felt that way about me . . . or your church elders."

Betsy's face took on fresh color. "For pity's sake, Mr. Determan, you have never grown up."

"'Whosoever shall not receive the kingdom of God as a little child, he shall not enter therein!'"

By now she felt two full beats behind her vexatious neighbor, and what was more, she knew he was enjoying himself to a colossal degree. While she strove for a fitting comeback to his revival preacher–style execution of that particular verse of

Mark's Gospel, he unsettled her yet again by continuing in the contemplative tone he had used just a short while earlier.

"I was grown once, Miss Elizabeth Wilcox, but when I met up with the Lord Jesus Christ, I decided to enter my second childhood." He sighed and stroked his beard. "You see, I didn't know how to laugh about anything back in those old days, and I sure as shootin' didn't know the first thing about finding joy."

"After your wife died?"

"Yes, after Meg died, and every year before that, numbering back to '29. That's the year I came into this world, but I like to think I *really* began living in '75."

"After you attended that revival," Betsy couldn't help adding dryly, her opinion of such events much on the same level with ring fights and that offensive Buffalo Bill Wild West Show that would soon be coming to town. She had never understood how even good people seemed to lose every bit of common sense at such assemblies, giving in to excessive sentimentality, emotion, and even histrionics.

"That's not the half of it. Would you like to hear about how Jesus—"

"Perhaps another time, Mr. Determan," she said, though not unkindly. She didn't care to hear about such zealous goings-on but hoped she hadn't hurt his feelings by cutting him off.

A short silence passed while the evening wind soughed through the cottonwoods. Betsy took another sip of lemonade, nearly choking at his next words.

"Miss Wilcox, do you think you might find yourself able to call me Elmore? I hear around town you're known as Betsy." His face lit with an appealing smile, and he continued speaking, not allowing her an opportunity to reply. "And while you're thinking about that, I'll give you something else to chew on. This might just be wishful thinking, Miss Betsy Wilcox, but I'd like you to be my companion next Tuesday to the Wild West Show."

Time seemed to stop in its tracks. Was he merely seeking a *companion* . . . or something more? Had Irvetta Auerbach actually seen smoke where there was fire? Of all things—the Wild West Show? Oh, good heavens, now what?

"Why me?" was all she could seem to articulate.

"Why you? That's a good question, indeed." His whole face lit with pleasure as he took in her perplexed expression. "Because you are a virtuous woman, and I can see that you have a fear of the Lord."

"But—"

"No *but*s until you hear me out." He held up his hand, his joviality mellowing into an expression that was somehow tender and penetrating all at once. "Let me say that I appreciate your company more than I've appreciated any woman's in a long, long time. You possess a particularly fine mind, and for some reason, that inspires me to ruffle your feathers. Yes indeedy, in the short time I've known you, you've given me great enjoy-ment."

She gave him *enjoyment?* When had she ever been told some-thing like that?

"You could choose any eligible woman in Lyon County, Mr. Determan. You need not choose me," she argued. Really, she was feeling a very odd throbbing deep within her chest as well as the inability to draw a full breath. Was *her* heart acting up?

"The Lord placed me next door to you, Miss Wilcox. I figure he must have done so for a reason."

"We hardly know one another!"

"We become better acquainted each time we see each other."

"But I'm too . . . *old* for such foolishness."

"Fiddledy-hoo."

"Fiddledy-hoo back!" she scoffed, seeing his features crease with delight.

"Will you take in the Wild West Show with me next Tuesday, Betsy Wilcox?" he proposed, eyebrows raised.

"I most certainly will not! I cannot abide such raucous, dusty, disorderly—"

"Hold up!" He raised his hand. His grin softened, and he inclined his head toward her. "I have one more thing to say."

"And what might that be?" Her retort was thorny, yet the tender expression on his face caused her to hold back the remainder of her opinions. She watched him sigh, and he turned back to face the setting sun.

"Betsy," he finally spoke, "I believe I am a little bit lonely."

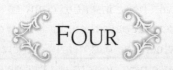

FOUR

"Only fifty cents' admission to see the greatest exhibition in the entire world! Twelve hundred men and horses in action! A veritable institution of heroes! For the very first time, see Roosevelt's Rough Riders in the Battle of San Juan Hill in the absolutely, positively most realistic reproduction of this famous battle you will ever see!"

As Elmore guided his buggy horse through the throng, Betsy cringed at the derangement into which the pleasant town of Marshall had fallen. Barkers were seemingly everywhere, blaring the marvels of Buffalo Bill and his traveling show. Already uncounted numbers of spectators had descended upon the city for this one-of-a-kind event, and they continued pouring in by all means possible. The noise and dust were indescribable.

"Have you ever seen such a marvel in all your days, Betsy? There have to be more than ten thousand here already, and it isn't even noon yet!" Seated to her left on the narrow surrey bench, Elmore radiated pure delight. Nearly shouting to make himself heard, he added, "The Northwestern and Great Northern have been running special trains all morning."

"I've no doubt the saloons are overjoyed for that," she responded under her breath, still not over her displeasure about Marshall becoming wet again after a two-year dry spell.

Why had she given her consent to come to such a frightful affair? In the past several days there had been countless moments during which she had nearly gathered her skirts and marched to the house next door to tell her neighbor that he could go on and see the western wildman and his production without her. But each time she resolved to do that, she remembered the expression on Elmore's face, the sound of his sigh, and his revelation after he'd asked her to accompany him to this extravagant show.

"Betsy, I believe I am a little bit lonely."

It made no sense that a single sentence could strike her so deeply. Yet in the space of those nine words, this man had taken the liberty of using a diminutive of her given name and had plucked uncomfortably at her heart as well. Was it because he had allowed her a glimpse of the humanness that lay beneath his cheerful, confident exterior, or was it because his admission, like a tuning fork, had caused a faint hum inside her?

Was she lonely?

"Isn't this a grand affair, Betsy? Look at the crowds! Smell that popcorn! Are you hungry? thirsty? What would you like to do first?" he offered gallantly, finding a spot to park in the hitching area. "Besides going back home," he added with a waggish grin as he set the brake and dismounted from the buggy. "If I know you at all, I'd guess that's what you're thinking right about now."

Lifting her eyebrows, she favored him with a reproachful expression while he assisted her to the ground. Unfazed, he chuckled and boldly tucked her arm inside his.

Taken unawares, Betsy gasped and pulled her arm free. "Mr. Determan! You can't do that!"

"I can't? I just did. And furthermore, you felt rather nice snugged up next to me."

If Betsy's heart had pounded oddly the evening he had declared his interest in her, it jigged to a breakneck tempo at this moment. His touch had lit through her like the electric lights the townspeople switched on at dusk—fast and bright. Kingdom come, what was happening to her? Swallowing hard, she glanced around to see who was in the vicinity.

With a wink, he inclined his head toward her. "Don't worry; I don't think anyone noticed."

"Oh . . . you!" she sputtered. "I never should have come!"

Still near her ear, his voice resonated with feeling. "Maybe not, but I'm awful glad you did. You're one dandy woman, Betsy. Now, if you're not hungry or thirsty, what do you say we investigate that row of vendors we just passed? I know your walls must be begging for a souvenir of this great day."

Elmore didn't try taking her arm again, but she was aware of his hand at her elbow several times as they perused what seemed like a limitless amount of merchandise. Accustomed to living the majority of her years alone, the closeness and touch of another human being—not to mention that of this dapper new neighbor—was far beyond disconcerting.

The mood of the crowd was one of suppressed excitement and festivity, but she scarcely noticed. Never had she imagined a man so attentive, and she found herself so distracted that she could barely think. At nearly every booth and stand, he tried interesting her in a trinket or two or ten. Finally, to appease his generous nature, she allowed him to purchase her three postcards of the Wild West Show.

"Now I have my souvenirs, Mr. Determan, and I thank you for them," she said, tucking them into the small bag she carried.

"You're most welcome." His smile was warm as he regarded her with those brilliant blue eyes. "You could have more than that, Betsy. All you have to do is—"

"Yoo-hoo, Elizabeth! Is that you, dear? I can't *believe* you're here!"

Turning her head, Betsy was dismayed to see Irvetta Auerbach bearing down upon them, her plump face aglow with pleasure. The uneasy, conspicuous feeling she'd had upon setting out with Elmore Determan returned instantly, making her wonder just when it had left her.

"Good afternoon!" Irvetta cooed upon reaching them. "You *must* be Mr. Determan. I've heard *so* much about you."

Lifting his hat, Elmore bowed formally. "And I sincerely hope I live up to each of the fine tales you've heard, madam. May I ask what you are called?"

Remembering her manners, Betsy made the introductions, hoping her giggling, clearly enchanted acquaintance would promptly be on her way. Fortune, however, did not smile upon them so.

"Did the two of you make the trip to town *together?*" Irvetta inquired, making no move to walk on as she glanced between the two of them. Her eyebrows lifted expectantly, as if she were about to hear the most interesting news in the world.

A beaming Elmore did not disappoint. "We did indeed make the trip together, Miss Auerbach. What's more, when I asked Betsy to accompany me to this dazzling display of horseman-ship, she accepted at once."

Accepted at once? Betsy nearly stamped on his foot. "I did no such thing! In fact, I very nearly did not accompany you at all."

A knowing smile developed on Irvetta's pink mouth, and not for the first time, Betsy thought that if the woman had a window in the center of her forehead at moments such as this, one could watch the wheels of her mind clacking round and round with ever-increasing velocity.

"Why, E-*lizabeth*," she gushed, "at our last sewing circle, I remember you sharing your opinion of the Wild West Show." Tilting her head toward Elmore, she added, "It must have been the *company* that changed her mind."

"You must be right, Miss Auerbach. I know I have greatly

enjoyed Betsy's companionship since we shared our first meal together. That would be the first of three, in case anyone might be keeping count." His smile broadening, he gave a conspiratorial wink. "The way I see it, time's a-wasting. This old ticker of mine could give out any day now, and then, as I always say, it'll be . . ."

Betsy grimaced as he delivered his quip and basked in Irvetta's delighted giggles. Things were moving too quickly, and in absolutely the wrong direction. Her mischievous, fantastical neighbor had no idea of what he was getting himself in for with a newsmonger such as Irvetta Auerbach.

And what was worse, he was involving *her* as well.

"Betsy, you have an absolutely *charming* suitor! This is the most exciting thing to happen in Lyon County since . . . since I don't know when!" Irvetta exclaimed, still flushed from her laughter. "I need to run along now, but I look forward to hearing *all* about your day at our next circle!"

Elmore chuckled as their visitor melted into the crowd. "She's a busy one, isn't she?"

"And you aren't?" Betsy snapped, raising her chin. "I don't suppose you know what you've just done."

"I have a pretty fair idea. And might I add that your loveliness is magnified with such color in your cheeks?"

Loveliness? Her outrage increased at his brazen compliment, while the word *suitor* burned in her mind. Why had Irvetta gone and said such a thing? And she would continue spreading her prattle to everyone with whom she came in contact. *Did you know I just saw Betsy Wilcox with that new man, Elmore Determan?*

Suitor, suitor, suitor.

Betsy drew in a breath and released it, feeling both helpless and out of control. At the age of sixty-eight she had no business entertaining a gentleman caller; she was far too old to be wooed and serenaded. Besides, she'd heard enough talk about widowers over the years to know the only thing they wanted was a woman to cook for them, clean up after them, and nurse them when they ailed. And really, what did she know of Elmore Determan . . . except that in all respects he resembled an overgrown, wizened, ten-year-old boy?

"Shall we find our seats? According to my other ticker, it's half past one."

"I think, instead, Mr. Determan, we should find your buggy."

"Really!" His eyes twinkled, merry and warm. "That's quite a walk if all you want is a little smooch. Why, I'd be pleased to save us both the trouble and give you a peck on the cheek right this minute."

Elizabeth felt as if she were outside of her body, watching in disbelief, as Elmore bent toward her. Light as a butterfly's touch, his lips grazed her cheekbone. Straightening, he wore an enormously satisfied expression. "There, now. If your Miss Auerbach is still watching, she'll have no doubt as to my intentions."

"Your intentions?" Betsy's disembodiment ended abruptly in a cascade of hot and cold shivers. Her eyes sought his, finding what she feared would be revealed there.

"Don't you know? I'm courting you, Betsy," he affirmed, his gaze both ardent and eager. "I had a long talk with the Lord about this, and he thinks my taking up with you is a splendid idea."

"W-well . . . ," she stammered, the crowd of several thousand, the dust, the noise all fading to the background of her awareness. "What if *I* don't?"

"Maybe you ought to discuss matters with him before you make any rash decisions."

"Who are you calling rash? I'm not the one going about kissing *you* in public!"

"You could, you know, if you really wanted to."

"I have not been acquainted with you even one full month."

Not deigning to respond to his repartee, she reasoned from another angle. "Besides what you have told me about yourself, I do not know the first thing about you. Perhaps 'Elmore Determan' is merely an alias for a man of unscrupulous character who moves from town to town, bilking unsuspecting women of their assets. You could be dangerous—even wanted!"

Elmore threw back his head and guffawed. "Dangerous?" he was finally able to utter, still chortling. "I can assure you I am not the least bit dangerous, but a fellow likes to fancy he is wanted . . . at least a little."

"Stop your . . . your *fiddledy-hoo*. I'm serious."

Raising his hands in a palms-up gesture, he shrugged. "I am, too."

"What have you ever been serious about?"

"Well, now that you've asked, for the first time in a quarter century, I find myself having serious thoughts of a certain woman. That would be you," he added with a wink.

"But why me? Why now?"

Where was the measured calm in her tone, the reliable voice that had carried her through more than three decades in the schoolroom? Her last words had sounded every bit as strident as something Irvetta might utter.

"Why you?" he mused, guiding her out of the increasing stream of foot traffic to an empty space between vending carts. With a buffer of canvas on each side of them, the rising din of the crowd was slightly muffled. His hand moved from her elbow, seeking her hand. This time, however, she did not pull away but allowed her fingers to lie limply between his. Perhaps she was in the midst of a dream; none of this was really happening.

Or was it?

"I believe I like you, Betsy, because of your honesty. Half the time, I think you'd just as soon tell me to jump in Lake Marshall as you would pour me another glass of your delicious lemonade.

But I also think, the other half of the time you like me coming over and rattling your cage."

Before she could form a reply, he went on. "I haven't pressed this, but I also think you're a beautiful woman. And it's not just your pretty little face that enchants me; it's what lies behind it."

To her mortification, tears sprang to the corners of her eyes. Jaws trembling, she swallowed. He had called her *beautiful*. Glancing at the wrinkled hands that covered hers, she wondered at the sense of a man saying such a thing during her waning years. Why not years ago—before the bloom of her youth had withered to dust?

He sighed, gazing wistfully into her eyes. "As for your other question, 'why now?' I don't have as clear an answer for you. It was like the Lord tapped me on the shoulder after all these years and said, 'She's the one, Elmore. I've been saving her for you.'"

"Impossible!" Betsy contended, swallowing past the thickness in her throat. "And for as long as you continue insisting that the Lord walks around all day with you, taps you on the shoulder, and whispers such flights of fancy in your ear, I cannot give you any more of my time. We have nothing in common."

"Balderdash. We have more in common than you realize. Now, this might just be wishful thinking, but I was hoping you would allow me to escort you to church this coming Sunday."

"I . . . no!"

"Why not? Aren't you going?"

With the memory of the sewing circle conversation burning afresh in her brain, she searched frantically for a reply. At the same time, she suddenly recalled that her hand was still sandwiched between his, and she snatched her fingers free. "I do not even know why I am here with you today."

He tipped his hat and made a slight bow. "Because today is my seventieth birthday, and I wanted the pleasure of your company as I celebrate."

Today was his birthday? Why hadn't he made mention of that before? And why had he sought *her* company during such a landmark day in his life? Once again, she was at a loss for words.

"Will you let me take you to church Sunday, Betsy? I'll behave . . . I promise."

"Why don't I believe you?" she disputed, alert to the growing flickers of ambivalence inside her.

"You could look at it this way, my sweet. If a man were granted the privilege of praising the Lord in the company of such a fine woman as yourself, wouldn't it follow that he would want to be on his very best behavior? And if he were denied such a privilege, mightn't he go on by himself and perhaps take it upon himself to act up a bit?"

"As in singing and shouting at the top of his lungs in a respectable house of worship?" She eyed him squarely. "Mr. Determan, that's blackmail!"

His eyes danced with mischief. "What time shall I come by for you?"

Just then, a cacophony of bugles sounded, heralding the start of the show.

"Tell me later!" he shouted with a grin, taking back her hands with the excitement of a small boy. "Come on, Betsy-fretsy, our adventure is about to begin!"

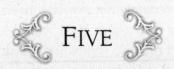

FIVE

Elmore couldn't remember when he'd passed a more glorious afternoon. The sights and sounds of the incredible show in progress far exceeded the descriptions that had been carried in the *Lyon County Reporter*.

The Wild West arena was enormous, and now, before their eyes, the charge up San Juan Hill was being reenacted—complete with a reproduction of the hill itself, a blockhouse, trenches, and barbed-wire fencing. To add to the drama, those on the imitation battlefield were not actors but valiant soldiers who had participated in the engagement in southern Cuba. Roosevelt's Rough Riders were represented, as were ex-regulars and volunteers of the United States Army, and even Cuban revolutionaries.

Finally the hill was taken, and the crowd erupted with wild emotion. Next to him, Betsy continued observing the goings-on quietly, without adding to the whooping and cheering from spectators on all sides of them. Even so, he would bet her sharp gaze hadn't missed a thing. A spreading feeling of contentment coursed through him as he continued stealing glances at the petite, dignified woman beside him.

Elizabeth Wilcox was really something.

At his age, he'd certainly not expected having his head turned and heart stirred in such a way. He'd been alone for so long, comfortably so, but now . . . something was drastically different. A long-extinguished spark had ignited upon making her acquaintance, and since then, thoughts of this pretty, prickly woman had filled his mind.

Though Margaret, his wife, had been much different, he had been deeply in love with her. Thirteen years his junior, Meg had been vivacious and sweet. She'd been an attentive and loving mother to Clarice, whom they had conceived during their first Christmas together, soon after their marriage.

Meg's barrenness for the next eleven years had been a great source of grief for her, and he remembered well their joy when she became certain she was carrying again. The months of confinement had gone well, with only the usual discomforts women suffered while with child. Even as she entered her labor, there was no forewarning of the hemorrhage that had come upon her, swift and deadly as a silent sword to her vitals.

He'd been forty-six when Meg had died; Clarice, twelve. Meg and the baby had been gone two months when he'd noticed a handbill for a traveling gospel event, promising abundant hope and new life to all who attended. From the depths of his despair he'd latched onto those assurances and gone to the assembly with his despondent, unwilling daughter in tow.

Once there, it hadn't taken even two hours for his spiritual conversion to occur. Even now, nearly a quarter-century later, tears sprang to his eyes when he recalled that moment of understanding: Jesus Christ had died so sinners such as he, Elmore Determan, could go to heaven. No sacrifice, ever, was comparable to the Son of God's death on the cross. How could he have walked around for so many years, oblivious to the Father's plan of salvation for mankind? Meg had known, he'd concluded in retrospect, but he'd been blind, deaf, and dumb to the truth.

How deeply he regretted his many years of unbelief—more than half his lifetime. While it was true he'd never been anything but hardworking and law-abiding, he had not honored the greatest commandment: to love God with all his heart and mind and strength. It wasn't until that night that the eternal significance of those words became manifest.

Who knew how things might have turned out if only he'd known the Savior before that?

But even after all these years of being a Christian, he still wondered if it had been a mistake to take Clarice to the revival that day. Not because she'd been too young to hear the gospel and decide for Jesus, but because it had overwhelmed her . . . and ultimately divided them.

As far as he knew, his daughter's heart continued to be locked up as tight as it had been the day they'd laid her mother to rest. Over the years he'd tried everything he could think of to reach her, but it was as if the more deeply he loved Jesus Christ, the further she'd retreated from him and the Lord.

Nonetheless, in gratitude for the gift he'd received, he resolved to spread the love and joy of the Lord wherever he went, until he no longer had breath to do so. Lately, there had been moments during which catching his wind was more difficult than it had ever been, making him wonder if that day might not be too far around the corner. At times, it seemed he could feel and hear his blood rushing through his veins. Though he had no fear of his own passing, he continued harboring worry for the loss of his daughter's soul.

"Have you fallen asleep again, Mr. Determan?" Betsy's distinctive voice tickled his ear, and his lips twitched at the unmistakable disapproval in her tone. She was as different from Meg as day was from night, but he knew there was a woman of great substance and intelligence beneath her prim and proper exterior.

Mentally shaking off his weighty thoughts, he opened his eyes and took in his companion's appearance.

It wasn't difficult to see past the network of fine lines on her face to the maiden she once was. Clear brown eyes sat over a straight, pert nose. Her cheekbones were set high, creating a most lovely plane extending downward to her jawline. Perched above the oval of her face and upswept silver hair was an understated black silk hat, finishing her appearance with grace and dignity.

"I can't thank you enough for accompanying me today," he declared in the waning roar of the crowd. "What a fine birthday this has been!"

"I should think your Buffalo Bill has more to do with it than I."

"You might be surprised, Betsy dear."

Eyes widening at his endearment, she made no comment. Her fingers twisted the cords on the bag she carried while the battle scene was cleared of its mock casualties and sharpshooter Annie Oakley was announced.

"Pardon me for a short while," he said, as nature called.

She waved him on, and he made his way to the row of back-houses behind the stadium, hoping he might be back in time to watch some of Annie Oakley. But on his return to the stands, a bit winded from his exertion, he stopped at a flower cart to catch his breath. While there, he selected an arrangement of chrysan-themums, cattails, and bittersweet to surprise Betsy.

Thinking he might save steps as well as disrupt fewer people on the way back to his seat, he decided to reenter the stands one entrance down from the one he exited. The report of a rifle rang out, followed by the cheers of thousands. He wished he could see more of the shooting exhibition, but at the same time, his steps seemed to be costing him much energy. Slowly climbing the wooden ramp up to the seating, he caught sight of a familiar

face out of the corner of his eye, and for a long moment, his gaze
locked with that of his daughter's.

Clarice Determan Wilson appeared as startled to spy her
father as he did her, but then, pasting a spurious smile on her
face, she lifted her arm in a nonchalant greeting, making no
effort to rise. She was perhaps ten feet up in the stands, only
twenty feet over and a row or two up from where he and Betsy
had been taking in the show. She sat amidst a group of finely
dressed women, and he surmised that she and her important
friends had come here on one of the special trains this morning
to watch the show.

Clarice now was older than Meg had been when she'd died,
and her resemblance to her mother continued to be remarkable.
But whereas Margaret had been petite and soft-spoken, Clarice
had grown to an ample size and was often corrosive. With a sad,
slight nod toward her, he continued back to his seat, his enjoyment of the day extinguished.

Had Clarice intended to make contact with him while she was
in town, or would she have slipped back to New Ulm as quietly
as she had come? he wondered, suspecting the truth was his
latter supposition. He'd written her twice since he'd moved and
had given her more than sufficient notice of his plans to move
before that.

Did she even remember it was his birthday?

His heart ached with both heaviness and pain as he slipped
back into his seat beside Betsy. Why was he so weary? Right this
minute, he wanted nothing more than to go home. Taking
several deep breaths, he tried gaining control over the shroud
of sadness that had settled upon him.

"Are those flowers for me, Mr. Determan, or did you intend
to hold them the remainder of the afternoon?"

Shaking his head, he handed the festive-looking spray to
Betsy. With questioning eyes, she accepted the gift and offered

her thanks. On the field below, Annie Oakley and Buffalo Bill began shooting down balloons that had been released to great heights. He watched, detached.

"Those two did the most senseless, dangerous things," Betsy offered when their display of skill had come to a close. "Can you imagine holding a silver dollar and allowing someone to shoot it from between your fingers? What if one of them should miss?"

"If they still have all their fingers, I would reckon they don't miss."

"Yes, but . . ." She trailed off, turning to look at him. "Are you well? You don't sound like yourself." Her gaze swept over his face. "Or look like yourself. Have you become ill?"

"I'm a little tired," he allowed, forcing a smile.

"You should be home." Her concern was clear. "It would be a sacrifice for me to miss the remainder of the show, but I would do that for you."

Despite his gloom, a brief, genuine smile replaced his artificial expression. "Miss Wilcox, I believe you just made a joke."

"I may have," she continued in what he assumed was her finest, take-charge schoolmarm voice, "but I truly do not think you look well. Your color has changed, and it appears to me that you're breathing harder."

"Well, then, Betsy-fretsy, will you take me home?" he asked, longing for the rest and comfort of his bed.

"I most certainly will." Gracefully managing the bouquet and her bag, she rose and extended her hand.

Even though Betsy insisted she was perfectly capable of driving the four miles home, Elmore took the reins when they were seated in his buggy. Gone were his optimism and jaunty manner; he drove out of town in a silence utterly uncharacteristic to everything she knew about him.

But what did she really know of Elmore Determan except that he was a widower who today celebrated his seventieth birthday? With another sidelong glance in his direction, she was even more troubled by the change that had fallen over him during such a short space of time. All day he'd been as exhilarated as a third-grade boy to see the Wild West Show, yet in the space of a quarter hour, he'd been ready to walk out without a backward glance. Had he become feverish? He stared straight ahead, his hat fixed low over his brow, his jaw set.

"Is there anything I can bring you?" she asked as they neared her drive. "I have a new bottle of Kodol's Dyspepsia at home."

Briefly his blue gaze lit upon her. "There's nothing the matter with me that a little tincture of time won't cure."

"You're certain?" Even his eyes were different, she noted, as if the brightness behind them had been doused.

She felt even more helpless when he dropped her off, thanked her for her company, and turned the horse and buggy around for home. Bent over the reins, he looked as though he was heading into a blustery storm rather than setting off in the pleasant September afternoon.

As she entered her kitchen, an idea sparked. She had saved a little chicken in its juices from the previous day, and she was well stocked with vegetables. Perhaps he would find a bowl of hot soup restorative. If she put some water on to boil right now, she could have it ready within the hour.

She removed her hat, pulled an apron over her head, and began bustling about the kitchen. Once a fire was going in the stove, she set out the ingredients she would use. The carrots, especially, would have to be finely diced so they cooked quickly, she thought, but then they would also have the added benefit of being more easily digestible.

Once again she found herself thinking of her blue-eyed neighbor, wondering at the cause of his indisposition. He had never

mentioned any health problems to her, save his wordplay about
his heart. That aside, the sudden disappearance of his normally
ebullient spirit caused her no small amount of worry.

When the vegetables were diced, she slid them into the steaming water. To save time, she boned the leftover chicken and
chopped the meat into tiny pieces, rather than boiling the meat
from the bones as she normally did. Adding a little hot water to
the roasting pan that had held the chicken, she loosened the rich
brown juices and carefully poured the concentrate into the soup
pot. Salt, pepper, and dried parsley followed.

Someday she would have to make Elmore a proper soup,
but this would have to do for now. Surveying her simmering
creation, she still carried the sense that something was undone.

Or was it sympathy because no one had made a fuss over his
seventieth birthday?

He might not feel like eating cake today, but she could just as
easily bring one over with his soup as not. The stove was hot,
and perhaps it would do his heart good to have some bites of
raisin-spice cake . . . to know she was thinking of him.

Just what are you thinking of him, Betsy?

A jolt went through her as she realized she had slid into
thinking of him in more than a neighborly sense. That wouldn't
do at all. He may have clearly stated his intentions toward her,
but that didn't mean persons of their age had any business
engaging in courtship. Why, they would be a laughingstock!
The talk of the town!

Thanks to Irvetta, no doubt you already are the talk of the town.

With a frustrated sigh, Betsy took a large saucepan out of the
cupboard and began gathering the items she needed to make the
cake. What was Elmore thinking? Where did he think his courtship of her would end? In marriage?

As if at sixty-eight years of age she would don a fine dress
and stand before a clergyman with Elmore Determan. What

bunkum. She poured a cup of water in the pan, sloshing a little over the edge, then added raisins, sugar, butter, cinnamon, and ground cloves. Once that had boiled five minutes, she would cool the fragrant mixture to lukewarm before adding flour and baking powder.

But even while she took a cake tin from the shelf and greased its inner surfaces, her mind spun at the whimsical thought of marriage to Elmore Determan. If such an impossible, improbable thing were to happen, didn't he realize they dwelt in the twilight years of their life span? One or the other of them could very well be meeting their maker any one of these years now.

Setting down the pan with a clatter, she realized she had to put an end to such outlandish thoughts at once. She was Elmore Determan's neighbor, and nothing more. Because she had always striven to be a good neighbor, she would bring Mr. Determan his soup and a fresh spice cake to acknowledge his birthday, but sick or not, he had to be set straight about the nature of their relationship. In her mind, she uttered a brief prayer that almighty God would help her neighbor come to his senses as far as realizing his age, as well as quash his desire to court her.

Dusk had fallen. After lighting the lamps and completing her food preparations, she read distractedly from a book of poetry until the cake had finished baking. The soup, too, was done, and smelling delicious. Carefully pouring half into a canning jar, she screwed on the top and nestled the hot container in a commodious basket amidst several tea towels and the entire cake still in its pan.

With renewed determination, she donned her cloak and lit the outdoor lamp, which hung on a peg near the door. Managing the lamp and the basket would be toilsome, but the sooner she made her delivery—as well as making things clear to Mr. Determan—the sooner she would be back home, enjoying her soup, and have this most disconcerting day behind her.

Full darkness had enveloped the countryside. In the east, a half-moon had risen above a backdrop of low clouds. The air had turned chill, a mild foretaste of Minnesota's coming winter. After clearing her drive, she walked down the road to her neighbor's and was nearly to his house before she noticed an unfamiliar conveyance parked outside.

Who would be visiting? Or had he fallen gravely ill? One of the horses nickered as she passed by; she approached the porch with quick steps, her anxiety stirred more greatly than her curiosity. Setting the lantern at her feet, she knocked at the door, shifting the weighty basket from her right arm to her left.

She felt, rather than heard, the approach of heavy, determined footfalls, and then the door was wrested open to a distance of no more than nine inches.

"Yes? What is it?"

The face staring outward at her belonged to a female in her middle years. At one time she might have been described as beautiful, but the twin tolls of time and excess weight, combined with the open hostility in her gaze, rendered her hard-featured.

Who was this woman? Why was she here?

Where was Elmore?

"What's your business?" the woman demanded, gesturing toward the basket.

"Mr. Determan was feeling poorly earlier, so I brought him some—"

"Wait—I remember who you are," the woman proclaimed with a censorious tone. Her pale eyes narrowed as she peered more closely at Betsy's face. "You're that woman who was with my father today at the show."

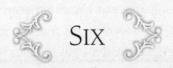

SIX

Walking home in a state closely akin to shock, Betsy tried recalling whether she'd ever been spoken to or treated in such a manner in all her born days. Elmore's daughter's words—*"you're that woman"*—echoed round and round in her head, for she had spat them forth with the abhorrence one might reserve for snakes or other hideous creatures. After that, she'd snatched the basket from Betsy's hands and briskly closed the door in her face.

Appetite forgotten, Betsy entered her good-smelling home with a heavy heart. How *was* Elmore? She'd never gotten to ask. Perhaps he was sleeping, and the daughter—had he once mentioned her name was Clarice?—was merely being protective of his respite.

The animosity on the woman's face, however, had told another story. Recalling the conversation she and Elmore had shared over lemonade last week, she realized he had never told her any more about his family and his life.

Oh yes, I have a daughter.

He'd been so full of mischief that evening that she'd almost forgotten that cryptic remark. In the silence that had fallen afterward, the expression on his face should have told her the subject was a doleful one for him. But he had started up with his tomfoolery again soon afterward, and between that, his invitation to the Wild West Show, and his unexpected disclosure about his lonesomeness, she'd all but lost her wits.

Yet again.

Keeping up with Elmore Determan was like attempting to watch every exploding kernel in a basket of popcorn. Never had she imagined such a person as he. Energetic, impetuous, mischievous, outrageous . . .

She recalled the cast of his features during the drive home. He had not been well. Had his daughter come to care for him? she wondered, rejecting that theory as she reasoned he had been perfectly fine until midafternoon.

What on earth was the matter with that woman? And what kind of care would Clarice give her father, anyway? Betsy was aghast to think of her kind neighbor being tended with so much bitterness. With such a person as his daughter about, his sunny nature would never be restored.

Though Betsy never said her prayers until she had put on her nightgown and brushed her hair, she made an exception in her routine and bowed her head. *Almighty God,* she began, searching for how she might best ask for help, *please grant Elmore your healing. If he needs to be tended, I suppose there's no reason I can't help him until he's better. Just send that dreadful daughter on her way. Amen.*

Sighing, she picked up the three postcards he had purchased for her that afternoon. Bold claims and busy, detailed illustrations covered the face of one. Another advertised the cities in which the Wild West Show had played. Buffalo Bill himself adorned the third—a tall, dignified man with a white goatee.

After looking more closely at each of the cards, she set them aside, her glance lighting on the spray of autumn flowers Elmore had brought her. The vivid chrysanthemum heads were full and flawless, set off by the striking scarlet blaze of bittersweet. With a sad smile, her finger stroked the velvety texture of the cattail.

She realized she had enjoyed their outing today after all.

❊ ❊ ❊

"Mr. Determan?" Betsy called after knocking. Opening his door a crack, she repeated his name.

"Come in, come in!" he invited, his voice sounding far off and sleepy. "Are you finished with church already?"

"I am. I asked the Gardners to drop me here so I could see if you needed anything." Letting herself in, she hung her cloak on the row of hooks inside the doorway and assessed her neighbor's modest home. He must be in his bed, for there was no sign of him in either the front room or what she could see of the kitchen.

She'd spent most of Wednesday alternately worrying about him and stewing about Clarice and her rudeness. Though she had not seen any further signs of the unfamiliar carriage, she told herself another driver could have left his daughter to stay with him.

But what if that was not the case? What if Elmore was ill . . . and alone?

By Thursday morning she was over her constraint. Besides wanting to lay eyes on her friend and ascertain his wellness, she was thoroughly incensed about his plump, dark-haired daughter snatching the basket from her hands—and she was determined to have it back. Bright and early she'd marched next door with a half dozen warm muffins, only to learn that Clarice had departed Tuesday evening.

Elmore, weak, wan, and apologetic, had answered the door. After visiting briefly, she'd gone home and made a proper soup, simmering beef, vegetables, and barley together to make a rich, nourishing noontime concoction. Each midday since, she'd called upon him, finding him a pale replica of the brash man who, only a month ago, had strolled up her drive with a bouquet of flowers he'd picked from her ditch. He continued insisting he was fine, merely a bit under the weather, but she was not satisfied in the least with his assurances.

"How are you feeling today?" she inquired, concerned that he had been abed this late in the day. His bedchamber was situated off the kitchen, so he appeared in the kitchen at the same time she did.

"I got the paper read and didn't find myself in the obituaries, so I reckon I can't complain." A grin creased his features, and to her relief, she noted his color was better today. Hair combed, cheeks fresh shaven, he wore a dark wool sweater, instead of his usual suit coat, over his shirt. "I was just having myself a little snooze."

"What do you suppose was ailing you?" Doing her best to ignore the flip-flops her heart made at his appearance and roguish smile, she couldn't help but think of his expression as the sun coming out from the clouds after a long spell of bleakness. "You didn't say much this week when I was over."

He shrugged. "I figure maybe the Wild West Show was too wild for this old man."

"I hardly think so," she commented dryly. "It has been my observation that you possess more energy than a sackful of Mexican jumping beans."

"Some days, Betsy dear. Just some days." In his blue eyes were tenderness and warmth. "Can I get you anything? A cup of tea?"

A pang went through her at his endearment, and she realized if she were to curtail his familiarity with her, she needed to do it now, before he grew secure in thinking her feelings mirrored his.

"No tea, thank you," she began, clearing her throat, "but there is something we must discuss before I leave."

"Might her name be Clarice Determan Wilson?" His smile

faded. "I notice you haven't commented on making my daughter's acquaintance. After suffering the remarks she made to me, I have no doubt she treated you in an equally unpleasant manner."

"It isn't my place to say anything," Betsy replied, feeling her blood rise at the memory of their meeting. *Even though she insulted me, snatched my basket right out of my hands, and slammed your door in my face.*

"I never did finish telling you about Clarice, did I?" He sighed and sat down at the table, allowing his weight to rest heavily against the back of the chair. "I recall beginning, but I don't believe I ever finished."

"That's correct, but you do not owe me an explanation." As she spoke, Betsy found her emotions in wild disorder. The curious part of her wanted him to elaborate, but her circumspect side knew if she sat down and listened, she would have even more trouble extracting herself from the tangled mess she was in.

"She and her husband live over in New Ulm. To my everlasting regret there have been no children, but they have themselves quite a little money," he continued, raising an eyebrow and gesturing toward the other chair. "A fellow might call them big fish in a small pond. . . ."

Against her better judgment, Betsy took the seat opposite her neighbor, telling herself she would redirect the conversation as soon as it was polite to do so. To her consternation, a full quarter hour had passed before she glanced up at the clock again. His account of his relationship with Clarice had been riveting, though sad.

"But you're her father," she protested, unable to believe a difference in faith could cause such division of close family members. "Doesn't she know how much you love her? It's quite apparent, even to me."

"I tell her, but she stopped listening to me years ago." Another sigh issued from him, followed by a slight cough. "Meg's dying was the beginning of the wedge between us. I think Clarice still blames me for her death . . . because of the baby, you understand. My acceptance of Jesus Christ only drove the wedge deeper. Besides that, she had it in her head that I ought to have remarried to provide a 'proper' home for her. When that didn't come to pass—"

"Why didn't you marry again?" Elizabeth blurted before thinking the better of holding her tongue. A man as handsome and outgoing as Elmore Determan should have had no difficulty finding a mate.

"Why? I never before felt called to take another bride."

Uncomfortable with his reflective tone, Betsy quickly remarked on the first thing she could think of. "You might have become a preacher, then. With your newfound faith and zeal, you would have been perfect for the job."

"Well, I can't say I didn't give that some thought, but again, I never received the call. You see, Betsy, a man's got to be clear about the Lord's leading before he makes such momentous decisions." His gaze was gentle and penetrating all at once. "I've been wondering . . . are you acquainted with the sound of his voice?"

For as long as she'd lived, Betsy had bristled at the notion of God speaking privately to individual persons. What inanity. Were such revelations preceded by a clap of thunder so one could be certain of the Almighty's identity?

Of course not.

The Creator spoke through his written Word and through various prophets of history. Over the years, it had been her observation that someone who said, "The Lord told me this, that, or the other thing," usually stood to gain the most by his or her supposed sign from heaven.

"Mr. Determan," she said with a sniff, "God rules the heavens and the earth, but he certainly does not *speak* to ordinary people."

"Are *you* certain, Betsy Lou? Have you never felt a particular stirring in your heart—"

"Aha! You admit, then, you do not *hear* a thundering, majestic voice coming down from on high?" Ignoring the license he had taken with her name, she was intent on making her point clear.

"No, I can't say as the Almighty has ever thundered at me, but he speaks to me all the same. His voice comes as the softest breath of breeze over a hushed stillness."

"You're saying God whispers to you, then?" Frustrated by his fanciful rhetoric, she couldn't help the edge that crept into her tone.

"You might say that," he replied earnestly, not appearing to have taken offense at her discourtesy. To the contrary, he seemed intent on explaining his experience to her in great detail.

"In fact, Betsy dear, I'd go so far as to say the Holy Ghost whispers right into my heart." Though fatigue lingered in his features, his eyes sparkled brilliant blue as he leaned forward. "Would you like to know what he told me about you?"

Acute nervousness eclipsed her inflammation, making her heart beat like the wings of a wren taking flight. Goodness, had her hands begun trembling as well? She shook her head, telling herself that now was the time to set him straight about the nature of their relationship. But her tongue remained tied in a row of knots as he continued speaking.

"He thinks we should marry . . . and I'm inclined to agree." Appearing quite satisfied with himself, he sat back in his chair and waited for her to speak.

Apprehension gave way to full-fledged panic. Springing to her feet, she scurried to the sink, putting as much distance between them in the small kitchen as she could.

If she was not mistaken, she had just received a proposal of marriage. "Mr. Determan," she began weakly, finding her voice. Why was it so difficult to draw a breath? "Do you think me lacking wits and common sense alike? I have lived on this earth in an unmarried state for sixty-eight years. I cannot suddenly up and wed a man whom I have known scarcely one month. What would people say?"

"Fiddledy-hoo! They'll talk less if we marry than if we keep courting."

"But why, after living twenty-four years as a widower, would you choose to marry *me*?"

The affection in his expression caused her racing heart to skip a beat. "Because, Miss Elizabeth Wilcox, you are a jewel among women, a rare treasure, a blossoming rose. You possess an abundance of both wits and common sense, and your mind is keen. You are not given to frivolity—"

"But—," she tried, feeling her cheeks grow as pink as wild columbine.

"And because neither of us is getting any younger," he continued sweetly. "I moved back to the prairie to live out my remaining years, but I never expected to find such a fitting companion to share them with. Betsy, I love you. In placing me next to you, the Lord has blessed me in my old age beyond my wildest dreams. To me, it feels like Christmas—and I'm getting the best gift of all—you."

With effort, he rose from the chair, then knelt. "This may be wishful thinking, Betsy Wilcox, but will you do me the honor of becoming my wife?"

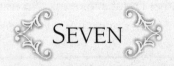

SEVEN

"I declare, Elizabeth, I don't believe I have *ever* seen you looking so down in the mouth. You've scarcely said a word today. Are you and your suitor no longer an item?"

With studied nonchalance, Irvetta pressed the bottom hem of the apron she had sewn. Her eyes sparkled, however, and the atmosphere in Betsy's home became electrified in the ensuing silence.

Elizabeth had avoided the September circle for this very reason, but as she was scheduled to host the October meeting, she couldn't very well not attend. Today, sixteen of the group's twenty-one members were present, packed into her small house like pickles in a jar.

"Why, last month at Emma's I told everyone you looked so happy together at the Wild West Show," Irvetta prattled on, "as if you were *made* for one another. I remember saying to myself, now *there's* a match if I've ever seen one." Addressing the group, she added, "Some of you may not know Mr. Determan has been coming to our Sunday services for the past three weeks, but he's been sitting four rows back from Betsy. And afterward? I notice she still rides home with the Gardners. Wouldn't it make more sense for Mr. Determan to bring her home? After all, they *are* right next door."

Tiny, elderly Mabel Dunn spoke up. "So he's turned up at your church now? I rather miss him. Does he still sing with as much gusto?"

Irvetta appeared nonplused. "Why no, come to think of it. I hear him, but not in the way Anna described. The way she told it, you'd have thought he was hooting and hollering while turning handsprings down the aisle."

"That's because he *was* all but doing those things," Anna Dilley pronounced, launching into a harangue about the silver-haired man's indiscretions during worship.

Betsy knew that somehow she had to make it through the sewing circle without saying much at all. Elmore had indeed begun attending her church the week following his illness, but despite his earlier gleeful assurance of misbehavior should she not accompany him, the gravest indecorum he had so far committed was being more animated than the majority of the congregants.

She had been right to refuse his offer of marriage . . . hadn't she? Why, it was sheer madness to rush into matrimony with a man she hardly knew. And at their ages! Practically speaking, how would they ever go about merging two so very different lives?

As they often did, her thoughts turned to that September Sunday afternoon back in his kitchen. She remembered the dignity with which he had arisen from his knees, the sad smile and nod he had bestowed upon her. Oh, why was there such a strange, squeezing pressure in her heart whenever she thought on that moment?

Anyone watching her afterward would have shaken her head at the sight of a woman in her Sunday best, scurrying home as if the hounds of hell were nipping at her heels. The tears had spilled down her cheeks once she'd reached the safety of her

dwelling, and she cried as though she hadn't cried in decades
. . . possibly ever.

Was it out of self-pity that she had wept so? she wondered,
feeling her throat grow thick even now. Or was it from a sense of
loss at the realization she would pass from this world without
ever being wed? She thought she had accepted her spinsterhood,
but perhaps deep down she hadn't.

Stop it, Betsy, she reprimanded herself, pushing her needle and
thread through the cloth she held. *Your life has been good. What a
privilege it is to have been charged with the teaching and formation of
so many young minds. That is the Lord's will for your life, not dashing
off to the altar willy-nilly now because you know you'll never have
another chance.*

In defiance of the stern talking-to she'd given herself, her mind
promptly served up a vignette of poignant recollections: Elmore
strolling up her drive in his dapper hat, a spray of rudbeckia
hidden behind his back; his sprightly grin, a pair of twinkling blue
eyes, an incorrigible sense of humor. Not to be forgotten was his
hearty laugh—and his equally uninhibited faith.

Of all the things about him, it was his religion that unsettled
her the most. The way Elmore talked about Jesus Christ was
pure exaggeration. Utter hyperbole. But still, the things he'd said
wafted through her mind at odd times, causing her both unrest
and confusion.

Ever since she was a little girl, she had gone to church each
Sunday, accepting Jesus as her Savior when she was nine. But
over the years that special relationship had faded, overcome, she
supposed, by the realities of life. Each night she said her prayers
without fail. Yet not once in all her years could she say she'd
ever experienced anything similar to her neighbor's fanciful spiritual adventures.

*Yessiree, I used to think all the Jesus-dying-for-my-sins business
was all a bunch of fiddledy-hoo, until I met the man. . . . Are you*

acquainted with the sound of his voice? . . . He thinks we should marry.

Enough! She knew she had to stop thinking on Elmore Determan before her heart became seriously involved. Though they were different as cat and dog, something about him had stirred her. Softened her.

Frightened her.

Why would he possibly want to marry her? she asked herself, unable to get him out of her mind. There was no way she could change her life so drastically now; she was too settled in. Too set in her ways. *"I can't,"* she'd blurted out to him, watching the hopeful light in his eyes grow dim. Since that day she had avoided him as much as possible, not understanding why memories of the times they'd shared should keep coming to mind. Nor did she understand the degree of grievance she felt about the dark-haired woman he called daughter.

At long last, the sewing circle ended, and she was left in quiet . . . but not peace.

❄ ❄ ❄

October passed into November while Minnesota readied itself for winter. Each morning frost gilded the fields and grasslands, while day and night a cold, cutting wind wailed over Lyon County. Long gone were the sweet-singing summer birds, leaving behind their hardier cousins to forage during the inhospitable months until spring.

A thick glaze of ice covered the horse's stock tank this morning, requiring a few blows to break through. After seeing to his outdoor chores, Elmore trudged back toward the house, observing the low-hanging clouds to the northwest. What he saw was only a confirmation of what his bones had already told him: a change of weather was on its way. His upper back ached something fierce.

As he did every time he was out, he gazed at Betsy's house and uttered a prayer for her well-being. Pausing to catch his breath, he studied her neat home and the curl of smoke rising from her chimney. Did she ever think of him? he wondered. He saw her bundled form outdoors from time to time, but she didn't spare a glance in his direction. How he missed her company, her companionship, their budding friendship.

After this many years, Father, why would you have me fall in love with a woman who wants nothing to do with me? You told me to court her; I know you did. But now I don't understand. I thought your plans for Betsy and me were to . . .

Entering the house, he hung up his hat, bringing his mental dialogue to a close. The Lord had heard it before. And as his respect for Elizabeth Wilcox demanded, Elmore would not press his suit. Perhaps he was wrong, but at times, he could have sworn she was secretly amenable to his courtship. The way she had fled his kitchen after his proposal spoke to the contrary, however, as did the many days and weeks of silence since then. After shucking out of his coat, he rubbed his arms, noticing that they felt heavy and achy, in addition to his back pain. A granddaddy of a snow-storm must be on its way. He had planned to attend the big foot-ball game this afternoon between the Marshall Eleven and their rivals from the sister town of Tracy, but he didn't fancy making his way home in a blizzard. He would have to keep an eye on the skies.

The pot of coffee he'd started before his chores was done, fill-ing the air with its rich aroma. Lately, coffee hadn't seemed to agree with him. Nor had many other foods. Even though he hadn't eaten yet this morning, he already noticed a twinge of the indigestion that had plagued him for the past several weeks. He hadn't felt right for a long while, and he couldn't help but won-der if his troubles with Betsy and Clarice had simply made him heartsick.

Though the situation with Clarice was nothing new, each time they associated he felt fresh pain about their estrangement. She had been particularly vitriolic the evening after the Wild West Show, doing her best to heap shame on him for having escorted Betsy to the event. He suspected, deep down, she felt guilty that he'd spotted her in town. Hence her unannounced visit later that day.

It was an encounter he could have done without, especially since he'd been feeling punk. If Clarice had noticed his affliction, she hadn't commented. He remembered being so weary, so tired, that he'd actually fallen asleep while she was talking. Once he'd awakened, she'd had more choice words for him, but then she had departed in a rush.

A dispirited smile touched his lips as he remembered finding the basket of food in the kitchen. At once he'd known it was from Betsy, and his heart swelled with gratitude.

How he missed her.

With a long sigh, he put a pan of water on to boil, deciding a bowl of mush was probably the best thing for him. Taking a seat at the table, he opened his Bible to Proverbs, seeking the Lord's counsel on all the matters of his heart.

❈ ❈ ❈

The past week had passed especially dolefully for Betsy, and she retired early Saturday evening. Even the prospect of seeing the eager faces of her Sunday school students failed to buoy her spirits because she knew, chances were, Elmore would attend the service afterward.

Oh, how her nerves stood on end each Sunday morning with the knowledge that he was seated behind her. Furthermore, the sound of his voice lifted in song never failed to elicit memories of the humid August day he'd walked up the drive and introduced himself. In the space of five minutes he had flirted with her, flattered her, helped with her churning, sung to her, questioned her faith, and invited himself to dinner.

There could be no man on earth like Elmore Determan.

Though she purposed not to think of him, she couldn't help it. And when she said her prayers at night, she couldn't seem to conclude without asking God Almighty to keep her neighbor safe.

"I've been wondering . . . are you acquainted with the sound of his voice?" What a strange question he had asked. Acquainted with the sound of God's voice? Did Elmore truly hear the voice of the Lord—and what's more, so often that he was *familiar* with it? Though she didn't really believe so, his question plagued her . . . made her wonder. From the still darkness of her bedroom each night she spoke toward the heavens, yet in her lifetime she had never heard a reply.

No thunderings, no whisperings.

Completing her preparations for bed, she put out the lamp and climbed between the smooth, chilly sheets. For some reason as she began her prayers, the Old Testament story of Samuel came to mind. Three times the boy was called in the night, and thinking it was Eli the priest who summoned him, he went to the older man each time, saying, "Here am I." Finally Eli discerned it was the Lord calling Samuel, and instructed him to say, "Speak, Lord; for thy servant heareth," if the child should hear the voice again.

"Speak, Lord; for thy servant heareth," Betsy whispered into the night, feeling as foolish and embarrassed as one of her students who had misspoken in class. There was a big difference between her and Samuel: God had already been calling Samuel. Quickly, she commenced with her usual prayers, brought them to conclusion, and closed her eyes.

It seemed she had been asleep only a few minutes when she was awakened by a persistent knocking. "Miss Wilcox," came an urgent male voice. "Are you there, Miss Wilcox?"

Alarmed and confused, Betsy sat up, reaching for her wrapper. "Who is it?" she called, her feet shrinking at the coldness of the floor.

"It's Pennington, your neighbor. There's been some trouble."

"What kind of trouble?" she called, her confusion waning as she hastened through the kitchen. The glow of her neighbor's lantern shone into the room once she'd unlocked and opened the door. His kind but angular features were grim.

"I hate to be the one to tell you this, Miss Betsy, but Elmore . . . well, he collapsed. Dr. Taft's got him, and Elmore was asking for you."

EIGHT

Never had the trip to town taken so long as it did tonight, Elizabeth thought frantically, scanning the dark for the first signs of Marshall's lights in the distance. Jim Pennington had filled her in on what he knew of Elmore's affliction—which was precious little—and now they rode in the buggy in silence, each wrapped in their own thoughts.

Apparently the men had met up at the Athletic Park to watch the high school football game. During the second half, Elmore had cried out and slumped forward. Fortunately, Pennington explained, Dr. Taft had also been attending the game in case any of the athletes should become injured. In no time at all, the physician had removed the stricken man to his office and residence.

"Yessiree, this old ticker of mine could give out any minute. . . ."

Along with the memory of her neighbor's playful words came the stabbing realization that perhaps he *did* suffer from some type of heart disease. He certainly hadn't *acted* like a man with a weak heart, but with him, who could know?

". . . and then, as I always say, it'll be no more Elmore."

What if he died—or was already dead? Betsy suppressed a rush of tears at the thought of her exuberant neighbor lying still and cold. No more Elmore? Life would be dreadfully empty without him. At the same time she wondered how this one man, met so late, could have managed to make such an impact on her life.

The night pressed down upon them without benefit of moon or stars. Though no snow had fallen, the sky remained as choked with clouds as it had been throughout the day. At long last she spied a glimmer of light ahead; minutes later they arrived downtown and parked in front of the physician's office.

An electric light burned at the entryway, emitting a strange, artificial glow. While she and Pennington approached the modest brick structure, she couldn't help but think that nothing about this night seemed real. Pennington knocked, and the door was soon answered by the town's newest and youngest physician.

"Come in, come in. You must be Miss Wilcox. I am Dr. Taft."

"How is he?" Pennington asked, dispensing with social niceties.

In reply, the younger man put his index finger to his lips before motioning them farther into his combination office and home. He had kind eyes, Betsy noticed before he turned, though he scarcely seemed of an age to shave, much less to have acquired any sort of competence in medical matters.

"Mr. Determan is resting," he announced after leading them into his personal office. Gesturing to the pair of chairs before his desk, he invited them to be seated.

"Have you settled in on what the matter is?" Pennington asked, still standing. "Can we see him?"

"In answer to your first question," the physician began, "I believe our patient has suffered a paroxysm of cardiac disease."

Betsy felt her heart sink. Cardiac disease. Tears welled in her eyes when she recalled her annoyance at Elmore's witticisms about his old ticker.

"You may see him *briefly*," Dr. Taft continued, "but I must caution you. In the treatment of such a condition, it is of paramount importance to keep the patient free from apprehension and anxiety. What you say and how you act before him could be of the greatest benefit or the most dire consequence. I must ask: are either of you aware of who his next of kin may be?"

"His daughter . . . Clarice Wilson," Betsy murmured, remembering the embittered woman who had answered her father's door. "She lives in New Ulm."

"Very good." The young physician nodded. "I'll notify her first thing in the morning. Now I can treat Mr. Determan here for a day or two, but my facilities are a far cry from a proper hospital. If he doesn't . . ." He paused, clearing his throat before beginning again. "Rather, should he become well enough to be moved, she may want to take him—"

"Just what are his chances?" Pennington interrupted, his brow furrowing. "You don't sound very optimistic."

"I'm doing what I can for him," Dr. Taft said simply. "We'll just have to wait and see how his body responds now to rest and medicine."

Icy fingers of fear squeezed Betsy's heart while the physician led them to the treatment room where Elmore lay. A wall sconce cast muted light from the side of the room opposite the bed, causing her ailing friend to be swathed in shadows.

Or was he already beyond his ailing?

He didn't appear to be breathing, and he lay so still. She was afraid to go nearer, not ready to learn what she didn't want to know.

"Mr. Determan," the physician said gently, taking his patient's wrist. After a few moments, he gave a satisfied nod. "Mr. Determan, your Betsy is here to see you."

Slowly, Elmore's eyes opened. Spying her, his lips traced upward in the faintest of smiles before he yielded to his body's demands for rest. As his eyelids fluttered closed, she couldn't help but wonder if that was the last of his smiles she would ever receive.

"Dr. Taft, may I stay here?" she blurted out, not able to bear the idea of her neighbor being alone, without loved ones near during such a time.

"Why, of course," replied the physician graciously, though his expression registered obvious surprise. "It isn't much to look at, but I have an extra room down the hall."

Tears sprang to her eyes as she bid Pennington good night and was led to a clean but starkly furnished room. "I'll call you if anything changes, Miss Wilcox," the younger man promised. "Mr. Determan's heart was feeble when he arrived, but perhaps his laying eyes upon you will strengthen its function as much as the medication I've given him." With a musing smile, he tipped his head and added, "He was most insistent about wanting you brought to town. He cares a great deal for you, I believe."

With a soft click, the door closed. Sinking onto the narrow bed, Betsy ruminated on the fact that Elmore's feelings for her had never been in question. It was her emotions toward him that were riotous and jumbled, painful and confusing.

With so many thoughts and worries swimming in her head, she thought she would never be able to sleep. But sometime during her prayers she must have nodded off, for she awakened to Dr. Taft's footsteps outside her room.

Startled, she gasped. "Is he . . . ?"

"Shh," he said, moving inside the room to cover her with a blanket. "I've just given him more medication, and I came to check on you too. He's the same. Go back to sleep."

Closing her eyes, she tried to do that. Several times she dozed, only to jerk back to wakefulness with the feeling that she was falling, falling from the sky. Strange dreams and disturbing thoughts visited her in the remaining hours until dawn. Each time she awoke, she did so with the sense that there was some knowledge a slight bit beyond her grasp, which, if she could have stayed asleep, she would have been able to discover.

When murky gray light began filtering into the room, she arose and lifted the window covering. It was snowing, thin and depressing flakes carried in swirling sheets on the northwesterly wind. What would today bring? she wondered, hearing footsteps in the hall. Had Elmore already departed this earth to be gathered at the beautiful, silver river of which he had once sung?

Oh, Elmore, her heart cried. *You tried to love me, and I wouldn't let you.*

"I have some warm water for you, Miss Wilcox," came the doctor's voice through the door. "Breakfast will be ready soon."

"Thank you, Dr. Taft," she called, overcome with relief at the news he hadn't borne. Opening her door, she found a pitcher of steaming water, a towel, and a washcloth waiting for her. The warm water felt heavenly on her face, cleansing away several layers of the physical and mental exhaustion that clung to her. She couldn't imagine how the poor doctor must feel this morning. Between serving her and tending Elmore, he probably hadn't gotten a wink of sleep.

A fresh spasm of worry gripped her as she thought about her good-hearted neighbor. Had he passed the night comfortably, or had he suffered? She wanted to do something—anything—to help him, but she felt so helpless, so out of control. If he died, she didn't think she could bear it, but in the back of her mind was also the fear that if he survived, Clarice would take him to New Ulm and then she would never see him again. With shaking hands, she removed the pins from her hair and did the best she could with a finger-combing before sweeping it back up into its usual style.

A short time later, in the kitchen, she bowed her head while Dr. Taft asked a blessing over their eggs and toast. Afterward, she learned that though Elmore had spent a fairly comfortable night, he was by no means out of danger.

"Mr. Determan is not a young man." The physician chose his words carefully, speaking with great tact. The skin beneath his eyes was swathed with shadows, testimony to his lack of sleep. "And I suspect the natural process of aging has advanced the organic changes within his circulatory system. He tells me he has

not suffered any disease of the heart, but the symptoms he has
described to me and has experienced over the past few months
relate another story. I also observed significant dropsy in his
lower limbs."

With a sigh, he set down his fork and pushed his plate
forward. "The good news is that there are some excellent medications available that can be tried."

"And the bad?" Betsy asked in a choked whisper.

His compassionate eyes met hers. "They may not be effective.
I promise you, Miss Wilcox, I will do what I can. However,
despite our best efforts, this may very well be his time."

No! she cried out from deep inside her soul while scalding
tears traced down her cheeks. Why did the thought of losing this
man hurt so much? *If you are willing, God,* she beseeched, *please
spare him.*

"Ma'am?" The doctor's concerned voice penetrated through her
grief. Glancing up, she saw he had extended his handkerchief
toward her. "When you feel ready, I'll take you in to see him."

Nodding, she wiped her eyes. When she was finally able to
speak, she thanked the physician for his many kindnesses. Now,
with her emotions under some semblance of control, she was
ready to look in on Elmore.

What she wasn't ready to do, however, was bid him farewell.

For a moment, Elmore had experienced the most dreadful fear. *I'm
dying,* he remembered thinking, feeling as though a lumber wagon
had suddenly parked itself across his chest. He had been aware of
his body pitching forward in the football stands, but he had been
powerless to stop himself, unable to breathe, unable to move.

Then, nothing.

He gathered he hadn't died when he'd awakened in this room,
a young man making an assiduous examination of his form. The

fellow had introduced himself as Dr. Taft, informing him that he'd had a bit of trouble with his heart. Over the physician's shoulder he'd caught sight of Pennington's face, and he knew the situation was much more grave than the doctor was letting on.

Is this it, Lord? he'd asked wonderingly. *This really isn't so bad after all. If you're taking me, though, I'd like to see Betsy one last time before I go.*

Dr. Taft had nodded to his whispered request, and Pennington had gone to fetch Elizabeth straightaway. To say good-bye, he surmised. Despite his hopes and wishful thinking, he realized she wasn't going to become his wife. She would have been a corker. Beneath her prim schoolmarm facade, he'd found her an utterly fascinating mixture of contradictions. Straightlaced and proper, yet not a bit bashful about speaking up and calling a spade a spade.

She was a strong woman and an intelligent one. He had also come to believe that the tenets of her faith in Jesus Christ were solid . . . if perhaps a bit *too* solid. Since making her acquaintance, he'd prayed for her to strike up a joyous, vibrant relationship with her Maker. It was his opinion that she didn't possess so much a bitter heart as one encased in a bit of crust.

How he'd longed to be the sandpaper that smoothed that brittleness away.

He read the fear in her eyes when she'd come in to see him, and he'd wanted to soothe her, reassure her he wasn't afraid to die, but he didn't have the energy. The medications Dr. Taft had coaxed down his throat throughout the night had eased his pain, made it a little easier to breathe . . . and made him so tired. He'd also found that if he lay perfectly still, the dreadful air-hunger did not come upon him. Only now did he remember that his father had died the same way. How could he have forgotten the elder Determan's cries for air—*Atemnot*—in his native German?

He slept again, and when he roused, Betsy was seated at his

bedside. Intent upon her reading, she didn't notice his wakefulness immediately, so he took the opportunity to study her
appearance. What a fine and lovely woman she was. Though
their courtship had not progressed far, he was deeply grateful for
the few months they'd had together.

"Oh!" she said with a start, glancing up at him. "You're awake.
Are you in pain? Shall I get the doctor?"

He shook his head slightly. With no small amount of effort,
he freed his hand from the covers and extended his fingers. A
strangled sound escaped her, and she took his hand between her
own. Twin tears fell from her eyes as she gazed at him, and then,
an instant later, she lowered her face to their entwined fingers.

"Oh, Elmore," she wept, her voice muffled, "I am so sorry—"

"Shh," he managed, squeezing her fingers with what little
strength he had. Her slender back shook as she labored to
restrain her tears.

"I . . . love you. Remember . . . love never . . . fails." His words
came slowly, in a whisper.

"But *I* failed." Her words were raw with regret. "How can I ever—"

He stilled her words by pulling his hand from between hers,
his fingers seeking the softness of her hair. One pin, then
another, hampered his efforts. How he wished he might have
made her his bride and seen her glorious silver hair down about
her shoulders, unfettered.

She turned her head toward him, a question in her tear-
dampened eyes. A long moment passed, and then, with shaking
fingers, she reached up and began removing the pins from her
hair. Elmore closed his eyes as the warm strands fell from her
twist, caressing his knuckles, his arm.

Thank you, Father, for the gift of this woman.

While he prayed, he was aware of her taking his hand in hers
again, bringing it to her cheek. Suffused with a perfect peace,
sleep overpowered him, and he remembered no more.

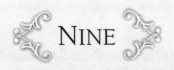

NINE

For Betsy, the next days passed with excruciating slowness. Dr. Taft continued treating Elmore with a combination of medications he hoped would increase the elasticity of his heart, remedy the dropsy, and relieve his pain. At times she was hopeful that the physician's medical regimen was working, but then she would sit at her friend's bedside, taking in his pallid complexion and frequent episodes of short-windedness, and her hopes would plummet.

Word about Elmore spread quickly. By Sunday afternoon, she'd had half a dozen invitations to dinner and offers to spend however many nights in town she wished, yet she could not bring herself to leave the doctor's residence. She wanted to stay—no, she *needed* to stay—as near to Elmore as possible. After the way she'd treated him, it was the least she could do.

What a fool she'd been to throw his affections back in his face. Not only a fool but a coward as well. He had offered her his very heart, and she'd run from his presence like a frightened pup. He'd scared her . . . her feelings had scared her. Though she hadn't been sure before, at this juncture in time she was certain: she loved Elmore Determan.

And now he might die.

Emma Graham and Irvetta Auerbach had called midweek, bringing a delicious assortment of foods. The day before, Emma had driven out to Betsy's and packed a bag of clean clothing and personal items, a gesture Betsy deeply appreciated. Jim Pennington had stopped to say he was seeing to both her place and Elmore's, and that he would be pleased to do so for as long as necessary. In addition, several women from church and from the sewing circle had also visited; consequently, Dr. Taft's kitchen was overflowing with good food and drink.

The young physician continued being a kind and generous host, but Betsy knew that having his home and medical practice turned upside down was taking a toll upon him. He had wired Clarice as he'd promised, and yet again, but no reply had come. On one hand Betsy felt relief, wondering if things might not be better for Elmore this way. She knew how their estrangement grieved him. But on the other hand, she worried about what would become of him. He couldn't stay at Dr. Taft's indefinitely, yet the physician did not believe he could tolerate a journey of any distance . . . even back to his home.

On Friday, a solution to the problem presented itself when Jane Pruitt paid call. She and her husband were perhaps the most well-to-do couple in the area, owning a large home three blocks from Dr. Taft's.

"Why don't we have Mr. Determan moved to our home?" she offered after listening to Betsy's concerns. "It's just a short distance away, and that way, Dr. Taft will be nearby. You'll come, too, Betsy. We have plenty of room."

In the end, that was exactly what happened. Dr. Taft gave his consent for Elmore to be moved to the Pruitt home and personally supervised the process. Once his patient was installed in a stately bedchamber of burgundy and yellow, he produced a written list of instructions. On it were times and dosages of medications to be given, a recommended diet, and a regimen of exercises for his limbs.

"Now, I'm sure this looks intimidating, but it really isn't," he said to Betsy and Jane over tea in the Pruitts' lovely parlor. "Miss Wilcox has watched me enough to have more than a general idea of what I've been doing for Mr. Determan."

"But what if he should—," Elizabeth began weakly, realizing she wouldn't have the doctor's presence to fall back on.

"Whatever it is, ring me on the telephone, and I'll be right over. I've already promised to stop by every day. Furthermore," he replied, leveling his gaze at Betsy, "I have the utmost confidence in your care."

"Perhaps we could hire a nurse," Jane suggested.

"Perhaps," Dr. Taft agreed, "but I have a feeling Mr. Determan will soon declare himself one way or the other."

A lump grew in Betsy's throat as she thought of her life without Elmore. *Oh, Lord,* she questioned, *why did you bring such a man into my life only to take him so soon?*

"As you know, Doctor, prayer can move mountains," Jane was saying, "and there are people all over Lyon County praying. If the Almighty is willing, Mr. Determan will be restored to health."

"I sincerely hope so," he responded, setting his cup in its saucer. After checking his watch, he stood. "Thank you for your hospitality, Mrs. Pruitt, but I must beg your leave. I have two more appointments scheduled this afternoon. And, Miss Wilcox," he said, turning toward her with a nod, "Mr. Determan is fortunate, indeed, to have such a devoted . . . friend."

Elizabeth felt herself color, but not because of the brief, awkward pause while the physician searched for a word to describe her relationship to Elmore. It was because his compliment was so far from the truth. If he only knew how she had run out on his patient weeks earlier, opposing the love Elmore had tried so patiently to bestow, he would have an entirely different opinion of her character.

At Jane's coaxing, she took a bath after Dr. Taft's departure. Elmore was asleep, and Jane promised to sit with him until Betsy bathed and refreshed herself. "Take a nap if you need to," she urged. "You must be exhausted. I have nothing pressing this afternoon; I'll stay with him as long as necessary."

Truly, Betsy hadn't intended doing more than washing up and getting back to Elmore, but the Pruitts' bathroom was a marvel of modern luxury. Running water—both hot and cold! The bathtub was like no other she'd seen, and once she filled it and slipped into its enveloping warmth, she could hardly think of moving again.

Oh, Lord, she thought, *here I sit in comfort while Elmore's life hangs in the balance. I've tried to show him I care for him, but what more can I do?*

As she closed her eyes and laid her head against the back of the tub, time seemed suspended. Could any of this really be happening? Here she was, Elizabeth Wilcox, bathing in a rich woman's home, grieving over a man who had just a short while ago declared himself her suitor. Her life, lived innocuously for sixty-eight years, had suddenly undergone a great upheaval. What more could happen?

Do you want him?

Yes! her soul resounded before she had even comprehended that a question had been asked. Opening her eyes, she found herself staring at the busy hearts-and-flowers wallpaper pattern. Though she knew no one had come into the room, she turned her head and glanced around. Nothing was different; not a thing was out of place. A round clock ticked steadily on a shelf. Her towel remained folded and undisturbed on its rack near the sink.

Had she heard a voice, or was her mind playing tricks on her? She sighed, the sound of her breath loud in her ears. She had heard that persons lacking sleep sometimes suffered hallucinations. After days of worry and interrupted slumber, could such a thing be happening to her? Though she didn't feel delusional, perhaps she was.

Do you want him? Do you want Elmore?

Again came the whispering question, somehow a part of her yet not a part of her at all. All at once, her heart began pounding like the hooves of a horse in full gallop. The story of Samuel leapt back into her mind, as did the self-conscious words she'd uttered into the night: *Speak Lord; for thy servant heareth.*

She wiped her face with a washcloth, aware her hands were trembling. Did almighty God deign to speak with her? Surely she hadn't heard his voice . . . or was this indeed the voice of which Elmore had spoken?

Gone was her exhaustion, her languor. She felt as though she could leap out of the tub and run a hundred miles. Did she want Elmore? With all her heart she did. But what did the question mean? she wondered, her contemplation cut short by an urgent rapping at the bathroom door.

"Betsy," cried Jane, "hurry! Come quickly!"

To Betsy's anxious query, there was no reply. Only a minute or two passed until she was out of the tub and back into her clothing, but it seemed like hours. *Oh, Elmore.* Had he taken a turn for the worse? Had Dr. Taft been summoned?

Heedless of the disarray she left behind, she opened the door and hurried through the Pruitts' princely bedchamber. As she entered the hallway, she heard not only Jane's voice but an unfamiliar female voice raised in anger.

"I don't know what you people expect of me. The doctor already told me he can't be moved."

Jane's reply was too soft to make out, but all at once Betsy knew to whom her friend was speaking.

"Well, does he need me right this minute?" Clarice fumed.

"Don't you understand how exhausted I am? We returned from Chicago yesterday, and I had to climb right back on another train today. As if I didn't have enough trouble finding the doctor's," she went on, "I had to *walk* all the way over here besides."

Taking a deep breath, Betsy rounded the corner. To her dismay, the two women stood right outside Elmore's door. How could he have helped but hear every word? she thought, feeling sick. Noticing Betsy's presence, Jane turned a grateful and pleading look her way, while Clarice's eyes narrowed.

"What is *she* doing here?" The question was blunt and rude.

"I've been helping to care for your father," Betsy replied firmly, stepping forward. With each step, her trepidation fell away, until she was standing before the pair of women. She might have been intimidated by Elmore's daughter before, but it wasn't going to happen again. Nor would she allow Clarice to upset her father.

"Dr. Taft wasn't equipped to keep him any longer, nor did he think a trip of any distance would be beneficial to his health. This good woman, Mrs. Pruitt, was gracious enough to open her home to both of us." With a nod toward their hostess, who appeared white faced and shaken, she added, "Perhaps we could have some tea prepared . . . in the parlor?"

"Yes, yes. I'll see to it at once." Only too happy to take her leave, Jane departed with swift steps.

A long moment passed while Betsy and Clarice regarded one another.

"Shall we go downstairs and wait for our tea?" Betsy forced herself to speak graciously.

"I don't want tea. As long as I've come all this way, I'm going to see my father."

With the physician's cautionary advice about not upsetting Elmore utmost in her mind, Betsy replied, "Of course, but perhaps we might have a word downstairs first."

Pushing past Betsy with a wordless glare, Clarice entered the bedchamber.

Now what, Lord? Betsy found herself praying as she stood alone in the hallway. *Elmore is already so ill, and this visit could very well be the death of him. On the other hand, this hateful woman is his only flesh and blood.*

Taking a fortifying breath, she stepped into the room. Elmore lay with his eyes closed, covers drawn up to his chin, looking helpless and pale. Clarice's progress had halted a full six feet from the bed, and Betsy noticed her shoulders shook.

"Clarice?" She spoke softly, feeling a rush of compassion for this hard woman. "Your father loves you very much. He told me so not long ago." Chancing to lay her hand upon the younger woman's arm, Betsy was surprised when it wasn't immediately shaken off.

A sound from the bed drew their attention. Elmore was awake, extending a trembling hand from beneath the covers. "Clarice," he entreated, his voice sounding as fragile as fine china.

"No!" she wailed, fleeing the room.

In the wake of his daughter's departure, Elmore's gaze locked with Betsy's. Tears brimmed in his brilliant blue eyes. A sob racked his chest, then another.

"Oh, Elmore," she cried, going to him, her heart breaking along with his. "For whatever it's worth, I love you." His fingers gripped hers fiercely as he wept. "I love you! I've been such a fool. Can you ever forgive me, my dearest? The Lord spoke to me today, and he asked me if I wanted you."

Raising her face toward the ceiling, she cried, "My answer is *yes!*" Tears slid down her cheeks as she realized the enormity of what had occurred this day, and she closed her eyes in awe of it all.

You really spoke to me, didn't you? All these years, and I never believed such a thing could happen. And on top of that, I'm in love. Glory, I thought this old body was dead! I never dreamed of feeling such a way! Oh, Father, what a hard-hearted, stiff-necked old woman I've been. I beg your forgiveness, as I beg you for a second chance with Elmore. Please heal his heart. I want to be his wife, and I want to live at his side until you choose to part us.

The pressure on her hand increased, and she opened her eyes, hoping to see Elmore's love for her reflected in his eyes. But to her horror, she saw his face gripped with pain, his chest flailing for breath. As she simultaneously shouted for Jane and reached for the medication on the nightstand, his grasp on her hand loosened.

Please! she implored first to the heavens, then to her beloved. *Not now! Please, not now!*

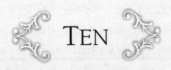

TEN

The town of Marshall was ready for Christmas. Decorations hung from streetlamps and storefronts, and cheery greetings rang in the frosty air. A soft snow fell, blanketing the streets and sidewalks with whiteness.

Betsy arrived at the church early, wanting some time to herself before the service began. She had taken great pains with her appearance, wishing to honor Elmore in every way possible. The air in the sanctuary was cool, smelling of candle wax and faintly of pine.

A crèche had been placed near the altar, a figurine of the Christ child lying in the straw. She bowed her head at the holy scene as she approached, remembering Elmore's words: *"Love never fails."* How was it she had gone to church all these years and never really understood how deeply almighty God loved each of his people?

How deeply he loved *her?*

Christmas had never meant so much to her as it did this year. The simplicity of the gospel teachings penetrated her soul and flooded her being with understanding. God loved his people so passionately that he came to earth in a way to which mankind could relate. Jesus was born, he lived among common folk, and he felt every human emotion. Above all, he loved.

It had taken a man, a one of a kind fellow with bright blue eyes and a joyful, mischievous spirit to teach her the truth about God's love. Oh, how her heart had been torn asunder these past months. In all her years, she had never experienced such things as she had since making Elmore Determan's acquaintance.

In her mind's eye, she again saw him strolling up her drive, presenting her with a bouquet of flowers he'd picked from her ditch. Tears moistened her eyes, and she knelt before the altar. *Oh, Lord,* she began, not able to find any words to express what she felt. Minutes passed, and she heard the door open and close, then the sound of hushed voices.

Was it time already?

Footsteps sounded behind her. "Betsy?" came Emma's gentle voice. "We came a little early for you, dear."

Rising, Betsy wiped her tears and gratefully received her friend's embrace.

"I brought you something," Irvetta offered, an unashamed tear trickling down her cheek. "Here," she said, reaching in her bag and producing an exquisitely embroidered handkerchief. "It was my mother's."

"Thank you." Deeply touched, Betsy wasn't surprised when more wetness spilled down her cheeks.

"Heavens, look at all of us standing around weeping," Irvetta said with a sniffle. "You'd think we were about to attend a *funeral* rather than your wedding, Betsy! Now, that handkerchief has a hint of aquamarine on the edge, so you can decide if you want it to be something old, borrowed, or blue. I *do* hope you've got something new."

Just then, Reverend Fraser entered from the side door, his face wreathed with pleasure. "Good morning, ladies. I see we have in attendance one bride. Has the groom arrived?"

"Not yet, Reverend," Betsy replied, her heart leaping as the big front door opened again. Turning, she felt a flush of pleasure and nervousness at the sight of Elmore's tall figure, flanked on either side by Ronald Pruitt and Dr. Taft. A bouquet of red and white flowers was tucked in the crook of his arm. Like a butterfly, Jane hovered about them, her face breaking into a wide smile when she caught sight of Betsy.

"Truly, we are beholden of a miracle," Reverend Fraser spoke out, watching Elmore's slow progress down the aisle.

"What better time of year?" Betsy said softly, glancing first at the baby Jesus, then at her husband-to-be. The virgin's words came to her: *"Be it unto me according to thy word."* Who could ever fathom the plans and goodness of almighty God?

A short time later, the guests were assembled, and the ceremony began. Betsy's breath caught in her throat at the emotion she saw reflected in Elmore's eyes. Since the day he'd collapsed, he had made an astonishing recovery. Even Dr. Taft had said there was no earthly accounting for the turnaround in his health. True, his strength was not complete, but he had progressed to being up for short periods of time without suffering.

As Reverend Fraser directed, Elmore laid his hand over hers and made his vows. Then, impossibly, at the age of sixty-eight, Elizabeth Wilcox was wed. Elmore's kiss was lingering, making her blush, and drawing laughter from the circle of friends gathered.

"There will be a reception and luncheon at the home of the Pruitts," the pastor announced, "to which you all are welcome."

From the corner of her eye, Betsy caught sight of a solitary figure at the rear of the church. Had Elmore noticed? she wondered, squeezing his hand. He had mailed a wedding invitation, together with a long letter, to Clarice, but there had been no reply.

"Well now, look who's here," he whispered to her as they carefully negotiated the steps down from the altar. "A little wishful thinking, a little more prayer, and look at the things that can happen."

"You and your wishful thinking," Betsy murmured as they received a hail of congratulations and well-wishes. Burying her nose in the spray of hothouse roses her husband had so tenderly presented to her, she smiled and urged, "Go to her, Elmore, before she leaves. I'll be waiting for you."

"Hallelujah! After all this, you'd better be!" His face creased into a grin that she knew would never stop turning her heart end over end. "I love you, Betsy-fretsy."

And I you, Elmore, my Christmas miracle.

Epilogue

Betsy Wilcox and Elmore Determan were wed on Christmas Eve 1899. Instead of settling in one home or the other, they sold both properties and purchased a snug house in Marshall. Electricity was installed, and a small addition was made, complete with a bathtub and water heater.

Elmore never regained his former vigor but lived happily and thankfully for another five years before departing peacefully in his sleep. During that time, a tenuous bond between Clarice and Elmore was reestablished, which grew stronger as the years went by.

After Elmore's death, Betsy was visited regularly by her stepdaughter until Betsy's passing in 1907. It wasn't until 1915, upon suffering ill health of her own, that Clarice opened the Bible Betsy had left to her. To her great surprise, she discovered within its pages a letter addressed to her in Betsy's hand, dated six months before the older woman's death.

Upon reading the tender missive left to her by her father's wife, Clarice put her head down and wept. Afterward, with her head still bowed, she sought the Lord for the first time in decades, unable to resist the legacy of love poured out upon her by her earthly father . . . and her heavenly Father as well.

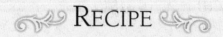

RECIPE

I'm not sure how far back this recipe goes, but I can trace it back at least as far as my mother's grandmother. When I was a little girl, I remember my Grandma Ivy telling me this was a popular cake back in the "olden days" because it did not require any eggs. It is easy to make, and your home will smell wonderful as the spices cook together with the raisins and brown sugar. Those watching their calories may want to finish the cake by sprinkling a little powdered sugar over the top. A recipe for penuche icing is included for anyone wishing to throw caution to the wind.

Sensational Spice Cake

1 cup packed brown sugar
⅓ cup butter
1 cup water
1 cup raisins
1 tsp. cinnamon
½ tsp. ground cloves
1 tsp. baking soda
2 cups flour
1 tsp. baking powder

In a saucepan, combine first six ingredients. Heat to boiling and simmer for five minutes. Set aside to cool.

In a small cup, dissolve baking soda in a teaspoon or two of hot water. Pour into above cooled mixture. Add flour and baking powder, stir until blended. Bake in greased 8 x12 pan at 350 degrees for approximately 25 minutes, until a toothpick inserted into the center comes out clean.

Penuche Icing

½ cup butter
1 cup packed brown sugar
¼ cup milk
1¾ to 2 cups powdered sugar

Melt butter in saucepan. Stir in brown sugar. Heat to boiling; cook and stir over low heat for two minutes. Stir in milk. Return to a boil, stirring constantly. Cool to lukewarm. Gradually stir in powdered sugar until icing is of a good consistency to spread.

A Note from the Author

Dear readers,

A woman from my town fell in love last year. Seemingly overnight, this very sensible, highly educated former missionary turned into the giddiest, giggliest, most exhilarated person I've ever seen. Some days I don't think her feet came within six inches of touching the ground! Her age might surprise you, for she wasn't in her teens, twenties, or thirties . . . but well into her sixties.

Even before I was privileged to watch this romance unfold, I had already submitted the proposal for "Wishful Thinking," complete with a sixty-eight-year-old heroine and a just-about-to-turn-seventy hero. I knew I was taking a chance with this far-from-typical love story, yet the scriptural theme I had chosen for the novella—*love never fails*—inspired me to press on.

All the confirmation I needed came the day my radiant friend confided her feelings for a certain gentleman. That morning, I knew beyond all doubt that the capacity in our hearts for romantic love does not diminish with age. I wondered then, and still do . . . does it perhaps become even greater?

Beyond the simple telling of a tale, I hope the elements of Betsy and Elmore's story inspired you in some way to love your dear ones even more dearly. My mother died just before I began writing this story, her body finally succumbing to the cancer against which she had fought so valiantly. I tell you this not to elicit your sympathy but to remind you that life is precious, and so are people. Our time on this earth is fleeting, and how well we love while we are here is at the heart of our Christian existence.

How do we love? First, we look to God and remind ourselves that we are created in his image and likeness. First John 4:8

gives us a very basic but oh-so-important tenet of our faith: God is love. Our calling as his children is to show forth his image and to be transformed into the likeness of his Son. This happens as we love our Creator, love our families, love our neighbors.

It is my prayer that none of us would be afraid to live—or love—fully. It may be difficult, and yes, it may even hurt, yet our heavenly Father has given us his word that such love will not fail. May his peace be with you as you do his will.

Sincerely,
Peggy Stoks

About the Author

Peggy Stoks lives in Minnesota with her husband and three children. A former registered nurse, she now enjoys working from home. Writing fiction gives her the opportunity to blend her faith in God, her love of history, and her knowledge of health, illness, and injury.

In addition to being an avid reader, Peggy enjoys a wide variety of outdoor activities. She is especially thankful for the woods near her home, where she takes many long walks. Peggy is an active member of her church family and has recently begun sharing her piano talent with its outstanding music ministry.

In the future, Peggy hopes to continue crafting rich and satisfying novels that weave together timeless truths about people, faith, and God. It is her most fervent hope that her work gives readers food for thought and inspires them to grow in holiness. Peggy's previous books include *Olivia's Touch, Romy's Walk,* and *Elena's Song.*

Peggy welcomes letters written to her at P.O. Box 333, Circle Pines, MN 55014.

Visit www.HeartQuest.com for lots of info on
HeartQuest books and authors and more!

www.HeartQuest.com

CURRENT HEARTQUEST RELEASES

- *Magnolia,* Ginny Aiken
- *Lark,* Ginny Aiken
- *Camellia,* Ginny Aiken
- *Letters of the Heart,* Lisa Tawn Bergren, Maureen Pratt, and Lyn Cote
- *Sweet Delights,* Terri Blackstock, Elizabeth White, and Ranee McCollum
- *Awakening Mercy,* Angela Benson
- *Abiding Hope,* Angela Benson
- *Ruth,* Lori Copeland
- *Roses Will Bloom Again,* Lori Copeland
- *Faith,* Lori Copeland
- *Hope,* Lori Copeland
- *June,* Lori Copeland
- *Glory,* Lori Copeland
- *Winter's Secret,* Lyn Cote
- *Freedom's Promise,* Dianna Crawford
- *Freedom's Hope,* Dianna Crawford
- *Freedom's Belle,* Dianna Crawford
- *A Home in the Valley,* Dianna Crawford
- *Prairie Rose,* Catherine Palmer
- *Prairie Fire,* Catherine Palmer
- *Prairie Storm,* Catherine Palmer
- *Prairie Christmas,* Catherine Palmer, Elizabeth White, and Peggy Stoks

- *Finders Keepers,* Catherine Palmer
- *Hide & Seek,* Catherine Palmer
- *English Ivy,* Catherine Palmer
- *A Kiss of Adventure,* Catherine Palmer (original title: *The Treasure of Timbuktu*)
- *A Whisper of Danger,* Catherine Palmer (original title: *The Treasure of Zanzibar*)
- *A Touch of Betrayal,* Catherine Palmer
- *A Victorian Christmas Keepsake,* Catherine Palmer, Kristin Billerbeck, and Ginny Aiken
- *A Victorian Christmas Cottage,* Catherine Palmer, Debra White Smith, Jeri Odell, and Peggy Stoks
- *A Victorian Christmas Quilt,* Catherine Palmer, Peggy Stoks, Debra White Smith, and Ginny Aiken
- *A Victorian Christmas Tea,* Catherine Palmer, Dianna Crawford, Peggy Stoks, and Katherine Chute
- *A Victorian Christmas Collection,* Peggy Stoks
- *Olivia's Touch,* Peggy Stoks
- *Romy's Walk,* Peggy Stoks
- *Elena's Song,* Peggy Stoks

COMING SOON (WINTER 2002)

- *Chance Encounters of the Heart,* Elizabeth White, Kathleen Fuller, and Susan Warren

- *Wyoming Skies,* Peggy Stoks
- *Autumn's Shadow,* Lyn Cote

HEART
QUEST®

HEARTQUEST BOOKS BY PEGGY STOKS

Olivia's Touch—Olivia Plummer desires nothing more than to honor God by using the healing touch he has given her. Eastern-trained doctor Ethan Gray, disillusioned by the pampered rich of Boston, risks his medical career to set up practice in rural Colorado. There he can help people who are truly in need. Immediately upon his arrival, he clashes with the town's "healer," Miss Olivia Plummer. But when his hand is injured, Ethan is forced to accept Olivia's help. Watching her work, he finds himself captivated by her bravery, her beauty, and her passion for helping the sick. And Olivia is drawn to Ethan's disarming tenderness. Still, he stubbornly refuses to support her efforts to obtain a state medical license. Must Olivia choose between the promise of love and fulfilling God's call on her life? Book 1 in the Abounding Love series.

Romy's Walk—Since moving to Washington Territory, teacher Romy Schmitt has secretly harbored tender feelings for the kind, handsome storekeeper Jeremiah Landis. But Jeremiah has secrets of his own. When a tragic accident forces Romy and Jeremiah to reveal their unspoken feelings, they make a hasty pledge that will take a lifetime to live out, testing their courage and faith. As Romy struggles to overcome her sense of loss and accept the gift she has received, Jeremiah's past threatens to shatter their newfound love. Together, they must learn how to surrender to God's plans, no matter what the cost. Book 2 in the Abounding Love series.

Elena's Song—After years of fame, love, and secret pain, Elena Breen finds herself on a dangerous precipice. With a singing voice damaged by misuse and a career cut short by the man who built her into a celebrity, Elena is haunted by her past and afraid to face her future. But Jesse Golden, the one man who holds the key to Elena's heart, is determined to reignite the love that once bound them together. As Elena heals from her emotional and physical wounds, Jesse discovers that there is much more to this woman than he had ever imagined. Neither of them is prepared for the depth of pain and height of love they discover as they experience the vastness of God's abounding love. Book 3 in the Abounding Love series.

HEARTWARMING ANTHOLOGIES FROM HEARTQUEST

Letters of the Heart—What says romance more than a handwritten letter from the one you love? Open these historical treasures from beloved authors Lisa Tawn Bergren, Maureen Pratt, and Lyn Cote and discover the words of love that hold two hearts together.

A Victorian Christmas Keepsake—Return to a time when life was uncomplicated, faith was sincere . . . and love was a gift to be cherished forever. These three Christmas novellas will touch your heart and stir you to treasure your own keepsakes of life, love, and romance. Curl up next to the fire with this heartwarming, faith-filled collection of original love stories by beloved romance authors Catherine Palmer, Kristin Billerbeck, and Ginny Aiken.

Sweet Delights—Who would have thought chocolate could be so good for your heart? A cup of tea and a few quiet moments are all you need to enjoy these tasty, calorie-free morsels from beloved romance authors Terri Blackstock, Elizabeth White, and Ranee McCollum. Each story is followed by a letter from the author and her favorite chocolate recipe!

Prairie Christmas—In "The Christmas Bride," by Catherine Palmer, Rolf Rustemeyer can hardly wait for the arrival of his Christmas bride, all the way from Germany. You'll love this heartwarming Christmas visit with friends old and new from A Town Called Hope. Anthology also includes "Reforming Seneca Jones" by Elizabeth White and "Wishful Thinking" by Peggy Stoks.

A Victorian Christmas Cottage—Four novellas centering around hearth and home at Christmastime. Stories by Catherine Palmer, Debra White Smith, Jeri Odell, and Peggy Stoks.

A Victorian Christmas Tea—Four novellas about life and love at Christmastime. Stories by Catherine Palmer, Dianna Crawford, Peggy Stoks, and Katherine Chute.

A Victorian Christmas Quilt—A patchwork of four novellas about love and joy at Christmastime. Stories by Catherine Palmer, Peggy Stoks, Debra White Smith, and Ginny Aiken.

HEART
QUEST®

OTHER GREAT TYNDALE HOUSE FICTION